T]
STAR THIEF

THE STAR THIEF CHRONICLES
BOOK ONE

JAMIE GREY

Publisher's Note: This is a work of fiction. Names, characters, places, and incidents are a product of the author's imagination. Locales and public names are sometimes used for atmospheric purposes. Any resemblance to actual people, living or dead, or to businesses, companies, events, institutions, or locales is completely coincidental.

Book Layout ©2013 BookDesignTemplates.com
Cover ©2013 Christa Holland

The Star Thief/ Jamie Grey – 2nd ed.
ISBN-13: 978-1492944843

ISBN-10: 149294484X

*To my grandmothers, Lois and Patricia, who encouraged
me to reach for the stars.*

ONE

Renna should have known better than to trust Boyd when he said the job would be easy. Her hand crept to the stolen pendant at her throat, squeezing it before tucking it back under her shirt. Damn Boyd and his powers of persuasion. If she'd known she'd end up spending four days crouched behind a stinking Dumpster, she would have thrown the contract back in his face. Nothing was worth having the smell of rotting garbage burned into your nose. Nothing except enough money to buy a small planet.

She shifted on her heels and studied the hulking steel building in front of her. The warehouse itself seemed normal—other than the deadly, high-tech fence surrounding it and the perpetual presence of four armed guards.

The blue glow of the laser locks on each door cut through the morning sunlight like a warning beacon. A few high windows let a little light into the cavernous building, but they were framed with thick, Saltani iron bars. No matter how much she stared, she wasn't getting in that way. Nothing cut through those suckers.

Renna sighed. At twenty-three, she was more than ready to get out of the mercenary business, but Boyd had asked her for one last job and retrieving the qualified gamma particle destabilizer was too big of a challenge to pass up. The newest tech from Aladea Science Investments could vaporize matter from long distances, even off-world. If anyone else found out it actually existed, it would start an intergalactic war.

And despite the olfactory assault, her stakeout hadn't been a complete waste. She'd memorized the routine of the warehouse down to the second. Two men on this side, the other two around back. Shift change every four hours. If she timed it right, she could sneak in the back door when Guard Number Four went for his daily constitutional.

She shuddered. Whatever the man ate kept him regular as clockwork.

Renna slung her black polythene bag over her shoulder and twisted her ponytail tighter. She should have cut off her damn hair ages ago, but the long, dark locks were her one claim to beauty and she was vain enough to enjoy the compliments.

Not to mention all the secrets she'd been able to pick up with a sultry flip of her head.

She crept from behind the Dumpster and down the filthy alley toward the back of the warehouse. The Cordozas owned most of the block, and she'd lived in this city long enough to know that a lot of their men were lazy slobs, more concerned with getting their credits than doing their jobs well. Definitely made her life easier this time around.

Her black leather boots made no sound as she cleared the corner of the compound. She smiled at the unguarded pillar grounding the entire electric fence. Stupid. The Cordozas thought they were invincible. That no one would dare steal from them.

They were about to find out differently.

She pulled a nanotech spanner from her jacket pocket, directed the beam at the thick metal casing on the pole, and adjusted the frequency until the metal hummed for a long moment. The mechanism gave way in a burst of sparks, and the metal door opened with a clang.

Renna smirked. Sleeping with the chief engineer of the V'Mani Electrical Company had been one of her better decisions. Give him a few drinks and the man never shut up.

A few adjustments to the coils inside and a small section of the fence buzzed and switched off. She tucked her spanner back in her pack and slipped inside the fence. She checked her watch as she darted across the courtyard. Guard Four would just be getting down to business in the bathroom. It would only take a few seconds to disable the glowing laser lock on the door, another hack she'd learned courtesy of the engineer's loose tongue.

Renna slipped inside the warehouse, nothing more than a dark shadow against the steel building. Triumph surged through her, hot and rich. "Utterly impenetrable," her ass. Sometimes the rush from this job was almost better than getting paid. *Almost.* Still didn't change her mind about wanting out of the business though. She'd made enough enemies since starting out seven years ago that there were plenty of people who'd love to slit her throat or lock her away in prison for the rest of her life.

She closed her eyes and let her senses reach out into the warehouse, gathering her bearings. The scent of spices, Hesperian wooden crates, and engine oil wove through the space like strands of silk. It smelled like home.

There was a beep as her cranial implant downloaded the building schematics from the net, and she opened her eyes, certain now of her path. On silent feet, she skirted past stacks of crates toward the back. The Cordozas had headquarters in every major city in the star system, but the city of Veth was their clearinghouse for the smuggled items and drugs they sent out across the universe. They were one of the biggest dealers of clay in the galaxy and always looking for a stronger foothold in the Outer Rim. When she had been nothing more than a tenement rat, they'd asked Renna to join their organization.

She'd not-so-politely refused.

Renna wrinkled her nose as she passed a stack of shiny plastic crates. The smoky, burnt-sugar scent of the drug reached her even from here. Almost instinctually, her hand moved to her pack to reach for the lighter inside. Each two-pound bag of clay sold for nearly a million credits on the black market, but stealing and selling it wasn't even tempting. Destroying every last bag, though? That, she almost couldn't resist.

On any other day, any other assignment, she might have done it. But today, get in and get out was her mantra, and setting fire to a billion credits worth of drugs would draw attention she didn't need.

The muscles in Renna's neck tightened, and she fluttered her fingers as she walked, keeping them loose and flexible. She rolled her shoulders, scanning the warehouse.

Her implant sent a couple of low frequency beeps to her ears as she passed the last row of crates.

Gotcha.

Renna dropped her knapsack on the floor in front of the gleaming iron safe and rummaged for her tools. A Saltani safe had sixteen manual tumblers, an electronic lock, and the most advanced internal circuitry out there, but once she got past the tumblers, it was easy work since all their safes had a weak point in the circuitry. You just had to know where to look.

"Ah, there you are, sweetheart," she said, probing with her tweezers. A few twists and she'd rewired the combination panel back to its factory settings. From there, all she had to do was enter the standard code.

The safe opened with a click, and Renna sank back onto her heels. Inside were three datapads, which she ignored. Instead, she helped herself to several stacks of credits and a sleek silver laser gun before finally spotting the box she needed buried under several bags of platinum coins.

She hefted one of the coin bags in her hand. Probably worth a hundred thousand credits. Not chump change by any means. It found its way into her knapsack.

The destabilizer was stored in a heavy wooden box about the size of her hand. She unlatched the lid and pushed it open. There was no way she'd make a mistake while retrieving this item. It was worth more than her life.

Red velvet cradled the globe of shiny metal, the electronic keypad on its face currently in sleep mode. She let out a breath, then locked the box back up and slipped it into her pack. She wouldn't want to be within two planets if that thing detonated. Luckily, she was handing it over to Boyd as soon as she got out of here. And then those shiny credits would be in her bank account and she could kiss this life goodbye once and for all.

Renna flipped the safe closed and locked it back up. She tweaked the wires again, resetting the combination back to what the Cordozas had set. Nothing quite like confusing the hell out of your targets.

Whistling softly, she slung the bag over her shoulder. Now all she needed was to slip back out the way she'd come in and turn the fence back on, with no one the wiser. But she had one quick detour to make first.

Her implant had detected a store of fibroseparators in the corner of the warehouse, and she'd almost danced with glee. Each device could fetch up to fifty thousand on the market, especially if you knew the right mercenaries—the ones who didn't want to report their gunshot wounds or blade slices. And, boy, did she know the right mercenaries. They would offer double if she could keep them in stock. Plus the couple she kept for herself. You never knew when a job would go tits up.

She found the stash without a problem and shoved a dozen into her pack with a smile. She'd already picked out the perfect cottage on a beach, far away from the drugs and stench of her current life. It would be peaceful. Relaxing. Safe. She'd change her name, and Renna Carrizal would finally be dead. She'd worked hard to put the past behind her, to break away from the tenement life and her abusive mother. Now it was time to figure out who she was without all that baggage.

Her hand played with the sapphire around her neck idly, and lost in her dreams, she barely registered the whimper until her implant squawked in her ear.

"Human presence detected."

Renna froze, hand on her pistol. She scanned the rows of crates, the shelves along the back wall, but the warehouse stood still and silent. Damn this implant. It couldn't be time for a new upgrade already.

"Report," she ordered.

"Thirteen meters to the left. Crate 107." The mechanical female voice was emotionless as always, but Renna's heart thudded in her chest. She turned and stared at the number 107 burned roughly into the wood of the crate. The thing looked barely big enough to hold a dog, let alone a human.

Another symbol was burned alongside the numbers: a strange eye crossed by two spears. She didn't recognize the mark. Maybe the crate was destined for one of the Outer Rim gangs. Were the Cordozas trafficking in slaves now, too?

The whimpering grew louder. "Is someone out there? Please help me."

She stared at the crate, lips parted at the young voice. She twitched her heavy bag higher on her shoulder, glancing toward the exit.

So much for getting in and out quickly. This was a complication she couldn't afford.

"Please! Help me! I know you're out there!" The terror in the kid's voice was thick and palpable.

Renna frowned. Took a step toward the exit. She wanted to help, really she did, but…

"Please. I've been here for days. I promise my uncle will pay you." The boy's voice broke on the last word, and she froze.

If that was the case, she would be more than happy to take the kid off the Cordozas' hands. Drugs and weapons were bad enough. She shouldn't let them get away with trafficking, too.

"Hold on, I'll have you out in a sec," she said softly, using the spanner to remove the nails from the crate. She stepped lithely out of the way as the front panel fell to the floor.

Renna's eyes widened, but she was too good a mercenary to let any other shock show. Inside the crate was a cage, and inside the cage was a small, dark-skinned boy, half-naked. The smell of unwashed skin made her stomach churn. He'd obviously been there more than a few days.

She gritted her teeth as he cowered in the corner, his dark eyes shadowed and haunted. Bruises and cuts marred his chest and arms. She dropped to a crouch before the laser lock.

"What's your name?" she asked gently, careful not to let her anger show.

"Myka. Myka Aldani."

"Nice to meet you, Myka. My name is Renna, and I'm going to get you out of here."

The boy nodded and crept forward from his corner.

"So where do you come from, Myka?" she asked as she tackled the lock with her tools. She tried to ignore how gaunt his bare chest was, every rib poking from his skin. Her fingers tightened around her nanospanner. If she ever ran into the Cordozas in a dark alley…

"I was living with my uncle in New Rome Colony, but my parents and I are from Banos Prime." His voice stayed expressionless, and Renna nodded. Banos Prime had been destroyed three years ago. Most of the population had been wiped out.

"Were your parents killed in the attack?"

The boy stared at her silently before nodding once.

"I'm sorry." Renna bowed her head over the last tumbler on the lock. What the hell were the Cordozas doing with this little boy?

The last tumbler fell into place, and the laser light shut off. "There we go. No problem." Renna smiled at the boy and tugged the cage front open. "You're free."

He stared at the open door as if he didn't believe his eyes.

And then the shrieking alarms began.

TWO

Shit." Renna glanced at the metal cage. How the hell hadn't she noticed the golden tripwire coiled across the top? This was why she didn't do jobs without prepping first. This was a rookie mistake, one she hadn't made since she was thirteen.

Growling under her breath, she reached into the cage to grab Myka's skinny arm. "Come on, kid. We need to get the hell out of here."

"Scan perimeter for heat signatures," Renna ordered her implant. "All exits." Her heart sank as it showed all four guards reacting to the alarm. She clasped the boy's hand and sprinted away from his cage. "Display alternate exits." Her implant obeyed, and she almost wished it hadn't. Multiple heat signatures at every entrance.

They'd called for reinforcements.

Beside her, the boy gasped, and Renna slowed her pace a little, remembering he'd been locked up for gods knew how long. She scanned each crate, each row of goods as they ran, looking for something to help them escape.

"Over here!" A man's voice echoed through the warehouse. "The boy's gone!"

Her heart skipped. Dammit. They were faster than she'd thought. Behind them, footsteps pounded against the concrete as the guards pursued. Myka gasped for breath beside her, his breath ragged and harsh. They had to find someplace to hide. And fast.

She frantically searched the schematics of the warehouse. *There!*

A maintenance bay was better than nothing. They could hide there until she figured out another route. Going on the offensive wasn't even an option. Her laser pistol would run out of charge long before she was done fighting her way out of here.

If she made it.

Stop that, Carrizal. There was always a way out; she just had to find it.

They slammed through the maintenance door, and she sealed it shut behind them with her nanospanner. That should keep the Cordoza thugs busy for a little while.

Renna quickly scanned the space, barely paying attention to the kid doubled over and gasping for breath. The maintenance bay was a rectangular box with cement walls and a solid steel garage door. A workbench lined one wall, the tools spread out with surgical precision. She counted three nanospanners like her own, a laser torch, a sonic screwdriver, and a set of electrow-renches of varying sizes.

And then there was the shiny Radiowing hovering in the middle of the garage. The chrome body and supple leather seat were pristine. By gods, it was gorgeous. She hadn't seen one in such good shape since she was a kid, and this was obviously one of the first gens. It looked a bit like the old motorcycles they'd had back in the twenty-first century, but instead of wheels, airlift wings jutted from the sides of the machine.

The perfect escape.

Renna grinned at Myka. "Ever ride one of those before?"

He shook his head.

"You're about to." She moved to the keypad on the garage door and began to hack it. Her fingers flew over the controls, trying to reset it to spec. It beeped, and the pad turned red. She tried again, a different hack this time. Nothing. Renna growled. She did *not* have time for this. A bead of sweat trickled down her forehead, and she swiped it away before trying a third time. This was unacceptable. She could hack locks like this in her sleep.

"Hey, lady?" The boy cleared his throat, and Renna spun around. He jerked his head toward the metal door. "I think they're here."

"Status check," she ordered. Her implant returned three heat signatures outside.

There was a hiss from behind the door as a torch kicked on. Blue flame licked through the metal, and her heart fell to her toes. They were going to cut their way in.

"Damn." She tried the keypad once more, but she knew it wouldn't do any good. She was going to have to do this the old-fashioned way.

"Get on the bike, Myka." Renna flipped open her holster as the torch cut through the door in a glowing line.

She swung her leg over the seat of the bike. Now if she could only remember how to start these things. They'd used something archaic like a trigger or key or...there! She spotted the switch near the base of the handles. She flipped it on, but nothing happened.

Myka glanced between her and the door but didn't move. "They're starting the second line," he said. Instead of getting on the bike like she'd ordered, he stood solidly, shoulders square and arms tensed at his side. Like he'd fight them all himself before getting back in that cage.

She might actually like this kid.

Renna tapped her finger on the chrome body. When she was a kid, Big George had owned one of the first Radiowing models in the city. He'd paid her to look after it one afternoon when he'd come to collect his earnings from the prostitutes in the tenements. She'd played lovingly with all the gears and switches while he was gone and threatened the other children who'd come around with her stolen blaster. Most of them knew better than to mess with her anyway.

"Right. Got it!" She placed her feet carefully on each wing and pressed her toes down. The machine rumbled deep in its belly. She pressed harder, throwing her weight into it and turning the grip on the handle. It roared to life, the vibrations tingling the insides of Renna's thighs. "Get on, Myka; we're getting out of here."

"Good. They're almost through." He swung a skinny leg over the seat behind her and grabbed her waist with a surprisingly strong grip.

Renna glanced behind them. The boy was right. She pulled her pistol from the holster and aimed at the keypad on the bay door. The explosion thundered through the space, the sound an almost-visible thing. Slowly, the mech bay door began to rise. Renna gunned the Wing's engine, ready to kick off as soon as there was room.

"Miss!"

She turned just as one of the guards kicked at the metal insert. But the bay door was still only wide enough for a child to sneak through.

"Screw this," she said, pointing her gun at the men. She fired off two shots, one hitting the first man in the arm, the other striking the man behind him. They both went down, immediately replaced by two more. And behind them, another dozen men waited in the wings. Her arm trembled. She'd never be able to stop them.

Instead, she directed her fire at the bay door. Her laser gun screamed as the beam passed through the door and weakened the metal. It would have to be enough.

Gunning the Radiowing, Renna leaned forward. "Hang on!"

The machine jerked and started forward, tipping and sliding drunkenly. She fought with the controls to right it. Then with a kick of her foot, the machine shot forward, directly into the bay door.

It crumpled with a screech. Renna ducked behind the windshield, letting the Wing bear the brunt of the damage. Flakes of shiny black paint sprayed over her as the fresh tint job disintegrated on impact. The bug screen shattered, glass flying in every direction. But the Wing was out of the bay and off the ground, soaring above the dozen men who ran screaming into the warehouse yard below.

It tried to roll beneath her as it climbed, and Renna tensed her muscles. They were still climbing too slowly for her to control it. Arms burning with the effort, Renna wrenched the Wing back in line. Below them, blasters shot at them from every direction. Her feet jammed into the accelerator, her hands twisting the handles to weave back and forth. Just needed to make it out of the compound. Once they were free, she could be back at her safe house in minutes.

The machine let out a low whine beneath her, and Renna glanced down at the controls. Her heart sank, suddenly as heavy as the Wing. "You have to be shitting me."

The fuel cell indicator was nearly at zero, and they still hadn't cleared the compound. That damn electric fence was getting closer by the second. And someone had turned it back on.

"Status update. Area map."

The implant showed her the surrounding area. Beyond the Cordozas' warehouse were three more empty buildings. If she could land this thing between two of them, she might be able to get them to safety. There was also a parking structure to the north. She chewed her lip and glanced back down at the fuel cell gauge, a plan working itself out in her mind. Could she risk it?

Bullets sang past them, the shouts of her pursuers echoing below. And then her blood turned to ice.

The hum of a hover car starting up. They'd overtake the Wing in no time.

At least it made her decision easy. She turned the machine north and kicked it into high gear, hoping to get some momentum before the engine stalled.

The ground below was a blur of men and machines and guns, but moments later, Renna and the boy cleared the fence and were free of the compound. Shouts of fury came from the men as they were halted by deadly electricity.

She risked another glance behind as the hover car shot from the garage bay. Dammit. She wasn't skilled enough to make this thing do what she needed, and the fuel cell was dropping by the second. Her hair whipped around her face, and Renna leaned forward, as if that would make the machine go faster.

The arms around her waist tightened. Right. The kid. She'd almost forgotten about him in their escape.

"You okay?" she called over her shoulder.

He nodded against her back, though he didn't loosen his grip. "Wish they'd stop shooting at us, though."

"We're almost there, but we're running out of fuel. It might be a bumpy landing."

"I can handle it." Her eyebrows rose at Myka's calm voice. Most kids would be a whimpering mess after all this. Of course, growing up on Banos Prime would make any kid tough.

Beneath her, the Wing jerked in midair, and she let out a hiss. They weren't going to make it.

The hover car hummed closer, the sound of its engine swallowing their own. Their only chance at escape now was getting to the ground. First stop: the parking structure. She could hotwire a car in twenty seconds flat, and she and Myka would be gone before the hover car even landed.

Renna pressed down harder on the accelerator. The scream of the Radiowing's engines cut through the air as it shot forward. Her belly fluttered. The structure was just yards away. And then the engine stopped.

The silence was deafening.

Renna slammed a hand against the fuel cell gauge, but nothing happened. The Wing started to plummet, making her stomach drop before the airwings on each side caught the wind and they glided forward.

"Come on, baby, just a little farther."

If she could keep the airwings steady, she might be able to glide the thing close enough to the structure to land it. Holding her breath, she tilted the Wing to bring it in at an angle. It continued to drop, the wind whistling past her.

There! The top deck of the parking structure was close enough to see.

She braced herself against the footpads and threw her weight into turning the machine. They were dropping fast now, but their forward momentum was dying as they got closer to the ground. Two more heartbeats before her pulse kicked into overdrive. They weren't going to make it.

The bottom of the Radiowing hit the edge of the structure with a bone-jarring thud. Renna clenched her muscles and threw herself from the bike, grabbing Myka's arms to make sure he followed.

The Wing balanced for an instant on the edge of the building, giving her just enough time to push off before it slid backward, scraping against the side of the parking structure as it dropped the thirty meters to the ground. It hit with a thunderous boom, shattering against the cement.

Renna and Myka landed almost as hard on the pavement of the parking structure. She tumbled over him, wrenching herself out of the way at the last second to avoid landing on top of him. Her body hit the ground with a thud, and the breath whooshed from her lungs. Her head slammed against the ground. A surge of electricity burst through her skull in a white-hot flash as her implant sputtered and switched off. Stars danced on the insides of her eyelids.

Beside her, she heard Myka moan and sit up. Curling into a whimpering ball sounded like a pretty good plan right now, but if the kid could get up, so could she. With a will she didn't know she had, Renna dragged air into her burning lungs and forced her eyes open.

"Are you hurt?" Myka asked, jumping to his feet.

Damn, was the kid made of springs or something? She slowly moved her head from side to side, and an odd metallic taste flooded her mouth. Her implant was definitely fried.

"I don't know," she said between gritted teeth. "Ask me in another hour."

"I still hear the hover car." The boy glanced back into the sky.

"Shit." She spat the word out, along with some blood, and forced herself to sit up, biting back a gasp as the world tilted crazily. Everything settled a moment later as she exhaled through the pain. She didn't have time for this shit.

"Help me up, kid." Renna leaned heavily on Myka's shoulder and slowly got to her feet. Each breath felt like someone stabbing her with a knife. "Grab my bag. We need to get out of here."

Myka slung her pack over his shoulder and let Renna lean on him as she limped across the cement. His shoulders barely sagged under her weight, though dark smudges shadowed his eyes. He'd already been through a lot, but you'd never be able to tell by the determined expression on his face.

"Just a little further." Her whisper was more for herself than for Myka. She'd spotted a sporty little Diskcar she could rewire in seconds. They'd be safe in no time.

"What's that noise?" Myka asked, pausing on the pavement. Renna had to pause, too. One wrong step and she'd be down for the count.

"I don't hear anything." Of course, the ringing in her ears from her destroyed implant meant she couldn't hear much.

"That."

She tilted her head, and then she heard it. The scream of an engine approaching, but not from the sky. A second later, a white magnacraft van barreled from the shadows of the ramp, straight for them.

THREE

G et behind me, Myka," she said, careful to keep her voice steady. She let the boy's arm fall away and forced herself to stand straight. She'd dealt with mob thugs like the Cordozas before. Show a glimmer of weakness and it was all over.

The magnacraft screamed straight toward them.

Renna held her breath.

It swerved at the last possible second, tipping on two wheels. She turned to follow it, keeping the boy behind her and reaching for her gun. Her fingers came away from her holster empty. *Godsdammit.* That, too?

The magnacraft's side door slid open, and she blinked. Instead of dirty Cordoza thugs, six people, dressed in black from head to toe leaped out, ninja-style masks hiding their faces. Two of the men charged at Renna and Myka, while the others raced across the parking lot.

"Stay back," Renna warned in her roughest, most mercenary voice. It usually worked well in bar fights, but these men seemed to be of a different caliber.

Their only identifying feature behind the masks was the cold glitter of their eyes. They moved with precision, each stride calculated and deliberate. One of the men stepped forward to take the lead, and her eyes widened at the handle of a long sword jutting over his shoulder.

What kind of thug carried a sword? That had gone out of fashion two thousand years ago.

"Who are you?" She reached behind her and squeezed Myka's arm, making sure he was close. Keep them talking long enough and maybe the Cordoza thugs would show up. The two groups could fight each other, letting her and the kid escape.

But the silent men didn't answer. The leader moved closer, the ice in his blue eyes and the smell of raw silk from his dark uniform making her take a step back. These weren't ordinary thugs. Her gut clenched and she tried to take a deep breath, but the still-searing pain from the crash made her gasp instead.

Maybe she should have left the boy back in his cage. This was getting to be entirely too much work.

Silence stretched between them until her whole body trembled with the urge to run. Renna's pulse sped up, and her gaze darted around the space, searching for escape. Before she could even take a step, the second man tugged his sword free of its sheath, the metal singing as he backflipped over them to land feet away from Myka.

The leader pulled his sword, too, the shining tip pointed directly at her. "Don't move."

"Like we had much choice," she muttered. She eyed the man's muscled frame and the strong arms that held his sword. She was impressed, despite the cold curl of ice in the pit of her stomach. If she wasn't mistaken, he was using Bumani. It had been a long time since she'd seen that style of martial arts training.

Renna shook her head, trying to clear it. The humming in her ears was getting louder, but it wasn't coming from inside her head any more. The Cordozas' hover car had finally arrived. The nose of the machine cleared the top of the parking structure. Two men hung from the open doors, guns pointed directly at them.

Her heart kicked, and she readied herself to roll out of the way. But she waited, watching the edge of the deck where the four remaining black-clad figures crouched, hidden against the ledge like shadows.

Moving as one, they pulled their swords free, the blades glinting in the morning sun. As the car glided overhead, they attacked, slicing into it from all four sides.

Renna's jaw dropped as the blades tore through the car like butter, the metal screaming and sparking at the impact. The men inside the car screamed, too, as soon as they realized what was happening, before bailing from the dying vehicle like lemmings.

The car shuddered and teetered on the edge of the parking deck before falling backward, landing with a boom that made the structure tremble. The Cordoza guards had barely found their feet before the other men had turned their blades to them.

Blood splattered like fireworks, turning the cement crimson and filling the air with iron and death. A head rolled past Renna's feet, bouncing down the gentle incline. She clenched her hands, forcing herself not to react. She'd seen some horrific things in her life, but the cold ruthlessness of these men made her stomach turn. The thugs were starting to look like the better option here.

Behind her, Myka gasped, and she spun to face him. He stared at the head as it left a trail of glistening blood behind it on the pavement. He still wore her pack slung over his shoulders, and she moved to hug him.

"Play along," she whispered as she slowly reached beneath the bag to the opening, pulling out the shiny metal blaster she'd stolen from the safe. The weight felt reassuring in her hand, and she gripped it tightly.

She pitched her voice so it was no more than a whisper of air in the kid's ear. "When I let go, run for the ramp. I'll distract them. Find Boyd in the merchant district. Sunshine building. Tell him Renna sent you." She felt Myka nod. "Good boy. Now *run*!"

Spinning on one heel, Renna kicked out, taking the first ninja guard by surprise. Her boot connected with his stomach, and he grunted, doubling over and clutching his abdomen. Before she could line up a shot, the second guard sprang at her with his sword. She tried to knock it away with the barrel of the gun, but the metal of the sword sliced right through it. She stared blankly at the blaster for a split second before ducking beneath his backswing.

She lashed out with her foot, catching him on the ankle. He twisted as he tumbled, grabbing her arm with his free hand and pinning it behind her.

The first man let out an angry hiss and grabbed her other arm, raising his sword. Renna stared down the length of the shining metal. She'd seen what it had done to those other men. She knew exactly how she was going to die.

"You boys sure like to play with your swords," she drawled breathlessly. It was hard to stay nonchalant pinned against the hard chest of a murderer.

The sword tip quivered inches from her chest, and she puffed it out even farther so that the tip touched the buttons on her shirt. "Sure would be a shame to ruin these perfect breasts. I can assure you they're all natural. No work done here, boys."

Dark blue eyes watched her from behind the mask, and she shivered at the man's cold glare. But the sword didn't move.

Her limbs tingled. Was this actually working? "If you let me go, I'm sure we can work something out to our mutual agreement." She smiled slowly, raking her gaze up and down the man's lean form.

"Get her to the van," he ordered, lowering the weapon. He had a voice like aged honey, rich and deep and almost familiar.

The man behind her grabbed Renna's arm. "Try to escape and I'll kill you."

She stood perfectly still, the five men garbed in black closing ranks around her. There was one missing. *Myka!*

On cue, the soldier strode up the parking ramp, carrying the struggling boy under his arm.

Myka pounded at him with his fists, screaming. "Get the hell off me, you fucker!" The man moved like he didn't feel a thing, dropping the kid in a heap of too-thin arms and legs in front of Renna.

"Tie them up and load them into the van," her captor ordered. The smooth metal of an exovise clamped around her wrists. At least he'd tied them in front of her. A flash of light in her peripherals told her Myka's soldier had done the same to him.

Once she was seated on the long bench inside the van, one of the soldiers leaned close to tie a blindfold over her eyes. She heard the boy struggling against him beside her. "Get off me!"

"Take them back to base. We'll stay and clean up this mess. And watch out for that one. She's dangerous." The door slammed with a thud, rocking the van, and Renna fought the acid burning her throat. In all of her years as a mercenary, she'd never been caught, never been in a situation she couldn't get out of. And here she was, trapped like a common criminal. She was better than that, dammit!

The van circled the parking lot, and she felt them descend the ramp into the parking structure. They circled round and round in silence for several long minutes before she felt the magnacraft straighten out. The sounds of other hover cars and wingcraft around them told her they were on a busy street, but after the circling, she had no idea which direction they were headed. Usually, she'd rely on her implant to track their movements, but it had been destroyed in the crash. She was working blind.

Beside her, Myka pressed his shoulder to hers, as if needing the human contact. "I'm not going back in that cage," he said fiercely.

Her hands twitched to comfort him. She wasn't one to get maternal, but for some reason, this boy got to her. Maybe he reminded her too much of herself at that age. Whatever it was, she had to get him to safety. If only she knew where safety was.

"So you grew up on Banos Prime? Were your parents miners?" she asked, hoping to distract him until she figured out a plan.

"No, they were scientists. The company sent them out there to track the ore levels and mining conditions. They were part of a large team."

"Weren't they evacuated off-planet when it was invaded?"

"It was too late. They got me into the last transport off-world. Women and children only. And Mom wouldn't leave Dad behind. They made sure my Uncle David knew I was coming. I don't think they knew the attackers intended to destroy the planet, not conquer it." He sounded so calm, so adult. Like all of this had happened to someone else.

"Tell me about your uncle. What does he do?"

"He's a scientist, too. Only he invents things. We live on Iniros. He has a lab there."

Renna froze. She only knew of one scientist who worked on Iniros. Most of the residents of the planet were ministers for the Cooperative Republic of Galaxies or wealthy businessmen who had vacation homes there.

"So what exactly does your uncle invent?" she asked, needing to confirm her suspicions.

"Scientific stuff. Like weapons and ships. I guess he's important or something."

By the gods. "Are you saying you're related to David Aldani? Of Aladea Labs?"

As in, the same people who'd hired her to retrieve the gamma particle destabilizer.

"Do you know him?" Myka asked hopefully.

"Enough!" a voice barked from across the van.

The kid stiffened beside her, and she frowned. "Who are you people?" she asked.

"You'll find out soon enough. Now both of you be silent!" His voice was low and sharp, like he hadn't wanted them talking about Myka's uncle. Was this all connected somehow? Had Boyd set her up?

Silence fell like a heavy blanket, only broken by the noise of passing vehicles. She still had no idea which direction they were headed, never mind where they might be going. Damn her cheap implant. She should have sprung for the nucleospatial model she'd thought was too expensive.

The car slowed, vibrating over a set of metal electrotracks in the ground. Renna tilted her head. Transit lines ringed the city center like a bull's eye, allowing the traincycle to traverse the entire loop in less than half an hour. They were traveling into the city.

She leaned back against the seat as casually as she could. She had an idea, but it would require perfect timing and balance. Renna let out a slow breath and lowered her shoulders from her ears. The van slowed again, swinging to the right. There was a slight pressure as it started down an incline.

Perfect. She let herself slide forward with the motion, her tight black leggings gliding against the metal bench. Momentum did the rest.

Renna braced herself for a tumble, but she underestimated the soldier across from her. Before she even hit the ground, he'd grabbed her, jerking her back on the bench. She flailed against him, which was easier said than done in the exovises gripping her wrists.

She slipped her arms over his head and pressed her face to his, trying to wiggle out of her blindfold. It slipped down a fraction, enough for her to see in the dim, windowless car. That was all she needed to slip across his lap and kneel on the bench beside him. The angle gave her enough leverage to tighten her arms around his neck. His breath wheezed in her ear as his bucking grew frantic. He pinched and grabbed at her, trying to push her off, but despite the pain, Renna squeezed harder, strangling him until his frantic movements slowed. He finally went limp against her, and Renna pulled her arms free with a shudder. Gods, she hated that. Killing never got any easier.

As the man slid against her to the floor, she tugged her blindfold off with shackled hands.

"What happened? What's going on?" Myka asked. He'd been perfectly silent during her struggle, but his hands were clenched so tightly together his knuckles had turned white.

"I'm fine. And now we're going to get the hell out of here." She ripped the blindfold from his face, and he stared at the man sprawled on the floor of the van.

"How did you do that?"

She shook her head. "No time for that now." Dim light filtered through the crack of the back door, and she fumbled for the latch. As the van slowed, Renna grabbed her pack off the bench. Somehow it had made it into the van along with them.

"When I give the word, jump. I'll be right behind you."

Hope crept into the boy's expression, and he nodded.

Renna pushed the door wide.

The van rocked to a halt.

"Jump!" she said, landing unsteadily on her feet. Myka followed but stumbled, and she grabbed for him before he could fall. The air in the shadowy space was cool against her flushed face, and smelled of metal. She'd bet her life it was another parking structure.

A man stepped from the shadows. "So nice of you to join us, Miss Carrizal."

FOUR

S he didn't recognize the older man's chiseled features or the uniform he wore, but he held himself like someone who'd spent his life in the military. And she knew what military men liked.

"I didn't know you were expecting me." Renna used her best seductive voice. If her hair had been loose, she would have given it a toss for good measure.

He raised an eyebrow, unmoved by her display. "We've been watching you a very long time, Miss Carrizal. I'm glad to see you've retrieved our package for us. I knew the Star Thief would be able to get the job done."

She froze at the nickname, and blood roared through her ears. That was supposed to be her dirty little secret. Only two other people in the galaxy knew she was the one who'd finished that job.

Before she could question him, half a dozen men dressed in the black ninja suits stepped from the shadows to surround them. A second magnacraft pulled up beside them, and more sword-wielding soldiers got out, taking up places behind her. Her stomach clenched as one of the men stepped forward, sword drawn. She recognized him even with his mask still in place; how could she forget those cold eyes? The same eyes that now raked over her, pausing slightly at the jagged scar on her neck before turning to focus on the older man.

He ignored the new additions and stepped forward to peer around Renna into the van. "I see you got the job done a little too well, my dear." He frowned at the body of the dead soldier lying on the floor. "A miscalculation on my part."

What had he expected her to do—sit back and pretend she was on vacation? She glared at him. "Who the hell are you, and what do you want with us?"

"All in due time, my dear. Right now, I'd like to get the little boy cleaned up and fed. I'm sure you'd agree." The man crooked a perfectly groomed eyebrow at her and then slid his eyes to Myka, who stood half-naked and shivering in the glare of the helo lamps. Dirt streaked his emaciated torso, but he held his chin defiantly.

"I'm not going anywhere without her," he said, moving closer to Renna.

"Nobody's going to hurt you here, son. You're safe now. Your uncle David works for us, and we promised to get you back for him."

Myka looked up at her with big, dark eyes, and Renna's heart twisted. For some reason, this kid trusted her. Nobody ever trusted a thief. She couldn't betray him after everything that had happened.

"Myka's not going anywhere with you until you tell me what's going on. What do you know of his uncle?"

"David Aldani works for us a consultant. Technically, it's his company, Aladea Science Investments, that works for us. But he personally helps us out on occasion." The man winked as if Renna was supposed to know what he meant.

She tilted her head to study him. "So why didn't *you* rescue the boy?"

"Do you think we haven't tried?" A wry grin twisted his lips. "Veth is the fifth city the poor boy's been to in the last month. We didn't think retrieving him would be nearly this difficult."

Renna squeezed Myka's hand. She would personally kill the Cordozas if she got out of this alive. "What did they want with him?"

The man shrugged. "Blackmail, we assume. Dr. Aldani is developing some extremely important technology. If an enemy system got hold of it…" He let the words trail off.

Renna already knew what would happen if Aldani's tech leaked onto the black market. The same kind of tech she currently carried in her pack. She shifted it closer to her body. It had to be a setup. Two birds with one stone and all that shit. She was going to kill Boyd when she saw him.

Renna studied the man's expensive uniform, the private garage, his own personal ninja army. "So exactly where do I come into this?"

"Wouldn't you much rather go inside and sit down? Have a nice cup of tea, perhaps? The boy looks positively exhausted." The man's smile was full of kindness and solicitude, and Renna almost believed him. Then she realized what he was doing.

"We're going inside whether we like it or not, huh?" She shook her head, tsking. "I thought you had better manners."

He spread his arms. "This sort of thing shouldn't be discussed in the open. Come along, please. Captain Finn, please accompany us." With a beckoning gesture, he urged Renna and Myka forward into the shadows at the back of the structure.

The leader of the ninjas nodded and pulled off his black hood, running a hand through his dark hair to make it stand on end. His angry gaze met hers, and Renna froze, the world dropping away as she stared at him, her heart banging out a staccato rhythm in her chest. The man's chiseled jaw. The bright blue of his eyes. The way the uniform clung to his muscles. She'd recognize him anywhere.

Dear gods.

"Hunter?" The word tangled in her throat. It wasn't possible. He couldn't be here. Alive. With them.

He ignored her and shoved his way toward a heavy metal door guarded by a glowing keypad. She couldn't tear her eyes from his hard body and the even harder expression he wore. He looked so different. So much…older. Maybe she was wrong. The Hunter she knew had died seven years ago in a raid.

Hadn't he?

She forced her gaze to the keypad he was using, and her heart sank as she recognized the technology. State-of-the-art biolock from Ohm Industries. It would take her exactly three-and-a-half minutes to hack. She didn't stand a chance against six sword-wielding ninjas and a well-armed military captain for that long. She swallowed, fighting the sick twist of her stomach.

Could this day get any worse?

Renna squeezed Myka's hand, making her voice light and cheerful. "Come on. I'm starving, aren't you?"

Captain Finn held the door open for them, and the older man gestured her inside with a slight bow. Renna ignored the courtesy but followed him down a short hallway. Captain Finn and his ninjas trailed silently behind. Only the rustle of their silk uniforms—and the crawling skin on the back of her neck—hinted at their presence. Whoever he was, Captain Finn's—Hunter's—dislike of her was almost a tangible thing.

They approached the end of the hall. With a whoosh of air, a set of frosted glass doors slid open, revealing a command center. Holovid screens and computers filled the room. One wall contained a vid screen with a map of the galaxy. A round table and half a dozen chairs sat in front of it.

The room buzzed with soft voices as workers spoke into their communication units or gave orders to their subordinates. Every one of them was dressed in the same dark gray uniform, with the symbol of a golden wing surrounded by a circle decorating the top left lapel.

Renna had been around long enough to recognize the signs. "What is this place?" she asked. "Does the Hesperian government know you guys are here?"

From the corner of her eye, Renna noticed the ninjas fanning out to take up posts near each door. She could feel their gazes on her. Watching. Assessing. Waiting for her to make one wrong move.

She curled her fingers into quick fists, then forced herself to turn back to the older man.

He smiled apologetically. "Do forgive me, I haven't introduced myself. I'm Major Erik Dallas, head of MYTH on Hesperia."

Renna hooked her thumbs in the pockets of her leggings and tilted her head. "I've never heard of MYTH. And I've heard of every secret organization there is. Been recruited by a couple, too. What does it stand for?" Maybe if she could get this guy to talk, she might have some useful information to sell to her clients, along with the qualified gamma particle destabilizer in her pack.

"Military Yield Tactical Horizon." He shrugged. "Don't ask me what it means though; the guys at the top came up with it. They needed a name that was impressive enough for a galaxy-wide organization tasked with protecting the Coalition of Territories from terrorists and outside attack." An unexpected dimple flashed in his weathered cheek.

Renna gritted her teeth. His boyish charm was not going to work on her. The guy had sent his highly trained ninja squad to kidnap her. After he'd used her to steal the destabilizer. It would take more than a friendly smile to get on her good side.

He turned to one of the uniformed technicians at a nearby console. "Lieutenant, please take Myka to get some fresh clothes."

The boy looked at Renna, his eyes so wide she could see the whites, but she nodded. "It's all right. They're not going to hurt you. And I'll be right here when you get back."

Reluctantly, Myka let go of her hand and followed the man through a nearby door. She tried to ignore the crawling of her skin and turned back to the major.

"A good name is always the most important thing when you're terrorizing the galaxy," she said, letting her gaze drift around the space, careful to not seem too interested in anything. She shifted her weight to the right and watched a series of numbers scroll past on the nearest holovid screen. The data made no sense to her. It seemed to be tracking ship movements in the outer traverse, but along no path she'd ever seen.

Beyond the vid, two more workers bent over a holographic simulation of a planet she didn't recognize. Renna played with the end of her ponytail. This was the most advanced tech she'd ever seen. The Coalition government was always screaming for money; there was no way in hell they could afford a facility like this. Whatever else MYTH was, they were obviously well funded.

But if they'd had all of this tech, why hadn't they been able to retrieve the kid themselves? Especially if they'd sent the ninjas after him. She'd seen those guys at work; they could have sliced and diced their way through that warehouse in seconds.

She tucked her hands into her pockets and nodded to the end of the room. "Mind if I take a look?" she asked Dallas.

"Of course." He waved her on.

The workers paid no attention to her, but Renna's scalp prickled as the ninjas' gazes followed her across the room. She squared her shoulders and made her way toward the map on the far wall to trace the curve of the traverse, the Outer Rim planets marking the edge of the Confederated Coalition of Territories.

They contained every form of life and every manner of race. Humanity had implemented space travel three hundred years ago, taking their place in the galactic government a mere hundred years later. They'd soon become leaders in defense and military action.

If nothing else, humanity excelled at war.

She chewed her lip as she studied the map. A glowing red line circled three planets grouped around a large star at the fringes of the traverse. Renna tapped her fingernail against her tooth. Something tickled the back of her mind, something about this cluster.

"Miss Carrizal, have you found something of interest?" Major Dallas asked.

She half-turned to look at him. "More than you can imagine." Her eyes drifted down the captain's trim figure. The guy was old enough to be her father, but she was willing to do whatever it took to get out of this mess.

Behind them, Captain Finn stood at ease, his blue eyes trained on her, taking in every subtle movement. Including her checking out the major.

Renna thought she heard him growl.

Dallas smiled, either oblivious to Renna's flirtation or ignoring it. "Would you like to have that cup of tea?" he asked, gesturing to one of the doors.

Renna followed him into a small, comfortable room. Instead of the office furniture she expected, there were two plush chairs and a low, white table. Someone had already set a tea tray on it with two ceramic cups. How very cozy.

"Please, have a seat, my dear. Captain, you can wait outside."

"But, sir…" Finn's lips thinned as he glared at her. The muscles in his jaw pulsed, like he had to grind his teeth together to stop himself from disagreeing with his superior. But the threat in his eyes, the promise of violence etched in every tense line of his body was all too real. And it was all directed at her.

She fought back a shiver. The Hunter she'd known had been different. Less serious. Kinder. He'd been one of the best soldiers-for-hire in their gang, but he'd never been so hardened. *This* man gave the impression that he'd kill first and ask questions later. What had happened to change him so much?

Dallas held up a hand. "Everything's fine, Captain. Renna is our guest."

Finn saluted and marched from the room, though the look he threw over his shoulder made Renna swallow as she sank into one of the chairs. She relaxed into its cushions and crossed her legs, trying to appear unruffled. In reality, her mouth was dry and her palms sweating as she scanned the room, taking in the smallest details—the lack of windows, the carefully neutral furniture, the slight bubble in the ceiling that showed her they were being watched.

She needed to stay on guard. She also needed to stay on this guy's good side. For now. "Where's' Myka?" She pitched her voice to seem unthreatening.

"In the next room. I thought you'd like to keep an eye on him." Major Dallas picked up a small remote control and pressed a button. The wall on the far side of the room, which had looked as solid as the rest, went translucent.

Myka sat at a long table, a bowl of some sort of food in front of him. He kicked his heels against the legs of the chair as he ate.

She bit back a smile. "Nice clothes." Someone had found the boy a spare uniform, with pants rolled up to his ankles and a button-down shirt long enough to be a dress on him. They had scrubbed him clean and at least he'd stopped shivering. Maybe MYTH wasn't all bad.

The major took a sip of his tea before setting the mug down on the table with a *thunk*. His amiable expression melted away. "Now that you're assured we're not harming the boy, why don't we get down to business?"

"I expected nothing else." Renna took a sip of her own tea, gazing at him over the rim of the mug in silence. Nothing like a long, purposeful pause to put a person on edge.

For such a high-ranking military man, Dallas cracked sooner than she'd expected. The faster they jumped to break the silence, the more important the situation was. Based on this, his organization needed her more than they'd like to admit. Men were always so easy to read.

His dark eyes bore into hers. "Miss Carrizal, I have a proposition for you."

FIVE

ow come I'm not surprised?" Renna took another sip and leaned back in her chair. "Was Myka's rescue a test?"

Dallas nodded. The bastard didn't even have the grace to hide his satisfied expression. "I had heard you were sharp. We used your fence Boyd to offer you a job retrieving the destabilizer, which we've been trying to track down for months. We made sure it was an offer you couldn't refuse." His pleased smile showed a row of shiny white teeth. "I don't know why I was surprised by your success. You did steal the Seralline Star Sapphire two years ago, did you not?"

Renna's throat closed at the mention of that job. She'd been so careful to keep her identity a secret. She forced her hand to relax around the handle of the mug instead of creeping to the sapphire necklace beneath her shirt. Her tone was carefully expressionless as she said, "I'm so glad I've met with your approval."

Dallas leaned back. "We knew the Cordozas were holding Myka captive. After chasing him across five different planets, we figured this was an opportunity to combine two projects into one. So we hired you to retrieve the destabilizer, hoping you'd also rescue the boy."

She raised an eyebrow. "Does that mean you're doubling my contract as well then?"

Dallas laughed. "Let's discuss money later, shall we? I think MYTH may have something better to offer."

Renna shrugged, swirling her rapidly cooling tea to mask the trembling in her hands. "How long has your organization been tracking me?"

"Long enough to know you're the best mercenary in the traverse. Your clients are always extremely satisfied with your work. So much so that they're extremely reluctant to talk about services rendered." His lips twisted into an amused smile.

Damn right they were. Most of the time, the things she retrieved were illegal on so many levels. A word from her and her clients could end up on a prison planet digging for minerals for the rest of their lives. "So how did you find out about my particular skills then?"

"We have many resources at our disposal. But honestly, it wasn't difficult." He dropped his hands to his lap, bracing his forearms on his thighs as he leaned forward to meet her gaze. "Five planets have permanently banned you, another three will execute you if you're caught on-world. Not to mention the standing warrant across the traverse for whoever did the Seralline job. You've made quite a name for yourself, Miss Carrizal."

Her pulse jumped, but she forced her face to stay expressionless. The whole Star Thief thing had been nothing but trouble since she'd finished the job two years ago. The money hadn't been worth her newfound infamy. Even if no one knew she was actually the Star Thief, she lived in constant fear they'd discover the truth. And yet she let Boyd keep talking her into contracts she knew she should turn down. That shiny retirement dream was looking further and further away by the second.

She let a strategic sigh escape her lips before saying, "Call me Renna. I think my detention is enough for us to be on a first-name basis."

Major Dallas inclined his head. "Because of your exceptionally impressive skills, we have another job for you, Renna."

"Let me guess, refusal is not an option?"

"Very astute of you. We need your help, and I'm afraid you're the only one who will be able to pull this off. The universe depends on you."

Renna rolled her eyes. Did he really have to be melodramatic? "The universe depends on a cutthroat mercenary who can't be bothered to care?"

"I think you'll find you care quite deeply after I tell you about the job. And what we can offer you."

She sat back in the chair, crossing her arms beneath her chest. It didn't hurt to emphasize her womanly qualities at a time like this. He was still just a man, and they always tended to underestimate her. Star Thief or not.

"Let's hear it then," Renna said with a smirk. "Make me care about the fate of the universe."

Major Dallas tugged at the collar of his jacket. "I'm afraid it's not that easy, Miss Carrizal. This information is so top secret even the President of the Coalition doesn't know about it."

Renna sat up, adrenaline rushing through her veins. This was going to be worth a small planet's gross domestic product to a couple of her clients. She was already calculating the new numbers in her bank account. "I give you my word that what you say will stay in this room."

He blew out a lengthy breath. "Unfortunately, your word is worth less than nothing. I'm not stupid, my dear. MYTH is offering you a choice." He stared at her for a long minute. "I don't want you to take this the wrong way, Renna. I assure you it's not a threat."

Her eyes narrowed. "When you have to say something like that, it usually means it is."

Dallas got to his feet and paced the room, his hands deep in his pockets. "The Seralline Star Sapphire heist is one of the most notorious unsolved crimes in the traverse. Until now, no one has been able to discover who did it." He paused, pinning her with a matter-of-fact stare. "I possess information tying you to the theft. I also have three orders on my desk for your execution. If you help us with this job, I can assure you all of your wanted ads will be pulled, the books wiped clean. We'll give you enough to retire comfortably to Paradisio Prime and live on the ocean for the rest of your life. We'll help you disappear."

Cold fingers wrapped along her spine. How the hell had they been able to find the evidence to pin this on her? She'd been more than careful. Did they know she'd done the job? Even worse, how had they discovered her retirement plans? She hadn't told anyone about them, not even Boyd.

"So, what I'm hearing is I can either be your pet thief, or I can learn to enjoy the benefits of prison food for the rest of my life. Doesn't sound like much of a choice to me."

"We need you, Renna. You're the only person who can pull this off. Your past just provides an appropriate amount of leverage to make sure you have proper incentive."

She arched an eyebrow. "And no hint of what I'm getting into before I agree? I can think of several instances where execution might be better than helping you."

Dallas stopped pacing and turned to face her. "If we succeed, I can assure you, you'll be set for life. Help us, Miss Carrizal."

"Renna," she said automatically. Her mind whirled. If she agreed now, maybe they'd let her out of this little compound to get the job done. And once she was out... She might not have enough money to retire the way she'd planned, but she could definitely disappear. Especially with the little security blanket on the chain around her neck.

"Fine. I'll help you. I don't really have a choice." She glared at him. "But don't think I'm happy about this." Wouldn't do to give in too easily. Dallas might get suspicious.

He grinned. "Good answer." He pressed the receiver in his ear. "Bring the papers, Captain Finn, Miss Carrizal has agreed to help us." Dallas sank into the chair he'd recently vacated, his shoulders relaxed and loose for the first time since she'd met him. "Now that that's settled, we can get down to business."

She shook her head. "No business on an empty stomach. I need food first or you're going to find yourself with one grumpy thief on your hands. And you really don't want that."

Dallas pressed the receiver again. "Finn, bring lunch as well."

"I'd like to introduce you to the rest of the MYTH team," Dallas said as he led her down another long corridor. "You've met Captain Finn already."

"Yeah, what's his story?" Renna patted at her hair, then dropped her hand. What the hell was she doing?

Dallas tilted his head. "I'm not sure what you mean."

"Having me on this team seems to be irritating that stick up his ass. If looks could kill—"

"Captain Finn has been a key member of MYTH for more than six years. He's led several successful, high-priority missions and has earned our respect. I was the one who recruited him."

"From where?" She kept her voice light as she slanted him a glance.

"I'm sure if Finn wants to tell you about his past, he will. All you need to know is he's the commanding officer in charge of this mission, and you would do well to find a way to work with him." Dallas frowned as he halted in front of a door. "Here we are. The team has sparring practice every day at this time. I thought it would be a good idea for them to get a sense of what you can do. Actions speak louder than words."

"You're making me perform? I'm not a fucking monkey."

"It's nothing like that," Dallas said, holding up his hands. "I just think it will help the team accept you more easily. Working with someone...like you...is in direct conflict to what most of them have spent their lives doing."

"Stopping ruthless thieves and mercenaries from ruining your carefully ordered galaxy?"

Dallas ignored her sarcasm and pushed open the door to a large, square space. Weight machines lined the walls, and a circular sparring ring had been set up in the center. Two men were currently fighting there, fists and feet flying as they attacked each other.

"Attention on deck!" someone shouted. Immediately all movement stopped and everyone stood at attention, their hands snapping up in a salute.

"At ease," Dallas said, striding into the room. "I'd like to introduce you to Renna Carrizal, the last member of the team."

All eyes focused on her, and Renna jutted her chin out.

"Renna, you've already met Captain Finn." Dallas gestured toward one of the weight machines where Finn stood. The captain was careful not to meet her gaze, his eyes staring over her head.

Beside Finn stood a tall, elegant woman with pale violet skin and silver hair pulled into a bun. Renna recognized her as a Delfine from the Preill system. "This is Staff Lieutenant Keva Li, our XO." The woman stood up straighter and puffed out her chest. Renna didn't think it was entirely due to pride. She did have a nice rack. Renna would have puffed them out, too.

Dallas turned to the massive man across the room who'd been bench-pressing his weights. His pasty skin was slick with sweat, but he stood at ease like the rest of the team. "This is Corporal Lynwood Bokal, our tech chief."

The man nodded at her. His light gray eyes were bright and intelligent, and he smiled at her with interest.

The two men standing in the sparring ring were the stiff, military types she'd expected. Major Dallas introduced them as Sergeant Doyle and Sergeant Santos. The final person in the room was a mousy woman with dark skin and black hair scraped back from a wide forehead. Her eyes never seemed to linger more than a second in one spot. She stood in front of a punching bag, but her hands hung limply at her sides. Hard to tell if the woman even knew how to use it.

"And this is Staff Sergeant Leslei Gheewala."

Renna noticed he didn't explain her purpose. Very interesting.

"Team, Renna is in charge of getting you in and out of the facility on Banos Prime. Your lives will depend on her skills."

They were too well trained to show their dismay, but Renna could feel it in the way they glanced at each other. She wondered how much Dallas had told them. How much they'd figured out themselves.

She squared her shoulders. Whatever they thought, they were damn lucky to have her. Might as well start off on the right foot. "Glad to meet you. I'm sure there are all sorts of rumors flying around about me, but here's the truth: I'm the youngest, most sought-after merc in the traverse. I've got more than ten years of experience in the field, and I can kill a man at ten yards with nothing more than my nanospanner. I suggest you stay on my good side." She grinned at the serious faces watching her. The only one who smiled back was Bokal.

Dallas cleared his throat. "Miss Carrizal has exceptional skills. I trust you'll all treat her with courtesy while she's on your ship."

The others exchanged more furtive glances before nodding. She didn't care. She wasn't here to make friends; she was here to get a job done. The sooner they all realized that, the better.

"I thought Renna could practice with a few of you. To help her get used to how MYTH trains their officers." Dallas waved at the sparring ring. "Any volunteers?"

She swiveled her head to look at Finn. Seeing him in action would give her an answer once and for all. Was he her Hunter? Or just a familiar-looking stranger?

Before she could suggest him as a partner, the Delfine stepped forward. "I'll be happy to fight her, Major." Keva's silver eyes narrowed, and Renna forced a smile.

She shrugged out of her coat and tugged off her heavy boots. Knocking out the woman's teeth with a misplaced kick wouldn't exactly win her any favors with the crew.

Across the room, Finn watched her, and when their eyes met, his lips twisted upward. On anyone else it might have been a smile, but the cold hatred on his face turned the expression feral. She swallowed thickly.

"Are you ready, Miss Carrizal?" the lieutenant asked in her slightly lilting voice.

Renna snapped her attention back to the sparring ring. The Delfine might look willowy and vulnerable, but Renna knew better. She'd fought with a Delfine on her first job. The woman had had balls of steel and had killed a man with her bare hands when he'd caught her stealing. She'd never stopped smiling.

Renna took her spot in the ring and rolled her shoulders a few times, working out the kinks. The other members of the crew circled the space, and she tried to ignore the heavy silence. She much preferred the shouting and chaos of a bar fight, but if this is what it took to prove herself…

Keva launched herself at Renna without warning. The alien's fist connected with Renna's jaw, and her head snapped back. Stars exploded across her vision. One of the bystanders sucked in a breath, shockingly loud in the silent room.

Renna glared at the woman as her jaw throbbed. So that's how it was going to be?

Ears still ringing, Renna attacked.

Her fists flew, and her body bent and flowed around Keva's punches. The woman had been trained well, and she moved lithely, almost like a bird. But Renna had learned her skills in the tenements, and the last thing she was worried about was form or looking pretty.

She was in it to win.

Renna ducked beneath a punch and swung her leg, catching Keva in the gut. The woman grunted and doubled over. Renna followed with an uppercut to the woman's jaw. Before she could strike, the alien grabbed her wrist and flipped Renna around, pinning her arm behind her back.

Her shoulder muscles screamed as Keva pulled harder. Sweat streaked down Renna's face and stung her eyes. Across the ring, Finn smirked.

Screw this.

Renna went slack. The unexpected shift of weight pushed Keva off-balance. Renna twisted out of the woman's grip and launched herself at Keva's midsection. They tumbled to the mat, twisting and punching and grunting. Sweat streaked down Renna's back until her shirt was soaked, but she didn't let up.

Keva's silver eyes glowed with rage as she tried to buck away from Renna's grip. But with one more flip, Renna had the woman on her back and her forearm pressed against Keva's throat. The thrill of victory started to build deep in her core.

The women stared at each other for a long moment, both panting. Both furious.

And then the Delfine scissored her legs around Renna's waist, twisting just enough to throw Renna off. They sprang apart, both back to defensive stances as they circled each other. They flew at each other twice more, hitting and striking out, both times breaking away before one or the other could get the upper hand. Renna's lunch churned heavily in her stomach. There was no way she was going to beat this woman.

The thought sobered her racing heart. But that also meant there was no way Keva would beat her. They were at a draw.

Dallas seemed to realize it at the same moment. He stepped into the ring with a wide smile. "That's enough. Thank you both for that display. You are worthy competitors."

Renna sucked in a lungful of air and smiled at Keva, holding out a hand to the woman. But Keva turned her back on Renna to grab the towel Finn held out for her.

Nice to see the crew was going to give her a fair chance after all.

"Quite a show," Dallas said, clapping Renna on the back. "I didn't know you'd been trained in Bumani."

"There's a lot you don't know about me." She used her sleeve to wipe the sweat from her face, shuddering as her clammy shirt clung to her back. "If you're going to blackmail me into helping, are you at least going to let me go home and grab some clothes?" She nodded toward the silky black garb most of them were dressed in. "Or even better, do I get a fancy ninja suit, too?"

Keva spun around, eyes flashing. "We're not ninjas. This is state-of-the-art armor fabric—light and moveable, but able to stop a bullet. We wear it on special jobs. It's not something you'll ever get to wear." The threat in her voice hung unspoken in the air between them.

Dallas cleared his throat. "Gheewala, take our newest member to the locker rooms and get her showered and geared up. I'll meet you all in an hour to debrief Renna on the rest of the mission. Dismissed."

Everyone in the room snapped to attention and saluted.

Captain Finn stepped forward. "Sir, I need to head to the armory and recalibrate my assault rifle. I can take Miss Carrizal. It's on my way."

Renna's lips twitched. Good. The sooner she was alone with this man, the better. Unfortunately, it wasn't for the usual lusty reasons. She needed answers from him. Now.

Dallas nodded as he left. "Very good, Captain. I'll leave her in your capable hands."

"Let's go." Finn didn't even look to see if she was following as she snatched up her pack and coat and hurried out of the room after him.

She studied him from beneath her lashes as they walked. Stubble shadowed his strong jaw, and his black armor accented the muscles of his chest. If it really *was* him, Hunter had sure grown up.

"So you going to tell me why you've changed your name and joined the Marines?" she asked as the silence stretched between them.

He glared at her and turned down another hall. "Inside. Now." He yanked open a door into a small room full of beeping tech and humming machines. The perfect place not to be overheard.

SIX

The smell of ozone and electricity tickled her nose, and a dull orange helolight did nothing to chase away the shadows in the room. Renna moved closer to the machines, her head spinning, and not just from the noise. By the gods, Finn really was Hunter.

Should she laugh hysterically or run for her life?

"What the hell!" She whirled to face him, preferring to go on the attack. "I thought you were dead."

He crossed his arms, his blue eyes hard as he gave her his best death stare. "Hunter is dead."

Once, she'd wanted to lose herself in their gorgeous depths. Now, they were full of hatred. "Why? What happened? Where have you been the last seven years?" *Why did you abandon me?* she wanted to add, but she pressed her lips together instead.

Finn stepped closer, menace rolling off every lethal plane of his body. Renna backed up until she bumped against a rack of servers, her fingers digging into the steel supports to keep her upright as his heat and scent enveloped her. Dear gods. Part of her wanted to jump into his arms. The other part wanted to strangle him.

"My life is none of your business," he snapped. "All you need to know is that I'm a MYTH agent now and I won't let anyone destroy what I've worked for."

"Hunter, please..."

"Don't call me that. Hunter died in an explosion seven years ago. I'm never going back to that life." His voice had dropped into a low growl, his eyes hard chunks of ice. "But I see it's done pretty well for you. Why am I not surprised? Even back then, you were the perfect little merc." Bitterness dripped from his words like acid.

"We both were." She shook her head as if that would chase away the fog that had taken her brain hostage. "You and Blur were the best in the traverse. What the hell happened to you? Everything went to hell when we were raided."

He raised an eyebrow, his lips twisting into a sneer. "Exactly."

Renna gasped. "You? You betrayed Blur and the gang?" She shoved him away from her, hard, throwing her weight behind it. "You sold us out, you son of a bitch!" Why would he do something like that? They'd been a family. The only family she'd had.

Finn barely moved, rocking back on his heels. Instead, his hand shot out and grabbed her arm. His fingers dug into her soft flesh like claws. "You deserved exactly what you got. You knew what Blur was doing. You knew how many lives he destroyed. And you went along with it. Hell, you encouraged him!"

She wrenched away, rubbing the tender skin of her arm. She didn't know what the hell he was talking about, but right now, she was too distracted by the fury surging through her to care. "I looked up to you, Hunt—Captain. You were my mentor. Do you know how fucked up your death made me?"

"Don't fool yourself, Renna. You were fucked up before you ever met me." His eyes flicked to the scar running across her neck, his lips curling ever so slightly. She fought the urge to cover it with her hand. She wasn't ashamed of her past. Not anymore.

His words stabbed into her like daggers. "Whatever our former relationship was, it's long dead. I tried to convince Dallas to find someone else, but he had to have you. If you even *think* about betraying me again, betraying the mission, I'll have you put away somewhere so deep no one will ever find you. Do you understand?" He snarled the last three words in her face.

She blinked at him. "Betray? You were the one who betrayed us!"

"Don't play dumb with me, Renna. You might be a lying bitch, but you're not stupid. I'll put up with you on my ship because I have to, but trust me when I say stay out of my way. Far out of my way." Finn spun on his heels and yanked the door open. "Move."

Emotions swirled through her—rage, hurt, sadness. She'd thought they'd been friends—maybe even something more as they'd gotten older—but he'd lied to her. Betrayed *her*. She was the one who should be furious, not him.

"I don't have all day, Renna," he snapped.

She stepped past him, careful to keep a large bubble of personal space. He was coiled so tightly, like a predator on the verge of pouncing, that the smallest wrong move might set him off. And until she could figure out what the hell had just happened, that was the last thing she wanted.

Renna followed Finn down another hall, careful to keep several steps behind him. Her head spun as she walked. Hunter was alive and a captain for a spec ops Marine force. The entire world had shifted, like she was Alice in fucking Wonderland and had just fallen down a giant rabbit hole.

Finn stopped suddenly in front of a door, and she almost tripped over her own feet to keep from banging into him. He grabbed her arm to steady her, but she crashed into the hard planes of his chest, their faces inches apart. His heart beat beneath her own, and the scent of his soap and skin wrapped around her in a wave of homesickness and longing.

Instantly, she was fourteen again, sparring with him for the first time. She'd felt so important, getting one-on-one training from one of the gang leaders so soon after joining. She almost hadn't minded that he'd easily disarmed her in three strikes and had pinned her to the floor with the solid weight of his body. He was four years older than her; there was no way he'd thought of her as anything more than a kid. But there'd been something about his kind eyes and the lopsided smile he'd used with her that had already had her falling in love with him.

He'd shaken his head at her and helped her to her feet. She'd stumbled then, too, and he'd caught her against his chest, the same scent wrapping around her, making her feel safe.

Renna blinked. Yanked herself out of the memory with a growl. Shoved herself away from Finn so hard he took a step back.

She met his expressionless gaze, ignoring the twist of lust in her gut. It was just residual, left over from a childish crush.

He nodded to the door behind her. "Inside is a locker room and an army surplus area with gear. Load up as much as you need. You have twenty minutes." Without another word, he turned and walked away.

She watched his rigid frame disappear around the corner and then pushed open the door and stepped into what was basically a very well-stocked surplus store. Uniforms of every rank and color were piled on tables, and one long wall was filled with racks of civilian clothes.

She spotted the locker room door and sighed happily. Before she did anything else, she needed a shower. She wrinkled her nose at the delicate perfume of rotting garbage that still clung to her clothes from staking out the Cordoza compound earlier, along with the faint tang of her blood from jumping from the Radiowing and her even more recent sweat.

Her face flamed with heat. Finn had probably smelled it, too.

Once she was clean and her embarrassment had faded slightly, she stepped beneath the ultraviolet dryer, and a moment later, her hair and skin were dry. Now to explore the most beautiful thing she'd seen all day: racks and racks of clothing.

She approached a table full of undergarments and held up a pair of panties, frowning at them. "What the hell are these? Do they actually expect me to wear this?" They were soft white briefs, military-issue—a far cry from her lacy thongs back home, the bras with the special enhancements and frilly cups. Her usual lingerie would make even a prostitute blush. Then again, she'd learned most of her fashion sense from them in the first place, so perhaps she wasn't so far off.

Sighing, Renna slipped into the boring underwear, then grabbed a satchel from the pile on the floor and stuffed it full of clothes. Panties and bras, tight-fitting shirts of some shiny dark material. Heavy leggings and fitted pants made from bulletproof fiber. Most of this stuff she'd only heard of or seen on the black market—military-grade, agent-approved street clothing. The kind they used to blend in off-world but could still serve as protection in a street fight.

She pulled on a pair of leggings and a shirt, then shook her head. The clothing she was nabbing probably cost more than three months' rent on her apartment in the city. When her bag was full of the necessities, she scanned the room again. No ninja suits, but she beamed as her gaze fell on a rack of coats.

As soon as she slipped the new coat over her shoulders, she knew it was the one. The knee-length black leather fit like it had been made for her, soft and supple against her skin. It had a military cut, with silver buttons lining the front and a slit in back. It looked almost ordinary, but she'd seen these coats before. There was a special weave added to the leather to make it bulletproof and element-resistant. Usually, they were reserved for commanding officers.

Even better, it felt like she was wearing nothing. Always a plus in her line of work, when one wrong move could mean getting caught. Or worse.

Like today.

She added a shiny new blaster and a holster to the pile, and a heavy dark sweater, just in case. Finally she snagged a brightly colored scarf from the table and wrapped it around her neck. Black might be her preferred choice of clothing, but a girl had to have a little pop of color once in a while.

She shoved her own pack inside the new satchel, along with the rest of the new clothes. Less than fifteen minutes had passed when she hefted the bag over her shoulder and approached the door to the hallway. To Hunter…Captain Finn.

Renna chewed her lip. She'd always assumed Hunter was his real name, but now that she thought about it, everyone in the gang had used a nickname. Blur. Edge. Chase. Hunter. They'd even called her Spyder, an Old-Earth nickname for a thief.

Pull it together. Whatever had happened between them was a long time ago. She looked out for herself now, especially since she was stuck in this situation for the foreseeable future. Her skin still prickled with anger, both at MYTH and at herself for getting caught. Now she'd have to figure a way out that wouldn't get her executed—or worse, exposed as the Star Thief.

But right now, she had to face Finn. And she sure as hell wasn't going to let him walk all over her again. She pinned a smile to her face and ran a hand through her long hair. Time to put all her experience over the last seven years to good use.

But when she pulled open the door, Finn was gone, replaced by a fidgeting woman with wide brown eyes and dark hair. Renna hid her relief and held out her hand. "Sergeant Gheewala, right?"

The woman nodded, though it looked more like a twitch. Her skin was soft and warm as they shook. "Captain Finn asked that I take you to the briefing room. Please follow me."

Sergeant Gheewala headed back the way Renna had come earlier. Her small, dancing steps were as far from military as possible, and her nervous tics could be deadly in the line of fire. This woman was as much of an anomaly on the ship as Renna.

"So, I noticed the major didn't tell me what you do on the team. Care to enlighten me?" she asked.

Gheewala gave a half-hearted smile. "I'm just the empath. I'm not important."

Renna forced her jaw to stay closed. She'd only ever met one other on her travels, and that woman had been bat-shit insane. The people with the gift—or curse, as it was—had a genetic mutation allowing them to sense things, depending on their skill or ability. The one she'd met on Krooss had been able to hear people's thoughts and had gone crazy with the constant bombardment. Only a steady dose of clay had kept her coherent enough to even function.

"Have you been with MYTH for long?" Renna asked, trying not to look directly at the woman. She knew most empaths preferred to stay in the shadows, to not be the center of anyone's attention. She totally understood the feeling.

"I was a founding member," Gheewala said proudly, her voice lilting with the accent of her home world. Renna placed her somewhere in the Inner Quadrant, those planets who'd first joined the Coalition. From the way she spoke, Renna guessed her family had been wealthy and well-educated.

"So that's how long?"

"Over ten years. Prior to that, I had a post on Vesper Nine, monitoring commuter traffic and interplanetary communications."

Renna's heart skipped. This woman was a tech empath. She'd heard of those, rarer than rare, who could recognize and intercept ship signatures, digital and light ray communications, and other particle sensory details. Most tech empaths committed suicide or overdosed on their choice of drug before they reached adulthood, but those who learned to control their abilities were highly sought after by the Coalition. The military was very lucky to have her.

She didn't have time to ask any more questions as they came to the main communications area where she'd first entered the compound. The same workers sat at their same stations, and a jolt shot through her. It had been less than two hours since her arrival at MYTH headquarters.

Two hours and her life would never be the same.

"Dallas has pulled together six of the best MYTH agents I've seen for this mission," Gheewala continued, interrupting Renna's racking thoughts. "I hope it's enough."

Renna raised her eyebrows. "You mean to tell me he's only sending *six* people to save the galaxy? What—did his budget get cut recently?"

"I don't think you understand. Six MYTH agents is like having a full platoon of other soldiers." The sergeant pressed her finger to a scanner, and a door slid open, leading down another corridor.

Renna cursed under her breath. MYTH's facility was huge, and she had no idea of the layout. Dammit. She desperately needed to fix her implant or find a new one before they left, but she'd bet her life MYTH didn't have the resources on site for something like that. Cyborg tech—especially black market—was frowned upon by most governments.

They walked for almost a minute in silence before turning down another utilitarian hallway. Gheewala finally stopped in front of a plain steel door. Inside was yet another standard-issue table surrounded by chairs made of some inexpensive but long-lasting polyplastic.

Dallas and the rest of the team were already waiting for them. "Please have a seat, Renna. We were about to get started with the debrief." He pointed to one of the empty chairs, and she slipped into it, crossing her arms.

"Is this going to take long? My feet are starting to get itchy." Always a good sign trouble was on the way, trouble she didn't want to be a part of.

"We have medicine for that," Gheewala said, pausing in her scan of the room to focus for a moment on Renna. She looked very concerned.

"It's a figure of speech, Sergeant," Renna explained kindly.

Across the room, Keva snorted and quickly pressed her fingers to her lips, turning away. Dallas took his spot at the head of the room, but Captain Finn stayed on his feet near the door. He'd changed out of the ninja suit into a crisp black uniform that looked almost as stiff as his spine.

The major paced, his shoulders around his ears. "Comm chatter has picked up in the last hour. We need to get you on your way ASAP. We've had reports that the planet they held Myka at prior to Hesperia has been attacked."

"Status?" Finn asked.

"Destroyed." Dallas tugged at his collar. "Dr. Aldani has been notified that Myka is safe. He assures us he has been working on the tech to get us inside the bunker. We need you to go to his labs on Iniros to pick it up and deliver the boy, but your route will have to be top secret. No one must know where Myka has gone. Even our own controllers will be told you are going to another planet. I will, unfortunately, be unable to communicate with you due to the sensitive nature of the mission and the chance of interception. Captain Finn has his orders and will fill you in on a need-to-know basis."

Dallas turned to Renna. "What I am about to say is not to leave this room."

She smirked. "I'm a thief. I know how to keep a secret."

"You also know how to sell them to the highest bidder," Keva muttered.

Renna clenched her hands in her lap. Someday she was going to knock that smug smile off that woman's beaky lips, and it wouldn't be in the sparring ring.

"I assume you've heard about the attack on Banos Prime three years ago?" Dallas asked, jerking her out of her dark thoughts.

She nodded. The murder of ten thousand civilians was always big news. "Myka said his parents had been killed there."

"Correct. They were there as scientists, ostensibly working for the mining colony doing research. In reality, they were part of the MYTH team investigating a strange mineral found on-world."

"And Myka didn't know?"

"Of course not. He's a child. But what his parents found put us on high alert a few days before the attack. Someone had built a station to take the minerals found in the Banos Prime soil and convert them into a new type of clay."

That drug seemed to be the cause of every problem in her life. She took a deep breath. "So someone killed an entire colony to keep production secret?"

"Partly. We also think the Aldanis had additional information about technology they discovered."

Renna tapped her finger on the smooth white surface of the table. "Well, you have the kid now, and I'm assuming the tech I retrieved was the stuff you were looking for. What else do you need me for?"

Dallas's lips tightened into a thin line. "Whoever was behind the attack on Banos Prime hasn't stopped. They're still after something, and we need to know what."

"I haven't heard of any attacks."

Dallas stopped pacing long enough to tap the holopad on the table, careful to keep his eyes averted from the screen. The map of the galaxy on the wall flickered and then disappeared, replaced by high-definition photo images.

Mangled bodies, smoking cities, blood, death, and destruction flashed by in a blur. Renna's stomach roiled, and she pressed a hand to her mouth.

"That's Nath. Or what's left of it. Two months ago, it was attacked without warning, and most of the humans on the planet killed. We don't know what the attackers were looking for or if they found it."

Renna dragged her gaze from the screen, swallowing the acid burning the back of her throat. "There's been no word of this. Not even a hint." She had contacts on every planet. There was no way the Coalition could have kept this a secret.

"MYTH is a powerful organization." Dallas's gaze fell to the table and his expression tightened. "And there were few survivors left to talk."

"But what do they want? Why are they doing this?" The pictures kept coming, and she wanted to scream at him to turn them off. She'd seen it all before, but there was something about the way the bodies had been gutted, the way their blood splattered everything around them… It was horrific.

"That's what we need your help to find out. We know the gamma particle destabilizer is part of it. So is Myka. Dr. Aldani agreed to help us if we rescued his nephew, but he refused to work on anything until Myka was returned. We think he knows more than he's telling us."

Myka's uncle seemed like a very smart man. "Nice to see someone able to stand up to you."

Dallas's face darkened. "We've found another manufacturing installation in the middle of the desert on Banos Prime, about twenty klicks from the city's ruins. We think it's the same people."

Renna's gaze rested on Lieutenant Keva and the two silent men sitting beside her. They all looked more than capable. She already knew the captain was. "I've seen how your space ninjas work. You're telling me they couldn't rescue a little boy from thugs like the Cordozas?"

"It wasn't that we couldn't. We just wanted to see if you could."

Her nausea faded away as every muscle in her body hardened. "You mean you used this kid as a frakking test for me?" she snarled.

Dallas raised a hand calmingly. "No, not at all. Myka was genuinely in danger, and we needed to rescue him. You were the closest thing we had to a stealth team. Had Finn's crew broken into the warehouse, it would have alerted the Cordozas immediately. And this way I was able to force my superiors into agreeing to give you those pardons if you helped us. It was for your benefit as well as ours."

"I don't much like your definition of benefit." Renna crossed her arms. "What I don't understand is what you think I can do at a manufacturing facility. I'm no scientist."

"No, but you can get into places no one else can. And this facility is...different." Dallas nodded at Keva, and she used the tablet in front of her to pull an aerial photo onto the screen.

A dull gray building sat in the middle of the desert. Keva flipped through several pictures, different angles. The walls were completely smooth. No doors, windows or other entrances. It looked like some sort of huge box.

"What the hell is that?"

Dallas frowned. "That's what we'd like to know. And we need to get inside. We're working on alternative solutions, but you're the only person who might be able find us a way in and help us uncover whoever is attacking these colonies and why."

Renna leaned forward to study the pictures. "I can't get into something with no opening. No matter how good I am. What makes you think there's anything in there to begin with?"

"Aldani says there is. He's developing the tools to help you get inside." Dallas motioned to Keva to turn off the holovid. "Our next step is for Captain Finn's team to take Myka and the particle destabilizer home to Aldani. Renna will work with the doctor to figure out the best way to get into the facility. Once we know what we're up against, we can figure out a way to stop the people behind these attacks."

He paused, letting his gaze drift over the team. "I know some of you are not happy with my team selection. I assure you that each of you has been handpicked for your exceptional skills. You all know what is at stake here and what needs to be done. I trust you'll do whatever it takes to ensure the end result."

Keva jumped to her feet and saluted. "We are honored to be part of this mission, sir!"

Dallas saluted back.

And then the earth trembled as an explosion rocked the room.

SEVEN

What the hell was that?" Dallas demanded into his communicator. His face blanched at whatever he heard, and he steadied himself on the back of a chair. The rest of the team watched him, too well trained to question him.

Renna had no such qualms. "What was it? Felt like we were hit with a bomb."

"We were." He ran an unsteady hand through his hair and started barking orders into his communicator unit. "Send Spec Ops 7 to intercept. We need men on the ground now! Get the cruisers into the air." He whirled on his heel. "Keva, get the boy and meet us on the ship. The rest of you move. Now."

The crew raced from the room in a thunder of boots and shouted orders. Renna turned to follow, but Dallas stopped her with a raised hand. He paced the room twice, shouting orders into his comm unit, before he turned back to her. "Okay. Follow me, Renna. I know you haven't had time to ask questions. What else do you need to know for this job?"

She expected the facility to be chaotic and crazy, but the workers still sat at their stations in the command center, speaking softly into their headpieces, moving things around on their holovids. She assumed those moving pieces were ships or people, but it was hard to tell as she and Dallas hurried past. He called out a steady stream of orders as they exited the room and headed down a hallway toward what she assumed was the hangar bay.

"How many troops?" Renna asked when Dallas was done issuing orders.

"Ours or theirs?"

Despite herself, she was beginning to like the major. "Let's start with theirs."

"Two destroyers have been spotted attacking the Warehouse District. It's gone. Everything is gone." He swallowed, his eyes flashing before he brought himself under control. "They're moving north through the city, looking for…whatever they've come to find." His hands clenched at his sides. "But how did they know? It's like they launched their attack as soon as we sent in Finn's team to rescue you and the boy. It doesn't make any sense."

Renna swallowed. There was only one thing she could think of that made sense if that was true, and it meant MYTH might have a leak. But Dallas's pale face made her hold her tongue.

Instead she asked, "What are our troops doing? Where are they focusing the attack?" She pushed aside the thought of Boyd, her fence and the closest thing she'd had to a friend. His apartment wasn't too far from the Warehouse District. He always said it paid to be close to work.

Her stomach ached, but she focused on Dallas's next words.

"We've sent three platoons of MYTH soldiers and two regular platoons of Coalition troops, and three starship cruisers are in orbit. Whoever they are, they won't get out of here without a serious fight." He cleared his throat as if remembering who he was talking to. "But right now, we need to worry about getting you off-world. The hangar is down this hall. The MYTH team and a small platoon of soldiers are already waiting."

"How big a crew do we have?"

"The *Athena* is a frigate with a service crew of thirty, plus the six MYTH officers. They've all served together on several missions now." His gaze was cold, and she could read the warning there. "I've read your file. You need to behave yourself, Renna. It's not a buffet."

She smirked and tossed her hair over her shoulder. "I am a professional. You don't need to worry. Much."

Dallas entered a code on the datapad at the hangar door, and it slid open with a *whoosh* of air. Renna inhaled deeply; the smell of starfuel, machinery, and space filled her lungs. Gods, it smelled like home.

And then she spotted the prettiest cruiser she'd ever seen gleaming in the helolights. The ship was long and silver, with a dark red stripe running down the center. Two long wings jutted from the back, and the nose of the ship was blunt and wide, all the better to jump to hyperspace with.

Her skin prickled. She recognized it as an Infiltrator-class frigate. One of the newest and stealthiest on the market. She was going to enjoy getting to know her new home.

Dallas smiled at her. "That's the *Athena*. She'll get you where you need to go and then some. Be nice to Finn and I can promise you, you'll get there unharmed."

"I planned on it. Anyone who captains a beauty like this deserves my best behavior." Or at least his pilot did.

Inside the ship, the familiar hum of the engines and the smell of recycled air greeted her like an old friend, but Dallas was moving too fast for her to get much more than an impression of the main deck. The crew was already sitting at their stations to man the ship controls. It might be a new frigate, but the ship couldn't fly itself.

She followed him to the command center, a circular space looking forward over the ship. Captain Finn paced back and forth, barking orders as they prepped for takeoff. Keva sat at a terminal beside him, her fingers flying across a holoscreen.

Major Dallas turned and clasped her hand in his. "Good luck to you, Renna. We're all counting on you." Then he strode over to Captain Finn. The two men spoke in hushed tones, glancing at her once before Dallas spoke into the ship's comm unit. His mellow voice filled the empty space around them. "The success of this mission depends on you. Be swift, silent, and deadly. And may the gods be with you all." He saluted before stepping down from the command center. Without a look back, he strode from the ship.

As the hatch closed behind him, Renna heard footfalls as someone sprinted toward her. She spun just in time for Myka to throw himself at her.

"I thought they were going to leave without you!" he said, hugging her around her waist.

She patted his back. "Can't get rid of me that easily, kid. They been treating you okay?"

He stepped back and nodded, scuffing one of his shiny shoes against the deck. "New clothes, a shower, some food and water. I'm much better now."

"Good. They really don't want to see me get angry." She winked at him, then nodded toward the bridge. "Come on, I have a feeling this is going to be a bumpy ride. Let's find somewhere safe." Renna waited for a pause in the action before calling up to Finn. "Captain, where do you want us?"

He glanced at her in surprise, as if he'd forgotten their presence. Her smile slipped. Was she that forgettable?

"Private Adams," Finn said, "Take these two to the observation deck and strap them in. Then get your ass back here."

One of the young men scurrying around paused when he heard his name and saluted the captain. "Sir. Yes, sir." He turned to Renna and Myka. "Follow me." He led them past the comm station, through a large meeting room, and into the port observation deck.

"Can you take care of him? I need to get back." Adams jerked his head toward the command center.

"We're fine. Go." So Finn still ran a tight ship. At least that hadn't changed. She swallowed away the memories. "Okay, kid.

Have a seat." She strapped Myka into one of the chairs, then took a seat by the window.

"I want to see, too." Myka struggled against the harness.

"Stay where you are," she said with a frown. "This isn't going to be pretty."

"But you're by the window." His voice rose to a whine.

"And I'm an adult."

The boy opened his mouth, but a look from Renna silenced him. She gripped the steady-handle beside the window and rested her forehead against the thick glass, letting her eyes drift shut for a moment. Who would want to destroy a planet just to find a little boy? It didn't make sense. She shivered. Would she ever see Hesperia again?

Luckily, most of her liquid assets were stored in off-world banks and other locations. She'd learned long ago that diversification was the best bet for someone like her. Having to go into hiding on a moment's notice meant always being prepared. Her free hand drifted to her throat where she carried her most prized possession, the Seralline Star Sapphire. She'd taken the job as a challenge, as a way to prove she was the best thief in the galaxy. Now she wished she'd never heard of the damn thing. It had caused her nothing but trouble.

Case in point: being blackmailed into helping on a suicide mission.

Unfortunately, the Star was worth more than the gross domestic product of all the Outer Rim worlds put together. It was her security blanket, her ticket to freedom. As long as she had it, she had an escape plan. And she always liked to have an escape plan.

Even that last day with Blur's gang, when the cops had arrived. She'd mapped a route out of the warehouse sometime during that first year with them, never thinking she'd have to use it. Three years later, slipping out the ventilation shaft had saved her from a life of hard labor on a prison planet. She'd worked alone after that. Getting involved was too dangerous. She could only depend on herself.

What would her life have been like if Hunter—if *Finn*—hadn't betrayed them? Would she still be working for Blur? Still tied to the gang by death and lies and violence? Renna let out a sigh. No sense in going down that road now. All of that had been a long time ago.

Beneath her feet, the engines rumbled to life, the ship's blood starting to pump and churn as they readied for take off. Sunlight streamed into the hangar as the doors above opened to the Hesperian summer sky.

Right. It was still daylight out here in the real world. Soon, they'd be in space, where time didn't matter, where the velvety darkness was a constant presence, wrapping her in its soft cocoon.

Captain Finn's voice came over the comm. "Stand by for takeoff."

Renna's stomach fluttered as the ship moved. And then they were out into the bright summer air, shooting upward so fast she gasped and clutched the grip as they went vertical, her ears screaming with the pressure of rising so quickly.

They cleared the MYTH building, then the other skyscrapers. Below them, the city of Veth was laid out in a grid. A smoking, crater-filled grid. She bit back a gasp, the image burned forever into her mind. The Warehouse District was gone, nothing but rubble. She craned her neck toward her apartment building, but there was nothing left. Even the less inhabited part of the city off to the east was now pocked with craters and smoking debris.

Strange destroyers churned through the city, obliterating everything in their path. They were unlike anything she'd ever seen: three stories tall, with double wings on each side and a long narrow tail.

Three MYTH battlecruisers shot past the *Athena*, their engines grinding as they banked toward the attacking fleet. Fire and missiles burst from the weapons bays of both fleets, streaming toward their closest targets in a blast of fire.

As one of the enemy cruisers pulled away, an explosion shook the air around them. Below, near the center of the city, a gaping crater had opened up, smoking and blazing with fire.

Renna unlatched her harness, her stomach tightening at the sight of the city below them. She had to clear her throat before the words came out properly. "Stay here. I need to check in with Finn," she said to Myka.

His eyes widened, and he put out a hand to stop her. "But Renna..."

"I'll be right back. I promise." She smiled reassuringly, waiting to pick up her pace until she was out of sight. She raced back to the bridge and heard Finn barking orders before she spotted him pacing in front of the holomap.

"Bank hard to port. Keva, patch through Dallas's comm feed. I need to know what's happening on the ground. Bokal, charge the guns. We're going to need them before we're out of Hesperia's atmosphere."

"Aye, aye, sir." Keva typed in a command at her console, and the crackle of static from the intercom filled the ship.

The roar of an explosion from the comm shook the bridge before Dallas's voice boomed out. "Evacuate! Get all support staff to the bunkers! Team Alpha to the ground entrance! Order the fighters to come around for another assault!"

Finn stared down at the console, his hands clenched into fists. "Dammit. They're getting killed out there. We have to do something."

Keva frowned. "You know our orders, sir. We have to escape with the boy."

Dallas's voice shouted through the comm. "Status on the *Athena*. Now!"

A woman answered. "Sir, they're approaching atmospheric release. They'll be away in three minutes." Her voice was cool and collected, a sharp contrast to the sound of explosions in the background.

"Keep the fighters on the offensive! Captain Finn has to get away. Evacuate all personnel from the facility. Then get to safety yourself."

The woman's voice came again. Renna assumed she was one of the technicians she'd seen in the command center. "What about you, sir?"

"I'm on my way. Now get going!" Ragged breathing sounded over the intercom, then Dallas spoke again. "Finn, I don't know if you're catching this, but the attackers are on the ground. They've destroyed most of the city center and the Warehouse District. They're looking for the boy. Keep him safe. We'll do our best from here."

The comm crackled again, a whine filling the air. The next second, a blast shattered through the comm speakers. A moment later, the ship shivered with the aftershock.

Renna dashed to one of the portals and pressed her forehead to the glass to peer down at the tiny city below them. A mushroom of smoke and fire rose almost to the atmosphere. The city of Veth was nothing but a smoking ruin now. There was no way Dallas had survived unless the facility had been made of bomb-proof material.

"Try him again!" Captain Finn shouted, pounding a fist on the control panel.

"Sir, we're almost out of the ground-to-air comms range. There's nothing there. We'll be clearing Hesperia's atmosphere in thirty seconds." Keva's gaze never left her screen, her lips a thin slash on her face.

"Dammit!" Finn slammed his fist down again.

Renna had one last glance of the enemy battleships starting to retreat before the *Athena* shot into the twilight of the upper atmosphere. Below them, Hesperia rapidly shrunk into a glowing ball.

Renna took a deep breath and released her death grip on the portal edge. It took her a moment to realize the trembles she felt in her limbs weren't vibrations from the ship. The icy rage that had silently crept into her belly as she watched those fuckers destroy her home and slaughter millions of innocent people rushed through her veins until she was shaking.

Boyd was dead. The crazy woman down the hall was dead. The guy who always walked his kids to school so they wouldn't be bullied by thugs was gone. And so were his eight-year-old twins.

The whole godsdamned city—nothing more than ashes of bodies and buildings.

Suddenly, she didn't care that she'd been blackmailed into boarding this ship. She didn't care that MYTH had enough information on her to send her on a one-way ticket to hell. None of that mattered anymore.

Because this? This act of war? Bombing her city?

It was personal now.

The intercom clicked on, and Finn's voice filled the ship. "MYTH headquarters is silent. We are on our own now. Let's take a moment to remember those whose lives were taken in the attack." There was a long pause before he spoke again. "Everyone, settle in for now. We'll land on Krooss in twenty-four hours, where we'll refuel before moving on to Dr. Aldani's labs."

He ran a shaking hand through his dark hair and snapped off the comm. His shoulders sagged for a moment, and he stared down at the console in a moment of despair. Renna wanted to go to him, to tell him it was going to be okay, but before she could move, Finn sucked in a deep breath. With that one action, his shoulders straightened, and he was back to the cool, unflappable Captain Finn. He wasn't the one who needed her now.

She spun on her heel. Dammit.

Myka.

EIGHT

Renna rushed back to the port observation deck just as Myka unhooked his harness. He slipped from his seat to gaze out into the darkness of space.

"You okay?" she asked, coming to stand beside him. The cool recycled air from the vents brushed her skin, made her hair tickle her face. She pushed it away, forcing a smile. The kid had been through enough already. He didn't need to see how pissed she was.

"What happened?" he asked. "All I saw was smoke."

"They hit Veth pretty hard, but we got away. You'll be back with your uncle soon. I promise." The word slipped out before she could stop it. Promises were few and far between in her line of work, and she never said it unless she meant it. It was a personal policy of hers.

From the corridor came the heavy thud of boots on the metal floor. Captain Finn stood in the doorway, his eyes shadowed and tired. Renna saw the effort it took him to keep his face friendly as he looked down at the boy. "Everything all right over here?"

Myka threw his shoulders back, head held high. "We're fine."

"Good. I thought I might take you on a tour of the *Athena* now before you get settled in. We're in the pre-FTL check phase so I have a few minutes." Although he spoke to Myka, his gaze flicked to Renna.

She nodded. "Sounds like a good plan. Myka and I could use a snack, too. We're both starving."

"First stop, galley!" Finn gestured to the corridor with a flourish. "Right this way, honored guests."

Renna's heart twisted at the lopsided grin he gave Myka. It was the same one he'd given her ten years ago, when she'd shown up dirty and hungry at Blur's warehouse. The same flourish he'd used as he held the door for her. She put out a hand to the cool wall of the ship to steady herself.

Stop it.

The mess hall was a long room along the port side of the ship. Several large community tables filled the space, and a service area lined the wall. A matronly woman in a crisp white apron stood guard over several pots of soupy liquid.

"My mate and I are looking for some grub; got anything space-worthy?" Finn asked with an over-exaggerated wink at the woman.

"You must be our new passenger—Myka, is it?" The woman's plump face beamed. "I'm Mary Wilson, but you can call me Miss Mary, if you like."

The boy nodded. "Pleased to meet you, Miss Mary."

She beamed again, her smile stretching her wrinkled face. "Isn't he just a doll? I have just the thing for you, Myka. How about a steaming mug of tea and a plate of my fresh molasses cookies? They're my great-great-gran's recipe; she was from Old-Earth." She moved away to get a plate and cup while Myka slipped into a chair at the nearest table.

"Are you going to stay here? Or finish the tour?" Finn asked, slanting Renna a reluctant look.

The last thing she wanted was to be alone with him again, but the sooner he realized she wasn't going to let him push her around, the better off everyone would be. She glanced at Myka, who nodded.

"Sure," Renna said. "I'm curious to see the rest of this beauty. This is one of the Infiltrator models, right?"

Finn led her away from the mess hall. "The *Athena*'s one of the newest starships in the fleet. Specially designed for MYTH operations with a near-silent quantum core, she's equipped with special cloaking material to get us in and out without detection." Finn ran a hand along the seamless metal wall, caressing it like he might a woman.

She forced away the image of his hand caressing her like that and cleared her throat. "It's gorgeous. Think Dallas might get me one, too, after this is all over?" She said it flippantly and then wished she hadn't when a shadow passed over Finn's handsome face. "I'm sorry. I didn't mean… I'm sure he's fine. He seemed like a tough old guy."

Finn shook his head. "Dallas's one of the best. I've known him since I first joined MYTH. I hope he made it out." His tone made it very clear he didn't want to talk about it. Instead, he led her to the bow of the ship where the pilot and first mate were prepping the *Athena* for the jump to hyperspace.

"This is Flight Lieutenant Mark Kojima. He's one of the best. Kojima, this is Renna Carrizal."

The guy looked about twenty-one or so, a few years younger than Renna. Finn let someone so young pilot his ship? But she hid her surprise and smiled at him as she held out her hand.

Kojima gave her an appraising once-over before grasping her hand. "Welcome to the *Athena*. Glad to have you aboard."

"Thanks. You handle this bird better than most of the pilots I've flown with. The way you escaped those cruisers with the thrusters was genius. I don't think even Herceg could have done it better."

Kojima's eyes widened. "You've flown with Herceg? He's a legend! Did you know he was the first to jump to hyperspace without needing the core fusion generator?"

"I was actually on the *Bluebird* when he did it."

Kojima opened his mouth, but before he could respond, Finn crossed his arms, his uniform jacket stretching over his shoulders. "Enough chatter. Back to your post, Lieutenant. You can compare flight notes with Miss Carrizal later."

"Yes, sir!" Kojima saluted, but winked at Renna when Finn turned around.

"Nice to meet you," she called before following the captain down another passageway.

The ship's interior seemed to be one long oval, with an elliptical corridor running the entire length and another smaller corridor in the center. The floors were made of corrugated metal, polished to a high shine, and the walls had been covered in some sort of thick polythene plastic to heat the space and cut down on the ship's noise.

It was gorgeously designed and obviously top of the line. Renna had some serious ship envy. Since the Seralline job two years ago, she'd had to stay out of sight, which meant giving up her own ship. It had been too easy to track. Using public transport or renting with a fake ID was safer. But someday...

Renna sighed. If she got through this damn mission first. "So where to next? Lower deck?"

"Staff quarters are on the lowest deck. There should be no reason for you to go down there."

She arched an eyebrow. "Whyever not? It's not that big of a ship. I'm sure I'll be down there once in a while."

Finn stopped in the middle of the corridor and turned his cold blue eyes to her. There it was again, the brief pause as he studied the scar on her neck. He'd always been fascinated by it, especially since Renna never talked about how she'd gotten it.

He dragged his gaze back to her face. "I've already told you I don't want someone like you on my ship—*or* fraternizing with my crew. I know you, Renna. I know how you work. But Dallas says you're the only one who can figure out who these people are and help stop them, so I have no choice." He lowered his voice and leaned close enough that his scent washed over her again. "Let me remind you: There's a chain of command here, and I'm at the top."

So much for working together. Whatever he thought he knew, she wasn't some raw recruit now. She was the best thief in the galaxy, and he damn well needed to remember it.

Renna lowered her voice to match his tone. "I don't mind you on top, darling. It's when you start pushing me around that we'll have a problem." She smiled at him coldly. "So I'll do my job, don't you worry. Just don't expect me to play by your rules. You know I was never very good at following orders."

"It's the only reason you're still free."

"What the hell do you mean by that?" she demanded, her hands on her hips.

"You should have been there when the police raided Blur's hideout. You were supposed to be back from the Peters job already." His eyes bored into hers, his top lip curling. "You should have gone to hell with the rest of them for what you did."

"If you think that should mean something to me, I hate to disappoint you, Cap, but I don't know what in the stars you're talking about." She leaned in close to him, her fingers itching to poke him in his chest. She curled them into tight fists instead and lifted her chin, throwing his own hard stare back at him. "But let me tell *you* something. Just because you knew me *seven years ago* doesn't mean you know one damn thing about me or my life now."

"I know enough to want you the hell off my ship. I would have been perfectly happy to have never seen you again." His raspy voice deepened into a growl, and his hands clenched and unclenched at his sides. "If I wasn't under orders, I'd leave you on the next planet."

"If I wasn't being blackmailed into helping your sorry ass, I'd be more than happy to go!"

"Then do it. I'll even write your discharge papers. I'll risk the court-martial; I just want you off my ship, Carrizal. I don't need a sticky-fingered whore distracting my crew."

"A whore? Is that the most creative thing you can come up with?" She shook her head and pursed her lips. "I'm so disappointed, Captain. The man I knew was much better with his tongue."

He grabbed her arms and yanked her to his chest. "The man you knew died seven years ago, along with any respect he might have had for you."

She leaned into him until she could feel his heart thundering beneath hers, his chest rising and falling in time with her own breathing. "Then why do you keep bringing him up? Why do you watch me like you're reliving the same memories I am?"

"I'm watching to make sure you don't steal anything. I know how you operate—everything is fair game to sell to the highest bidder. You never could be trusted."

Her fingernails bit into her palms. She'd knock the smug look from his face if he said one more word.

Footsteps vibrated on the metal floor of the corridor as Keva darted around the corner. "What the hell do you two think you're doing shouting at each other? The whole ship's going to hear you!"

A muscle jumped in Finn's jaw. He pushed Renna away, stepping back so the width of the corridor separated them.

Renna forced her hands to stay at her side. "Isn't that too bad?" she drawled, feigning calm despite the hammering in her chest. "Maybe your crew will finally see you for what you are."

"And what's that?" he asked dangerously, lowering his voice.

"You're as mercenary as I am," she said, matching his low tone.

"Watch yourself, Renna. The truth is a double-edged sword, and last I knew, swordplay wasn't your strong suit." The ice in his words could have frozen the deepest lake on Hesperia.

"Things change, Captain. I've grown up. I know how to play with lots of new toys."

Murder flashed in his eyes, and he took a step forward. Renna hastily swallowed her next witty quip.

"Betray me again, and I'll make sure you serve the rest of your life on a hard work planet."

This again? Renna's smile was icy. "Do you really want to talk about betrayal, Cap? Because I have a few choice words regarding your own actions. I'm happy to share if we're going to play that game." She leaned back against the wall, arms crossed. Despite her relaxed pose, she held herself tightly in check. One more word from him and she'd attack, prison planet be damned. "And if you ever call me a whore again, I'll make sure you never have the luxury of enjoying a real one."

Finn growled and spun on his heels. "Keva, show the thief to her cabin. I'm done here." He strode away in the opposite direction, anger rolling off him in tangible waves.

Keva's jaw dropped open, her purple, beak-like lips parted in shock. "I've never seen the captain so angry. What did you do?" the lieutenant demanded.

"I have no idea." Renna shook out her hands and cracked her neck, trying to relax the muscles in her body that were still coiled like springs. She hadn't felt so out of control in years. Not since the last time she and Hunter...*Finn* had sparred.

Damn him and damn her past for finally catching up with her.

NINE

That night, Renna fell asleep to the hum of a ship's engine in her ears for the first time in almost six months. It was the smoothest, steadiest sound she'd ever heard, and she fell a little more in love with the *Athena*.

Despite the blow-up with Finn and the destruction of Veth, she slept like a rock. She always did while traveling, and when the morning bell rang for the crew to switch shifts, she stretched in her bunk and snuggled more deeply under the covers. There was no reason for her to get up. She wasn't an official member of the team. Finn had made that very clear last night.

An hour or so later, the ship trembled as it came out of FTL, and she jerked awake. They'd reached Krooss. She'd been on the planet once, five years ago, for a job. It was a backwater planet, the space port barely a scrabble of clay buildings and steel warehouses, but it was one of the last stops in the Thassa system to fuel up.

She stretched and glanced around her room. The berth they'd assigned her was small but comfortable, with a bed, a holovid on the wall, and a table and chair in the corner. A low leather couch sat across from the holovid, and another door led to a bathroom. The place was nicer than her first apartment.

And the shower was amazing. The bad thing about space travel was how dirty it always made her feel—the recycled air, the metal coatings, the space particles. But after a quick rinse, she felt almost human again.

Renna peeked in on Myka, but he was still sleeping and she didn't want to wake him. Gods knew the last time the kid had had a good night's sleep.

She headed toward the bridge, passing crew members busy at their stations, mechanics on their way to the engine room, even a private wiping space dust off the walls. As she approached the center of the ship, she heard Finn talking with the crew. There was no way she was dealing with him before she'd even had her coffee, so she changed routes and made her way to the flight deck where Kojima was on duty.

At least he didn't look at her like she was diseased.

"Good morning, Miss Carrizal." He smiled as she climbed the stairs to his cockpit.

"Call me Renna, please."

"Then what brings you my way this fine morning, Renna?"

She raised an eyebrow. "I didn't think I'd exactly be welcome on the bridge after my little fight with the captain yesterday."

"I heard about that." He chuckled. "I've never seen the guy lose it, and I've served with him on three missions now."

"Yeah? How long have you been with MYTH?" She studied the holoscreens and consoles in front of him. He might look young, but he had some serious skills to run this complex navigation system.

"Four years. They recruited me straight from the academy. Been with Captain Finn almost the whole time. He's one of the best."

"I'll take your word for it."

Kojima gave her a sly look. "It's got to be your reputation that's got him up in arms. It's not every mission we get to host the Star Thief."

Her face went carefully expressionless. "What are you talking about?" By the stars, had Dallas told everyone?

"I know everything that happens on this ship. Including all personnel files. Don't worry, I'll never tell. But if the rest of the crew knew…"

"They'd put me in the brig." Or even worse, turn her in for the billion-credit bounty on her head.

He smiled but didn't deny it. "So what was it like? Being on Treze? Stealing the sapphire?" He tapped at his console before turning back to her. "Those aliens are weird, right? Four arms? Gills and scales?"

She leaned against the hatch frame. "The Trezian military is unlike any other in the galaxy. It puts MYTH to shame. I mean, what could you do with four arms?"

Kojima slanted a glance at her from the corner of his eye as he adjusted one of the nav points on his screen. "So how did you do it?"

A small smile curled her lips. "Sorry, that's classified."

"Come on, just a hint?"

"Sorry, kid, some secrets are best kept."

"Hey, you're not that much older than me." He sounded pouty for a moment before he realized it and grinned. "Fine. But next shore leave, the guys and I are going to take you out. Maybe after a few drinks, you'll spill."

"I can drink you under the table," Renna said with a laugh.

"What the hell are you doing up there, Flight Lieutenant?" Captain Finn's voice cracked through the intercom, and Kojima jumped. "We're on approach to Krooss. Have you radioed for our landing berth yet?"

"No, sir. Doing that now, sir." Kojima turned back to Renna. "You'd better get out of here before I get in trouble."

She took a deep breath and steadied her nerves. The *Athena* wasn't that big. She was going to have to see Finn sooner or later, and putting it off made her feel like a coward. And that pissed her off. Renna squared her shoulders and marched to the bridge.

Finn sat in the captain's chair watching the holo as the *Athena* approached Krooss. His gaze flicked to her briefly as she stood at the railing, but he said nothing. Together they watched the spaceport appear and the *Athena* head to her berth on the west side of town.

"We'll be here for three hours. I expect you to stay on board while we refuel." Finn still didn't look at her.

"I thought you wanted me off your ship."

"I want you to do your job," he said, slamming his fist down on the arm of the chair. "And that means following my orders."

Well, well. The supposedly unflappable captain was still angry at her. Interesting. Men usually only stayed that angry for one reason: injured pride.

"Whatever you say, Cap. You're the boss." She wandered away, hands shoved into her pockets and her shoulders relaxed. Wouldn't do for him to see how annoyed she was. She had no desire to see the dirty spaceport, but damn she'd wanted to argue. Just to prove to him that she didn't do blind obedience.

Instead, she walked to the officers' quarters and woke Myka to get some breakfast. Miss Mary already had food ready and waiting for him when they got to the mess, but she wasn't as kind to Renna. She had to dish up her own plate of rubbery-looking scrambled eggs and some dry toast.

Mary's gaze lingered over the boy as she lowered her large frame into the seat across from them. "How'd you sleep, Myka? Is your berth all right?"

Myka nodded, too busy stuffing himself with breakfast.

Mary smiled at his obvious appetite. "The *Athena* is the best ship I've ever served on. And that's been quite a few."

Renna paused, fork halfway to her mouth. "Don't you have a family? Children?"

Mary's gaze dropped to the table, and her fingers traced a gouge in the steel. "My Harold and I didn't have children. And now it's just me. It's why I joined MYTH. Figured I'm the best cook out there, why not cook for those'll appreciate me?"

"Noble sentiment." Renna paused. "Have you been with MYTH long? I thought they were top secret."

"You're not the only one they recruited. I've been with them six years now. And I must say their offer came at an auspicious time. I'd been planning to leave Logaaine anyway. Things were getting a bit too hot for me to take on any more jobs."

Renna felt her eyes widen. "You were a mercenary?"

Mary nodded. "In my younger days. Left it all behind me when I was with Harold. He was my moral compass. After he died, it was easy to slip back into the old ways, but I'm getting a bit too old for it now. Wish I'd saved more for my retirement." She looked wistfully at the boy, then heaved herself to her feet. "MYTH's been good to me. I'd hate to see anyone double-cross them." She pinned Renna with a cool stare before returning to her kitchen.

Renna watched her go. Would that be her in another twenty years? Cooking or cleaning for someone else just to scrape by? Slipping back into mercenary work if nothing legal came up?

The weight of her empty life made her chest ache. She flitted from planet to planet, never getting attached to anything or anyone. She'd been working toward retirement from the day she'd run away at thirteen, from the day she'd realized this business would kill her just as drugs had killed her mother.

But no matter what she told herself after every job, she kept getting dragged back in. The promise of credits, the thrill of the chase, proving she could tackle and win the hardest jobs.

Oh, she'd had relationships—one-night stands or flings with the hunk of the month, but nothing serious. She'd never let herself slip into that trap. And it had felt like a trap, no matter how much she was looking for a connection. Letting herself become vulnerable had never felt safe and rarely even crossed her mind with the kinds of guys she picked up.

Except once. With Hunter. Finn. Whoever the hell he was.

She'd been a kid and there hadn't been anything more than friendship between them, but he'd understood where she'd come from and seemed to accept her as she was. It'd scared the shit out of her.

And then it had all changed the day the compound was raided. Blur had gone down, a bullet ripping through his chest as she'd watched from her hiding place. Hunter had fallen next, bullets piercing his chest, too. With the two leaders dead, the rest of the gang had given up without a fight, the police rushing in to arrest them all. She'd run for miles to get away from the death of her mentor and the destruction of the only family she'd had left.

With nothing holding her on that world, she'd stowed away on the nearest transport ship to a distant planet and started over. She'd never looked back. But in her heart, she'd always wondered what might have happened between them if Hunter hadn't died.

Renna sighed and took a sip of her tea. Now, here he was. Alive. On the same small ship in the middle of a galaxy. And he hated her. Something had happened all those years ago to turn him from friend to enemy, something big enough to make him betray them all. She just wished she knew what.

One way or another, it had to do with Blur and whatever games he'd been playing. But she'd been a grunt; she hadn't had any choice in the jobs she was assigned. She was going to have to confront Finn about it sooner or later, but right now, getting the kid to his uncle was her only job.

"You all right?" Myka asked, poking her arm.

She smiled, locking the memories up tight in the back of her mind. "I'm fine, just daydreaming. Finished with your tea?"

"Yes." He got to his feet. "Now I need a bathroom."

"I think that can be arranged."

They were headed back toward Myka's room when she heard the shouting from the bridge.

Boom.

The sharp report of a gun echoed through the ship. The walls closed in as Renna tried to suck in a breath. Dammit. If her implant had still been working, she would have instantly known what was going on. Instead, her sixth sense screamed at her to run.

"They're here for me, aren't they?" Myka's voice trembled, his earlier self-assurance vanishing in an instant.

"I'm not sure. But until we know, I think you should hide." Renna scanned the corridor. Most ships had electrical panels at regular intervals to access the guts of the electrical systems. She ran toward the stairs, searching for a big enough space to hide the boy. *There!*

She pulled her nanospanner from her pocket and got to work on the screws holding the panel to the wall. Moments later, she had the panel pulled off. She shone the spotlight on the spanner into the space. Electrical wires ran across the top and there were fuses and fixtures along one wall, but it was big enough for Myka to crawl inside.

"Okay, this is going to have to do it. Get in and I'll screw the panel back on."

He stared into the dark stuffy hole, then glanced back at her, shaking his head. "I can't," he whispered, his face suddenly as pale as the polyplastic covering the walls.

Shit. He'd been trapped inside that cage for gods knew how long. She couldn't make him do it again. Renna squeezed his hand and fought back her own panic. There was no place else for him to hide here, and there was no time to find another place. "Myka—"

A scream came from the front of the ship, and she jumped.

"We're running out of time. You're going to be fine. You can do this, okay? I promise I won't let anything happen to you." She cursed under her breath as that word slipped out again. She didn't know if this was a promise she could keep.

Myka squared his shoulders, swallowing thickly. "I can do it." He stared at the hole in the wall. "I'm tough."

She could have kissed him, but she merely smiled and squeezed his hand again. "You're the toughest kid I've ever met. Now get in and stay quiet no matter what."

Myka nodded. "I promise." He climbed into the dark hole.

Renna could barely see the whites of his eyes as he stared up at her. "Take my spanner. It has a light on it. Use it if you need to." She shoved it into his hands, then lifted the panel back into place, tightening the screws with her fingers.

She pressed a hand against the metal grate. "Be safe, kid. I'll be back as soon as I can." There was no answer as she rose to her feet. Myka was already wrapped up in his own nightmare.

Another shout echoed through the ship, and Renna's heart thudded in her chest in time with her pounding feet. Whatever the hell was going on, she needed to get to the bridge. She needed to find Finn.

Rough arms yanked her to a stop before she could clear the passageway. "Going somewhere, lady?" The man towered over her, and when he smiled at her, a black hole gaped where his front tooth should have been. Her gaze fell to the tribal markings tattooed on his forearm.

Pirates. They must have been waiting for the *Athena* in the fuel station.

She immediately forced herself to relax and give him her sexiest look. "Guess not, big guy. Who do you work for?"

He leered at her and yanked her down the passageway. "Does it matter?"

"Actually, it does. I know most of the mercs in this star system."

"This isn't a social visit, lady. We're here for the kid."

She shrugged, which was difficult with his meaty hand holding her arm. "We don't have any kids on board. You've got the wrong ship." By the gods, did Myka have a tracker on him or something? How did these people keep finding him?

"Boss says it's the right ship. Now stop talking and move!" He jerked her down a set of stairs to the lower deck. "The rest of the crew's already inside." He gestured his blaster at the brig door.

She stopped just inside the room and frowned. Of course. Because that's how today was going. Captain Finn and the rest of his team pressed against the bars of the holding cell.

She'd left her own pistol in her cabin, and Myka had her nanospanner. There was no way she could fight back.

The merc opened the cell door and shoved her inside. Corporal Bokal caught her before she fell.

"Thanks," she said, tugging at her jacket and righting herself.

He nodded. "Any time."

"Where's the cargo?" Finn breathed into her ear.

"Hidden." She eyed their captor, who lounged against the door. His leather pants were well worn, and his black shirt looked like part of a gang uniform. There were only a few crews who operated this far out in the system. Fetah and her team of pirates, but they usually focused on in-space raids. Brencic, whom she hadn't heard from in over a year. And then her stomach clenched.

These men belonged to Viktis.

TEN

Just her frakking luck. She took a steadying breath before turning to Finn and leaning close enough that she could smell his shampoo, the scent of his skin. Her lips barely moved as she whispered, "I know these mercs. And I can get us out of this, but you need to trust me."

"You run with some nice people," Keva muttered, her eyes flashing with anger. "Criminals and pirates. And Dallas expects us to work with you?"

Renna gave the woman a withering glance. "He does. Because I'm about to save all of your lives."

As she spoke, a tall Ileth alien, with broad shoulders and amber skin highlighting his chiseled face, strolled into the room. Cranial ridges sloped back from his forehead like hair, and his violet eyes scanned the captives in the brig.

"Good day," he said, sketching a bow. "I do apologize for this intrusion, but you are carrying cargo we need. Where is the little boy?"

Viktis had changed in the four years she'd last seen him, but his voice was still smooth and polite. Not the voice of a merc, but a politician. If his family hadn't been murdered, he eventually would have taken a seat in the Coalition Senate. But his parents had been too influential, too popular with the masses. They were a threat that had been eliminated by the other houses on Ileth.

Luckily, Viktis's silver tongue had spared his life, and the merc who'd been hired to kill him took the boy on as an apprentice instead. When Renna met him a few years later on a job, Viktis had taken over the merc's territory. He'd even shown Renna a few things himself.

Until he'd tried to kill her.

She stepped forward, tugging at her shirt. Why hadn't she done something better with her hair this morning? "By the gods, someone up there sure has a sense of humor," she drawled, leaning against the cell door.

Viktis's expression froze, shock flashing across the harsh planes of his face before he masked it. "Renna Carrizal. I thought you were on some Outer Rim world, living in luxury."

She smiled sweetly. "Or dead?"

He shrugged apologetically. "You know I didn't have a choice, my dear. The job paid well, and you were getting a bit too close to my territory for comfort."

She felt Captain Finn's disapproval like a hand pressing against her back. She ignored it and let her gaze travel across Viktis's broad shoulders. "And here I thought saving your life all those years ago had been a good deed. Ah, well, all good deeds are punished in this business, aren't they?" She let her eyes drift down to his lips, then licked her own. Slowly.

Viktis chuckled. "Nice to see you haven't changed, my dear."

"Nice to see you have." Her gaze lowered deliberately down his lean body, the leather jacket and tight breeches he wore showing off his lithe frame. The Ileth were a handsome race, and Viktis had definitely aged well.

"You still running that old bucket of junk?" she asked.

"The *Monet* was a beauty. But, no, I have a new cruiser. Won her in a card game."

She laughed and tossed her hair. "That's so cliché."

Viktis grinned. "For a reason. It seems to happen more frequently than you'd expect." He turned to the mercenary guarding the door. "Get her out of there."

The man obeyed. A moment later, Viktis grabbed her arm and pulled her into a tight hug. "Damn, it's good to see you again, Renna."

She hugged him back, making sure to rub her hands along his torso. Not only was he impressively muscled, she discovered he had two guns strapped to his waist and a knife slipped into a side pocket. He'd come well-armed. She expected no less.

When she stepped back, he seemed reluctant to let her go, keeping one of her hands in his. His amber fingers were long and rough, and even back then, he'd known exactly how to use them to pleasure her.

"What in the stars have you been up to these past few years?" he asked.

Renna shook her head, clearing away those long-forgotten images. "Not really the place for catching up, love. How about you tell us what you came for and then we can send you on your way."

He scowled and ran a hand over his jaw. "We're here for the boy. Once we have him, we'll let the rest of the crew go. As long as they don't try to be heroes." He paused, his lips tightening as he studied her. "How about you come with us, Ren? I know you can't really be part of a bunch of Marine stiffs."

She laughed, fighting to keep her voice light. "Afraid so. And we don't have a boy here, aside from Kojima, our pilot. I think you have the wrong ship."

From the brig, the pilot protested her choice of words, but Finn shushed him.

A smile tugged at Viktis's lips. "You're lucky I like your games, Renna." Still holding her hand, he turned to his men. His face went hard, like he'd pulled on a mask as he barked his orders. "Search the ship. Kill anyone who gets in your way. When you find the boy, bring him to me immediately."

"I promise there's no boy here, Viktis." Renna nestled against his arm. "But you do have me. How about we go get reacquainted?"

He smiled down at her. "My thoughts exactly." Viktis headed back toward the stairs, but Renna paused and frowned at Captain Finn, shaking her head ever so slightly. She'd take care of Viktis and then come back and rescue the crew. As long as they didn't do anything stupid in the meantime.

Finn's eyes widened, and he nodded back.

With a sigh, Renna followed Viktis from the ship. Good thing she'd washed her sexy underwear.

Viktis's new ship, the *November*, was docked in the next bay. It wasn't as pretty as the *Athena*, but it was a serviceable beast, large and heavy. The stench of men and sweat and carbonite hit Renna in a wave of choking fumes as she followed Viktis to the commander's quarters. She wrinkled her nose. "This place reeks."

"I thought it best to stick with male mercs for this job. None of them will come down with any maternal feelings for the boy. Unlike you." His eyes raked over her like a physical caress, and Renna shivered. "By gods, woman, you still make me hard just looking at you."

Renna glanced up at him through lowered lashes. "You'll make me blush, Viktis." Heat twisted her insides, but she wrenched her mind back to the task at hand.

"That was my plan." He pressed a finger to the switch on the wall, and the door swished open. "How about a drink? We've got some catching up to do. I want to hear about what you've been up to."

"Since you tried to murder me?"

He draped a heavy arm around her shoulders and grinned wickedly. "Since you escaped."

His quarters were comfortable and sleek, just like Viktis. She threw herself down into a threadbare chair and reached for the whiskey bottle on the table, along with one of the glasses sitting beside it. She held the glass for a moment, testing its weight before she tugged down her sleeve and used it to wipe out the inside. "Since I have no idea if this thing's ever been washed," she said with a laugh when he raised his eyebrow. She poured a splash of whiskey, then handed the glass to Viktis.

He smiled as he watched her pour another measure for herself. "To old times." He held up his glass in a toast and sank into the chair across from her.

Renna mimicked the movement, then took a gulp of the amber liquid. The burn of the alcohol slid down her throat like silk. Damn, she hadn't had Preill whiskey in years. It instantly set her insides quivering in the best possible way. But instead of enjoying the pleasant buzz, she had business to conduct. And she'd have to be careful with this one. He knew most of her tricks.

She also knew most of his.

With a twitch of her wrist, she reached up and pulled the band from her hair. It spilled in dark waves around her shoulders, and she shook it free.

Game on.

Viktis had always been a sucker for her hair. She needed every advantage she could get if she was going to get out of here and save the kid.

"Ah, Renna. You can still make a man forget to breathe." His eyes drifted down her body, lingering appreciatively over her chest before he took another drink.

"You've filled out quite nicely yourself, Viktis." Renna tilted her head just a little, letting her hair spill down past her breasts. "I'm surprised I haven't run into you before now."

"I keep to the Preill system. Plenty of work over there for me and my men. We've been busy with some smuggling runs and the like. Nothing too glamorous until I got this job."

"So you're branching out into the slave trade? I thought you had more sense than that, Viktis."

"You know better than to ask questions in our line of business. The job paid handsomely, so I took it. I'm sure you understand."

Of course she did. She was a merc; she knew how the business worked. She'd never allowed herself to take jobs with slavers, but most of her counterparts had at some point. It was a fast, easy way to make some quick credits, and they all found themselves needing the payout at one point or another.

But a girl had to have her principles, and slavery didn't fit into her moral code.

Renna crossed her legs. Her tight leggings clung to her thighs, highlighting her carefully toned muscles. Viktis's gaze dropped lower for a moment, and she bit back a smile. Thank the gods for MYTH's well-stocked supply room. "Who hired you to find this kid? And why's he so important?"

He smiled but shook his head. "You know I'm not going to tell you. It's unprofessional."

Renna scoffed into her whiskey glass. "I'm not trying to steal your job, asshole."

"Doesn't matter. Someone wants the boy, and they're going to get him whether I find him or not. Figured I might as well be the one who gets the reward."

Renna shrugged, mentally changing tactics. She'd have to do this the long way. Ah, well, there were worse things than having to seduce a handsome mercenary who obviously still had feelings for her.

She tilted her head and traced a finger across the lip of her glass. "So how's Serenita? You two were still a thing last I heard."

"We had a falling out." Viktis grimaced and took another sip of whiskey. "She's changed since you knew her. Hardened."

Not surprising. Serenita had always had an edge; it had made her one of the best mercs out there. But the woman had never known when something was a lost cause. She'd see it through until the end. It had almost killed her, more than once.

"How long has it been?" Renna asked.

"She left about a year ago. Said she wanted to see new things, take on jobs my crew wouldn't touch. I haven't heard from her since then." His shrug was indifferent, but she'd swear there was hurt in his eyes. Who would have guessed Viktis the Pirate had a heart?

There was her opening.

But Renna paused, chewing on her lip. A girl had to have her morals, but where should she draw the line? Sleeping with him to get what she wanted? She'd certainly done it before, but this time…? This time she couldn't afford to make mistakes.

Renna set the glass down on the table and leaned forward. "So I wouldn't be poaching on her territory if I made a move on you?"

His smile deepened as his gaze wandered south again. "You'd forgive and forget? I tried to kill you, Renna."

"And I escaped. It would take a better merc than you to actually kill me." She gave him a slow, predatory smile. "Besides, it's been a long time, Viktis. And by the look of you, you've gotten some experience since last we met. Maybe a few new scars?" She licked her lips, brow arching.

Viktis set his glass down as well and stood up. "This is a dangerous game you're playing, Renna. It could backfire."

"Dangerous games are always the most fun." She stood and slipped out of her jacket. "Besides, I know how much you like to gamble."

"Ah, you still know me, don't you?" He unlatched his holsters and shrugged out of them, setting them carefully on the table. His violet eyes glowed in the flurolamps on the ceiling. "You know I don't trust you."

"No more than I trust you. But that doesn't mean we can't enjoy ourselves." Her gaze flicked to the bedroom door, then back. "A secret for a secret?" She tugged her shirt free of her waistband, flashing him a small patch of her stomach.

"Agreed." Viktis pulled off his belt, the leather whispering against the fabric of his pants. He coiled it up and set it next to his guns. "But first, let's make sure we're not interrupted." He strode to the door and snapped the lock into place. "If they find the boy, they'll bring him to me immediately. I'd hate to miss that." He paused, his expression feral. "I'd hate even more for them to walk in on us."

"There is no boy," Renna reminded him, popping open the button at her waist.

Viktis crossed the room to stand before her. He played with the hem of her shirt before tugging it over her head in one smooth move. His graceful amber fingers caressed the bare skin of her waist, and she bit back a moan. Dear gods. Her whole body felt like it was on fire.

"If there's no boy, what are you doing on that ship?" His voice was a warm murmur as he sucked her earlobe. "I saw the registration. It's government-owned."

"I'm working for them now," she whispered as she returned the favor and tugged his shirt over his head.

Viktis laughed. "You'd never work for the government. No lies, Renna."

She stared at the golden trail of hair peeking above his waistband. Ran a finger across the softness. Tried to calculate the odds. "Fine. I'm their prisoner. They caught me after my last job. It was a setup." Her voice had a growl that even she couldn't fake. At least there were a few kernels of truth woven in with her lies.

"Are you losing your touch, love?" Viktis traced the long scar on her neck. "I can't believe you still have this. Can't the doctors take care of it?"

She swallowed. "I like it. Gives me character." Desperate to change subjects, she blurted, "Viktis, Hesperia is gone. Destroyed in an attack." She bit back a groan. *Stupid, Renna.* Death and destruction were not the best way to seduce someone.

His hand froze as it traced her collarbone. "Gone? How is that possible? Who was it?"

"Don't know."

"That's why there was radio silence so suddenly." He shook his head. "We'd been tracking a government compound, but then there was nothing."

His eyebrows furrowed, and Renna reached up to smooth away the wrinkle. "It's not safe in this system anymore. No place is safe until we know who they are or what they want. We barely escaped the planet before it was destroyed. The boy is probably dead if he was on-world."

"Shit."

She smiled, languidly stretching her body until it brushed against his, trying to bring him back to the moment. She slipped a hand down his hard stomach, sliding it lower beneath his pants until she could touch him. Velvet and steel, just like she remembered. His hips jerked as he groaned, and a burst of heat built in her midsection.

He lowered his lips to her neck, his tongue flicking and caressing the sensitive skin beneath her ear. She sucked in a breath. A girl had to have her morals, but that line was getting further and further away the more he touched her.

"Who hired you to find him anyway?" she asked again, now that he was distracted. Now that they *both* were distracted.

He leaned back slightly so she had better access. "A third party mediator. I don't know who the actual client is."

Renna's hand stilled against his swollen member, and Viktis moaned again, pushing against her. If she knew Viktis, there was way more to it than that, but she'd get the truth from him soon enough.

"Why don't we get a little more comfortable?" she said, tugging on the waistband of his pants to propel him toward the bedroom. She led the way, making sure to swing her hips as she walked.

After three steps, Viktis growled and reached for her, but Renna moved out of his reach. It was time to rein this thing in. She needed to be in control. "Patience, love. Good things come to those who wait."

"You're killing me, woman."

Her smile was wicked as she turned away and unlatched her

bra. The straps slid down her shoulders, and Renna glanced back with a half-smile as she let the lacy black thing dangle from her fingers.

"Gods I've missed you," Viktis growled, yanking her into his arms and pressing his lips to her collarbone. She shivered as his coarse hands glided against her bare skin.

Her gaze drifted down to his erection, and she smiled. "I can tell."

The amber color of his skin and the muscles rippling beneath it made her mouth go dry. The angular planes of his legs and stomach. The hardness of his body against hers. He was perfect. And yet…

"Things were never the same after you left," he whispered. His lips brushed against the skin of her breast before his tongue softly caressed her nipple.

She moaned, her fingers tracing the rigid plates on his head as they stumbled backward toward the bed. "You mean after you tried to kill me."

"You know it wasn't personal." He flashed her a quick grin before resuming his tongue's careful exploration.

"It never is, is it?" Damn him, he knew exactly what to do with it. Heat curled lower in her belly, and she forced herself to ignore it.

"This seems pretty personal to me." His hands drifted lower, splaying across her stomach. She swayed, tugging him to the bed. She was running out of time.

And then he sucked in a breath. "What the…" His eyes widened a split second before he collapsed on the mattress.

Sound asleep.

ELEVEN

Renna pulled her clothes back on as Viktis snored loudly, his bare legs draped over the side of the bed. The man would sleep like the dead for at least another hour. A dash of sleeping powder from Antivia Nine when she'd brushed out his whiskey glass with her sleeve had done the trick. That poison bracelet had been a very good investment.

Her body still hummed from the Ileth's touch, and she ignored the heat pooling between her legs. She quickly pushed away the tiny bit of disappointment that curled through her. It had been way too long since her last fling; some good, old-fashioned stress relief might have been nice. Romping in bed with a handsome man was never a hardship, but she was on a job and it was time to get what she'd come for. The cold shower could come later when she was safe on the *Athena*.

The desk was the only part of the room Viktis kept tidy. She slid into his chair and pulled open a few of the drawers. Nothing but a worn notebook with a list of past jobs and a few ratty receipts. Not surprising. Viktis had always kept most of his info on his tablet.

She picked up the device from its stand and switched it on. Encrypted, of course, but easy enough for her to hack. Less than a minute later, she was scanning through his messages.

"Dammit." The message she needed had no identifying data, no electronic signature she could use to track down the sender. A few clicks later, she discovered the company who'd contacted Viktis, NavStar Industries, was a front. She didn't recognize the name, but the information still might come in useful later, so she sent the rest of his messages to her own device. She'd go through them back on the *Athena*. Never hurt to know what the competition was up to.

Renna sighed and tucked the device back in its stand on the desk. Well, that'd been a waste of time. She turned to stand, and her fingers knocked into a pile of notes. A piece of paper fluttered to the ground.

Well, well, what was this? The paper was heavy and smooth against her fingers as she picked it up. Dr. Draven Navang. Bioethics and Biotechnology Specialist. NavStar Industries. The name and company were stamped in embossed black ink, and in the corner was a small logo: an eye with a two spears bisecting it.

Renna stiffened. Where had she seen that logo before?

But the flicker of recognition died, and she shrugged. Maybe it would come to her later. She tucked the card into her pocket and got to her feet. Across the room, Viktis grunted in his sleep, and she smiled. He was going to be so frakking pissed at her when he woke up. Good thing she wasn't the kind of girl who held grudges, or he'd be in serious trouble right now.

But despite the urge to get back at the merc for trying to kill her, the *Athena*'s crew was locked in the brig, and Myka was still in hiding. It was time to get the hell out of here.

Renna unlatched the door and peeked into the hallway. *Empty*. She crept down the passageway, her boots making no sound against the metal floor. It would be easy enough to find her way back to the hatch, but what might be a little more difficult was calling back Viktis's mercs and escaping the spaceport before they realized they'd been scammed.

The bridge lay straight ahead, and a smile curved her lips at the squat console sitting in the middle of the space. That would do just fine. Her fingers flew over the keypad as she hacked the propulsion system and disabled the ship's engines.

Viktis and his crew were dead on the ground. Perfect. By the time he got the ship working again, the *Athena* would be long gone.

Now all she needed to do was program a simple recall message in the merc's communicators and set it to go off in sixty seconds, so she had enough time to get back to Finn's ship. There. A few taps on the console and it was done.

She peered down the corridor, then sprinted for the cargo ramp. Outside the ship, the fuel station was shadowy and silent, and Renna sucked in a deep breath. Viktis neutralized. Check. One team rescue, coming up. She paused. Team, huh? Since when? Most of those people hated her or, at least, didn't trust her further than they could throw her. She wasn't part of their team. She was on her own. As usual.

Renna shook her head and started toward the *Athena*. A moment later, a low tone sounded throughout the warehouse. Dammit! She darted behind a stack of crates, dropping low to hide from the gang of mercs who stomped down the *Athena*'s loading ramp.

One…two…three…. Shit. She had no idea how many were left on the *Athena*. Dealing with them herself was going to be tricky.

Renna crept from behind the boxes. She was running out of time. She needed to move now. Sprinting on silent feet, she sneaked through the landing hangar and back onto the *Athena*. Men's voices echoed from the other side of the ship, and she crept in the opposite direction, toward the lower deck.

Laughter rang out, and she froze, pressing herself against the wall. A few more men stomped down the ramp, some chuckling, some grumbling, as they returned to Viktis's ship. Once their voices faded, she moved again, making her way to the stairs.

Get Finn and his crew free. Get the hell off this planet.

She took the stairs slowly, making no sound. Carefully, she peered around the hatch and into the brig.

Dammit. The meaty mercenary was still there, leaning against the wall, picking his fingernails with a knife. Renna pulled back and chewed her lip. She had two options: attack the guy and hope she took him by surprise, or trick him into returning to the ship. She probably couldn't take the guy without a weapon, so that left option two. Her stomach jumped, and she took a deep breath. It was now or never.

She marched into the room like she was following orders.

Mercenary Man jumped as she entered, gripping the knife and glaring at her.

She kept her whole body at ease, smiling her best I'm-in-the-mercenary-club-too smile. "Relax. Viktis sent me."

The man's eyes narrowed. "Oh?"

"Didn't you hear the recall tone? They found the kid. Viktis wants you back on the ship."

"And who the hell do you think *you* are?" He shifted on his feet, his gaze flicking to the *Athena*'s crew still behind bars.

Renna flipped her hair, focused on keeping the man's attention. "You saw me leave with Viktis. We go way back. I've agreed to help him with this haul...and a few other things."

Someone whispered "*bitch*" from the brig, but she ignored it.

His suspicion was almost palpable. "Yeah? So where's Viktis then?"

"On the bridge getting ready to take off. You want him to leave you behind?" Renna turned to go with a shrug. "Whatever. You don't believe me, that's your problem. You can stay here and wait for the Marines to find you."

The man frowned, then slid his knife back in its sheath. "Fine. Let's go."

Renna let him go first out the door, grabbing one of the crew's pistols from the officer in charge's desk. She slipped it into the waistband of her pants before following him back to the cargo ramp. She'd only use it if she had to.

The merc stepped outside the ship, but she paused, pressing her finger below her ear like she was taking a call on her communicator. "Right." She paused for a beat. "I'll make sure." Another pause. "Yes, he's on his way now."

The man turned. "What was that?"

"Viktis wants me to search the captain's quarters, but he wants *you* back on the ship to help with prep. I'll be there in a minute."

He shrugged. "Whatever the boss wants." Without a glance back, he tromped down the gangway and disappeared into the docking bay.

Renna spun on her heels and slammed a hand against the hatch panel. As soon as it started to close, she dashed back down the deck to the brig.

"What the hell is going on?" Finn demanded as she fumbled with the lock on the cell.

"I just saved your asses. We need to get the hell out of here now before Viktis's crew realizes what's going on."

"Everyone! Stations, now! Prep for takeoff." The crew streamed from the room, running to various parts of the ship.

Renna ran behind Finn and Keva to the bridge where the two immediately began shouting commands.

Seconds later, the whir of the engine filled the ship. "Flight status, Lieutenant?" Finn demanded.

Keva's fingers flew across her display. "Take off in forty-five seconds."

Around them, the ship rumbled and vibrated as the engines warmed. Renna's stomach jumped as the ship surged into motion, speeding away from the spaceport before beginning its ascent back into the stars. They were safe.

Captain Finn finished giving his orders, then leaned back against the railing beside her, his arms crossed. "What did you do?" he asked. "What happened to the merc?"

"Don't worry about it, Finn. I took care of him."

"You were gone for almost an hour." He sounded sullen and annoyed.

She blinked at him. "Is there a problem? I thought you'd be happy I was finally earning my payment." Renna turned to walk away, but Finn grabbed her arm.

"Did you sleep with him?"

Renna gritted her teeth and slung his hand off her. "By the stars, why do you even care? You already think I'm a whore, re-member?"

Finn's lips thinned. "I didn't think you'd come back."

Renna arched an eyebrow at him. "I don't know why you keep making those kinds of assumptions. It's obvious you don't know anything about me, Captain. Not anymore."

He shifted his weight, eyes sliding away from hers. "Well, whatever you did and however you managed it, you have my thanks. We managed to escape with the boy and with no casual-ties. Where is Myka by the way?"

Her lips parted. The last thing she'd expected was for Finn to thank her, even if he was obviously uncomfortable doing it. "He's down on the officer's deck, locked away tight. I'll go get him."

"I want to see this," Keva muttered, getting up from her chair and following them through the ship.

Renna's stomach tightened as she picked her way through the clothes and bedding that spilled from the rooms out into the hallway. The mercs had been ruthless. Mattresses had been ripped to shreds, and any furniture not bolted down had been toppled. Even locked doors had been sliced through with lasers, leaving only twisted metal.

Exactly how much was this kid worth to them?

She thudded down the stairs to where she'd left Myka and froze in her tracks. Blood roared in her ears as she stared at the metal screen covering his hiding place. The panel was bent and seared, ripped through like a piece of paper. Renna dropped to her knees and touched the navy fabric snagged on one of the jagged pieces of metal. Myka's new pants.

"You hid him there?" Keva asked.

Renna stared at the hole, ignoring the other woman. Acid burned the back of her throat. How had they found him? Had he been so terrified he'd given himself away?

"He's gone," she whispered, yanking the metal screen away and peering inside to make sure. Metal glinted on the floor, and she reached for her nanospanner with a shaking hand.

"What do you mean he's gone?" Finn's voice was low and dangerous as Renna rose to her feet.

Her hands trembled, and she clenched them into fists. "Somehow they found him. Took him." First on Hesperia and now the ship. What was it about Myka that drew these people to him? What did they want with the boy?

Renna's mind raced. They had to go back. Had to find him. How the hell had the mercs gotten past her with the kid?

A muscle jumped in Finn's jaw as he glanced at the destruction around them. "So your whoring around did nothing to help us. And now they've got the kid." His voice went flat. "Or was that all part of your plan? Act like you're playing along with the pirate when really you've had this worked out all along? How else would the mercs have known where we were refueling? Or where Myka was hiding?"

Renna's fingers itched to grab the gun from her belt. So they were back to this again. Gods, this man had more mood swings than a pregnant woman. "You think I betrayed you? That I gave up the boy for a fat paycheck?" She glared at him, her temper slipping farther out of her control. "If that's the case, why would I have come back to free you? Why not stay on board and escape with Viktis?"

He dismissed her with an angry shrug. "Because it looks better this way. Because we can't prove you had anything to do with it. But I know the truth. I know you're only in this for the money. Like always."

"I'm here because I didn't have a choice," Renna growled. "But now that I am, the only thing that matters is getting Myka back. With or without your help."

TWELVE

Before anyone could stop her, Renna dashed through the ship, heading to the flight deck and Lieutenant Kojima. Finn and Keva shouted at her as they followed, but she blocked them out. Viktis wouldn't hurt the boy, not if he was the pirate's ticket to getting paid, but she wasn't going to let Myka go through that again.

"Flight Lieutenant Kojima! Turn the ship around. We're going back."

He spun around in his chair. "What happened?" His gaze flicked to Captain Finn, who pounded up the stairs behind her.

"Hold your course, Kojima," Finn ordered.

"I am not leaving Myka with that man," Renna said. She sucked in a jagged breath. *Get it under control, Carrizal.* She wouldn't do Myka any good by getting herself killed.

"Then you should have thought about that before you decided to screw Viktis."

The breath whooshed out of her lungs at the fury in his words. "It's none of your business who the hell I sleep with."

"It damn well is if you put our mission in danger. And surprise, surprise, you already did. I warned Dallas that bringing you on board was a mistake." The words dripped from his lips like acid, and Renna growled.

"Well, if you could do your damn job, I wouldn't have to take matters into my own hands!" She crossed her arms so no one would see how badly she was shaking. "Turn the ship around, Kojima. We're going back for the boy." Renna was not going to fail him. Not now, when he'd already been through so much.

She blinked. Where had all this maternal concern come from?

Finn curled his lips back, baring his teeth. "No. We're not." He bit off the words through a clenched jaw. "I'm commanding officer on this mission, Carrizal. You would do well to remember that."

Her ears roared with her racing pulse, and she fought to keep her voice under her control. She'd promised the kid he'd be safe, dammit. She didn't break promises. "Listen to me, Captain. You don't know what they're going to do to him. He can't go through that again." Despite her efforts, Renna's voice went shrill, echoing through the flight deck.

"I can't risk what's left of the mission. Viktis's ship has an advanced class ship-to-ship missile. They'll destroy us if we go back. We need to focus on getting to Aldani and stopping the attacks. If we don't, more people than Myka will die."

"He said he wouldn't help you until he had his nephew back. Why the hell do you think he'll help you now?" Renna put her hands on her hips, carefully sliding the gun from her waistband.

"We found Myka once; we can rescue him again. But what we can't do is let another planet be destroyed. Millions of people are dead because of these attacks." Finn raked a hand through his hair, his voice lowering to a frustrated growl. "The doctor has to understand that stopping these people is the only way to accomplish his goals. My mission is to break into the facility and find the truth. Once we have that information, we can focus on Myka. I'm sorry to say it, but the boy isn't our priority right now. Getting the particle destabilizer to Aldani is."

A muscle twitched in Finn's jaw as he placed a heavy hand on the back of Kojima's chair. "Flight Lieutenant, get us to Iniros. The sooner Aldani knows what's going on, the sooner we can end this thing."

They were going to end this thing right now if she had her way. Renna aimed her blaster at the captain. "Don't make me do this, Finn." She turned to Kojima. "Take us back to Krooss."

Beside her, Keva pulled her own gun, and two other MYTH agents swarmed the bridge, their blasters pointed at Renna. "Put the gun down now!" Keva ordered.

"Not until we have Myka back."

"I will not have mutiny aboard my ship." Captain Finn crossed his arms, his blue eyes snapping between the two women. "Renna, put your gun down. Now. Before you do something you regret."

She kept it pointed at his heart. "No."

Finn's voice softened. "I understand how you feel. I want to go after Myka, too. But we need to stop these people. They've gone to great lengths to find this boy; they're not going to kill him now."

No, but there were things worse than death. "Such a *mercenary* way to look at the world, Captain."

Finn nodded once.

Strong arms grabbed her from behind, wrenching the gun from her hand. She struggled against her captor, tried to smash her head against whoever it was, but the grip around her chest tightened.

"Now, now," a man's voice said in her ear. "Didn't you ever learn to play nice with others?"

She froze for a moment, pressed against his bulk. Corporal Bokal, the tech chief? Where had he come from? For such a massive man, she'd never even heard him coming up the other set of stairs.

Renna thrashed again, heart pounding frantically at the feeling of being trapped. She was not going to let Finn win like this. "Let go of me!"

"Put her in the brig. We'll deal with her when we get to Iniros," Keva ordered, holstering her gun. The Delfine's beautiful face twisted with scorn. "Nothing like a little poetic justice, eh, Carrizal?"

She'd shove that poetic justice up the alien's ass if Keva kept looking at Renna like that. But Bokal was too big and held her too tightly, so she said nothing, just glared at Finn and his XO.

How the hell had this happened? Everything had gone wrong from the moment she'd taken this damn job. And now Finn had taken away everything from her. Acid rose to her throat, and she swallowed it back. She just needed to bide her time. Revenge was a bitch, and the captain and his crew would be in plenty of trouble when they showed up at Aldani's labs without Myka.

She just hoped she was around to see the man's reaction. The captain deserved everything that was coming to him.

Bokal's hands were firm but gentle as he pushed her into the brig. He locked the door and frowned at her. "Didn't think we'd be back here so soon. I'm sorry about this. Can't blame you for wanting to go back for the boy." His voice was low and rumbly as he rubbed a hand against his wide jaw.

"Then why didn't you stand up to Finn?"

"Because he's the boss. I'm just a corporal." He shook his head. "You've never been in the military, have you? You don't disagree with a superior offer. That's grounds for court martial."

Renna sighed. Since when had she gotten so soft? She'd never cared this much about a job before, but something in the boy's dark eyes haunted her. And she'd promised to keep him safe. That damn moral code was going to get her killed one of these days.

"They're going to hurt Myka if we don't go back."

Bokal frowned. "I know, but there's nothing we can do until the captain gives the word. And who knows? Aldani might have a better idea than rushing in and attacking. I hear he's a smart guy. Did you know he created a time machine? He's still testing it, but if it works…" Bokal's voice trailed off, but Renna didn't need him to continue. She could only imagine the ramifications of time travel. Hell, she could go back and stop Myka from being kidnapped in the first place.

"Let's hope it's true."

"I can't wait to meet him. I've heard all of his intergalactic broadcasts, read his treatise on antimatter and particle destabilization. The man's brilliant."

"He'd better be. The entire galaxy is in his hands right now." Renna had met plenty of brilliant men on her jobs. They were usually about as stable as a three-legged chair. And right now, a single crazy act could blow the traverse sky high.

Bokal shifted his weight. "I'm sorry about this, Miss Carrizal, but I need to make sure you don't have any other weapons on you."

A smile tugged at her lips. "Are you asking if you can pat me down, Chief?"

His pale face flushed deep red. "No, ma'am. I'd prefer you'd just hand everything over."

She shook her head. "I was teasing, Chief. I wouldn't do that to you." She paused. "Unless you want me to?"

He flushed again and held out his hand. "Weapons, please?"

Renna pulled the gun she'd grabbed earlier from her waistband and handed it over, then, sank down onto the lumpy mattress.

Bokal smiled at her. "I'll have Miss Mary bring you down some food. We'll be at Aldani's lab by dawn. I'll come and get you for the fireworks." He winked and lumbered from the brig, leaving Renna in silence.

Or at least as silent as being on a moving ship could be.

The hum of the engines and the whisper of the air recycler soothed her ragged nerves. She pulled her knees to her chest, resting her chin on them. Where had everything gone so wrong?

How far back did she want to go?

She shook her head. No sense in going down that road. Just because she was here with Finn didn't mean she had to relive that part of her life. She'd moved on. Obviously he had, too. Someday maybe she'd get the story out of him, but right now...right now she wanted to give him a good roundhouse kick to the gut. Her muscles tightened until they felt like rocks, and she rubbed the back of her neck.

The person she was angriest at was herself. That was twice now she'd been careless. And Myka was going to be the one to suffer.

She sighed and let herself slide down onto the mattress to stare at the ceiling. Better get some rest while she could. When she got out of here, she'd have plenty of work to do.

THIRTEEN

The sudden silence woke Renna several hours later. Blinking against the bright lights of the brig, she rubbed a hand over her face. The engines were off, and the faint echo of voices drifted down to her from above. There was the commanding treble of Finn's voice. He sounded pissed. Good. Keva's lighter tones rose in response. Neither appeared to let her out.

With a yawn, she got to her feet, tugging a hand through her tangled hair before pulling it back into a neat ponytail. She slipped back into her leather coat and tugged at her shirt. Gods she hated sleeping in her clothes. She always felt so dirty afterward.

Almost ten minutes later, Bokal finally came to let her out. "Sorry it took so long. Had to finish the captain's orders."

Renna followed him through the empty ship. Bokal stopped her at the hatch by putting a hand on her arm. "I know you're only looking out for the boy, but don't let Finn fool you. He's as worried about Myka as you are. His hands are just tied."

"Sure. Whatever." Finn had his orders. She got it. But she wasn't under any requirement to follow them.

The ship hatch slid open with a *swoosh*, and she stepped out onto a metal landing pad in the center of a huge industrial space. Her jaw dropped. The place was at least five stories tall, with a retractable glass roof. Other ship bays dotted the area, dwarfing the one where the *Athena* sat. Dr. Aldani must do very well for himself.

Bokal led her down the pad's ramp to the floor of the hangar. Her boots clicked against the cement as they headed toward a double door she guessed led to other areas of Aldani's lab. Bokal held the door open for her and she stepped across the threshold. Only to stop short inside the hallway.

Two men seemed to take up the entire space: Captain Finn, standing at attention in his uniform, and the tall, dark-skinned man shouting at him. They were of similar size and build, but the scientist's fury made him seem even more dangerous than the military man.

"Who the hell do you think you are telling me how this is going to work? I'm the one who can stop them. Not you." Aldani jammed a finger into Finn's chest, but the captain held his ground. "And you haven't completed your side of the bargain."

"Doctor, we did have Myka—"

The man's mahogany skin mottled. "And then you lost him. And instead of rescuing him, you decided to leave him with those bastards!"

Keva moved forward. "Doctor, if you'd just listen—"

Aldani whipped around, his eyes narrowing on her like twin laser beams. Keva swallowed and stepped back at the raw anger on his face.

"No, you listen to me. I'm not giving you a thing until Myka is back safe and unharmed. Do you understand? I don't care what it takes. The boy is the only thing that matters."

Renna moved from behind Bokal.

Like a lion sighting its prey, Aldani's dark gaze immediately snapped to her.

She froze. He had Myka's eyes.

"Who the hell are you?" he demanded. "Wait, don't tell me. You're the merc who lost my nephew."

"I'm the woman who rescued him. Renna Carrizal. Pleased to meet you, Dr. Aldani." She held out her hand.

He stared at it as if was dirty. After a long, awkward moment, she finally dropped it.

"I don't know which of you is worse." His gaze flicked between her and Finn. "I want you all gone from my lab within the hour. Tell Dallas to send someone else to get my nephew."

Finn shook his head, and he swallowed once before saying, "I'm sorry, sir. I'm afraid that's impossible."

Anger blazed in Aldani's brown eyes. "Don't you tell me what's impossible, boy. I'm done dealing with ineptitude."

She totally got the doctor's anger, but this had gone far enough. Renna interrupted before he could take his next breath. "Hesperia is gone, Dallas is likely dead, and the MYTH facility on that planet is destroyed. I'm afraid you're stuck with us."

Aldani opened his mouth, then closed it.

"They're all dead." She swayed as the image of the crater in the middle of the city filled her memory, the mushroom cloud of destruction the invaders had caused. Tamping down her anger with everything in her, she took a deep breath. "Whoever is looking for Myka attacked the planet. I'm not sure if anyone survived."

Aldani whirled on his heels, the tails of his lab coat flapping. "Why didn't you tell me this, Captain?"

Finn spread his hands. "I tried, sir, but—"

Renna nodded. "He's a popular kid. You need to tell us exactly what's going on and how this is related to us breaking into the facility on Banos Prime."

Aldani let out a low growl. "Fine. If you're all I get, I'll have to make do. Let's take this inside, Captain." He stabbed a finger at Renna. "You too, Miss Carrizal."

Finn nodded at Keva. "Prep the ship to be ready at a moment's notice and finish the repairs on the sleeping quarters. Then make sure the crew gets some rest." He gave her an encouraging smile. "I'll call if I need you."

"Aye, aye, sir." She saluted and marched back toward the ship.

Bokal winked at Renna, then followed the lieutenant back through the doors.

"This way." Aldani headed in the opposite direction, down a wide, sterile hallway. White walls lined the corridor, stretching down to meet the shiny, white tile floors. Even the grout was white.

His maid had to be spectacular.

As they walked, they occasionally passed sliding glass doors that led to various labs, all full of shiny metal machinery and masked workers in lab coats and gloves.

"What exactly do you do here, Dr. Aldani?" Renna asked. Based on the gamma particle destabilizer she'd retrieved, she had a pretty good idea, but it was always illuminating to see what someone said about themselves.

He arched an eyebrow at her but didn't break stride. "I don't see how that is any of your business, Miss Carrizal. You were hired to bring me my nephew, and you failed. Until he's returned, I don't trust either you or Captain Finn with my secrets."

"Unfortunately, you might not have much of a choice," Renna said with a shrug. "This is a lot bigger than just a little boy now. In case you hadn't heard, five planets have been attacked. If you ask me, I think you know a lot more than you're letting on." She arched an eyebrow at the doctor. "Who knows, maybe they'll show up here next. If they know who Myka is, I'm sure they know you're his uncle. Maybe someone wants to clean up loose ends."

She felt Finn stiffen beside her as they walked, but he stayed quiet.

Aldani gritted his teeth so loudly she thought she heard his jaw pop. "Not here, Miss Carrizal."

He turned down another corridor. This one felt slightly less clinical, with an occasional picture dotting the wall or a soft chair and table stashed in an alcove. Finally, they stopped in front of a rich wooden door with a brass plate bearing Aldani's name. He pushed it open and strode to the hulking desk in the middle of the room. It was a monstrous piece of mahogany, the surface covered in papers and books. A digital picture of him and Myka sat in one corner, while a holovid blinked on the other corner of the desk. She thought she spotted detailed plans for some medical device before he turned it off.

"Sit down," he ordered, pointing at the two chairs in front of his desk.

Finn folded his tall form into the chair nearest the door. Renna flashed him a look of annoyance. That was always her preference, an easy escape route if she needed it. He'd taught her that.

Renna slid into the other seat, turning it so her back wasn't to the door. Now that he wasn't raving like a madman, she took a moment to study Myka's uncle.

She'd never have guessed they were related except for the eyes. They were the same liquid brown, full of life and sadness, but that's where the resemblance ended. Aldani had a sharp, hawk-like nose, bushy eyebrows, and a cleft in his chin that dimpled when he spoke. He also had an air of authority around him that even Dallas hadn't been able to command. This man obviously expected to be obeyed. She found his self-confidence appealing, even if she didn't much like the tone of voice he'd used with her.

Her gaze slid to Finn. The doctor was an interesting contrast to the self-contained military captain sitting beside her. Finn's expression was relaxed, but he sat straight, feet on the floor. His posture couldn't hide the tension she still felt rising from him. The constant vigilance was both reassuring and annoying at the same time. While some of the big things had changed, Finn's personality was still the same: duty and honor before everything else. And gods help you if you did something he thought was dishonorable. More than one member of Blur's gang had been kicked out for doing something not in Finn's code.

She was pretty sure the same thing had happened since he'd gotten his own command, too.

"Dr. Aldani, I get the feeling there's more to the situation than Dallas told us," Finn said, leaning forward slightly. "What I can't figure out is how Myka and the gamma particle destabilizer and this facility are all connected. Does it have to do with what Myka's parents were researching on Banos Prime?"

Aldani steepled his fingers and stared at Finn, letting out a sigh. "Dallas was the only one who knew the truth."

"Unfortunately, he's now out of communication range or dead. If this mission is need-to-know, I think we need to be fully briefed now."

"Can't MYTH send more help?"

Finn shook his head. "Only a few commanders at the top know how to get in touch with the other branches. Keeps it safer that way."

"So what are you supposed to do now then?" Aldani sounded dubious as he watched Finn.

The captain squared his shoulders. "Finish our mission. The universe is depending on us."

Aldani's interest turned to Renna. She shifted in her chair as he studied her, his dark eyes taking in her unkempt hair, her clothes wrinkled from sleeping in them. Finally he turned back to Finn. "And where does Miss Carrizal come in?"

Finn's voice was expressionless. "I leave it to you. If I had my choice, she'd be executed for treason, but she was recruited specifically for this mission because she has an exceptional skill set.

She was the one who was finally able to retrieve Myka after our other teams failed."

Aldani's gaze drifted back to her. His lips lifted into a smirk. "Tell me about yourself, Miss Carrizal."

"Call me Renna, please." She smiled at him sweetly, ignoring Finn's glower. "Despite what the captain thinks of me, I do have principles. I always finish a job. No matter what." She chuckled at Aldani's expression. "Shocking, I know."

"How did you get involved in this, Renna?"

"I was hired to retrieve your gamma particle destabilizer, but I ended up rescuing Myka, too. MYTH said they needed me, and I was strongly *encouraged* to join the mission. Despite the disapproval of much of the crew." She slanted a look at Captain Finn. That was as polite as she could keep it without betraying her real feelings. Aldani didn't need to know everything.

"You were the one to lose him to that...pirate," Finn growled.

She rolled her eyes. "If I hadn't scammed Viktis, you'd still be trapped in the brig. But it's easier to stay angry at me, I get it."

A muscle jumped in Aldani's jaw. "You know the man who took Myka?"

"Most mercenaries know each other, at least by reputation. I happened to know Viktis personally, though it's been a few years."

Finn's relaxed posture was gone as he sat stiffly in the chair. "She used her connection to the pirate to get on board his ship, but while she was gone, Viktis's men found the kid. We escaped, assuming he was still hiding on the *Athena*. When we realized our mistake, it was too late. If we'd gone back for him, the pirate vessel would have destroyed our ship or at least grounded her.

They had an advanced class ship-to-ship missile. We'd never have gotten close enough to rescue the boy."

"Myka. His name is Myka." Aldani slapped his hands down on the desk. "And he's the only family I have left, so your feeble excuses don't exactly reassure me. A MYTH agent and a galaxy-renowned mercenary should have been able to rescue a small boy from a bunch of pirate scum."

"I tried. And got thrown in the brig for mutiny," Renna said with a shrug. "Now we're here, and your accusations and recriminations aren't exactly helpful. What do you suggest, Dr. Aldani? You seem to be the man with all the answers. You might even be the man these people are after and Myka's just bait. Did you ever think about that?"

He stared at her. When he said nothing, she continued, pinning him with a cold glare. "Viktis was working for an organization, but it's a front." She pulled the heavy business card from her pocket. "Who's Draven Navang?"

At that, Aldani went perfectly still, his hands clutching the table in front of him. "Navang is my former business partner."

"Former?" she asked. "What happened between you?"

The lines around Aldani's eyes deepened as he frowned. "I didn't agree with his research methods. He didn't agree with mine. We dissolved the partnership. Now we're competitors, though I'm sure he'd say we're just old friends with differing opinions."

"You'd disagree?"

Aldani shrugged. "We don't have anything to do with each other. I haven't heard from the man in years."

"Why would Viktis be working for him?"

"I wish I knew," he said softly.

Renna's palms started to itch. She could tell from Aldani's expression that he was lying to them. But why? What was his end game? Why would he protect his ex-partner?

Finn glanced at her, and she knew he was thinking the same thing. He might be military now, but a merc never lost those skills.

"Could Navang have kidnapped Myka? To get back at you, perhaps?" he asked.

"I doubt it. We haven't worked on the same sort of research in years. He's more focused on his business."

Renna leaned back with a frown. "All the more reason to go after Aladea Scientific Industries."

Aldani shook his head and glanced over at the picture of Myka at the corner of his desk. "There's nothing that would please me more than putting an end to Navang and his…business. But I don't think he's involved."

Renna thinned her lips. Lies were a dangerous necessity in this business, but they could also get you killed. And she did not plan on dying for this man. "Then, as I see it, we have two options," she said. "Go after Myka and try to rescue him from Viktis if we can find him. Or we can continue with our mission and investigate the facility using your technology with the hope we can figure out what's going on before more people die. Which do you suggest, Doctor?"

Aldani pinched the bridge of his nose. "Myka is my nephew. How can you ask me that?"

"Because we can't do anything without your cooperation." Finn leaned forward, his expression earnest. "I'm worried about him, too. But we have an obligation to figure out what that facility is and how it's connected to the attacks. Myka can't help us with that."

Renna's gaze rested on the picture of Aldani and Myka. The doctor stood with his arm slung around the little boy, while a rough, stony mountain jutted up from the plain behind them. The dun-colored sand was dotted with burgundy rocks. Banos Prime.

She studied the picture more closely. Myka looked to be about six and had a bandage around one arm, though his happy expression said he wasn't in any pain. Aldani himself looked younger, too, less gray at his temples and fewer lines around his eyes. She guessed at that moment nothing bad had yet happened. Myka's parents were still alive. The attack still a few months out. But even then, Aldani had obviously cared for the boy.

The guilt of Myka's kidnapping made her stomach clench, but she had to put her unexpectedly maternal feelings aside. Finn was right. They had to focus on getting into that facility if there was a chance it would stop the attacks. She'd have to trust that whoever wanted the boy wouldn't harm him. "Doctor, I know it's a lot to ask, but our original mission still stands. Millions more may die if we don't stop these people, and that facility is our only lead right now. Can you tell us what Myka's parents were working on before they died?"

Aldani sighed and stood up. He turned to look out the window onto the golden fields surrounding New Rome colony. "I can't see that it matters now."

She gritted her teeth, forcing herself to speak calmly. "Because any clue you can give us might help us figure out if there's a connection between all this. Right now it feels pretty feeble to me. We're snatching at straws. We need more to go on than a mysterious facility, a kidnapping, and some doctor's gut feeling."

Finn glared at her, but she ignored him. The doctor knew something else, something that could help them. She'd played nice so far, but maybe Aldani responded better to threats.

He nodded once, as if he was making up his mind. "My brother and his wife were working on an experimental drug for MYTH. More than that, I don't know." He turned back to face them with a frown. "I do know I can't have anyone else's blood on my hands. Send the gamma particle destabilizer to my assistant. I'll have my team finalize the machine. Let's just hope the answers you're looking for are in this place, or it might be too late for my nephew."

Aldani pressed a button on his datapad. "My assistant will show you and your officers to the sleeping quarters. Unless you'd like to stay on your ship?"

Finn shook his head. "Quarters here will be fine. I'm sure Lieutenant Keva and the others will be grateful for the change of scenery."

A squat gray alien with a thick, fleshy neck and four large eyes spread horizontally across his face appeared at the door. "This is my assistant Syna. He'll take you to your rooms. I'll order dinner to be served in two hours."

She recognized Syna as a Conyara alien; they had some of the brightest scientific minds in the galaxy. She'd known several who'd made names for themselves creating the most dangerous weapons she'd ever used. Aldani must have more influence than she'd thought to have a group of them working here.

An idea sparked, and she hung back, casting one last look around Aldani's office. It just might get her the hell out of this mess and into hiding. All she'd have to do was forget those two little words.

I promise.

FOURTEEN

Syna led them through the quiet hallways of Aldani's complex, his short legs flashing as he trotted in front of them. The alien was silent, but then again, the Conyaras weren't known for being talkative. Unfortunately, it meant the only sound accompanying them was Finn's boots echoing loudly as they walked.

Renna cringed with each noisy step. "Do you have to stomp around like a wounded buffalo?" she snapped.

He raised an eyebrow. "Not all of us can have the grace of a thief."

She let her gaze slide down his muscled chest and carved thighs. "I seem to remember a time where you moved as silently as I did. But I'm sure I could still teach you a few things."

His face flushed unexpectedly, and he looked away. "I don't think so."

She bit back a smile. Gods, she loved baiting the man. He was so easy to rile.

Syna's light voice interrupted. "Miss Carrizal, your room." He pushed open the door, then gestured to Finn. "Captain, you're down the hall."

The two walked away, leaving Renna staring into the luxurious space. Now this she could get used to. Imported silk rugs covered the tile floor, while lush silks draped the large bed. She let out a happy sigh. She could get lost in that bed. Even better was the holoscreen on the wall. It was bigger than her window back home.

Too bad she wasn't here on vacation.

She spotted her satchel on the table in the corner. Someone had brought her things from the ship. And there was a gorgeous bathroom tucked into the corner of the room. Right now, a shower was the only thing she wanted.

She stripped out of her clothes and climbed into the tiled space. Steaming water blossomed from the overhead spigot, and she stood beneath the spray, letting the events of the last few days wash away. Gods. It felt like years.

And seeing Finn again...

That was a shock she was still reeling from. And his obvious hatred. But those shoulders... She pushed away the image, the memory of the way his stubble shadowed his strong jaw. Whatever had been between them was long over. Right now she had to focus on getting in that damn building and then getting Myka back.

She finished washing her hair, then switched the shower controls to dry. The ultraviolet light evaporated the water from her skin and dried her long hair in under a minute. And the warmth from the lamp eased some of the tension from her shoulders.

Clean and dry, Renna pulled on a new pair of leggings and a tight-fitting black shirt before shrugging into her holsters. She slid back on her knee-length leather jacket and stared at herself in the mirror. There were dark smudges beneath her gray eyes, and her coffee-colored skin looked dull and lifeless. She was twenty-three, for fuck's sake. If she wasn't careful, she'd start looking old.

She needed a vacation. She needed to retire.

If only this had been a regular job—return the particle destabilizer, get her last fee, sell the sapphire, and vanish to another planet. That had been the plan, at least. But now here she was, trapped on some gods-forsaken research station, plagued by guilt over Myka's kidnapping and trying to figure out how to stop an unknown attacker to save him.

This was exactly why she didn't establish relationships with her clients. It was too complicated. Too messy.

Her code wasn't as black and white as most people's, but it had always kept her sane in the messy mercenary world. As soon as she started breaking it, in her mind, she'd be no better than a common criminal. As much as she wanted to flee, she had to keep her promise.

That didn't mean she couldn't keep an eye out for her own opportunities. Just walking through the lab, she'd seen tech she could sell for millions of credits on the black market. Stealing a prototype or two would pad her nest egg quite nicely. That meant she needed to get back on her game. No more softie-Renna.

Like Viktis had said, this was business, not personal.

She turned on the holoscreen and pulled up a map of the facility. The place was larger than she expected, with three levels of labs and a storage area deep underground. The main level consisted of living quarters and Dr. Aldani's personal lab space.

Renna tapped a finger against her chin. Now there was a place where she could find some interesting information, but she'd glimpsed his security earlier as they'd walked to his office. His lab was probably locked down even tighter, and she didn't have time to do her homework. She'd have to go after the less secure labs in the level below, though they'd be difficult enough to get into on their own.

She glanced at her watch. Just a little over half an hour before she was supposed to meet the others for dinner. More than enough time to get "lost" and look around a bit. It wasn't as much prep as she'd prefer, but she'd make it work.

Renna retraced her steps to the elevator she'd noticed on the way to their rooms and took it down to the lower level. The doors swished open, and she stepped out into an industrial-looking hallway lined with chrome and gray tile. A quick sweep of the space showed that the bulk of the labs were located to her left. She started toward the doors.

Most of the workers had gone for the day, but a few hard-working souls still moved about in their labs, examining vials of liquid or typing on their datapads.

She walked along slowly, like she'd gotten lost, knowing the cameras along this corridor were recording her every movement. Stupid implant. She could use an internal map of this place right about now. It was a maze.

There!

A heavy glass door barricaded a room full of small medical implants, and she smiled through the glass. Bionic dimensional probes if she wasn't mistaken. She knew the perfect fence for those—a smarmy little doctor on one of the Outer Rim worlds. The mob he worked for was notoriously hard to patch up.

All she had to do was sneak back later and deal with security.

"Excuse me, miss. Can I help you?"

Renna spun around at the sound of a woman's voice directly behind her. A tall alien with bright green hair and three eyes set in a triangle on her forehead studied her with interest. A Xestu.

Renna pulled her lips into a smile of relief, playing the game. It felt good to slide back into something she knew. "Oh, thank the stars. Somehow I got myself lost. Can you direct me to Dr. Aldani's dining room?"

The alien nodded. "Of course. I still get lost myself sometimes. Let me show you back to the residential quarters." She gestured for Renna to follow and led her back down the corridor. "You're with Captain Finn's team? David said you were supposed to be rescuing Myka."

Part of Finn's team? Hardly. Only Dallas's orders were keeping her out of prison now. But she nodded. "Yes. We had him, but he was captured again." Renna paused. "Have you known Dr. Aldani and his nephew long?"

The alien blinked her three eyes. There was a small, half-second delay between each eye blinking. "I've been with David for about ten years now. He recruited me from university before I even graduated. He's wonderful to work with. Very smart. And amazingly kind. I've always felt like part of the family." Her smile was soft and full of affection.

Renna's chest tightened. It had been a long time since she'd had anyone she could depend on. She quickly pushed that thought away. "What do you develop here? Aldani said he's currently working on several large projects."

"Oh, yes," the Xestu woman said with a bob of her head. "His pet project is his space-time continuum machine, but we also build weapons and computer tech. He developed a tiny device that lets you network with any holovid in the galaxy from your armchair using the dark matter principle. Even though it hasn't been implemented yet, the government paid him handsomely."

"I bet they did." Renna's pulse quickened. She didn't need the money necessarily, but the thrill of getting that kind of find to the black market was almost irresistible. And that's where she kept getting in trouble. Every time she thought she was done, one last job came up.

But…there were at least half a dozen buyers who'd easily meet her asking price. Besides, it was unfair to give the government such an advantage. They'd create a communications monopoly no one could break. Selling a few of the devices to one of her fences would even the playing field a little. She'd be doing it for the good of the galaxy.

"Could I see it? It sounds amazing."

"Unfortunately, no. We're still in development mode. Testing should be done this week." She pointed to a lab as they passed. "The specialists are working around the clock to make sure the devices are manufactured by the deadline. I think they only get a few hours of sleep a night. Probably not a good thing, but we want to make sure they're perfect."

Renna nodded sympathetically. "I understand." Wouldn't hurt to make a note of the lab number for later, though.

"Here we are. Take this elevator up one floor, and the dining room is the third door on the right."

Renna smiled. "Thank you for your help. And good luck with everything."

The Xestu disappeared back the way they'd come. That had been more productive than she'd expected. Guilt tugged at her, but she ignored it. Stealing from Aldani wasn't breaking her code. The man was lying to them. In her book, stealing some of his tech was merely an insurance policy for when he screwed them over later.

But right now, she still had a game to play. Renna paused in the corridor and adjusted her jacket.

Aldani rounded the corner, coming from somewhere else in the facility. He smiled when he spotted her. "Right on time. I like punctuality," he said. He'd taken off his lab coat and wore a dark suit that highlighted his athletic build and broad shoulders.

"I aim to please," she said with a grin.

"That's what I hear." Aldani's jibe made the smile slide from her face, and he cleared his throat. "My apologies. That didn't come out the way I'd intended."

Why was she offended? The guy was only stating a fact. But she was so tired of being that person. So tired of people not being able to see past her game. Maybe she was a bit *too* good at her job.

"Please, after you." Aldani held the door open for her. The officers from the *Athena* had already gathered in the long, richly furnished dining room. A sleek glass table groaned with porcelain and silver, and the polycarbonite chairs were covered in thick cushions. Captain Finn sat with his legs outstretched, looking relaxed and at ease, but his navy uniform was neatly pressed and his dark hair had been tamed. The stubble that had shadowed his jaw, gone. Lieutenant Keva perched on the edge of her chair, hands moving as she talked to him.

Corporal Bokal and two of the other officers were deep in conversation, and Sergeant Gheewala sat near the door with her eyes closed.

"Give me a quick rundown," Aldani said as they paused in the doorway. "Who am I dealing with?"

"Gheewala, the one over there, is a tech empath, and the big guy is Bokal, tech chief. The two other men with him are special ops. Haven't seen them work yet, but I'm sure they're dangerous. Dallas said they were all the best of the best. I haven't seen otherwise yet."

"And what about the captain?"

Renna watched the man in question for a moment. Now that was a loaded question. When she was thirteen, she would have said he couldn't get any more handsome, but age had been good to him. His dark hair and blue eyes were the same, but his strong jaw and the five o'clock shadow along his jaw were new.

He seemed like a good captain. His crew respected him—always a sign of a good leader. But there was something else going on behind those eyes of his. Something secret that had everything to do with their past.

She chose her words carefully. "Finn is a respectable sort of military man. Does his job, runs a good ship. I think he's trustworthy."

Aldani arched an eyebrow. "You two don't get along, I take it?"

She grinned despite herself. "Was it that obvious?"

"Just a little. What I don't understand is how someone as obviously skilled as the captain and his team could have lost my nephew. It does not bode well for the rest of this mission." Aldani sighed and, before she could answer, strode into the room, arms wide.

"Good evening, everyone." Gheewala let out a little shriek and jumped from her chair. Aldani ignored her and made his way to Captain Finn. "I trust you're all comfortable in your quarters?"

Renna paused to touch Gheewala's arm. "He didn't mean to startle you, Sergeant. Were you listening for something in particular?"

Gheewala shook her head, worry lines wrinkling her forehead. "How did you know I was listening?"

"I've met other empaths before. I recognize the look."

Gheewala's eyes darted around the room, never landing in one place for more than a few seconds. "There's another voice out there, just out of range. I can't place it, but it's been following us since we escaped Hesperia."

"Is it dangerous?"

"I can't tell. It's unlike anything I've heard before."

"Did you tell the captain?"

"I told the lieutenant. I'm sure she thinks I'm imagining things." Gheewala shrugged. "Perhaps I am."

"Well, I believe you. Will you tell me if you hear anything else strange?" Renna held the other woman with a steady gaze, hoping it would calm her.

Gheewala's darting eyes finally stilled, and she nodded. "I'll keep you posted. And thank you for believing me." Then she scurried off to stand with the rest of her team, though she kept to the fringe of the group. Separate and apart.

Aldani stood at the head of the table and gestured to everyone. "Why don't you all take a seat? I'll have my staff bring in dinner, and we can discuss our next steps." Captain Finn and Lieutenant Keva took seats on either side of him, like guards. The rest of the officers fanned out on either side.

How very strategic.

Renna sat in the last open seat at the far end of the table. She preferred to stay out of the way and watch without being noticed. She always got more information that way. And it was going to be interesting to see how the rest of the team interacted. Enjoying a civilian dinner was completely different from being on a military ship.

The two special ops guys—she vaguely remembered their names were Doyle and Santos—ignored the rest of the team and talked only to each other. Finn and Aldani chatted easily, but Keva sat stiffly, as if she were still on duty. Bokal and Gheewala sat on the other side of the table, both silent and watchful.

She studied Finn as he and Aldani made small talk. The man made her pulse race, and not entirely in a good way. He'd yelled at her, thrown her in the brig, called her a whore, and yet despite all that, he still fascinated her. Maybe it was the contrast between the Hunter he'd been and the captain he was now. Maybe it was something else. She didn't really care to find out.

Keep telling yourself that, Renna.

She let out a sigh and took a bite of the seaweed salad in front of her. Interesting that, despite Finn's lounging pose and the slight smile he wore, something told her he was still perfectly aware of everything going on in the room.

And that included her.

Finn met her gaze down the length of the table as if he knew she'd been watching him. His expression held a hint of challenge.

She smiled slowly. Intimidating her wasn't going to work. He should know that by now. His answering smile held a thousand threats. A shiver made its way down Renna's spine, and she glanced away.

She pretended to be absorbed by her food, but her eyes kept drifting Finn's way. He had such strong hands. Aldani's fine tungsten utensils looked so delicate when Finn held them. And despite her dislike of the man, she couldn't keep the thought of those hands drifting over her body from popping into her head.

She took a gulp of wine, then coughed as it burned her throat. Her face reddened, and she looked away, still trying to cough away the sting of the alcohol.

Aldani laughed from the head of the table, noticing her discomfiture. "Terribly sorry, I forgot to mention I'd asked for moonwine from Purgatory. It's a little stronger than what you might be used to."

Finn smiled down at his plate. There was a sparkle in his eye that made Renna wonder if he'd guessed what she'd been thinking about.

The wine might be powerful, but by the gods was it good stuff. Even burning in her throat, she could taste the sweet ripeness of the grapes grown especially on the desert planet. The acid in the earth there led to an exceptional vintage.

Aldani's staff brought out the rest of the food. She sighed lovingly at the thick, juicy steak in front of her. It was a far cry from the takeout or hastily radiated plate of noodles she usually ate.

Renna tried to block out the conversations around her so she could concentrate on the amazing food. It worked until the blasted Lieutenant Keva brought up Myka again. Renna couldn't stop herself from listening in. The boy's name seemed like some sort of switch for her. By rescuing him, she'd forged some sort of strange bond with him that she really needed to get over. She wanted nothing more than to steal those prototypes and bolt to the nearest big city. She could disappear for a few months until all this blew over. But she'd promised…

Renna chewed angrily. Damn her stupid code. Damn Myka. Her gaze wandered back to Finn.

And damn him. Yet another reason to get out of here. The man had betrayed her. Betrayed Blur's gang. And given the chance, he'd lock her away in a prison for her crimes. She had to stop getting involved.

Emotions were just too deadly.

FIFTEEN

After Aldani's staff took away the dessert plates, Renna wiped her lips with the soft-spun napkins. Nothing quite like classic chocolate cake to end a meal. At the end of the table, she watched Keva lean forward, smiling at Captain Finn and the doctor. The alien's silky hair hung loose around her shoulders instead of scraped into a bun, and the silvery tresses shimmered softly in the helolights. Renna also noticed dark kohl highlighting Keva's slanted eyes and a berry stain on her lips.

Renna sat back a little in her chair, watching the three. She'd bet the sapphire around her neck that Keva had on slinky underwear beneath her dress uniform.

"Captain, Dr. Aldani, we need to talk about our plans for the mission," Keva said after a sip of wine.

"Our mission is rescuing Myka." Aldani's voice went cold, his

158 | JAMIE GREY

jovial expression gone. "I thought you understood that."

Finn shook his head, lips pressed together in a thin line before he spoke. "But sir, earlier we agreed that getting into the warehouse was our priority."

Aldani crossed his arms. "I changed my mind. Your mission is not mine. Myka is the only thing I care about."

Renna played with the stem of her wineglass, rolling it between her fingertips. Aldani had changed his tune faster than she'd expected. What had happened between their earlier meeting and now?

Keva shook her head. "The captain's right, Doctor. Rescuing the boy right now doesn't make sense. With radio silence coming from MYTH headquarters, we can't afford to split our team. And if the kidnappers come after him again, we don't have any additional support to protect. Even Renna's...special...skills won't work this time." Disdainful derision dripped from Keva's words.

Renna forced herself to loosen her grip on the wineglass before it shattered. Bitch. What was it with these people? She was proud of her skills; she'd worked hard to become good at her job, even though she wanted nothing more than to get out. But they wouldn't see her as anything but a greedy mercenary.

Aldani glanced over at Renna, then arched a mocking brow at Keva. "I suppose competency is one of those 'special' skills, seeing as how Renna's the only person in this room who's actually done her job."

Keva's pale violet skin flushed pink, and she dropped her gaze.

"Excuse me, sir?" Corporal Bokal's voice rumbled pleasantly through the room, breaking the sudden tension. "I understand you've been working on tech to get us inside the facility. How close are you to finishing it?"

The doctor studied each of the crew in turn, as if he were gauging his response. Finally he answered, "It should be finished tomorrow. I have one last test to complete."

"What is this thing, and what exactly does it do?" Renna asked. She knew it had something to do with the gamma particle destabilize she'd retrieved, but ever since she'd stepped inside the MYTH headquarters, everyone had been specifically vague about it. Did anyone actually know the answer?

"That's on a need-to-know basis," Keva snapped, casting an angry glance in Renna's direction.

"Really?" Renna raised an eyebrow. "I'd say I'd need to know. You know, using it to break into a facility no one else can figure out…"

Captain Finn nodded. "Renna is right. She needs to know the details before we can plan our attack."

Renna smirked. Agreement from Finn was the last thing she'd expected, but it was worth it just to see Keva's shocked expression.

Aldani picked up a fork and drew hash lines in the tablecloth as he spoke. "The device uses the gamma particle destabilizer that Renna retrieved from the Cordozas to rearrange the dark matter between molecules, making them pliable. Once I configure it into my technology, it should get you inside the otherwise impenetrable facility."

Finn continued. "After that, it's Renna's show. We'll have to rely on her to guide us." He turned his head to catch the doctor's gaze. "If Dr. Aldani agrees, of course, that this is the next logical course of action."

The doctor seemed to deflate, the wrinkles around his eyes standing out as he frowned down at the tablecloth. "You don't understand. Myka is all I have left of my brother. He's special. We *must* get him back."

Renna leaned forward. "And we will. I promise." She froze in her chair. Dammit. Why the hell did she keep using that frakking word?

"But only if I allow you to investigate the facility first." Aldani's shoulders slumped. "I know I am being a sentimental old man, but the fate of the universe doesn't seem very important when your only family is missing." He rubbed his eyes. "Very well. Continue with your mission. I will have my staff finish work on the destabilizer device. But please, please find Myka as soon as you can."

"We will," Renna said.

Aldani inclined his head. "Thank you, Miss Carrizal." He rose to his feet, setting his napkin on his plate. "If you'll come with me, I have something else I'd like to give you that may help you once you're inside the facility. Everyone else, please feel free to stay and enjoy your wine."

Across the table, Finn stiffened, like he was going to get to his feet and follow. Aldani waved him down. "Stay with your crew, Captain. Renna will be perfectly safe with me."

"It's not her I'm worried about," he said dryly.

Aldani chuckled, and Renna smiled tightly at Finn. If looks could kill, he'd be in a heap on the floor.

With a sigh, she trailed Aldani from the room, leaving Finn to stare after her.

"Have a seat on the table," Aldani said as he shut the door behind them. They'd come to one of the labs on the lower level, and the doctor had quickly led her to a private room and pulled out a tray of sterile tools from the cabinet on the wall.

Her heart jumped at the variety of scalpels laid out across the tray. "What are you doing?" she asked, her voice a touch too high as she eyed the shiny metal instruments.

"Upgrading your implant."

"I don't have—"

"I saw the incision site on your neck earlier. Am I right in guessing it's not currently working?" He pinned her with his gaze, and Renna found herself nodding.

"It broke while rescuing Myka." She paused. "Don't you care that I have illegal tech?"

"I only care that you have the right tech to rescue my nephew." He pulled out a small handheld computer and tapped the screen. "What model do you have?"

"It's a Compass X-3 from Imperial Medical Systems."

He touched another series of buttons on the screen. "All right. I'm going to numb you up a bit. It shouldn't hurt, but I don't want you to be uncomfortable. Then I'm going to restart the cybernetics and see what the damage is."

She didn't trust him. He was obviously holding something back about Myka's abduction. He could be planting a tracer or sabotaging her implant.

Aldani must have seen the unease in her expression. "Please don't worry, Renna. On my honor, it's a simple repair and upgrade." He flipped the screen around to show her the diagnostic tool he was using. She recognized the manufacturer's software.

"All right. Go ahead." Even if she didn't trust him, she needed every advantage she could get to break into that facility. She'd just have to hope he was telling the truth.

Renna's stomach lurched at the sight of the needle, threatening to revisit dinner once more. She squeezed her eyes shut as it pricked the skin at the base of her skull.

"That's a nasty scar you have there. Ever think about getting it taken care of?"

She knew he wasn't talking about the implant site. She opened her eyes, forced her fingers not to trail the white gash running across her throat. "Don't you like it? I think it gives me character. My clients are always very impressed."

He chuckled. "Every beautiful thing needs a flaw."

"Doctor, are you flirting with me?" She smiled up at him, and Aldani shook his head.

"If I were a younger man, most definitely. Now lay back and turn your head to the side. This will just take a minute."

Renna obeyed. While she couldn't feel whatever Aldani was doing to her implant, she could occasionally feel his fingers as he brushed against the skin of her neck or smoothed her hair out of the way. He hummed softly under his breath as he worked, and Renna's eyes drifted shut.

"Earlier you said I was familiar with your work. Care to explain?" he asked after a few minutes of silence.

She let out a soft sigh. Before this job was over, the entire traverse would know who she was. But Aldani needed to know she was good at what she did, and this was the one way to convince him. "I did a job a few years ago that got a lot of attention. You may have heard of the Seralline Star Sapphire heist?"

His fingers froze on her neck. "That was you?"

"Yes. But I would never have taken the job if I'd known it was going to be so high profile."

"You stole a priceless heirloom from one of the most dedicated military planets in the galaxy and you didn't think it was going to cause waves?"

She resisted the urge to shrug. "I didn't realize it was going to capture the imagination of the entire galaxy. I also thought the Trezians would keep quiet about it, not wanting to lose face."

"For anything else, you would have been right, but the sapphire is too important culturally for them not to go to any lengths to get it back."

"Yeah, I figured that out." She ignored the flecks of blood coating the tweezers Aldani set down on the tray beside her. "So what's your story? How did you end up as Myka's guardian?"

"My brother and his wife had no other family, and when Banos Prime was hit, they sent him to me. I expected they would follow, but they were killed before they could get off-planet."

Poor Myka. Renna chewed her lip as a thought occurred to her. "Could it be possible that the attack on Banos had something to do with Myka?" Maybe it was the *first* attack. Maybe someone had been after him longer than they'd thought.

The doctor shook his head. "I don't know, but I'm starting to wonder."

"Dallas said Myka's parents had found some interesting technology. Do you know anything about that? Did it have to do with whatever drug they were developing?"

Aldani frowned as he moved to stand behind her. "Hold your head still, please."

Renna clutched at the edge of the table as a buzzing sound filled her head and the room spun. She squeezed her eyes shut and tried to breathe through the electric flashes of pain shooting through her skull. Lightning bolts danced across the back of her lids. She'd been knocked out the first time her implant had come online. This was hellish.

"Hang in there, I'm almost done." Aldani rested a warm hand softly on her forehead. "All right. It's working again. Just needed a little rewiring. Now I'm going to install the upgrades. You may feel slightly dizzy while they install."

Dizzy was an understatement.

Something cold pressed against the back of her neck, and she tried not to jump.

"Easy there. Just a few more moments."

Renna's eyes fluttered as Aldani finished the software upgrades and her brain accepted them.

"So where does one even go to find a black market implant?" he asked. She could hear him tapping on his tablet near her ear, but she kept her eyes closed a little longer.

"I have good connections. IMS supposedly stopped making cybernetics after the ban passed, but if you know the right people…"

"Seems dangerous. Back alley surgery can lead to complications."

"Oh, it wasn't back alley. There are a few private hospitals on the Outer Rim that will perform the surgery if you pay well enough. With no paperwork left behind." She smiled at the memory. The doctor who'd installed the implant for her had been young and handsome. They'd spent a week together after she'd "recovered." He'd had an amazing bedside manner.

"I'm glad it wasn't a hack job. There. That's the last download." He swiped something cool and wet across the incision site on her neck. "Keep an eye on this for the next day or so, but I think you should be all set."

Renna sat up slowly and turned her head from side to side. The familiar overlay across her vision was back. She grinned at Aldani. "Amazing. There's a whole new suite of comm tools here."

He nodded, the corners of his mouth lifting. "I've upgraded your omega-net access and local scanning systems as well." He moved to the sink and scrubbed his hands, talking over his shoulder. "I trust you'll remember I helped you and not use those tools while you're in my facility."

Renna stiffened on the table before forcing herself to relax. "Of course I'll remember. I appreciate the help. I'm going to need all the tools I can get to break into that facility."

Aldani dried his hands under the UV light and turned back around to face her. "I need to go check on the progress of the gamma destabilizer. Can you find your way back to your room now?"

"With this back on, I sure can." She hopped down from the table and held out her hand. "Thank you again, Doctor."

He shook it, his large hand swallowing hers. "Don't make me regret helping you, Miss Carrizal."

SIXTEEN

Aldani left her at the elevators and headed off to his private lab. Renna watched him disappear around the corner, his flapping white lab coat at odds with his more formal dining attire. She frowned. She had two options now: go back to her room and get some rest or continue with her plan.

Guilt coiled heavily in her chest, and she stared down at her hands. The hands of a thief, her mother had always said. It hadn't been a compliment.

Aldani had trusted her enough to fix her implant, but if Dallas had been killed, maybe no one left at MYTH knew the terms of their agreement or her pardon. She'd have to take care of herself like always.

This was no time to go developing a conscience.

Renna glanced down the hallway. Empty. She wouldn't get a better chance. As if on their own, her feet headed down the corridor. When she spotted the first security camera, she paused, careful to stay out of its range. She watched it rotate back and forth and, with a zap of her nanospanner, stunned it in a position where she could sneak beneath it. The second camera was as easy as the first. Even better, when security reviewed the feed in the morning, all they'd think was that the mechanics had malfunctioned. It might keep suspicion off her for a little while.

With her implant working again, Renna found the lab she'd noticed earlier easily enough. A few minutes at the touchpad had her inside without a hitch. The last tech had dimmed the lights. Only a few weak helobulbs lit the long metal tables and the gleaming test tubes. A double-walled safe room had been built in the center of the space, and through the tempered glass walls, she could see the computer chips. Row after row of pinhead-sized dots of metal.

The Coalition government would be pleased with Aldani's work. Once implanted in a server, these chips would be able to infiltrate any network in the system, gathering data, spying on terrorists, keeping watch on the net users and hackers who threatened national security, allowing communications to travel even more quickly between distant systems.

A few of these on the open market would even up the score a bit and allow the hackers a way into government systems as well. The net should be a two-way street. It was never fair to have all the power on one side. And like Viktis had said—someone was going to make a buck off the job. It might as well be her.

She crouched at the door of the safe room and gazed at the glowing pad. Well, well, what was this? The tech was something she'd never seen before. Homegrown, probably developed in-house by Dr. Aldani's team.

Renna grinned and cracked her knuckles. Tumbling a new lock was like having sex with someone for the first time. Sure, it was a little awkward learning all the ins and outs, but the thrill of discovery more than made up for it. Carefully, she sliced into the system, each movement checked and double-checked before she proceeded with the crack. Wires and cyberware wove throughout the device in elegant circuits. Challenging, even for her.

Renna's stomach fluttered, and she took a deep breath. She hadn't felt like this in years. Since her first major safe crack, to be exact.

It was her first job after joining Blur's gang, and she'd lied to get the contract, assuring the mark she'd broken through dozens of chemocyclic locks. She'd practiced at home for a week before going in, memorizing every circuit, every route through the lock, every wire and pin. And when she was there, crouched in the CEO's office, she'd felt it. The surge of adrenaline, the feel of power that kept her coming back for more. It had taken her forty-five seconds to get through the safe and retrieve the datapad. Another two minutes to get back outside undetected. And three days to come off the high she'd gotten from finishing the job.

Blur had bought her a bottle of Scottish whiskey to celebrate.

Renna steered her mind back to the task at hand. One slipped wire could alert the whole compound. A few more seconds, and she heard the dulcet sounds of the safe turning off. She was in.

She slipped a single case of the microchips into her pocket, and a rush of adrenaline made her whole body tremble. No need to be greedy. Each of these babies would earn her a small fortune. She could hold onto the sapphire a bit longer, let the legend grow before cashing it in. She'd never need to work again.

Quickly, she reprogrammed the system, backing out and removing any sign of her presence. The safe clicked, then hummed again, and she stroked the metal pad fondly with one finger. Dr. Aldani had a devious and brilliant mind. If only she had a little more time to probe it more deeply.

She slipped out of the lab and made her way back to the elevator. The hallway to her room was empty, and she finally let herself relax. She'd made it. Hopefully they'd be long gone tomorrow before Aldani's staff discovered the theft.

She didn't bother to walk quietly, and the tap of her boots on the floor echoed off the marble floors. As she passed, one of the doors slid open, and Finn stepped out, his face stern.

"Where have you been?" he demanded.

She frowned at the accusatory tone. "With Dr. Aldani. Is there a problem?"

"I can't imagine he wants someone like you wandering around his facility."

Her muscles tightened every time the blasted man even opened his mouth. If only she wasn't so aware of the other things that tightened as well. "Dr. Aldani trusts me. Maybe you should, too."

His words matched the ice blue of his eyes. "Trust you? I wouldn't trust you if you were a Priestess of Preill."

"It's a good thing I don't look good in green then, isn't it? Those habits aren't at all flattering for a girl with my figure." She turned to walk away, determined not to let him get to her, but Finn grabbed her arm. His fingers dug into her skin. When she tried to yank away, they only tightened.

"Get your hand off me. Now." Steel laced her voice, her entire body coiled to attack.

Finn's hand fell away from her arm, but he didn't step back. He crowded her, threatening and hard as stone. "I want to know what game you're playing," he said, staring down at her.

"Games? You want to talk about games, Hunter?" She emphasized the title ever so slightly.

His eyes widened a fraction, and he glanced down the hall. "I told you that part of my life is over. I'm one of the good guys now. Unlike you and your merry band of misfit mercenaries."

"Jealous?" she asked sweetly. "Do you remember how it felt after the rush of a dangerous job? The adrenaline of getting through an impossible situation? I can't imagine being in MYTH is nearly as exciting."

"I've had my share of excitement since joining, I promise." He emphasized the last word in an echo of her earlier tone, and she flinched.

Dammit. He'd been the one to drill that code into her head when she'd joined the gang. He knew she didn't use the word lightly.

"Tell me what you were doing with Aldani," he demanded.

"It's none of your business." Her shrug was dismissive, but his closeness made every cell in her body quiver with awareness. Anger and desire surged through her in equal measures. She hated that she was still attracted to him after all this time, even more so now that he was acting all alpha male on her.

"Everything regarding this mission is my business. Including you."

Her lips quirked into a smirk. "Is that so? Then maybe instead of making assumptions about me, you could do me the courtesy of asking. I haven't done a damn thing to make you distrust me, so what the hell is your problem?"

"You are my problem. Have been from day one. I don't want you on my ship, on my team, or in my life."

"Let me make one thing very clear." Renna jabbed her finger into his hard chest. "You may not like me personally or the fact I've spent most of my life as a thief, but I am exceptional at my job and I take pride in doing it well. I've already saved MYTH's ass twice, and it looks like I'll be doing it again. So either get over yourself or get out of my way because I don't fucking care what a washed-up coward thinks of me."

"Coward?" he snarled, leaning over her threateningly. "You think I'm a coward for turning in Blur and his gang? You knew what he was selling! How could you go along with that?"

The heat from his body scorched Renna's skin, and her pulse pounded in her ears. The headache she'd been fighting since Aldani had fixed her implant sliced through her brain, and she swayed on her feet.

Finn's hand shot out again, but this time to steady her. "What's wrong?" he demanded. "What did Aldani do to you?"

She shuddered as Finn touched his fingers to her neck, and when he pulled them away, blood coated his fingertips.

"Dammit." Renna clapped her hand over the incision site and swallowed back the nausea from the pain. "Let me go. I need to take care of this."

He scowled and shook his head. "Inside. Now." Finn steered her into his room and forced her down into a chair before disappearing into the bathroom.

Finn's room seemed much like hers, with the same plush rugs and soft fabrics. And the amazing bed. Just looking at it made her sleepy. There were no signs of its occupant, nothing personal to show who stayed there except the slight musky sandalwood smell of Finn himself.

She hated that she recognized his scent. Hated even more that it made something warm and safe curl through her.

Stop that, Renna.

Finn returned a moment later with a tube of Burmec and some gauze. "Hold your hair up. This'll stop the bleeding."

"It's fine. I can take care of it myself." She moved to get up, and he clamped a hand on her shoulder.

"I've got this."

Renna shrugged and sat back in her chair, pulling her hair out of the way. "Do you patch up all of your crew like this?"

He paused, looked at her. "No. I don't."

She blinked, but he moved behind her before she could come up with a witty response. Finn's warm fingers smeared the medication over her incision site. Her eyes drifted shut as he massaged the stiff muscles in her neck. *Heaven.*

Then she snapped them back open. She needed to stay focused. "What did you mean about Blur? What was he selling?"

"Are you telling me you honestly didn't know? You ran those jobs for him." His fingers stilled, and she fought the urge to ask him to continue.

"I didn't know what the hell was going on with Blur and his top mercs. I just did what I was told. Most of my jobs were retrieving paperwork from a safe in the merchant district. I never read the stuff, just handed it over. That's why Blur trusted me."

There was a long moment of silence. "I assumed since he used you so often you knew the business." He stopped and met her gaze with a tortured expression. "Blur didn't just take retrieval contracts or other jobs no one else would touch. He was a slaver. The intel you brought him was on new victims—people who were in debt, people no one would miss. People like you, when you first came to us."

The air in Renna's lungs vacated, as if vaporized on impact. All she could do was stare at the dark screen of the holovid on the wall as waves of horror washed over her.

"It's not true. Blur wasn't like that." He'd been kind. Always had time for her, even though he was busy running the business side of things.

"I didn't believe it at first either, but I saw his books. I saw the documents you brought back to him. They were all the proof I needed to crack open the biggest slaving ring on the planet. I had to go to the police." His voice was so low she only heard him because he was still crouched behind her, fingers grazing the back of her neck.

Renna swallowed. "Why did you think I would have gone along with that? Why didn't you ask me?"

"You were a kid. And you were Blur's prize pupil. I thought you were…involved."

She would have laughed at his carefully chosen words if she hadn't been so horrified. He still had no clue he was the one she'd crushed on back then. All the times she'd asked for a private training session in Bumani fighting, just so she could be close to him. "I thought you knew me better than that."

"Blur said he had plans for you. You were sixteen, and he talked about how you and he…" He sucked in a deep breath. "Evidently he was lying about that, too."

Finn's fingers resumed rubbing the gel into her incision site. The silence stretched between them, but Renna had no idea what to say. No wonder he'd hated her. He'd thought she was part of the slaver ring. Thought she'd been sleeping with Blur. She would have felt the same.

"I'm sorry, Renna. I should have given you the benefit of the doubt. My only excuse is I didn't trust *anyone* back then."

"I get it." She didn't add that he'd been the only one she had trusted in the gang. "It's over now. I need you to know I have never taken a job that involves the capture or selling of slaves, and I've turned in the few sent my way. It's not part of the code."

He chuckled, a warm raspy sound that made her stomach dance with butterflies. "The code. I can't believe you still follow it. You were a quick study back then."

"Some things haven't changed." She grinned, her shoulders relaxing like a weight had fallen from them.

His fingers rubbed at her sore muscles, and she finally let herself sink into the feeling. "And some things have. When did you get the implant?" he asked. "There wasn't any mention of it in your file."

"I'm sure there are a lot of things about me not in your file." She could sit here all night if he kept doing that. He was actually rather pleasant when he wasn't sniping at her.

"I'm starting to wonder," he said in a low voice. Finn opened one of the gauze packs and pressed it to the wound. "You ever going to tell me what happened here?" He traced the scar across the front of her neck with a finger, and she jerked away as goose bumps flashed across her skin.

"Doesn't matter. It was a long time ago." She jumped to her feet, all relaxation driven away. "Thanks for patching me up. I've got to go."

"Renna, I…" He stood there, staring, obviously wanting to say something else, but she needed to get away.

"Thanks for the patch job." Without looking back, she sped from his room and back to hers.

Calling herself a coward the whole way there.

SEVENTEEN

I've had the destabilizer device brought to the ship. We ran the last tests on it this morning, and everything seems to be working as expected." Aldani led Finn and Renna back to the hangar bay where the *Athena* was waiting. "We've also fueled her up for you and restocked some supplies. I'm hoping this will be a quick in-and-out job, but it's best to be prepared for anything."

"Thank you, sir." Finn kept his gaze carefully directed ahead, his long legs carrying him ahead of Renna and the doctor. "I appreciate your help. I know we didn't get off to the best start yesterday."

"Just make sure you find something out. We can't rescue Myka until we know what's in that facility."

"Don't worry. It's under control," Renna said.

Aldani had shown her how to use the small globe of metal that would get them inside earlier that morning, but she still didn't know what they'd face. It didn't matter. She had a job to do, so she'd figure it out one way or another.

Finn paused long enough to salute the doctor. "I comm'd Keva to have the ship ready to go. We should be on Banos Prime by this afternoon and hopefully back here within twenty-four hours with more information. If you'll excuse me, I need to go make final preparations." He turned, marching up the gangway and into the *Athena* without waiting for them to respond.

Renna and Aldani watched him in silence until he disappeared inside, then the doctor turned to Renna, one eyebrow canted. "Is everything all right between you two?" he asked.

"Of course," she lied. But Finn's behavior said otherwise. Snippets of the previous night rushed through her mind, the feel of Finn's fingers against her neck sending a shiver down her spine. With an inward groan, she pushed the thought out of her mind. Last night, she thought they'd finally come to a truce, but maybe she was wrong.

"Well, I'll give you my farewell speech then. Watch the destabilizer. It will only work long enough to open one door, then it must be recharged. And by the stars, don't let it fall into the wrong hands. It won't blow up a planet now that I've adjusted the settings, but it could do some serious damage."

"Understood. Thank you for everything, Doctor." She held out a hand, and he shook it. "We'll be back to find Myka in no time." There. No promises, just nice and vague. Too bad it was already too late for semantics.

"I believe you. And, for what it's worth, I think you're an asset to this team. They need someone like you to think outside the box." He cleared his throat and stepped back. "Go on. The sooner you leave, the sooner I'll have my nephew back."

"Yes, sir." She smiled at him, and he winked at her before she boarded the ship.

Renna spent the ride to Banos Prime time scouring the omega-net for news about other attacks, Myka, or Hesperia. She also moved some of her liquid assets to new accounts and rearranged her portfolio. Things were about to get messy, and she had no idea if she'd get the chance again. Thank gods she'd paid attention when Blur had stressed the importance of diversifying.

"Approaching Banos Prime. Landing in thirteen minutes." Kojima's voice came over the intercom, and Renna closed down the hololink in her interface. Aldani had seriously upgraded her implant, and despite a few twinges of pain as it readjusted to her neural patterns, everything ran like clockwork.

She pulled on her coat and grabbed the bag with her tools. Time to get the job done.

The *Athena* touched down in a golden valley between two rock formations. The outcroppings looked like gnarled burgundy fingers reaching up from the desert. According to the surveillance maps, the facility they needed to find was more than two klicks away, but Finn didn't want to land too close and alert anyone inside.

Renna tugged at the pack on her back as she surveyed the arid desert surrounding them. She'd packed her tools, Aldani's device, and a few other necessities that might come in handy when she got into the facility. Only she and Finn were going inside, but Keva and one of the other sergeants—Doyle, she thought—were coming along as backup on the journey.

Not exactly how she would have chosen to run the mission. Having three other people with her made her skin itch with unease. More people meant a greater chance of detection.

She shivered as a gust of wind blew sand across the surface. Banos Prime might have been a desert world, but it certainly wasn't warm. The blazing sun overhead looked welcoming, but they were too far away for it to heat the atmosphere above freezing most days. And at night…they'd be completely screwed if they had to be out here after dark.

"Open planet map," she ordered her implant. A moment later, the surface of Banos was laid out for her, the facility blinking red. She turned to Finn and Keva, who were whispering about something or other. She didn't much care. "We need to head north. Looks like there's a line of rock outcroppings we can follow to stay out of sight."

They both nodded, and Renna started north without a glance behind her. Let them follow if they wanted. She'd spent way too much energy worrying about Finn and his crew already. Ever since they'd left Aldani's lab that morning, everyone had been acting strange. They'd greeted her in the passageways by name, acknowledging her for the first time since the missions had started. Their sudden friendliness made her twitchy.

It also made her wonder what exactly Finn had said to them.

The group walked in silence for a few minutes, the whistling of the wind across the sand the only noise until Finn's long strides caught up with her. Even then he didn't speak.

She definitely wasn't going to be the one to break the sudden awkwardness between them.

"Any hint yet as to what's out there?" he finally asked, shooting her a sideways glance.

"This area of Banos seems to be completely deserted. No life signs anywhere, not even at the colony to the north."

"That's where Myka's parents were stationed. MYTH had a small team posted there for years, investigating the area. Dr. Thana Samil led the expedition. She's one of our best scientists." He frowned. "It wasn't the hardest hit, but everyone was killed. They didn't even find most of the bodies."

Renna paused, then said, "I wish I knew how the colony and this facility were connected because I don't think it's a coincidence."

Finn didn't comment, just kept pace with her for a few more minutes before glancing at her again. "MYTH lost a lot of important people in that attack. Thank gods Dr. Prince escaped with much of their research or we'd have no idea what our teams had found."

"And what's that?"

"Banos has special minerals deep in the soil. I wonder if the facility was created so someone else could continue that work."

"But who? Only MYTH knew the real reason the team was here, correct? Do you have enemies? Could someone have found out what you were doing?"

He shrugged. "I have no idea, but that's what I'm hoping to find out."

They walked a few more moments, Finn slanting glances at her from the corner of his eye. She felt his gaze like pressure against her skin. She couldn't decide if it was pleasant or annoying.

"Out with it, Captain. Why do you keep looking at me?"

"How long have you had your implant?" Finn asked.

She looked at him warily. He wanted small talk? Now? "Five years. I knew someone who cut me a deal. Best investment I ever made."

"Is it one of the nucleospatial models from Stagg Industries? I hear they're exceptional for mapping and schematics."

Renna blinked at him. Since the ban fifteen years ago, cybernetic implants were forbidden in Coalition territory. A few of the richest mercenaries she knew had them and a few dirty politicians, but the military absolutely forbade them and had implemented random body scans to keep everyone compliant.

"I didn't know you'd kept up with them. No, it's a Compass X-3. I wish I'd held out for the nucleospatial model, but mine's been extremely helpful, so I can't complain too much. And the upgrades Aldani installed are amazing."

"Must have cost a lot of money, even with a deal." Finn walked with his hands swinging easily at his sides, his shoulders relaxed and at ease, but she got the sense there was something else on his mind, something worrying him.

"What's going on? Want to make sure it won't hamper me from being able to do the job?"

A frown tugged the corners of his mouth down and caused the skin between his eyebrows to pucker. "You know, you could ease off a bit. You think everything I say is a criticism."

"Isn't it?"

"Look, Renna. I'm trying to apologize. I'm sorry for everything that's happened, but it was a long time ago. We need to work together here, not be enemies."

"I already have plenty of enemies. What's one more?" She threw the words out like a slap and instantly regretted it as Finn's jaw tightened. She sighed. Evidently, she wasn't very good at apologies either. "Look. I've worked alone all my life. It's how I operate. And yet here I am, blackmailed into helping a big group of military do-gooders. And to top it off, you made it perfectly clear I was more worthless than the shit in the vacuum sewer. It's going to take a while to get used to the change."

He rubbed a hand over his face before looking at her, and she noticed how tired his blue eyes looked. "Can you? Forgive me, I mean?"

She shrugged. "I haven't shot you yet. That's always a good sign."

Finn chuckled and looked slightly relieved. "Truce?" He held out his hand, large and capable and strong.

There was an instant where she wanted to ignore it. If she forgave this man, everything would change Was she really ready to take a step in that direction? Before she could talk herself out if it, she took his hand, the warmth from his fingers soaking into her skin.

Something shifted inside her, something that felt almost like friendship. Or at least respect.

"Truce, Captain."

His expression cleared. "And just think, if you hadn't joined up with us, you never would have gotten Aldani's upgrades."

"Trust me, if Dallas had given me any other choice, I would gladly give them up."

He nodded. "I know. It was kind of a shitty thing for him to do. But I know Aldani feels better that you're going to help us find Myka."

"And what about you? Ready to put your money where your mouth is?" She gave him a wicked smirk. "If you're so happy to have me on the team and willing to forgive and forget, how about a little wager on how long it takes me to get inside?"

Finn shook his head, a twitching smile on his lips. "I make it a point to never bet against a sure thing."

"Smart man." Their gazes locked, and she almost forgot the job she was here to do. Dammit. She could not let herself go down that road again. Being involved with Finn and his team already broke every rule she'd set for herself, and the job was suffering for it. But something in her was still drawn to this man—the way the muscles in his chiseled jaw clenched when he was angry, the blue eyes that seemed to cut past her barriers.

"The facility is over this ridge," Keva said, stalking past them with a glare to crouch against an outcropping of burgundy stone. "Are you coming?"

Renna snapped back into job-mode and called up a map of the area with her implant. "I'm detecting heat signatures from inside the building, but I can't get a read on how many or where."

She frowned at the rough rock surface as if it could answer her. "Usually my implant can get a better sense of numbers." Maybe Aldani's upgrades had affected something else. Or maybe the heat signatures weren't actually human. Whatever it was, they'd have to be careful going in.

"Is there a place where we can get inside without anyone spotting us? We need at least four minutes to use the destabilizer to open a door," Finn said.

She peered over the ridge at the facility below. It sat in a wide, sandy valley, with jagged hills surrounding it. The place was a lot bigger than she'd expected, maybe almost as large as a city block back on Hesperia. She had no idea how it had gone unnoticed for so long. Especially when the dull metallic material of the building stood out against the golden sand like a scar.

The sun shimmered off the walls, highlighting the perfectly smooth façade. There were no doors, windows, or blemishes standing out anywhere.

"Download schematics," she ordered.

"Error. No schematics available," her implant said in its soft, robotic voice.

"Download area map."

"Error. No map available."

She tapped her foot against the sand. "Download building material list."

"Error. No list available."

Renna gritted her teeth. What the hell was going on? "I can't get any information on this place," she said, turning to Finn. "I hope Aldani's upgrade didn't break my implant."

"I suppose there's nothing else we can do but take our chances. At least MYTH surveillance hasn't found any trace of people going in and out of the place." Finn ran a hand through his hair. "Keva, Doyle, get back to the ship and prep for takeoff. I don't want you hanging around here too long. Just because we haven't seen anyone doesn't mean we're not being watched."

"But sir..." Keva's face twisted with indecision. "I'm not leaving you behind."

"I'm not important; the mission is. If we're not back within six hours, get back to Aldani's lab and contact MYTH HQ on Preill. They're the closest branch to this system. They'll send backup."

Keva's jaw tightened, ready to argue, but Renna interrupted. "Captain, this isn't necessary. I can go in alone. There's no reason for both of us to risk it."

"I'm going with you. There will be no discussion." He pinned both women with a steely gaze, and Renna threw up her hands.

"Whatever you want, Captain. It's your call." Part of her was relieved, but she couldn't ignore the other voice that whispered suspiciously at the back of her mind. Was he really coming with her because he still didn't trust her?

"Be careful, sir," Keva said. She opened her mouth as if she was going to say something else, but shook her head.

Beside her, Sergeant Doyle saluted. "Good hunting, sir. Ma'am."

EIGHTEEN

Finn and Renna snuck down the dune toward the building. As they got closer, the building seemed to tower over them, at least two stories high. It was a lot bigger than it had looked from a distance, and the closer they got, the more the strange material threw her off.

She rubbed at the prickling skin on her arms. "Do you feel that?"

Finn pulled his gun from its holster. "What the hell is it?"

"Some kind of force field. I think they're blocking all communication in and out of the place. Probably why my implant isn't working." But there was something else there, too, just below the low hum. Something simmering at the edges of her mind.

They crept toward the building. Finn scanned the area, his gun at the ready, while Renna studied the structure in front of her. She scooped up a handful of cold sand and let some of it stream between her fingers. Then she threw the fistful at the side of the building.

Nothing happened. The sand slid off the strange material as if it was perfectly smooth. Not even a grain left behind.

"What do you think it is?" Finn asked, peering at the wall.

"I wish I knew. I've never seen anything like it before." Whoever had built this facility had gone to a lot of trouble and expense to create this material. But why?

"We're not going to figure out what's going on by standing here. Are you ready?"

Renna moved closer to the building, trying to ignore the energy that cobwebbed against her skin. She pulled the particle destabilizer from her pack. The globe was smaller than her fist, and the silver metal seemed to move and shiver the closer it got to the building. She gripped it and twisted the top and the bottom away from each other, pulling it apart to reveal a core of glowing elemental antimatter.

"Here goes nothing." She pressed it against the strange metal wall. Surges of electricity ran up and down her arm, and she forced herself not to jerk away.

"What's wrong? Are you all right?" Finn moved closer, but she stopped him with the shake of her head.

Slowly, the point at which the device touched the wall started to glow blue, the light moving in circles from the center outward, growing larger by the moment.

"What is it doing?" Finn asked, peering over her shoulder.

"It's agitating the molecules. Aldani said it could take up to three minutes to burn through, depending on the material."

Finn's lips tightened, but he simply nodded and glanced back toward the hill where Keva and Doyle were hiding.

The strange blue ring was almost as big as a plate now, and the energy shimmered just enough that she caught a glimpse of the facility beyond. "I think it's working," she said, leaning forward.

Finn's presence was warm against her back as he moved to stare at the wall. His MYTH uniform was covered in a fine dusting of the sand, dulling the navy fabric. Her own clothes were probably covered in it, too.

The ring of light was as large as a person now, and it had finally stopped expanding. Slowly, the molecules of the wall started to go translucent.

"Looks like there are some large boxes and crates on the other side. I think they're hiding our entrance."

"No sign of an alarm?" Finn asked.

"Not yet." She paused and said, "Facility schematics please."

"Facility schematics not found."

"Still nothing." She let out a sigh in frustration. "Whatever this building is made of, it's still blocking any signals."

Finn shifted his weight. "This whole situation feels wrong."

Renna nodded. For once, she was in complete agreement with the captain. Then she froze. The wall had gone completely transparent. She could see into the facility like she was gazing through a window.

"Finn."

Together they peered inside. Stacks of boxes and crates lined the walls of the warehouse. Bright helolights hung from the ceiling, giving everything a hard, cold glow.

"It's empty? I thought, with this kind of security, it would be full of workers." Finn craned his neck to see further in, his voice sounding troubled.

"Maybe they're in another part of the building? Once we get inside I think we'll have a better sense of the place."

He nodded. "I'll go first. Once I verify it's all clear, you can follow me in."

"Wait just a minute. I'm the thief here. Let me go first."

Finn shook his head. "We are not going to argue about this. I'm in charge of this mission. You need to listen to me."

He definitely hadn't gotten less bossy with age.

"And I'm here because of my exceptional skills. Might as well let me use them to make sure there's no one around to catch us." Carefully she pulled Aldani's device away from the wall, half-expecting the hole to snap closed. But it stayed open, the edges shimmering slightly with the strange blue light. She slipped it into her bag, then straightened from her crouch.

"Are you ready?"

He scanned the scene one last time. "I'm right behind you."

Renna stepped silently over the edge of the wall. Inside the facility, the temperature was a good twenty degrees warmer. The air hung heavy and sluggish, the scent of metal making her nose itch. There was another scent there, too, just at the edge of recognition, but when it didn't come to her, she focused on scoping out the rest of the facility.

"Schematics," she whispered.

"No schematics found."

Dammit. So much for Aldani's upgrades. She was going to have to do this blind.

As Finn stepped through the hole, she inched around the side of the crate to see better. Inside, the room was a maze of boxes and machinery. A conveyor belt ran along the ceiling of the room, but it didn't seem to be turned on at the moment.

Instead, silence pulsed around them.

Finn pushed past her, his gun still in his hand. "Where to?"

Renna swallowed. Tried to stretch out her own senses to get a feel for the place. After years of doing this, even an implant was only a little better than her intuition, but somehow, this was different. Whatever the building was made from, it messed up more than her implant's sensors. She'd be damned if she let the captain know that, though. Instead, she squared her shoulders, pulled her own pistol from the holster, and moved forward toward the next stack of crates.

"We need to check the perimeter. I can't tell if the whole facility is one large room or broken up into smaller areas."

Finn nodded. "On your six."

They snuck around boxes toward the north end of the facility. Renna's feet were noiseless on the concrete floor, but Finn moved like a soldier, methodical and precise. But not silent.

If this was a real job, she would have fired his ass.

"Can you pick up your feet a little, soldier?" she asked as they paused at another bank of crates. "You sound like an elephant."

"What are you talking about? I'm moving as quietly as I can." He stared down at the heavy boots he wore.

"It's not working. How about I give you some lessons when we get out of here? Evidently your time in the military has dulled a few skills." She smirked at him and pushed past to scope out the rest of the area. She might have let her arm brush against his on purpose, but she'd never admit it.

He stiffened at the touch but didn't say anything as she headed for the far side of the room.

Her implant buzzed in her ear, and Renna froze in front of a narrow doorway leading off the space. "Warning. Heat signatures detected."

"Show heat map."

The implant still couldn't display an image of the facility, but the red blobs of heat that appeared seemed to be dead ahead through the door. They weren't moving, but that didn't mean anything. They could be waiting for Renna and Finn to get close enough to attack.

"What's wrong?" Finn's words were hot against her ear, and she shivered, ignoring the surge of…something that shot through her midsection.

"There's something beyond the door, but I can't tell what it is."

"Then let's find out." He crept closer, pressing himself against the wall. Renna followed. She recognized the keypad on the door as one of the SEU series. She'd have to be careful with this one.

Pulling out the small nanotech pliers she used for jobs like these, she carefully slid them into the hidden port on the bottom of the lock and fished for the grounding wire. Her first connection made the keypad scream in protest, and Renna jerked back, heart pounding.

Finn hissed at her. "Quiet!"

She glared but didn't respond. Renna let out a breath and tried to calm her racing pulse. Rookie mistakes would get them both killed. There was no excuse to be jittery now. She wasn't thirteen with a crush on her mentor anymore.

She slipped the pliers back into the port and tried again. This time, the connection took, and the nanotech ran through the security program, searching through the holes in the code. A few seconds later, the red glowing light clicked over to green.

"We're in," she said with a grin as she pressed her back against the wall and gripped her gun. "Ready?" He nodded, and she shoved open the door.

Finn popped into the doorway, did a quick scan of the room, then popped back. He shook his head.

Renna moved into the room, her gun at the ready. It was empty, but the blob of heat signatures still showed on her implant scan.

"What the hell?" Maybe her implant was broken. The room was the size of the command center back on the *Athena* and was completely deserted aside from the three holo lights hanging from the ceiling and a few worn crates in the corner. The walls and floor were the same dull gray as the rest of the facility.

Renna moved her gaze slowly through the room, searching for anything that might give them a clue as to who owned the facility or what the owners were doing here.

Finn followed close behind. His presence felt warm, like sunshine on her back. When she was younger, she'd gotten really good at knowing when he was close. That skill had come back faster than she'd expected. Old habits died hard.

"I don't get it." Finn shook his head. "There's nothing here."

"What about the crates?" It was the only possibility. And she didn't like what it implied.

They exchanged a glance and headed for the closest of the large metal bins. Renna pulled out her nanospanner sonic screwdriver and loosened the bolts holding down the top of the crate. "Okay. It's off. Help me with this."

Finn took the other side, and they lifted off the panel and set it on the floor. "What in the seven gods is that doing here?" Finn's eyes widened, and Renna glanced down into the box.

A mech—a human-like robot—was curled into a crouch. The shiny metallic body had limbs made of the same dark metal as the walls of the facility. She couldn't stop herself from glancing back out the door they'd come through, into the main facility. There were hundreds of these crates in there. Were they all filled with mechs?

Her hand trembled as she ran a finger over the lifeless form's skull. She found the control pad and turned on the diagnostics. "They haven't been programed with an AI yet, but they're primed and ready to go. Finn, they're equipped with weapons. State-of-the-art weapons."

Finn stared down into the box. "So this facility is building robot soldiers? But the Treaty of Thermesium…"

"When has that stopped anyone?" Renna shook her head. "Look at my implant. And the Empyreans are still selling programmable AIs on the black market for personal use. It's a matter of affordability. If you're rich enough, you can buy anything."

She moved to the next crate and unscrewed the top. This one was full of robot parts, arms and legs and heads jumbled together. A pair of lifeless eyes made her shudder, though she'd much prefer that to the cold glow of an activated mech.

"What do we do now?" Finn scanned the warehouse space.

"There has to be something else here. It doesn't make sense. Why would they build an impregnable facility to build robot parts?" Renna headed through the stacks of crates toward the other end of the building. She didn't bother masking her steps or waiting to see if Finn followed. If someone else was here, she would have heard them by now.

She passed through a large arch and into another wide room. The facility seemed to be divided into sections: storage, assembly, prototypes. In this room, the crates were gone, replaced by machinery and conveyor belts holding mech parts in various states of completion.

At the end of the assembly line, she spotted a faint glow in the floor. "Finn, over here."

A perfect glowing square appeared in the dark material. It was the size of one of the crates, and if she didn't know better, she would have dismissed it as a stain. "It's some sort of hatch. This facility has a lower level."

She crouched over the space and ran a finger along the seam. The cement was slightly raised, like the two pieces didn't quite fit back together after being cut. "There doesn't seem to be any way to get it open from here. I think it's an access panel."

"And that means there's bound to be a door somewhere around here." Finn spun slowly on his heels, while Renna paced back and forth trying various commands to get her implant to upload building plans or updated heat signatures. Anything that might give her a sense of what was going on here. "Dammit. Nothing's working."

The weight of Finn's gaze made her shoulders hunch, and she forced herself to stay calm. This is what Dallas had hired her to do. If she couldn't do the job, they had no reason to hold up their end of the bargain.

Finally, she stopped and turned to the captain. "There's got to be another way down. Search the south side of this room and keep your eyes open. The doorway will be hidden like this one." She headed to the north side of the room and started in the corner, raking her gaze over every inch of the wall. She just needed another seam. Or a keypad. Or something.

Renna's whole body still thrummed with the electricity that ran through the facility. Her heart raced like she'd consumed too many energy drinks, but her senses felt dulled. This place was dangerous, and the sooner they got out, the better.

"Renna, over here." Finn's voice carried across the warehouse. She was at his side in seconds. "There's a control pad here, and it doesn't seem hooked into any of the machinery." He gestured at the nearby conveyor belt. "I can't figure out what it does."

"Then let's find out." Renna jacked in her device and ran the program again. It hummed and vibrated in her hand as it worked, and she'd almost given up hope when the code finally broke and the light turned green.

But still nothing happened.

Renna chewed her lip and studied the keypad more closely. It had unlocked…something. But what? Finn stared at it, too, as if their combined brainpower could figure it out.

She felt jumpy, her body on alert, as if an ambush could happen at any possible minute. She was so distracted it was probably only a matter of time before that actually happened.

Pull it together, Renna.

She closed her eyes and forced a familiar sense of calm back into her center. Breathe in. Breathe out.

When she opened her eyes, she ignored Finn's curious expression and focused on the keypad. She let her fingers drift over the numbers.

Ever so faintly, some of the metal pads caught at her fingertips. The ones used most often. Renna made another pass. This model used a clockwise entry order for the security code. She let her fingers tell her which pads to press, until she'd made a complete circle on the device.

There was a whirring noise as one of the machines started up. The conveyor jerked and screamed into motion, and the wall beside them slid back to reveal a long, dark corridor.

Finn's eyebrows shot up as he glanced from the now-apparent door to Renna and back again. "Dallas might have been right about you."

"Captain, that's the nicest thing you've ever said to me." She flashed him a smile as she moved into the corridor. Lights on the ceiling flickered to life, illuminating a metal ladder at the far end. "Looks like we found our way in."

Finn nodded. "Good job. Stay alert. If there's anyone here, they're bound to have heard us by now." He started down the ladder, his broad shoulders disappearing into the darkness before Renna followed.

Finn's boots clanked against each rung as they descended. She counted each step as a way to pass time, and after forty rungs, Renna's legs were burning. Weak hololights glowed every twenty rungs or so, but the watery light made the climb even worse. Her breath hitched, but she forced herself to stay calm. The image of being trapped beneath tons of earth was not helping.

"Finally," Finn muttered. Renna heard his feet hit the cement with a thud, and in the dim light, Renna felt more than saw him step away from the ladder.

Three more rungs and then she stood on solid ground again, too, arms wrapped around her waist so he wouldn't see her trembling. "I hope we find another way out of here. I'd rather not have to do that climb going up."

Finn nodded. "I'm with you there." He pulled his gun out, and Renna did the same.

They were in another narrow corridor, colored pipes running along the walls. The lights flickered on as they walked, obviously motion sensitive. She guessed they were heading south through the complex.

"Hang on. Let me make sure these aren't tied to a security system." She pulled down one of the wires and studied the electrical components. She'd only seen one security system like that, but it had always stuck with her as ingenious and something she'd do when she had her own place.

"Looks clean." She tucked the wires back in and shrugged. "I'm actually surprised there isn't more security in this place."

"I'm pretty sure they figured they had an unbreachable facility, what with no doors or windows."

"Right. But we have Dr. Aldani. Bonus points for us." A few steps further and she made out the shape of a door panel. "I think this is it. Are you ready?"

"I wish we knew what was behind there." A muscle jumped in Finn's jaw, and his fingers tightened around the handle of his gun.

"Damn, so do I." Renna tugged at her jacket and stretched her arms. "I can't remember the last time I went in blind on a job." She rolled her shoulders, then pulled her gun from its holster. "Guess it's now or never."

Finn gave her the ghost of a smile. "Let's do it."

Renna pressed her fingers lightly against the door, and it slid open without a sound. She stepped through…

…and froze as a dozen pairs of eyes turned to her at once.

NINETEEN

Renna turned to dart back into the corridor, but a man grabbed her arm and yanked her into the room before she could even struggle. "Let me go!" she demanded, but the Ileth just glared at her.

She froze. Dear gods, what was he? Instead of violet pupils like Viktis had, this man's eyes shone with an odd metallic glow. More machine than biological.

Another one—human this time—tried to grab Finn, but he'd had enough of a warning to fire off a shot. The bullet hit the man's thigh, penetrating the skin with a spurt of blood, but he kept coming like he didn't even feel it. The air filled with an iron-rich sent, almost like blood, and Renna gasped as the bullet pushed back out of the entry wound and bounced on the floor.

The hole in his skin knitted closed a second later, leaving only a smear of crimson behind on his pants.

Finn threw a punch, his fist connecting with the man's jaw, but the hulking mercenary had Finn's arms pinned behind his back in three moves. The captain jerked and thrashed against his captor, but the man stood steady, unmoving. Like a rock.

Or a machine.

Renna let her gaze rake the rest of the room. The mercenaries seemed to be a mix of human, Ileth, and Trezian, but each of them had something that seemed off. A robotic hand. Glowing cornea implants. Half a face full of metal.

One of the Trezians stood up and crossed two of his arms. "Well, well. Someone must have found some seriously high tech to get in here." The scales on his skin glinted sliver in the light. One side of his face was completely gone, replaced by a metallic mask. His other two arms he shoved into the pockets of his uniform pants. "The boss isn't going to be happy about this."

"What do we do with them, sir? Kill them?" the merc holding Renna asked. She wrinkled her nose as he moved, the scent of sweat and dirty clothes rolling off him in a cloud of stink. And beneath that, he carried the strange undertone of metal that permeated the air here.

She struggled against him, trying to arc her body as far away from his chest as possible. The man's fingers curled into the skin of her arms. She grunted at the pressure.

If he left a frakking bruise, she'd make sure he never touched a woman again.

"Hold still," he ordered, jerking her bag from her shoulder and dropping it on the floor to get a better grip on her.

The leader started pacing. "We need information from them before we do anything. The boss will be the one to decide if they live. He may want to use them for other things."

Renna's brain spun. She didn't recognize their uniforms, but these men were mercenaries. Her people. Maybe she could get the captain out of here at least.

She shifted into her role, like putting on an old jacket. Her lips lifted in a conspiratorial smile. "I know you guys aren't Iron Elite; you're too well-funded for that. But I'm not sure who you're with. The Star Raiders? Phi? Who's running this part of the traverse now?"

The leader narrowed his eyes. "You've never heard of us."

"Try me. I have more connections than you can dream of."

"Who are you?" he asked. "You look familiar."

Renna shook her head. "Uh-uh. You first, love."

The alien's neck slits flared, and all four fists clenched in front of him. "Answer me, dammit. Or I'll make you."

The guy was wound tighter than she'd expected. What the hell had they stumbled into? Renna swallowed and kept her face expressionless. "How about you let this guy go," she nodded toward Finn, "and I'll tell you whatever you'd like to know? He's not important, just one of my bodyguards. A smart woman never travels without one."

"A smart woman wouldn't need one in the first place." The leader glanced between Finn and Renna, then motioned to one of his other men. "Why don't you convince the lady to tell me what she knows?"

One of the human mercs stalked toward Finn, a satisfied smirk twisting his face. Without warning, he slammed his fist into the captain's stomach.

Finn grunted, his body bowing, eyes closed, but a breath later, he straightened his spine and stared straight ahead. As impassive as a glacier.

Renna's muscles screamed to stop these men, to fight back, but she forced herself to stay still. There was no way they'd win a physical fight against them.

"You gonna talk, beautiful?" the leader asked. The metal plate on his face caught the light of the helolamps and glowed silver. She looked him in the eye and simply smiled.

He gestured, and the man punched Finn again. Aside from the violent sound of air leaving his lungs, the captain remained silent. He squeezed his eyes shut and took a shuddering breath before straightening again.

Damn him. Why did he have to be so stoic? If he collapsed into a quivering mess, these guys were more likely to believe he was nothing but hired help.

"Again," the leader ordered.

The thud of the man's fist connecting with Finn's jaw sounded through the room, echoing off the scattered card tables and chairs. Renna gritted her teeth as Finn spit out a mouthful of blood.

Obviously this wasn't working. Time for Plan B.

"Fine," she drawled. "I'll tell you what you want to know."

The leader held up his hand to stop his merc from hitting Finn again. "Go on."

"My name is Renna Carrizal."

The man's lips parted. Good. Hopefully her name would be enough. In certain circles, she was legendary. For several reasons.

He raked his gaze up and down her body, his expression two parts cunning, one part lethal. "Well, well. I can think of quite a few people who'd love a chance to talk to you, beautiful."

Renna suppressed her shudder. "I'm sure we could all sit down for tea and cookies. Sounds delightful." She tried to yank her arm away from the man holding her, but he didn't let go.

The Trezian chuckled. "I can't believe I caught the best thief in the galaxy. I'm going to be famous. And you're going to be the boss's new plaything as soon as we ship you off to him." He rubbed his hands together, his teeth gleaming as his lips stretched into a triumphant grin.

Renna shrugged and examined her nails. "Sounds like I get the better part of this deal. I'm leaving this planet, one way or another. You guys are trapped here with—what—a bunch of half-finished mechs and a team of dirty men? Doesn't sound like much fun to me."

"Oh, don't you worry. Things just got a lot more fun." The brilliance of his smile dimmed from elated to sadistic. "We're not just building mechs here. It's a whole different type of army. And I think you and your friend here will make excellent additions."

Two of his arms pointed to the back of the room where there was a thick wooden door that looked surprisingly out of place in the high-tech facility. "Take them to the holding cell. I'll contact the boss. I'm sure he'll be happy to have Miss Carrizal on his team."

"In your dreams, love. The only team I work on is my own." She forced a slow smile to her lips. She'd been in enough oh shit situations to know better than to show her nerves. Even if they were screaming loud enough to deafen her.

The man holding her arms yanked her toward the door, and the other man did the same with Finn. She struggled, using the motion to scan the rest of the room without them noticing. An arms bench sat on the far side, next to a half-opened crate full of assault rifles. Starmasters if she wasn't mistaken.

The two mercenaries dragged them down another corridor. Their boots echoed loudly on the cement floor, and the walls were built of the same gray stone as the rest of the facility. A series of alcoves were cut into the walls, and Renna's merc stopped in front of one. He typed in a number at the keypad, and the metal door slid open.

He shoved her inside, and she stumbled a few feet. Finn followed a heartbeat later.

"Don't worry, we'll be back for you soon," the merc called just before the door swished shut.

The captain took two shuffling steps, then fell to his knees. His eyes widened at her before he toppled sideways.

Shit. Renna raced over to him and collapsed by his side. "Are you all right?" Her fingers itched to touch him, to wipe the trickle of blood away from his lip, but instead she folded her hands in her lap. "How bad is it?"

He took a shuddering breath and opened his eyes. The blue depths had lost their usual sparkle. "I think he broke my rib."

Renna pulled her knees to her chest and wrapped her arms around them. "I'm sorry. I thought I could get them to release you if they thought you weren't important."

"I figured. Too bad it didn't work. Besides, do you really think I would have left you here?" He touched her arm. "I know we didn't start out on the best terms here, but I haven't changed that much. I don't leave my crew behind."

Her heart twisted strangely. Having someone looking out for her was something she hadn't experienced since she was a kid. But at the same time, it was nice to know someone had her back.

Finn dropped his hand like it had suddenly gotten too heavy. "You shouldn't have told them who you are. You're not exactly anonymous in this galaxy, even if they don't know you're the Star Thief." He gasped as he struggled to sit up.

Her heart stuttered at the pain etched on his face. Dammit, he was really hurt. She slid an arm beneath his shoulder and helped him lean against the wall. His body against hers was hard and muscled, and even injured, she got the impression he could still kick her ass.

"Thanks," he said once he was propped up. Deep lines gouged the space between his eyebrows, and his skin had taken on a shiny, waxy tone, like he was made of plastic. But he tried to smile at her anyway. "So what's the plan?"

Renna jumped to her feet and paced the room, careful not to look at him. Finn was hurt, and it was all her fault. Whatever she came up with had to get him out of there and quickly. Those punches had been vicious. She wouldn't be surprised if he wasn't injured more than he let on.

The cell wasn't much bigger than her bunk back on the ship. It only took six strides before she hit the wall and needed to turn back around. She made three passes before she let out a long sigh. "I have no idea." She shoved her hands into her pockets. "They took my tools and the destabilizer. The only thing that might work is attacking the next guard that shows up and hope we can get away."

Finn shifted against the wall and winced again. "I'm not going to be much help."

"I can take care of myself." His eyes looked strangely sunken, and she made her voice light and joking. Maybe it would be enough to distract him. "You haven't seen me in a bar fight. Your lessons came in handy."

"I don't suppose that's where you got the scar on your neck?" Finn studied the white line running from below her left ear around the front of her neck. She usually tried to hide it with her hair, but when she pulled it back like now, it was clearly visible. Heat crept across her skin at the curiosity in his gaze, at the way she could almost feel it like a caress.

She laughed awkwardly. "You know it's not. I had it when I first met you." She never talked about that night. Even after more than ten years, just thinking about it still made her skin crawl. Renna wrapped her arms around her waist and sank down the wall to sit on the floor beside Finn. It was better to not have him looking at her. To not feel so exposed under his steady gaze.

"You going to finally tell me what happened?" he asked gently.

The metal was cool against her back, even through her leather jacket, and she tried not to shiver. She stared straight ahead. "It was nothing."

"Right. And I'm not a space Marine." Finn sighed. "Want to know how I got this one?" he asked, unbuttoning the top of his uniform to uncover a puckered white circle on his shoulder.

Her eyes widened. "Gunshot?"

"Even better." His smile was wicked. "One of my first missions out after joining MYTH, we got shot down on Devon Alpha. I was only a corporal then, trying to prove myself. We were trapped in the jungle with only our blasters and a few days' rations."

"Damn. That is not a friendly planet."

"You're telling me." Finn refastened the buttons, then rubbed his shoulder as if bothered by phantom pain. "The remaining crew and I decided to make for the main spaceport and hope we could get there before the supplies ran out. Halfway there, a gang of Krongs attacked. Have you had run-ins with them before?"

Renna shook her head. "They're fairly primitive, aren't they? Live in huts in the jungle? No space travel?"

"Yeah. They still use spears and bows and arrows. And when they attacked us, one of the spears found the weak patch in my armor where the mesh meets metal. I've never been in so much pain. I had to walk around with half a spear sticking out of my shoulder until they could get me to a medicenter. The team called me 'Pincushion' for months."

Renna chuckled. She couldn't imagine Finn as a raw recruit. Even back in Blur's gang, he'd been the one to order them around. He'd always seemed so together...so military. "At least it wasn't poisoned. I hear the stuff they use has...special effects."

"You mean the penis-shriveling kind? Yeah. I got lucky. I can assure you there's no damage there," he said with a sly smile.

Renna's stomach dropped. If he grinned at her like that again, her insides might spontaneously combust. To distract herself, she shrugged out of her jacket and pushed up her sleeve. A long, jagged scar stretched up her forearm.

"I had a job go tits-up on Enill when I was eighteen," she said. "The boss thought because I was a girl, he could cheat me out of my payment. He sent his men after me when I left his headquarters. One of them tried to relieve me of my earnings by threatening me with a laser knife. He got one swipe at me before I cut off his balls with it. I made sure the boss understood it would happen to him if he tried that again."

They grinned at each other for a long moment before Finn unbuttoned his uniform jacket and tugged up the bottom of his shirt. "Okay, one more. I think I might have you beat."

"Let's hear it."

He exposed the flat ridge of his stomach, and the muscles rippling there made Renna's mouth go dry. *Wow.* She forced her face to stay expressionless as he pulled the shirt up higher.

"That scar, there?" He pointed at a thin white line high on his ribcage. "I grew up on Forever Station. When I was nine, my parents were killed while running patrols in the western traverse so I went to live with my aunt. There was a gang of us kids who ran together. Not much to do on the station, so we invented our own game. Vent diving."

She shook her head. "Do I even want to know?"

"Probably not," he said with a smirk, "but I'm going to tell you anyway. We would make up these elaborate races through the venting system on the station. Whoever could get from Point A to Point B in the shortest amount of time using the vents won."

She chuckled. "Sounds like my kind of game."

"I'd bet you'd be good at it. The thing was, you could only race through the vents not currently being used for air flow. And they switched those up at random times. When the hissing started, you had sixty seconds to find the nearest escape hatch or you'd find yourself sucked into the furnace area, or worse, vented into space."

Her eyes widened. "Did that ever actually happen?"

He nodded. "Just once. A few months before I started playing the game. One of the older boys got stuck in a vent and couldn't get out in time. A patrol found his body in space."

Renna shuddered. "That's awful."

"Yeah, looking back on it now, we were idiots, but when you're that age, you're invincible. And I was the king of vent diving. I knew those things in and out. Good thing, too, because it saved my life. One time I got stuck in a vent that was turning on. Shirt snagged on something, and I couldn't move. Longest twenty seconds of my life was trying to wiggle out of that damn thing. I made a mad dash to the hatch and, on the way out, sliced open my ribs here. I was lucky it wasn't worse." His voice dropped lower as he sobered. "I'd barely gotten into the main tunnel when the air was sucked out of the vent."

"Did you stop diving after that?"

"Scared the shit out of me, but I was too stubborn to stop. Finally gave up a few months later when I got too big to fit."

She ran a finger along the thin scar, his skin searing beneath her fingertip. Their gazes locked, and something warm and tight coiled in her midsection. She licked her lips as his gaze darkened. Whatever they'd fought about before, whatever conflict they'd had was gone. In its place, a haze of desire hung between them, so strong it felt like a magnet.

"Just a few more scars than the last time I knew you," she said, her voice husky and low.

Her fingers slid higher, her palm flattening against the ridged muscles of his chest. Beneath her hand, the thump of his heart was as staccato as hers. Every inch of her tingled with awareness. And by the stark need in his eyes, he felt the same way.

Finn growled and cupped the back of her neck, crushing her mouth to his. His lips were hot and insistent as they tortured and teased her until she was gasping for air. His fingers tangled in her hair, pulling it from its ponytail so that it tumbled between them, creating the illusion of safety, of privacy.

He tasted exactly how she thought Finn would, like warmth and sweetness and strength. And when his tongue touched her lips, she opened her mouth to let him delve deeper, to stroke and caress until she moaned against him. Her hands moved lower to trace the muscles of his stomach, the chiseled spot where his hips met his torso.

Finn shifted so he could deepen their kiss, and Renna swung her leg over his to straddle him. His warmth soaked into her skin and made her shudder. Careful not to jar his ribs, she moved closer until there was only a breath between their bodies.

Finn cupped her face with one hand, then traced gently down her jaw. When he stroked her collarbone with his fingers, a shot of pure lust spiked through her, and she stifled a moan. She wanted him to touch her, to feel his fingers everywhere, but there were too many clothes between them, too much space.

His own desire pressed against her core through her clothes. Any rational thought she might have had flew from her mind, leaving her with only one mantra: *Must. Remove. Clothes.*

Her hands found the waistband of his trousers, and she slowly unbuttoned them, sliding her fingers lower into the soft hair there. He moaned softly.

And then the sound of the keypad beeping echoed through the room.

TWENTY

On pure instinct, Renna shot to her feet and threw herself against the wall near the door. She sucked in a shuddering breath. Her whole body still hummed and buzzed with desire, but she forced herself past it. Using that pent-up energy now was the only way they were getting out of here.

"Okay, you two, boss wants you taken to the lab right now." One of the mercs stepped into the room. "Come with—"

Renna kicked out, catching him in the groin. He crumpled to the ground with a gasping scream, clutching his balls.

The second merc darted into the room with gun drawn, and Renna lashed out again, this time with the side of her hand. A wet, crunching sound came from his throat as her hand connected. He clutched his broken windpipe and gasped for air, his gun clattering to the floor as he collapsed, writhing in pain.

"By the gods." Finn struggled to his feet and grabbed the gun. "Remind me never to piss you off."

"Good call." Renna stooped to rifle through both men's pockets. She found a keycard and datapad on the man who'd never have sex again. He writhed and moaned on the floor, but didn't try to stop her.

The other man wasn't going to make it. She frowned down at his gurgling, gasping form. She hadn't meant to kill him. But if that's what it took…

When he was silent, she patted through his pockets. Empty. "We need to find the destabilizer and my tools and then get the hell out of here." She moved back to the living guard and nudged him with her foot.

"Where did you take my things?"

He shook his head, tears streaming down his face.

She arched an eyebrow. "Do you want to end up like your friend?"

"They'll kill me," he gasped.

"So will I."

"D-d-down the hall. To the left. Last door on the right."

She took the gun from Finn and nodded. "Thank you. I appreciate the help." She turned and pistol-whipped him in the temple with the butt of the gun. The merc sprawled unconscious on the floor, a trickle of blood seeping from his scalp.

"Was that necessary?" Finn asked, limping toward the door.

"Did you want him sounding the alarm?" She pressed the gun into his hand and helped him into the hallway, then used the keypad to lock the cell door. "Hopefully this buys us some time."

"Lead the way," Finn said.

They reached the end of the corridor and the door the merc had pointed out. She eased Finn against the wall, and he curled into himself, holding his side.

Renna frowned at the metal door. She'd been more distracted by Finn than she'd thought. Why hadn't she asked if there were guards inside?

"Be careful," he whispered.

Her eyebrows rose, but she quickly schooled her features. "Always am." She slid the merc's keycard through the reader and took a deep breath. Time to earn her salary.

She kicked open the door, then spun into the room, gun at the ready. She slumped, relaxing her stance when she saw that it was empty, except for a bank of holoscreens which were obviously tied to the security system.

And the small safe in the corner.

She'd bet her last credit that's where her things were. "It's clear. Come on." She helped Finn into the hard seat at the desk.

He grimaced as he lowered himself into the chair but waved her away. "Get your things. We need to get out of here before they find we've escaped."

"Work on seeing if you can call up the *Athena*." Renna crouched in front of the safe and cracked her knuckles. It had been a long time since she'd done this manually, but a thief never forgot her skills. At least, a good thief didn't.

She rested the pads of her fingers lightly against the face of the safe. It wasn't a Saltani safe, thank the gods. Even she couldn't break into one of those without tools. This was an old-school laser lock, with tumblers and pins. She closed her eyes.

It only took her one try.

The safe *whooshed* open with a blast of air when the seals unlocked. She let out a breath as she spotted the familiar black bag and destabilizer inside. "Got it." She also shoved a small metal box into her bag before slinging it over her shoulder. If the mercs had put it here, it had to be important.

Finn shrugged. "I should stop being surprised. You were good back then. You're even better now."

She smiled at him, pleased by the genuine compliment she heard in his words. "I really am."

"Looks like whoever built the facility spared no expense on this surveillance system." Finn pointed to the screen of the large warehouse where they'd entered. "There are cameras in every room."

On the other screens were images of the smaller room where they'd found the robots. A third room on the ground level—which they'd missed—was filled with smaller cargo containers.

Renna tapped on the console to change the camera view. "Dammit." There was a brand on one of the containers. One that made her stomach clench. "That's clay." But were they shipping it out or bringing it in?

"What do they need clay for?" Finn asked. His voice sounded far away, and she glanced down at him in concern.

"Hey, you all right?"

He shook his head. "Don't worry about me. I'll be fine."

Sure he would. If Finn went any paler, he'd be dead. Renna turned back to study the monitors. There had to be a way out of here that didn't involve fighting. The destabilizer was spent; it needed a full twenty-four hours to recharge. It was going to be up to her to find them an exit.

She scanned the room where the mercs had caught them. Most of them still seemed to be there, with their strange implants and even scarier leader. The last two monitors held very different views. One seemed to be watching an empty wall, but she spotted the keypad at the edge of the screen and her heart thumped. It had to be the way out. But where was that room?

Based on the way the monitors lined up, it had to be on this level.

Renna adjusted the camera view, pulling it back to see if she could get a better sense of the space. *There.* The edge of the door shone glossy and high-tech, like the ones they'd just passed. Okay. She could work with that.

The image on the final screen was another long room full of machinery, but there seemed to be some sort of vat or mixing container tucked into the corner. As she watched, several of the mercs marched into the room, guns drawn on a trio of men dressed in white lab coats. The mercs took up posts along the wall, while the scientists moved to either end of the assembly line. One of them hunched over a keyboard, typing something into the machine's computer, while the other two donned breather masks and moved toward the vat.

She frowned. Did this have to do with the clay?

"Renna," Finn whispered. "We have to go."

Her gaze snapped to his ashen face. "What's wrong?" His whole body trembled as he sat in the chair, and his eyes had a glassy sheen.

"I don't know," he said through chattering teeth. "But...I don't feel right."

"Hold on." She slipped an arm beneath his shoulders and helped him to his feet. His skin felt cool and clammy as her fingers grazed his arm, but she forced her voice to stay light. "I think the exit door is in this corridor. We just have to find it. Did you get a hold of the *Athena*?"

"No. That facility is still blocking all signals coming and going. We're going to have to call for help once we get outside."

She risked another glance at Finn as he sucked in a wheezing breath. Maybe he had more than a broken rib. Internal bleeding? Punctured lung? Whatever it was, he needed medical help. Immediately.

She opened the door and peeked out into the hall.

Still empty.

Letting Finn lean heavily on her, she led them down the hall. Her muscles screamed at her to hurry. Capture could be seconds away. But Finn could barely shuffle forward, his breath coming in labored gasps. He wasn't going to make it much farther if she didn't do something.

"You turning into a pansy on me?" she growled. "I expected better from a Marine. What, are they letting anyone in now?"

He grunted, then sucked in a sharp breath. "Get moving, Carrizal. I can keep up."

"I don't believe you. Move your ass, soldier." She forced herself to pick up the pace, dragging him along with her, even though Finn's sallow face looked like he was about to pass out. She spotted the door at the end of the corridor. If she could get him through it and outside, the *Athena* could come for them.

They reached the door, and she propped Finn against the wall. She swiped the dead merc's keycard through the lock, but it didn't so much as blink, let alone open. "Dammit," she muttered. Maybe whoever owned this facility didn't want their people coming or going either.

A few frantic hacks later, the door finally slid open, and she pulled Finn into a small elevator. He swayed on his feet, and she shoved her shoulder more firmly under his. "Buck up, soldier. We're almost there."

Her stomach lodged somewhere in her throat as the metal box shot upward.

"Stay here," she said when it stopped and the doors slid open. She slipped from under his arm and leaned him against the wall, but Finn didn't answer. Renna's heart jack-knifed. This was not good at all.

She crept forward into another one of those strange little rooms that looked empty. But she knew better. There was a door here. She just had to find it.

"Scan for imperfections," she ordered. Her implant returned a faint rectangular outline glowing against the image of the wall. "Oh, thank the stars."

As she searched, another smaller outline appeared. The keypad.

Renna glanced back at Finn, who was still propped against the elevator wall. His eyes were closed, and air whistled from his lungs with every breath. His skin had turned the color of a dead Ileth—gray and green. She swallowed, tasting the bitter acid coating the back of her throat, and turned back to the wall. How the hell did she get the keypad to appear?

She ran a finger along the wall where her implant said the controls were. It felt perfectly smooth, but by the tingling in her fingertips, she knew something else was there. Her fingers traced it again, searching for anything that would give her a clue. Then her implant beeped softly in her ear.

"Class C electronic device recognized." Something whirred in the wall, and the keypad rose to the surface, the material sliding off of it like water. Whatever her implant had done, she could have kissed it. A moment later, she'd hacked the door open. The wall here reacted the same way as the material on the keypad, flowing back from the center of the space like a bathtub draining until there was a square door. And beyond it, the dun-colored sand of Banos Prime.

She hurried back to Finn. "Let's get you out of here," she muttered, slipping her arms around his waist. He groaned but barely opened his eyes.

His lack of response was like a nanospanner to the heart.

Renna and Finn slipped out into the cold, dry air. "Contact the *Athena*," she ordered. She had no idea how much time had passed while they were in the facility. *Please let them still be on the planet.*

And then she froze. Two of the mechs she'd seen in the crates stood guard in front of them. The machines turned stiffly to face the escapees, their round eyes glowing red.

"Warning. Intruders detected. Please hold while you are scanned for compliance."

Oh shit. Renna whipped out her gun and shot the first one in the head. It erupted in a blaze of sparks and metal, a bloodcurdling scream ripping from its mouth as it went down.

The second mech's hands melted, then each hand reformed into a blaster rifle. It raised the gun at them, but Renna was faster. Her bullet hit directly between the mech's eyes. The machine froze, then exploded, sending shrapnel flying.

Renna's skin crawled at the long, wavering, almost-human scream it gave before collapsing. She covered Finn's body with hers and turned away from the blast.

Shit. Shit. Shit. That noise would have alerted every merc on the planet.

They needed to get out of there.

Now.

TWENTY-ONE

"Athena, this is Renna Carrizal. Are you there? We need an extraction ASAP."

She forced Finn to start moving toward the rock outcropping where they'd left Keva and Doyle earlier. She hauled his dead weight as best she could, her muscles quaking in protest. She slipped on a patch of sand, and Finn groaned.

"Finn, you need to tell me what's wrong. Where does it hurt?"

He shook his head. "Everywhere. But it doesn't matter. We need to find someplace to hide until the *Athena* comes."

She risked a glance at his pale skin. They weren't going to get much farther with him in this shape. He was going into shock. She tried calling the ship again, her voice catching at the words. "*Athena*, this is Renna Carrizal. We need you at our location ASAP. Captain Finn is injured."

Static.

Renna shifted Finn's weight so she could help him up to the outcropping. By the time they'd made it, he was gasping and trembling in her arms.

"Need rest," he whispered haltingly, casting a glance back at the facility. They were still too close for her comfort, but they wouldn't make it much farther if he didn't take a break.

She helped him down to the sand, letting him lean back against the rocks. Finn closed his eyes, and his head fell back as if the effort to keep it up was just too great.

Her pulse felt like a living thing inside her, clawing to get out. She needed to keep moving or the panic would take over. "I'm going to see if I can hail the *Athena* from that pile of rocks over there. I won't be far."

He didn't respond. After another long stare, she turned and jogged away through the sandy soil. When she'd gone far enough that she couldn't see the facility anymore, she tried again.

"*Athena*. Do you hear me?"

Static crackled in her ear. And then a voice. "Renna! Where the hell are you?" Keva demanded.

Renna let out a shaky laugh. "Thank gods. Keva, we're at the outcropping. I know you can't bring the ship that close, but you have to send the shuttle. Finn's hurt. Badly."

"We'll be there ASAP. Hang on."

"I'm going back to Finn. I'll keep an eye out for you. Just get your ass moving."

"Got it. See you soon, Carrizal." The woman's voice held the hint of a smile.

Renna hurried back to Finn and dropped to her knees beside him. He hadn't moved at all, his head still leaning back at an awkward angle against the rock.

"Dammit." He was injured badly, and she needed to see what was going on. Her fingers trembled as she pushed aside his jacket and shirt. This time when she sucked in a breath, it wasn't at the sight of his washboard abs, but at the dark bruise spreading across his ribcage. She wasn't a doctor, but she'd bet her last credit he was bleeding internally.

"No fair," Finn said with a weak smile. "It was your turn to show me a scar. Or could you just not keep your hands off me?"

She brushed a lock of hair away from his forehead. Dear gods, he was so cold. "Just sizing up the competition. I wanted to make sure my scars were more impressive than yours."

He chuckled, then winced and clutched his side. "How bad is it? I'm afraid to look."

Her lips thinned. If she were hurt, she'd want the truth. "I think 'fist-of-steel' may have crushed something, and you're probably bleeding somewhere internally. We need to get you to a hospital."

"Probably a good idea." He coughed, and a trickle of blood dribbled from the corner of his lips. "Where's the *Athena*?"

"Keva is on her way. We'll get you somewhere safe and get you taken care of. Promise."

He nodded. "Go to Lenue. There's a MYTH outpost there. They can help. Code word: Prometheus." His eyes drifted shut, and she touched his shoulder.

"Stay with me, Finn."

He nodded again but didn't open his eyes. "Tell me about your scar."

"Only if you stay awake." She swallowed back the burn of tears when he opened his blue eyes and nodded.

"Deal." He reached up and touched the scar running from her ear to her jaw, and her skin erupted in goose bumps. His hand fell heavily back to his side. "Tell me."

She sat back, leaning against the rock beside him. "I grew up on Old-Earth. In New York City. Never knew my dad, though Mom said he was military. After she had me and he left, she…lost herself. Lost her job first, lost our apartment next. When I was five, something changed. She came into some money. Bought a place in the East Village. Started seeing these strange men every night. But we had food on the table again, and I had clothes to wear to school."

"East Village? Isn't that…?"

Renna nodded and clenched her fists together in her lap. "Where the prostitute slums are. She'd become an escort. She was making good money, too, until one of her Johns decided he didn't just want to screw her, he wanted to destroy her. Luckily one of the service owners was in the building and saved her, but he scarred her pretty face. After that, no one wanted to hire her. We got kicked out of our apartment, but she still had friends in the business. They hooked her up with a new pimp."

She stared down at her hands. She'd never talked about her childhood before. Wasn't sure she wanted to tell anyone about it, let alone this man. He already knew she was damaged. Now he'd know how badly

"Must have been hard for a kid your age," he said softly. "How old were you?"

"I was seven when we moved to the tenement. The ladies there became surrogate mothers to me. Took care of me when Mom was…busy. Showed me how to cook and clean and dress myself. They were so kind. Even some of their boyfriends looked out for me. Mom had a few regulars, too. One of them showed me how to pick locks. Another taught me how to shoot. We lived in a dangerous area. Kids had to learn to take care of themselves."

"Especially girls, I imagine. And pretty girls at that."

Her lips curved into a wobbly smile, but she shook her head. "You never would have known I was pretty, with greasy, ratty hair and my face covered in dirt. It probably saved my life, though." She sobered, stared out at the desert, not seeing the sand, only the cramped room where her mother had tried to raise her, the tiny bed tucked into the closet that was her room. She'd hated it there. Had spent as little time in that apartment as she could. She and the other kids in the block had run roughshod over the neighborhood. They'd been her real family.

Finn squeezed her hand and didn't let go. "It's okay. You don't have to talk about it."

"No. It's just a memory I thought I'd forgotten." She swallowed before continuing. "My mom, like most of the prostitutes who worked in the East Village, was addicted to clay. All of them used it before a visit. After a visit. Whenever they felt low. Most of the women kept it to a minimum as it could affect their performance, but Mom didn't care. And when she was on it…she wasn't herself."

Tightness built in her chest until it was hard to breathe, but she made herself continue. "I walked in on her shooting up with one of her Johns, and she lost it. I don't know if it was a bad batch or I startled her or what, but she went into a frenzy, screaming and throwing things around. The John got out of there as fast as he could, so Mom took the rest of it out on me."

Renna's voice shook, and she cleared her throat. "She didn't know what she was doing. Honestly, I believe that now. But she grabbed a knife from the kitchen. She was screaming about how she wouldn't let me grow up to become her. That I'd be better off dead. And before I knew what she was going to do, she tried to slit my throat."

A gust of wind caught her words, and they drifted out into the cold air of Banos Prime like a wisp of memory. Finn's hand was still in hers, and he stroked his thumb over the back of her hand. She was grateful he didn't say anything.

"One of the other ladies heard the screaming and got me away from her before she could do anything more than cut me, but we couldn't afford to go to the hospital, so she patched me up the best she could and let me stay with her for the next few days. Mom eventually came down from the drug and tried to apologize, but I didn't want anything to do with her. I spent the next three years learning everything I could to get the hell out of there."

"How old were you?"

"I was ten when she attacked me. I hopped a ship when I was thirteen and landed on Antibes Prime. That's where I met you and Blur. Never saw my mom again."

Well, not that Renna would admit. She'd looked her up once, last year, to see if the woman was alive. She was. Renna didn't need to know anything more.

"I'm sorry. I remember how messed up you were when Blur found you out outside the warehouse. We weren't sure if you were entirely sane for the first few months."

She shrugged, still not willing to look at him. She didn't want to see the pity on his face. Or worse, disgust. "Hey, I hear the shuttle."

A moment later, it came into sight, flying directly for them. She jumped to her feet in time to see the door on the facility slide open and a wave of mercenaries stream out.

She ducked down behind the rock and pulled out her gun. "Give me yours, too. We've got company."

Finn handed it over and tried to get to his feet.

"Stay down. You're in no shape to hit anything but the side of a barn." She peered over the top of the rock, aimed, and took out the first two mercs with a clean headshot. The rest of them pulled up slightly, giving Keva enough time to land the shuttle. Two of the MYTH agents dashed out and lifted Finn between them. Renna fired a few more shots to cover them before turning to dart into the shuttle herself.

"Get us the hell out of here, Lieutenant," she called over the whir of the engine.

The door slammed shut, and they were off a second later. A few dings sounded as bullets ricocheted off the side of the shuttle, but none of them penetrated the thick material.

"What happened?" Keva demanded as she steered them toward the *Athena*.

"I could ask the same thing. Where were you guys?"

She glared. "The hole closed as soon as you went into the building. We waited as long as we could before going back to the ship. I prepped the *Athena* for a fast getaway, but we wanted to wait to see if you'd be able to get back out. We were getting ready to leave when your comm came through."

Renna nodded. "Good timing then. We got caught, and they beat up Finn pretty badly. He needs serious medical help. There's a MYTH outpost on Lenue; that's where we need to go."

Keva's only response was to radio the ship. "Prep for launch. We're one minute out. Set course for the Clare system."

TWENTY-TWO

W hen the *Athena* touched down in the spaceport on Lenue, a team of doctors were already waiting for Finn
with a hover car. Keva insisted on going with them to the hospital, but Renna hung back. Things had gotten intense with Finn
back on Banos Prime, to say the least. And he'd almost died.
Again.

She needed some time to sort through her feelings. Away
from his distracting presence. Already, her mind was whirling,
trying to process the thousand and one different emotions he'd
dredged up. Emotions she'd thought were long gone. But when
he'd kissed her…

She stepped out of the ship and inhaled, the scent of dusty
earth and starfuel washing over her and clearing her mind. The

babble of voices from the market filled the air, shouts and calls echoing off the squat steel and plastic buildings.

She shifted her pack on her shoulder. It felt heavier than she remembered, as if laden with the weight of her own guilt. What she was about to do went against every bit of her code, but what had happened with Finn made it very clear that this whole situation was beyond anything she'd dealt with before. She knew better than to get involved or let her feelings get in the way, but this mission—with Myka, the facility, the mechs and the clay—was based on nothing *but* feelings. Running was her only option. Promises be damned.

She'd packed the microchips she'd stolen from Aldani's labs, as well as the destabilizer. Once she sold them, she'd be able to hire a transport and disappear. If she was smart, she'd wait to sell the goods later, on a non-MYTH planet, but she was running out of time. If she stuck around much longer, the guilt would devour her insides.

She tried to ignore her gnawing unease and joined the crowds of humans and aliens as they wandered past the market stalls. The scent of unwashed bodies and decaying fruit hung like a fine fog over the square, coating everything it touched. Renna wrinkled her nose as she slipped between a pair of short, round aliens from the Clava system. Their six eyes turned to her, then slid away, dismissing her as nonthreatening.

If they only knew the truth.

She moved through the crowds like a shadow, weaving past people who never noticed her. She'd always loved the feeling of disappearing in a crowd, of becoming invisible. Gods knew she'd had plenty of practice. And it had saved her life more than once.

"Download area map."

Her implant overlaid it across her vision. The market sat at the center of the spaceport, surrounded by the alien barrios. Now, she just needed to find the right contact to buy her merchandise and she'd be free.

She rubbed a hand across her chest, as if she could ease the tension that hung on her heart like lead weights.

MYTH trusted her. It would be hours before they suspected she'd run. When they finally came looking for her, she'd be nothing more than a ghost. She could disappear. Leave all of this behind her.

Leave Myka behind.

Leave Finn behind.

Her fingers twitched, and she forced them into her pockets. The kid had been nothing but trouble since she'd found him. And Finn...he'd already left her once. Why stay and watch a repeat performance?

She let out a growl and turned away from the market. She needed a drink before making any decisions. And she could use the time to contact the right buyer.

The closest bar was a seedy place tucked into a dank alley. When she pushed through the doors, the smoky, dark space welcomed her like she'd come home. The scent of spilled alcohol mingled with disinfectant, and her boots squelched against the floor as she made her way to the bar.

"New in the area?" the bartender asked. The Delfine smiled before leaning toward her to rest an elbow on the bar. "What'll it be, gorgeous?"

She passed over a few credits. "A shot of Jade Sour and a beer, please."

"Anything for you, love." He reached under the bar and produced a small glass cylinder, snapping the top of the beer off before placing it on the counter in front of her. Then he grabbed one of the larger bottles behind him, flipping it between fingers. His spiky purple hair swayed as he tossed the amber container in the air, then poured her shot. "Anything else to go with that? My comm number perhaps?"

Renna tried not to roll her eyes. It took more than some fast fingers and smooth moves to get in her pants. "Thanks. I'm full up on my quota of bartenders for the moment, but I'll let you know if that changes."

She grabbed her drinks, then wove between tables to the empty booth she'd spotted in the corner. Renna sank into the seat, taking a position where she could keep an eye on the door. Wouldn't do to get careless.

She downed the shot, chasing it with a sip of beer. The familiar warmth burned through her, and the muscles in her shoulders finally relaxed. Everything was going to be fine. She'd done this a million times before. Find the fence. Sell her stuff. Buy passage on the next ship out of here. Leave all her troubles behind.

Most of all, she needed to ignore the tickle of memories at the back of her mind. Places like this always reminded her of home, of running with the gang. Of the first time she'd met Finn and Blur and the rest of them. It had been a long time since she'd felt like that, a long time since she'd let herself trust anyone else.

Yet here she was working with another team. With Finn again. This one just followed the rules a bit more.

Godsdammit.

She raked a hand through her hair, letting her head rest in her palm for a moment. Running made her a coward, but staying...staying made her stupid.

"Call Keva," she ordered her implant, finally looking up again.

"What is it, Renna?"

Keva's voice hitched, and Renna's stomach dropped. "How's the captain?"

"Still in surgery. He's got three broken ribs, a punctured lung, and they're trying to stop the internal bleeding."

Her eyes squeezed shut for a moment before she asked, "Will he be okay?"

"They haven't said yet. Nurse says they should know more in an hour or so."

Renna nodded, though she knew the lieutenant couldn't see her. "Keep me posted, okay?"

"I will. Thanks for getting him out of there, Renna. Finn said you saved his life." She let out a long exhale. "I was wrong about you, Renna. I'm sorry for being such a bitch."

Keva's words wrapped around her, tightening like a noose. Renna had to clear her throat before she could speak again. "Thanks. I appreciate that. And...I was just doing what Dallas brought me into do. Anyway, I'll see you back on the ship." She turned off her comm and drained the rest of her beer.

What the hell was she going to do?

Renna sighed. She had to stop saying that she was going to quit and just do it. Once and for all. After she'd sold the Star and the items she'd taken from Aldani, she could more than afford her luxury-garden-world dream.

Renna rummaged through her pack until her fingers closed around the strange box she'd found in the facility's safe. What was important enough to the mercs to lock away in the middle of an impenetrable facility?

She stared at the squat metal box on the table, then flipped the latch and opened the lid to reveal a plastic bottle full of orange pills. What the hell? Renna shook one out onto her palm and studied it. Simple gelatin coating, orange grains inside. She sniffed it, but there was no scent, no clue as to what it might be. Was this what they were making in the underground lab?

Renna dropped the pill back into the bottle and locked the box. Maybe the fence would have a suggestion for a back alley clay lab that could run an analysis for her. There had to be one on this planet somewhere. At least it would give her something to do while she tried to find a buyer for her haul. And maybe it would squash the guilt crawling through her gut.

Renna drained the last of her beer and got to her feet. Then ducked back down to hide behind a large Trezian when she spotted the familiar broad shoulders hunched over the bar.

By the gods. *Viktis.*

What was he doing on Lenue? Did that mean Myka was here, too?

The alien downed a shot of something and made a joke with the bartender that had the Delfine laughing.

Her heart kicked as all her plans shot out the window faster than a speeder car. If she stayed, she might be able to fulfill at least one promise. The most important promise. But Viktis couldn't know she was here.

Viktis slapped a few credits on the bar and shoved his way to the door. Several of the other patrons glared at him but gave him a wide berth when they got a full dose of his fuck-off expression.

Renna followed at a safe distance, hanging back in the doorway of the bar for a long minute as Viktis headed down the alley away from the main street. With any luck, he was going back to his ship. And that would lead her to Myka.

Viktis walked at a sedate pace—not fast enough to look like he had a purpose, but not slow enough that people would jump him. Renna held back, keeping to the shadows.

Eventually, he turned down another street, navigating toward a three-story building that had seen better days. Boarded-up windows looked like blind eyes in the flaking wooden façade, and garbage had drifted against one side, piling up higher than her thighs. The place fit Viktis's personality perfectly.

He stopped and looked behind him. Renna flattened herself against the building across the street. Her stomach tightened as his gaze raked the alley where she hid. A few moments later, he turned and went inside. Renna let out a breath. Viktis knew most of her tricks. If anyone had been able to spot her, it would have been him.

She darted across the alley and studied the building. There weren't any open windows she could use to sneak in. No basement access panels or ventilation shafts. She was going to have to go in the front door. Blind.

Again.

Somebody seriously wanted to test her skills.

"Building plan," she ordered. The schematics downloaded, showing her the first floor was one large room, with a staircase off to the right leading up to the second floor. There seemed to be a back entrance opening into a small garden. Maybe she should try sneaking in that way. But if Viktis caught wind that she was coming... She couldn't risk him fleeing with Myka.

"Heat signatures."

"One individual detected."

Renna rolled her shoulders and cracked her neck. Viktis was unpredictable, and after her stunt with the sleeping drugs... Well, he wasn't exactly going to welcome her with open arms.

Her hands were steady as she pushed open the door. She did a quick sweep of the space with her gaze. It had once been the first floor of a house, but the plaster had been removed, leaving only the wooden frame behind. Wallpaper peeled from the few perimeter walls left, and the floor was scraped wood, worn and dusty with age. It smelled of must and mold and something else she didn't want to think about.

Across the room, Viktis froze, his violet eyes widening. "Renna."

"Miss me, Viktis?" She shifted lightly on her feet. Her gun was still in its holster at her waist, but she could get to it in a split second if he made any sudden moves.

"You have no idea." His smile was cold. "You should have killed me when you had the chance."

"Where's the boy?" She moved farther into the room, and Viktis circled away from her, maintaining the fifteen or so feet that separated them.

"He doesn't matter. You and your new employer owe me a ship."

She shook her head. "Why? Did you lose it playing poker?"

His hands clenched at his side. "I lost it when they frakking *attacked* me."

He lunged forward, breaking into the no-man's land between them. One golden arm arced out, aiming for her head.

She stepped out of the way, and he swung wide. "What are you talking about? The *Athena* didn't attack you."

He struck out again with a combination jab and uppercut. She feinted to the side, then blocked his blow, countering with a right hook to his jaw. Pain raced down her fist at the impact, and she tried not to wince.

His head snapped back with a growl. "They were waiting for us when we landed here. My men went to drop off the kid, but it was a trap. They killed the crew, blew up my ship. I only escaped because they thought I got caught in the blast." He doubled back, his gaze cold and steady. Without warning, his fist shot out and caught her in the stomach.

Sparks blossomed in her vision, and she danced away. Renna gasped, but she almost enjoyed the pain. At least it made her feel alive. Her words came out in a raspy gasp. "Sucks to be you."

"You have no idea. Everything I had is gone. The kid, my ship, my haul. You owe me, Renna. Big time."

"I don't owe you anything. I didn't have anything to do with that. Who are these people you think attacked you?"

"Think? You think I made up the destruction of my entire life?" With a roar, he charged her again. When his fist flew out, she caught his forearm and wrenched it to the side, leveraging their difference in height to put an additional strain against his elbow.

"I'm going to kill you," he snarled.

The hatred in his voice made her skin shiver. She'd only heard that tone once before. When he'd killed his parents' murderer.

"You couldn't do it five years ago. You certainly won't be able to do it now." Renna forced herself to stay calm, loose. If Viktis got a hold of her, it would be all over. "Listen to me. I just want to know where the boy is. I swear I had nothing to do with your ship being destroyed."

"You're an awful liar, Renna. I saw their uniforms. Same as what your crew was wearing."

"You're wrong. The people I'm working for are the ones looking for Myka." She flexed her fingers and looked for a way to end the fight, but Viktis's words swirled through her mind. Maybe the branch of MYTH stationed on this planet had been looking for the kid, too.

Maybe they'd found him and he was already safe.

Viktis took advantage of her momentary distraction to jerk out of her grip. "I don't care who did it. I want revenge," he growled. "These people are going to pay." He grabbed her by the throat. "*You're* going to pay."

The air wheezed from her lungs as he tightened his fingers. Before panic could claw its way into her chest, she twisted and swept her leg under him.

They toppled to the floor together in a pile of arms and legs and bruises. She lashed out as he scrambled to grab her again, and her fist connected with the hard muscles of his stomach. Viktis's hot breath whooshed out against her face in a grunt. He looped an arm around her waist and flipped her over so he was on top of her, straddling her hips.

Renna grinned up at him. "Feels familiar."

"Shut up." His arm came up again. Before he could strike her again, she twisted, throwing him off-balance enough to slip from beneath him and jump to her feet.

"I don't know who destroyed your ship or why, Viktis. But if you help me find the kid, we both get what we want. Revenge and justice."

A muscle twitched in the tawny skin of his jaw, but he didn't go after her. "How are you going to find them?" he asked.

"I have connections. You scratch my back, I scratch yours."

"I think you've done more than scratch, my dear." He wiped a trickle of golden blood from beneath his nose.

"You're lucky it wasn't worse." Her gaze fell on her bag, dropped on the floor when Viktis had first attacked. Maybe she could kill two birds with one stone if she was going to be sticking around a few hours longer. She shrugged her shoulders. "How about we work out a deal? I need to find an unregistered lab on this planet. I have something I need tested."

"And what do I get out of it?"

"A clean shot at the people who destroyed your ship and killed your crew. Once the kid is safe with us. And I'll owe you. You know I always make good on my debts."

He growled and turned away, shoving his hands into the pockets of his leather jacket. As he paced, Renna kept her hand on the butt of her gun. They hadn't come to an agreement yet, and she fully believed in keeping her friends close and her enemies closer.

Finally, Viktis spun on his heel. "Fine. I'll help you with this. But I want restitution from the people you're working for."

"I can't promise that. I honestly don't think they were in-volved in destroying your ship. But I promise I'll talk to them about it."

Shit. Another promise she might not be able to keep.

He sighed and rubbed a hand over the ridges on his head. "That will have to do. Come with me. I know a clay dealer who has a lab in on the outskirts of the city. He should have the tools to analyze whatever you have."

"No traps, Viktis."

"No traps. I want to kill those people more than I want to kill you. Right now at least." He smiled, but it didn't erase the cold fury swirling in his eyes.

Viktis was more upset about the death of his crew than she'd imagined. Maybe he'd grown up since the last time they'd worked together. Maybe he'd actually started taking responsibility for the people he worked with.

Unlike her.

The Warehouse District crowded the edge of the spaceport like a tumor on the city. It was little more than a dingy circle of concrete buildings and steel roofs protecting the rest of the city from the winds blowing across the rocky plain. In the distance loomed the large mountain that provided work for most of the residents in the city. Miners dug into the rocky soil, searching for voidonite, a mineral used in developing medicines.

It was also a key component in clay.

Viktis knocked at a thick wooden door, and a six-inch window at eye level slid open. A brown human eye gazed back.

"I need to see Wall," Viktis said. "I have some business for him."

The eye blinked once before the small window shut and the door rattled open. A short, dark-haired man with a scar over one bushy brow grinned at them. "He's in back. With his guards." He let that little tidbit of information sink in before suggesting, "Behave."

"I always do," Viktis said. "A word of warning, Ren? The guy fancies himself a philosopher. Speaks in quotes half the time. Just ignore him."

Renna nodded as they passed into the musty building. "I'll just go with it. He can't be any odder than that pair of Synesian twins we met up with on Clava Six. Speaking in rhyme does not work well when you're under attack and trying to issue orders."

Viktis chuckled. "I forgot about them. Drove me insane every time they opened their mouths."

They walked the length of the warehouse, past dinged crates and wooden boxes full of straw. A smoky, burnt-sugar smell hung in the air. It made Renna's skin crawl and her eyes water.

Clay.

She tried to ignore the bins of it stacked in the corner, the faint orange dust covering the floor. Her fingers curled into fists as she walked through the warehouse. She'd never get over the slightly sweet scent, the way it seemed to clog the very air, as if its mere presence was enough to contaminate it. Or the nightmarish memories it evoked.

But right now she had other goals. And this man, despite selling the stuff, could help her reach them.

Wall greeted them at the door to his lab, his massive frame taking up most of the space. "Viktis." He clapped the Ileth on the back with a meaty, ochre-colored hand. "What the hell are you doing here? And I'm on a deadline, so as the Bard says, 'Speak on but be not over-tedious.'" He smiled behind his thick brown beard and pushed up the wire-framed glasses that slid down his hawk-like nose. The light of a data stream glowed from one of the lenses.

Viktis leaned against the lab table, arms crossed. "We needed some help, and you were the first person I thought of."

Wall's chuckle rumbled through the room. "Doesn't that make me feel warm and fuzzy? Who's the doll?"

Viktis's eyes flicked to her, a smirk making his thin lips curl up at the corners. "Renna Carrizal."

Wall's eyes widened. "You have to be shitting me."

Renna shifted her weight and looked away. She always hated this part. She never knew how to react when people realized who she was. She'd worked hard to earn her reputation, and part of her wanted to preen at the obvious attention, but unease made her shoulders tense around her ears as she shook his hand.

Wall beamed at her. "By the gods, you're the last person I ever expected to show up in my warehouse."

"Thanks for seeing us." She smiled back at the man and forced herself to relax. This was no big deal, just a business transaction.

Wall shook his head. "Not every day you get to meet one of the best thieves out there. What can I do for you two?"

She opened her bag and pulled out the bottle of pills. "I need a drug analyzed. We need to know what it is and what it does. And it needs to stay completely between us."

"You have my word."

She placed a single orange pill on his well-lined palm. Wall's thick fingers were surprisingly delicate as he turned it over and studied it. "Homemade. No pharma signature on the casing." He took it to one of his superscopes and pulled out a slide. With a sharp knife, he split the pill in half, and fine orange sand spilled out onto the glass. He poured some of it into a beaker and the rest onto the scope's pad.

"Give me a few hours and I'll have an analysis for you. I'll get a hold of Viktis when I'm ready."

"How much is this going to cost me?" she asked. Men like him charged a premium for their services. Maybe she could talk him down.

"'No profit grows where is no pleasure taken,'" he replied with a smile. "Shakespeare again. *Taming of the Shrew*."

Viktis's bark of laughter echoed through the warehouse. "My friend, you have no idea how true that is."

Renna glared at him. "Keep it up, Ileth. I know where your soft spots are."

Wall leaned back against the table and studied her. "I enjoy solving mysteries. Consider it a favor."

Owing favors to men like him was dangerous, but did she really have much choice? Finally she nodded. "Deal. We'll be back in a few hours."

"'We only part to meet again.' John Gay." Wall saluted. "I'll be in touch."

TWENTY-THREE

Outside, Renna gave Viktis an appraising once-over. "Thought for sure you'd set me up."

"I'm hurt you don't trust me," he said, pressing his hand against his heart. "I told you. I'm more interested in revenge right now. The men who killed my crew need to pay."

"Who is this new Viktis and what did you do with my old enemy?"

He shrugged. "Things change. You can believe me or not. In the meantime, I'm going to go wait at the bar. Care to join me?"

Renna shook her head. "I have some things I need to do first. Comm me when you have Wall's info."

Viktis paused to study her. "When's the last time you got some sleep? You look like shit."

She scowled at him, rocking back on her heels. "You sure know the way to a girl's heart, don't you?"

"Get some rest before we go any further, Ren. These people aren't screwing around. We need you at your best."

"I'll try." She walked away, waving goodbye over her shoulder. Viktis's gaze burned between her shoulder blades until she turned the corner. Once she was out of sight, her whole body slumped. He was right. She was exhausted, mentally and physically. And no closer to an answer than she had been earlier.

Run now or stay and save the galaxy?

She wandered toward the hospital. Maybe she'd make sure Finn was all right before she decided. A few more hours couldn't hurt, and she had to wait for Wall anyway…

Excuses, excuses.

Renna found Lieutenant Keva pacing the hallway outside of Captain Finn's room. Her usually immaculate uniform hung in wrinkles from her thin frame, and she'd pulled her silver hair back into a messy ponytail. Dark smudges framed her eyes.

Gods, was the prognosis that bad? Renna had to clear her throat before asking, "What's the news, Lieutenant?"

Keva's head snapped up at the sound of her voice. "He's out of surgery. Doc says he stopped the bleeding. Captain's going to make it."

The muscles in Renna's stomach unclenched in a giddy wave of relief. "That's great news. Hey, why don't you go get some rest? You've been here all day. I'll watch him for a while."

Keva glanced at Finn's door, then down at the floor. "I don't know. I think…"

"I think you should get back to the ship, update the crew, and get some sleep. Finn will be fine, and I'll make sure he knows what's going on the second he wakes up."

"Okay." Keva nodded slowly. "I'd like to make sure the crew is all right. There were some repairs we needed to make." She smiled at Renna before turning to leave. "I'm glad you were around to rescue the captain. I know we didn't get off to the best start, but I'm happy I was wrong about you." Even exhausted, the woman still marched like a soldier as she walked toward the elevators.

Renna sank onto one of the benches lining the wall and played with her implant, downloading the schematics of the hospital, plotting out where the lab safes were, even inspecting the rankings of this place compared with the other galactic hospitals in the traverse. A few nurses bustled down the hallway, not paying any attention to her. Then a gurney bearing a familiar body rolled by, pushed by two orderlies.

She shot to her feet, pulse hammering in her ears. An ugly purple bruise shadowed Finn's jaw, but the thing that shook her was how still and waxy he looked lying motionless on the bed.

He looked dead.

The air left Renna's lungs in a violent whoosh. Had Keva been wrong? Did the doctor give her the wrong information? Had something else happened?

She couldn't do this again. She'd already lost him once. Her hands curled into fists, her nails digging into her palms as she fought the wave of nausea that threatened to take her down.

"Miss? Is everything all right?" one of the orderlies asked. He put a hand on her arm, jerking her out of the spiraling panic that threatened to take hold.

"What?"

"Are you all right?" he asked again, looking concerned.

"The captain. How is he?" The words came out on a shrill whisper, but she didn't care. She could only stare, wide-eyed, as a smile washed over his face.

"Yes, of course." He shook his head. "Don't worry, he's still asleep from the surgery. It went very well. We stopped the internal bleeding, and his ribs should be mended in a few days. We're going to get him comfortable before you go in to see him."

Her knees went weak, and she sat down heavily in her chair. Finn was going to be fine. But as the fear drained away, the tsunami of relief was even more unsettling.

She cared what happened to him. Too much.

Pain bit into the palms of her hands. She looked down to crescent-shaped marks embedded into the skin where her nails had nearly broken through. She glanced over at the exit. If she was smart, she'd get the hell out of here right now before she got sucked in any further.

Renna rose to her feet. She couldn't afford to get involved with a man like Finn. He stood for everything she'd fought against: law, order, blindly following the rules.

But instead of leaving the hospital, her feet took her into Finn's room.

One of the nurses adjusted the Temifen IV and ran a small machine up and down Finn's body. "Vitals stable. He should be coming out of the anesthesia momentarily." The drone by her head flashed a bright light across the bed, and Finn blinked.

The latest surgery drugs used ultraviolet light as a catalyst to remove the medication immediately from the system, instead of leaving the patient groggy and confused. Most of the time, the patients were completely awake and normal within minutes.

"How are you feeling, Captain?" the nurse asked, hovering over him.

He blinked again and licked his lips. "Better than I expected." His voice was hoarse, but there was still a hint of humor there.

"We have you on some pain medication for now, but the surgery was successful and you'll make a full recovery. The facial swelling and bruising should be gone by tomorrow." She patted Finn's shoulder. "Try to get some rest now." The nurse bustled out of the room, leaving Renna standing awkwardly near the door.

Across the room, Finn's gaze met hers. "You're still here?"

His blue eyes were the right color again.

Renna smiled. "Where else would I be?"

"I don't know. Halfway to some garden planet? I wouldn't blame you."

"That hurts, Captain," she teased. But inside, guilt snaked around her heart. How had he guessed the truth?

Finn's head fell back onto his pillows, and he closed his eyes briefly against the movement. "I'm glad Dallas was right about you. We never would have gotten out of there without you." He took a few seconds to catch his breath, then asked, "What happened? I don't remember much after the beating."

She pulled up a stool and sat beside his bed, her mind whirling. Did he not remember their kiss? Or the stories they'd exchanged?

She didn't know whether to be relieved or disappointed.

Some emotion must have flitted across her face because Finn raised his eyebrow. "Did I do something embarrassing?"

"No, not at all. We managed to subdue our guards, find the security room, and escape the facility. It was all very exciting."

"I get bits and pieces of memories, but it's all kind of blurry. Hopefully it'll come back soon." He sighed and gingerly touched his swollen face. "We do not have time for me to be laid up like this."

"You'll be better soon. I'm working on a few leads right now myself, so hopefully by the time you're back on the *Athena*, we'll have a plan."

"I think I remember robots," he said with a frown. "Was that real?"

She nodded. "And we discovered they were making some sort of drug there. I have a contact analyzing it now. Hopefully it'll help us figure out who owns the place and what it is they're doing."

"Thank you." Though Finn was still slightly groggy from the drugs, she'd swear there was something else there behind his eyes. Friendship perhaps? "Seems I owe you another apology—and my life."

"You don't owe me anything." Renna got to her feet. "You need to get some rest. I already contacted the MYTH office on this planet like you said, but we still haven't heard back from them. Hopefully they'll find us soon."

"We've already found you." A thin man with gray hair strode into the room. Even though he wore brown pants and a button-down shirt, he carried himself like a soldier. Like Dallas had.

Finn struggled to sit up. "Major Larson."

"At ease, Captain." Larson shut the door behind him, then approached Finn's bed. "We received the *Athena*'s transmission several hours ago but had to verify the electronic signature. I'm sorry it took so long. With the destruction of the Hesperia branch, we've been cut off from a lot of our operatives."

"I understand, sir. I wasn't in a position to question the delay."

"I see that. Miss Carrizal will fill me in on the latest mission report. I think you should focus on getting some rest."

Her gaze snapped to the major's, and he gave her a ghost of a smile. She wasn't military, and she certainly wasn't MYTH. Why wouldn't he ask for a debrief from Keva?

Finn shook his head. "I'd like to be present, sir. It was my mission after all."

"Permission denied. I've already lost too many good men this month. You need to focus on getting better. Miss Carrizal will be fine with me, I promise."

Finn frowned at both of them, but didn't say anything.

Major Larson nodded. "We'll debrief tomorrow. Goodnight, Captain." He turned to Renna. "Shall we?"

She followed him from the room, glancing back at Finn at the last moment. He was gritting his teeth so hard she could almost hear it from the door.

"I took the liberty of requesting a conference room here, Miss Carrizal," the major said, opening a door down the hall. "You'll forgive me if I don't trust you with the location of our headquarters yet."

"Why should you? I just saved the lives of your entire team." Her tone was unexpectedly bitter as she took a seat at the small conference table. Damn Finn and damn her stupid feelings for him.

"I am very aware of your contributions, Miss Carrizal. I am also very aware of the company you keep."

Of course. They'd seen her with Viktis. She'd been so busy following him she hadn't even given a thought someone might be following her.

"Viktis has agreed to help us track down the boy. Since he was the last to see Myka, I thought it was a good idea to use him."

"Very resourceful. I just want to make sure you don't decide to join him once the boy is found." The major sat across the table from her and regarded her with a cool expression. "I'm familiar with your work, Renna. I must say you've had some very impressive jobs in your past. MYTH can definitely use someone of your skill level."

"That's what Major Dallas said when he…convinced me to join this mission."

"Erik was a smart man. I'm glad to see you took his conversation seriously. Now, tell me what happened at the facility. We've had three surveillance teams on that place for months, and no one has been able to crack it."

Renna gave him the bare bones of what had happened, leaving out the kiss with Finn. She figured the robot army was bad enough.

"So what are your next steps?" Larson asked.

"I was hoping you could tell us," she said, leaning back in her chair. "Do you have any intel on the boy? Or who the facility might belong to? It feels like we've reached a dead end."

She could play this game as well as he could.

Larson shook his head. "Not at this time. We have reports of an attack on Chasa Nine and have sent a team to investigate."

She frowned. Chasa was close. She'd assumed the attacks were related to the kid, but if they had Myka already, what else were they looking for? "Why that planet?"

"Right now we have nothing besides a small clay manufacturing facility. It's barely a blip on the black market radar."

"So what do you want me to do?" Renna shrugged. "I'm not MYTH. I don't have any resources."

"I want you to keep digging for who created the robots you found at the facility and how those drugs are connected. And because you're not MYTH, you can do it without anyone the wiser. We need your skills, Renna. And when your friend uncovers whatever it is you sent him to find, we'll let you do what you need to. Just keep Captain Finn out of it. He's one of our best. I need him to stay that way."

"You think I'm going to corrupt him? Or recruit him to be a pirate like Viktis?" She shook her head with a chuckle. "I promise you're safe there. Finn's one hundred percent military. He'd never do that. But thanks for suggesting I'm that talented."

"I don't think it—I know it. You forget we've been following you."

She leaned forward and rested her elbows on the table. "Right. Then let me ask you a question. Dallas offered me a deal if I did this job. Are you going to make good on it when this is all over?"

"Dallas had permission from the highest level of our organization to bring you on board. We will honor your agreement with him." Larson shifted in his chair. "Do you intend to honor your agreement?"

And there was the question. The chains of responsibility tightened across her chest until she couldn't breathe.

"Miss Carrizal?"

"Yes, I intend to honor my agreement." The words felt like stones falling from her lips, each one heavier than the next. Tying her to these people. And yet there was a part of her that seemed lighter somehow, knowing she'd be part of the team a little longer. Knowing she'd be around Finn.

Larson got to his feet. "I'm glad to hear it. Now go get some rest, you look like you could use it. I'll check in on Captain Finn tomorrow. The doctors say he'll be ready for duty again in two or three days. We'll hold a debrief with the rest of the crew then."

"Yes, sir." She resisted the urge to salute as Larson left the room. If she wasn't careful, she'd end up thinking she actually *was* one of these people.

TWENTY-FOUR

Viktis found her a few hours later in the same bar where she'd first spotted him. He pulled up a chair at her table and plunked down two beers. "You look like shit. I thought you were going to go get some sleep."

"Why does everyone keep asking me that?" She rubbed her gritty eyes and glared at him.

"Never mind. Forget I said anything." Viktis's expression turned smug. "Wall found something interesting in those drugs you gave him."

"He's done already?"

"Told you he was good." Viktis took a sip of his beer, as if he knew the delay would whet her appetite. At this point she didn't care. She needed some good news for a change.

"What did he find?"

"He's never seen the chemical compounds before. Doesn't know what they're supposed to do. But the base material is clay. Someone is using the drug as a carrier."

"So clay and…"

"That's the interesting part. It's a mixture of elements Wall's never seen. It's got a structure similar to the voidonite used in developing implants, but there's an added component he can't identify." Viktis scanned the room before dropping his voice. "He thinks it could be some sort of anti-rejection drug. Like the old kind humans used to use back in the twentieth century. From what he can tell, it's a cytotoxin that seems to lower the immune system and allow this new chemical to integrate into the nervous system."

Renna stared down into her beer. The mercs at the facility all had had implants. Could this drug be an experimental new development to make the tech better?

"Does he have any idea where the new mineral comes from?" she asked.

"Only a few planets even contain the trace chemical. Banos Prime, Lenue, and Vall. A few others."

Her fingers tightened around the glass as something pinged in her memory. The feeling was gone a moment later. But it was certainly convenient some of those were the same planets that had been attacked.

"What? I recognize that look. You know something." Viktis leaned forward to stare at her.

Renna wished the Ileth were as easy to read as humans, but their angular facial structure made their expressions inscrutable most of the time. Could she trust him? Viktis always had his own

256 | JAMIE GREY

agenda. As soon as it didn't line up with hers, she'd need to watch her back.

She chose her words carefully. "The people I'm working for who want to find the boy? They're also investigating attacks on certain planets. Some of which—if you're right—are the same as where this chemical is found. We need to figure out how the two are connected."

Viktis ran a hand over the bone plates on his skull. "Interesting. I bet this information would be worth a lot to them."

"I'm sure it will. Too bad I'm not charging them for it." She narrowed her eyes. "I work for them now, remember?"

"Right. Renna's on the straight and narrow. An era has ended in this part of the traverse."

"And you'll be more than happy to step in and take my place?"

"Of course. I may not be as pretty as you, but I do have exceptional…skills." The smirk twisting his lips left her in no doubt of the innuendo. "How about we go back to my place and I can fill you in on what I've learned? I promise it'll be even better than last time." His voice dropped to a rough growl.

For a split second, she wanted to take him up on his offer. Viktis was safe. She wouldn't have to worry about her heart with him. And a little stress release was exactly what she needed. The things he could do with those clever fingers…

She squirmed in her seat and shook the thought away. She'd gone down that road once already. Then he'd tried to kill her.

Besides, it wasn't Viktis that her body desperately craved. And she damn well knew it.

She smiled reluctantly. "I think I'm better off getting some of that sleep you all keep telling me I need. But thanks for the offer. Catch up with you tomorrow? We can pay a visit to Wall."

Disappointment flashed across Viktis' face, but he nodded. "Want me to walk you back to the ship?"

"Nah, I'm fine." She stood up and cracked her knuckles. "I'm itching for a fight. I hope some fool decides a woman is easy prey."

Viktis chuckled. "I feel sorry for anyone who gets on your bad side. Have a good night, love."

Renna walked through the darkened city, inhaling cool air scented with metal and sand. Bright helolights shone down from the buildings, illuminating spots on the sidewalk, casting shadows outside the circle of light. The streets were still full of people bustling past on their way home or to the nightclubs serving as entertainment on this planet. Hover cars sped through the sky, beeping and swerving to avoid traffic. This spaceport was a backwater hellhole, but even here, the march of technology moved on. She'd spotted three new Starzales already, and they'd only been on the market for six months.

Was she an idiot for turning down Viktis? Even if it slipped into something past one night, she already knew what life would be like with him—full of adventure, good jobs. It would be so easy to slip back into that, to postpone her retirement. She wasn't really the type to lounge on a beach anyway.

Renna sighed and shoved her hands into her pockets. She knew this urge, knew exactly what it was; she was running again. She did it every time things got too complicated. And this situation with Myka and Finn and MYTH was pretty much the definition of complicated.

What the hell was she going to do about Finn?

When she was a kid, he'd been an unattainable crush. The four-year age difference had been a chasm between them, even when she was sixteen and he was twenty. And then he'd died, and she'd buried all those feelings, as well as her desire to trust. His abandonment had been the last straw after a lifetime of other rejections.

She'd kept a tight rein on her heart since then, but now, here she was with a team behind her. With Finn at her side. And she hated to admit it, but it felt good. She'd been strong on her own, had loved the freedom. But it was exhausting, always having to watch her back, waiting for the next up-and-comer to come gunning for her.

A gust of wind blew a loose piece of paper down the street, bringing the smell of starfuel and exhaust from the traffic lanes. Her hair whipped around her face, and she pushed it behind her ears. Could she give up everything she'd worked for to be part of this team?

The *Athena* was docked at one of the landing bays nearest the city center. MYTH status would do that for you. She blinked in the bright helolights as she entered the hangar and made for the ship. The facility was clean and well-lit, with mechanics and security both on staff twenty-four hours a day. Quite a bit different from the seedy ports she was used to using.

Renna pressed her hand to the scanner at the door of the ship and the automated voice responded, "Welcome, Renna Carrizal. Please enter your security code."

She typed in her code, and the door slid open with a swoosh.

Most of the CIC deck was empty, just a few techs still manning the computers or performing last-minute checks. She ignored them as she made her way down to her cabin. All she wanted was a shower and bed. In that order.

Keva appeared instantly in her doorway as Renna passed. "Renna! How's the captain?"

Had the woman been waiting for her all this time? "He's doing well. Doc says he could be back onboard in a couple of days."

Relief flooded the woman's features, and Renna wondered again about Keva's feelings for her boss. A sudden twinge of sympathy flooded through her. The man was easy to lust after, despite being infuriating. And Keva was exactly the type of woman he needed in this life. Honorable. Trustworthy. Someone who followed orders. Maybe it would be better for everyone if she left now. Before anyone else got hurt.

Before she got hurt.

Keva smiled. "That's such great news. I'll have to go check on him first thing in the morning."

"I'm sure he'll be happy to see you." Renna stifled a yawn behind her hand. "Night, Lieutenant."

"Goodnight, Renna."

Sergeant Gheewala stopped Renna before she could leave the ship the next morning. The woman twitched even more than usual, her eyes darting round the command center before pulling Renna into an empty navigation pod.

"What's going on, Sergeant?" Renna asked.

"I've been hearing things."

From anyone else, Renna might have laughed, but from Gheewala, that meant trouble.

"What kinds of things?"

The sergeant shook her head. "That's the problem. I don't recognize them. Whatever it is has no signatures to read. It's just white noise, different than the rest of the galaxy. And there's something beyond it. Something coming this way." Her voice quivered on the last word.

Renna frowned. "Have you told Keva? They need to make sure the ship is ready to go if we're attacked again."

"I told her."

"Good. I'll make sure to let Major Larson know, too. I think we should be prepared for anything."

Gheewala nodded. "I'm glad you're here, Miss Carrizal."

"Renna, please." She smiled at the sergeant. "One of these days you will all remember to call me by my first name."

Gheewala laughed, a nervous, schoolgirl twitter. "I'll try my best."

"Good. Now go find Corporal Bokal and tell him what you told me. Also, tell him I said to ready the *Athena* for takeoff. We need her on standby in case what you heard shows up."

Renna left the ship, making her way through the port toward the Warehouse District. She didn't like Gheewala's news. It meant whoever was attacking the planets might be on their way here. She needed to get her information and get the hell out of here before they arrived.

As she reached Wall's warehouse, her implant beeped with an incoming transmission.

"Just knock. Runner will let you in," Viktis's voice said in her ear.

"How did you know I was here?" she asked.

"I have my ways."

She could hear the smile in his voice and shook her head. She'd have to search for a tracking device. Knowing Viktis, he'd slipped one on her yesterday. If she'd been thinking, she'd have done the same to him.

She knocked sharply on the metal door, and it swung open.

"Go on back, they're waiting for you," Runner said with a grin. She noticed he was missing a front tooth since yesterday.

"Must have been a hell of a fight."

He nodded. "But you should see the other guy."

Renna made her way through the warehouse, pausing in the doorway to Wall's lab. The other men who'd been working there yesterday were nowhere to be seen. The place felt eerily quiet. Even the crates of clay she'd spotted were gone, leaving faint outlines of orange dust on the floor. And only a lingering trace of the burnt-sugar smell.

"What's going on?" she asked. Her palms itched, and she let one of her hands drift down to the pistol at her hip.

Wall looked up from his microscope. "Just a precaution. Whatever it is you got yourself involved with is big time, Miss Carrizal, and I'm not going to take any chances with my business. I've relocated."

"What makes you say that?"

"I've never seen a drug like this before. And I've seen it all. Whoever created this was a genius. Or a madman. On the surface it seems like a refined version of clay in pill form, but laced throughout is a strange element that makes the clay act differently."

"But you're not sure what it does?"

Wall shook his head. "No. It seems like it could be an immunosuppressant or an anti-rejection drug because of the clay and the cytotoxins laced throughout. But until I know what this new element does, I couldn't even begin to guess."

Renna sighed and tugged at the ends of her hair. "And the only planets it's found on…"

"Are the ones I told you about last night. Still hasn't changed, Renna." Viktis leaned against one of the empty work tables, suddenly materializing as if out of thin air. "I did a little more research since I had plenty of time to kill." He raised a mocking eyebrow. "Whatever it is, nobody's seen it before. At least not that I could find."

But he was wrong. Someone knew what this drug was. Dr. Aldani's words came back to her in a rush: "*My brother and his wife were working on an experimental drug…*"

He'd lied to them about everything.

She needed to get back to the ship and set up a holo call. "I might know someone who can help us, but we need to go. Now." She turned to Wall. "Thank you for your help on this. I owe you."

"Yes, you do. But I'm always glad to help a master at work. I'm sure we'll meet again, Miss Carrizal." He pulled the slide from his microscope. "I'm assuming you don't want this floating around?"

"I'm sure you took your own sample, but yes, I'll dispose of the rest of this." She slipped the slide into her pocket. She had no illusions as to Wall's trustworthiness; she would have kept a sample herself if she'd been in his position. One never knew when something like that might come in handy.

Wall shook her hand, his monstrous paw swallowing her own small fingers. "Good luck. I hope you find what you're looking for."

Outside, Renna headed for the hospital. Viktis strode to catch up with her, a frown pulling at his lips. "What's going on? What else do you know that you're not telling me?"

She shook her head. "Not here. I need to talk to Finn and Major Larson."

"Then I'm going with you. I'm not going to be cut out of getting my revenge."

"I'm not sure that's a good idea, Viktis. This is the military we're talking about. They're not exactly fans of yours. Or mine, for that matter."

"The feeling is mutual. But none-the-less, I'm coming with you."

TWENTY-FIVE

Renna knocked at Finn's door before pushing it open. Her eyes widened as he turned away from the window where he'd been standing to face her. The bruise on his jaw was nothing more than faintly darkened skin now, and his ribs were obviously on their way to being healed. The accelerated healing regimen had worked.

"You're up! That was fast. How are you feeling?" she asked.

Finn's welcoming smile slid from his face as Viktis pushed his way into the room "I was better until he showed up." Finn gritted his teeth. "What the hell are you doing, Renna?"

She swallowed and glanced between the two men. One at a time, she could deal with, but the two of them together in the same room made the walls start to close in on her. "Viktis has been helping me. One of his contacts analyzed the drug we found on Banos Prime. I have a feeling Aldani knows more about this than he let on."

Viktis slouched against the doorframe and crossed his powerful arms. "I'm just along for the ride. And to avenge the murder of my crew. Don't mind me."

Finn ignored him, turning to Renna with his cold blue eyes. "Does the major know about this?"

"Not yet. I just found out myself. But there's something more. Sergeant Gheewala stopped me this morning. She heard something out in space. Something she couldn't identify and it's coming this way."

Finn stopped pacing. "We need to warn Larson. If they attack this planet…"

"I had Gheewala tell the crew to prep for takeoff. I know you'll be in the hospital a few more days, but I wanted them to be ready. Just in case."

He nodded. "I think that's wise. I'll send for Larson, and we can debrief together. Without your…friend." Finn paused and for the first time looked directly at Viktis. A muscle jumped in his jaw before he said, "I'm sure he won't mind waiting in the jail down the street."

"Clever. I can see why Renna's so hung up on you," Viktis said with a sneer.

Finn raised an eyebrow as heat flooded her face. Damn Viktis. If he wasn't trying to kill her, he was acting like a three-year-old boy.

And the fact that she'd made her interest in Finn obvious enough that Viktis had seen it… What the hell had she been thinking?

Renna cleared her throat. "Enough. We have more important things to worry about than who's got the bigger dick. Viktis, get down to the hangar and see if they can use your help. I'll comm Keva and let her know you're coming so she doesn't shoot you."

Viktis bowed. "Your wish is my command." As he straightened, he winked at her. "And I mean that in every way possible," he added before disappearing down the corridor.

Renna rolled her eyes and fought another flush of heat to her cheeks. He must have been seriously put out that she hadn't fallen into bed with him at his request. Men were the same no matter what species.

"Nice to see some things don't change," Finn said. He had that haughty tone back in his voice. She could practically see him donning his holier-than-thou armor.

She'd be damned if she let him go back to treating her like that.

"Viktis and I have an understanding. When he's not trying to kill me or sleep with me, he's a decent guy. I think he can help us with this."

"Help you, maybe. I don't want anything from a dirty merc who kidnaps children." Finn crossed his arms and turned back to look out the window.

Renna studied the stiff line of his spine, the clench of his strong jaw. Something else was going on here. Could he be jealous of Viktis?

With a growl, Finn spun around to face her. His whole body was coiled like one big spring, and in two steps, he was close enough to grab her arms. He shook her slightly, forcing her to look up at him. "Seeing you standing there with him, with that smirk on your face—it all came rushing back. The facility, the beating. The *kiss*."

His fingers curled into the soft skin of her biceps. She'd have bruises tomorrow. But she couldn't face the blazing questions in his eyes, so she looked away. Lifted her shoulders in a shrug. She wasn't ready to admit the truth, so she said, "Because you were there? Because we both needed comfort?"

"Liar."

The word was barely a whisper, and her gaze snapped back to his like a magnet.

"You wanted me. As much as I wanted you. I felt it." He challenged her with his cold stare—with the twinge of hurt she could read in the furrow between his brows. But why did he care? It was just a kiss.

She tilted her chin in defiance. "So what if I did? What does it matter?"

His eyes flashed as he yanked her to his chest. Beneath her fingers, his heart thundered, echoing the racing of her own. The heat from his body curled around her until her skin tingled.

"It matters," he growled, before crushing his lips to hers.

His touch lit a fuse that burst into flame, all the untamed desire building up inside her erupting in a coil of heat and longing. She instantly responded, deepening the kiss, stroking his tongue with hers. He buried his fingers in her hair and pulled her closer until they were pressed together as tightly as two people could get with clothes on. This was no gentle kiss for an injured man. This was a devouring—a pent-up release that had been too long in coming.

Her hands curled into the fabric of his shirt as their tongues tangled and warred. Heat pooled in her belly. What the hell had this man done to her? She'd never wanted someone as much as she wanted him. And from the feel of his hardness against her, he felt the same way.

Finn's fingers stroked trails of heat across her collarbone, then slid lower, thumbs brushing against her already aching nipples. She moaned against his mouth and arched her back, trying to get closer to his touch.

He broke away from their kiss to stride to the door and lock it, and Renna took the brief reprieve to gasp for breath. Her whole body sang with sensation, and when Finn returned, he yanked her shirt over her head in one smooth move.

The cool hospital air sent her skin erupting into goose bumps, and she shivered before Finn pulled her back into his embrace. His mouth found hers again, hot and wet and wanting. Claiming her for his own.

Her hands gripped the back of his neck, pulling him closer. The silk of his hair slid between her fingers, thick and soft, and she clutched at his strong shoulders as his lips slid down her neck, tasting and licking. Setting her skin on fire.

Renna moaned as he pulled aside her bra so his tongue could swirl against her nipple, and her head fell back in pleasure. He teased and sucked until her knees trembled and all she could do was whisper, "Finn."

He paused and looked up at her, his blue eyes dark with desire. That was all she needed. She grabbed his shoulders and tugged him to the bed. When he fell back against the pillows, she climbed on top of him, straddling his legs, yanking at his shirt. It slipped over his head, and she sat back to take in the ridged planes of his stomach. The scars marking him as a warrior. A hunter.

She smiled as he panted beneath her, his fingers digging into her hips. She could get used to seeing that every day.

"I don't like that look in your eye," Finn said after sucking in a breath.

"Smart man."

"Do you…" He glanced down at her and she knew what he was asking.

"Yes. I've had a birth control implant since I was thirteen." She leaned forward to capture his mouth in a kiss before stroking her tongue against the rough skin of his jaw. Then lower, to his neck. He tasted clean, like soap and something indescribably Finn. She inhaled deeply, letting his scent wash over her. Then she traveled lower, her tongue swirling over his nipple like he'd teased her.

Finn's breath exploded out on a moan, his body bucking beneath her tongue as he buried his hands in her hair. "Renna," he groaned.

White-hot need surged through her, zipping straight between her legs in a pool of wet heat. She sat up and struggled with the zipper of his pants, shifting her weight aside so she could tug them down. If she couldn't have him right now, she was going to spontaneously combust.

She ran a hand down the velvety length of his erection, smiling with power as his head lolled back and he grunted in pleasure. Gods, this man was magnificent. Even better than she'd imagined.

She slipped out of her own pants, and he watched her silently. But this time she didn't care about putting on a show or making him work for her. She wanted him. Now. Inside her. Seconds later, she was back on top of him.

He reached up and touched her face. "You sure?"

"You have no idea." She'd wanted this from the day she'd met him. From even before she knew what this feeling meant. She positioned herself until she felt him pressed against her, then slid slowly down, feeling him stretch her. Fill her.

Finn's eyes rolled back in his head, and he moaned again. "Oh my gods, Renna." His hands gripped her hips as she began to move, sliding up and down, each stroke building the pressure at her center.

She glanced down to find him watching her, their eyes meeting in a jolt of electricity, shaking her to her core. Finn's lips curved into a satisfied smile, and she arched her back, letting him slide even deeper. Her whole body quivered with the sensation of his hands on her skin, of the feel of him beneath her. She'd slept with plenty of men, but somehow, this was different.

Finn's hands slid up her torso to cup her breasts, his thumbs circling her nipples. A shot of pure pleasure made her whimper and press herself against him. "Do you like that?" he asked softly.

She nodded, and he sat up, bringing his lips to her breast, using his tongue to flick and suck her until she thought she'd explode beneath his touch. She rode him harder and harder, her hands tangling in his hair, pulling him to her, locking their bodies together.

Pleasure coiled tighter and tighter, until her skin felt like it was made of pure light, each touch more intense than the last. "Don't stop," she whispered against his hair.

Her fingers curled into his muscled shoulders, and her eyes drifted shut as the sensations built. Finn's dusky skin glistened with a sheen of sweat, and his breath came in ragged gasps, hot against her skin. He tore his mouth away from her breath and claimed her lips for his own. Their tongues slid and stroked each other, mimicking their bodies' motion.

Renna could feel him, deep inside, stretching her, filling her. And she wanted more. She wanted this to last forever. She rocked harder against him. A husky moan escaped his lips, setting Renna on fire.

They moved together faster, more urgently. Finn's whole body tensed beneath her, and he slid his fingers between them to touch her most sensitive spot.

Stars exploded in her vision. Heat and pleasure and release shattered her into a million tiny pieces. Two breaths later, Finn clutched her hips, jerking upward and driving into her one last time before he came with a moan.

He sank back onto the bed, and Renna fell onto his chest, panting as his arms came around her. His heart thundered beneath her ear, and she could hear the air moving into his lungs as he gasped for breath himself.

She let her eyes drift closed.

"I've missed you," Finn whispered against her hair.

Something warm and sweet twisted its way through her heart. "I missed you, too. I'm so glad you're not dead."

He chuckled, and the vibration of his chest against her ear sent goose bumps through her. His skin was warm beneath her cheek, and she snuggled in, tracing her fingers over the scar on his arm. "I'm assuming the hospital staff wouldn't approve of all this exercise. Aren't you supposed to take it easy for a few more days?"

"I think this was exactly what I needed."

She raised her head to grin at him. "Well, it does release lots of endorphins. And they're really good for you, right?"

He smoothed a piece of hair away from her face. "Definitely."

There was that jolt again, as their eyes met. She felt naked and exposed, not just because she was lying on his chest, but because he seemed to see her. And she'd been hiding for so long.

She cleared her throat and sat up. "We should probably get dressed before one of your nurses returns and gets ideas about you. Though I'm sure they've already had plenty," she said, taking in his flat stomach and muscled arms.

"Stop, Renna," Finn said, leaning on one elbow and frowning at her. "I know what you're doing."

"I have no idea what you're talking about." She rescued her underwear from the floor and slipped into them.

He let out a noisy sigh and swung his legs over the side of the bed. She forced herself not to get distracted by the sight of his carved thigh muscles.

"What happened between us freaked you out and now you want to dismiss it. Run away from it. I get it. But I'm not going to hurt you."

"This has nothing to do with you, Finn. We were just having some fun." Her chest constricted, and she could feel herself gearing up for the it's-not-you-it's-me conversation she'd had so many times before.

"It was fun, wasn't it?" he asked with a wicked smile. "Nice change from the sniping and fighting we've done so far. I'd like to do it again."

Her heart kicked with unease, and she nodded. "I feel the same way. But I can't be distracted right now. We have a job to do." She shrugged into her jacket. "Let's keep it casual, okay? We can figure it out later if we need to."

He slid off the bed and stalked toward her. Completely naked. She forced her gaze away, focusing on his strong chin, the hint of a dimple as he talked. Renna shook her head and realized his lips were moving.

"When this is all over, we're going to have a lot to talk about. I'm not going to let you run, Renna. Not this time."

He tilted her chin up so their eyes met for one long, intense moment.

And then he kissed her.

Gently.

Before letting her go.

TWENTY-SIX

She left Finn and made her way back to the ship. Partially to escape Finn and partially because she needed to talk to Aldani about the drug they'd found. She wanted the truth, and this time she wasn't letting him get away with vague half-answers.

Renna made her way to the comm room, nodding at the crew as she passed. Somewhere in all this they'd come to accept her as one of their own. Maybe because she'd saved Finn's life. Maybe it was something else. Either way, it felt...nice.

She frowned at the thought. These men and women would give their lives for him. That they respected her now meant something.

She just wasn't sure what.

Renna patched into the comm system and waited for Aldani to answer, drumming her fingers against the table. The steady beat slowed as her mind crowded with images of Finn's naked body beneath hers. Her skin start to burn, and she pressed her hands to her cheeks. She could still smell him on her skin. Feel his hands on her.

Aldani's voice jerked her out of her daydream. "Miss Carrizal. I assume you're calling about a status update on the mission?"

Renna cleared her throat. Thank the gods he couldn't see the flush staining her cheeks. "Actually, Doctor, I'm not. I need information. Have you heard of this compound before?" She rattled off the formula Wall had given her.

There was silence at the other end of the communicator. Then Aldani cleared his throat. "Where did you find that?"

Dammit. She was right. "Does it matter? I know this is the same drug Myka's parents were working on. It's the only thing that makes sense."

He let out a weary sigh. "You're correct. But their work was based on something my ex-partner Draven Navang and I developed years ago. We thought the compound could be used for creating a new medical device, but it never worked properly. When a new chemical was found on Banos Prime, my brother remembered our research. He and his wife began working on a new chemical formula containing that mineral."

"Their drug was an inhibitor, right? To help the body receive retrofitted body parts and transplants?"

"Exactly." He paused for a moment before asking, "How did you know what Navang's original work was to be used for?"

"Because it's now being used on a robotic army."

Aldani sucked in a breath. "What did you say?"

"The facility was full of robotic parts and cybernetic implants. Whoever is behind this is creating a mechanical army."

"Damn him," Aldani whispered. "He promised."

"Doctor?"

"The formula you shared is slightly different from the one my brother developed. Someone's been working on it since he was killed. Altering it. My ex-partner has to be behind this. He's using his NavStar facility on Vall. It's the only place in this part of the galaxy with that kind of tech."

"I thought you said Navang wasn't involved."

"I'd say anything to keep Myka safe, including lying to you." His voice dropped, worry in every syllable. "Navang threatened my nephew. Blackmailed me into keeping quiet about his involvement with the promise to return him, unharmed."

She squeezed her eyes shut, exhaling forcefully to temper the sudden frustration swelling inside her. "Don't you realize you've put him in even more danger? What does Navang want with him? Is he using the kid as blackmail to get you to cooperate with his research?"

Before he could answer, sirens screamed through the ship and the emergency lights flashed.

Renna shot from her chair.

"What is that?" Aldani demanded.

"I don't know. I need to go, but this isn't over. You owe us the truth."

"I know. I'm sorry, Renna. I didn't have a choice. Just be careful. Navang is more dangerous than you can imagine. Don't trust a word he says."

"Noted." Renna snapped off the communicator before sprinting to the CIC.

"What's going on?" she demanded.

Keva spared Renna a brief glance between barked orders. "We just caught four ships on our system scanners. They're coming in fast."

"Lieutenant Keva." Flight Lieutenant Kojima's voice boomed over the comm system. "The ships are headed right for the main part of the city. They're deploying bombs. Impact in t-minus ten minutes."

"Dammit!" Keva tapped something into the computer. "I can't get through to warn Larson and the captain. If this is anything like Hesperia, the port will be destroyed in minutes."

The crew kept the panic to a well-ordered minimum, but Renna's muscles throbbed with the urge to flee. "Keep trying to raise him, I'm on my way to the hospital now. There's a landing pad on the roof. Be ready to meet us there."

Keva nodded. "Be safe out there. We don't have much time."

Renna tore through the ship, adrenaline lending her speed. As she ran through the docking portal, a roar filled the warehouse and the whole ship shuddered. But Renna continued her sprint. She'd spotted a vibrobike in the corner. It was a beautiful machine, with sleek lines and a five-hundred horsepower engine. Hopefully it would get her to the hospital in one piece. She'd have to pay the owner back for it later.

If any of them survived.

She threw her leg over the bike and kicked it into gear. With a squeal from the tires, she took off. She pushed the machine as fast as it would go, until the buildings and cars she passed were nothing but a blur. The machine seemed to have a mind of its own, and she gripped the seat with her thighs as it rounded corners and dodged debris at her slightest touch.

Fires burned whole blocks where the bombs had already hit.

A boom sounded in the distance, and the ground vibrated as one of the buildings collapsed in a plume of smoke and rubble. Screams and shouts filled the air as people fled the destruction, searching for safety. Wherever that was.

Renna coughed and tugged her shirt over her mouth, keeping her head down as she passed through a wall of smoke. The scent of sulfur and ash filled her lungs and stung her eyes until everything around her wore a hazy halo.

She wove the bike between emergency vehicles and scattered bodies, urging it to go faster. The hospital was only a few kilometers away, but it felt like she was running a gauntlet as more bombs rained down onto the city.

When she glanced behind her, starships shot one after another from the spaceport like a flock of birds, their silhouettes black against the purple sky. Maybe they'd had enough warning to evacuate the population.

And maybe she'd actually be able to retire to that paradise world she kept dreaming about.

Renna swerved as a man ran screaming from the building beside her, his clothes blazing. He made it five steps before collapsing in flames. She gritted her teeth and looked away. There was nothing she could do for him. Getting to Finn was the only thing that mattered right now.

She kicked the bike into a higher gear just as an explosion erupted on her right, sending a shock wave full of debris at her and the motorcycle. The impact sent the bike spinning, and she flew off, landing with a bone-jarring thug against another building. Pain sledgehammered through her body, her bones and muscles rebelling against the collision. She lay there, paralyzed and gasping, each breath a thousand tiny knives. Renna stared up at the sky and forced herself to relax, to breathe through the agony.

She focused on the tiny black bird soaring high above her in the purple sky. Her eyes narrowed and focused. It wasn't a bird. It was a ship, growing larger and larger as it approached. The sheer mass of it made her jaw drop. It was double the size of the *Athena*, with strange wings on the sides, almost like the old airplanes they'd made before space travel. The dull, metallic color glinted in the weak sunlight. Instinctually, she knew it was made of the same strange material they'd found at the facility on Banos Prime.

And it was coming in fast.

Renna staggered to her feet. *Hospital. Captain Finn. Athena.* Her head swam, making the road beneath her feet jump and move. She focused on standing straight. If she didn't hurry, none of this would matter anyway. They'd all be dead.

She took one slow step and then another. As she moved, the fire in her lungs eased and her muscles loosened. The hospital was close. Hopefully it was still standing.

Less than two minutes later, she rounded the alley and her shoulders sagged in relief as she spotted the hospital. It hadn't been hit yet, despite the bombs falling all around. Maybe that meant Finn was all right.

Renna burst through the front doors and headed for the stairwell, climbing two at a time. "Find Captain Finn," she ordered her implant. It returned a heat signature in the fourth floor conference room where she'd met with Major Larson yesterday. She made for that corridor, skirting past the medical personnel scurrying in every direction, trying to stabilize and evacuate patients.

She slammed open the conference room door. "Finn!"

The captain and Major Larson jumped at the thud of the door against the wall, but she didn't wait for them to answer.

"What the hell are you two still doing here? The attack is getting worse by the second." Renna's heart threatened to pound through her ribs. She hadn't run like that in months. Something warm trickled down her face. She raised her fingers to the cut throbbing on her cheek, and they came away wet with blood.

Major Larson frowned at her. "We couldn't get through. Comms are down."

Why did the guy look so unhappy to see her?

"Doesn't matter now," she said, shaking her head. "We need to get to the roof. The *Athena* is on her way."

Finn nodded. "Major, come with us. It'll be safer onboard."

Larson shook his head and strode toward the door. "I'm heading to HQ. We have a bunker there. I'll be in contact soon, Captain. Be safe, both of you, and stop these bastards. Whatever it takes."

Finn's eyebrows furrowed, but he and Renna followed Larson out into the hall. "Yes, sir. You can count on us." Finn saluted.

The major returned it. "Go on. Get out of here before it's too late. That's an order."

Renna grabbed Finn's arm and headed back to the stairwell.

"What are you doing here?" he asked as they ran toward the roof.

"We couldn't get you on the comms, and Keva wouldn't leave without you." Renna ignored the other part of her that said she didn't want to leave without the blasted man either.

"Larson and I were trying to patch into the *Athena* as well. Seems like the first thing the attackers did was disable all communications on planet." Finn shook his head. "What are these people after? Lenue is nothing but a backwater spaceport. There's no value here. And Myka's not here. I thought these attacks were tied to him."

"That's what we need to find out." Renna sucked in a breath, trying to calm her pounding heart. "Aldani's been lying to us. His ex-partner is behind this."

"Dammit." Finn raked a hand through his hair. "I should have known. Dallas had me investigate Navang's biomedical device company, NavStar, almost six months ago. Everything came up clean. A little too clean."

They climbed the last flight of stairs, and Renna shoved open the door to the roof. The flight pad was empty, and she scanned the sky for the ship. Finn turned and searched in the other direction. The echoes of screams filled the air, even this high up. Each blast of a bomb striking its target made her jump. She forced herself to block the noises out. If she let herself think about what was happening, how many people were dying, she'd be paralyzed. And now, more than ever, she needed to stay strong.

"There!" Finn pointed off in the distance. "That's the *Athena*." He pulled Renna back into the stairwell, and they watched the ship approach.

"Thanks for rescuing me," he said softly. "You could have gone without me, finished the mission. No one would have thought badly of you."

She gaped at him. "Is that what you think of me? That I'd steal your ship and your crew and disappear? I thought you trusted me. Or was that all a lie, too?" Anger and disappointment licked across her skin like the fire in one of the buildings below, burning away the fear and exhaustion that threatened to make her collapse.

"No. That's not what I mean." Finn pinched the bridge of his nose before trying again. "That didn't come out right. I just meant that I knew you'd do the right thing."

She glared. "I don't have time right now to work out if I should be offended or not. Not to mention, your crew would never leave you behind."

"I still appreciate you risking your life to find me." He gently touched the skin beneath the cut on her cheekbone. "We'll get you patched up as soon as we get back on board."

Her gaze drifted past his head to the dark form sweeping toward them. "I think we're going to have a few other things to worry about first." She pointed at the other ship, and her blood turned to ice. Had the *Athena* seen them?

She stepped around Finn and pressed below her ear to turn on her comm. "Renna to the *Athena*. Do you read?" Dear gods, let the comms be working at close quarters. "*Athena*, do you copy?"

A burst of static sounded in her ear before she recognized Kojima's voice. "This is *Athena*. What's your position?"

"We're on the roof of the hospital, but there are hostiles incoming. Watch your left flank. They're going to attack."

"I see them. Evasive maneuvers in place. We'll loop back around to pick you up when we've lost them."

The *Athena* changed course, curving away from the hospital and causing the other ship to shoot past them.

"What the hell is that?" Finn asked, staring at the onyx machine. "I've never seen that ship designed before."

"It's made from the same material as the facility. I have a feeling Navang designed it. I just wish I knew why." She held her breath as two white streaks burst from the belly of the enemy ship and snaked toward the *Athena*.

The ship banked, slipping behind a high rise, and the missiles hit the building in a fiery explosion, blowing out all the windows on the block.

"Shit. All those people." Her hands were shaking, and she clenched them in front of her.

"It was empty. They evacuate tall buildings like that first." Finn's fingers pried hers apart, and he held her hand tightly as the *Athena* came around behind the enemy ship.

"There! Kojima won't let them get away. Watch this." Finn squeezed her hand as the missile bay doors on the *Athena* opened and the main gun fired at the other ship. It started its turn to escape, but it wasn't as agile as the *Athena*. The MYTH ship fired four shots. They hit the side of the enemy in a waterfall of sparks. A moment later, an explosion ripped through the air.

Renna clasped her hands to her ears as the ship blew apart in a volley of shrapnel and fire. Down below, she could hear people cheering at the *Athena*'s victory. At the destruction of the enemy.

Less than two minutes later, the *Athena* touched down on the roof. Renna and Finn raced for the hatch, which slid open to meet them. Keva and Viktis were waiting for them.

Finn stopped short inside the airlock and glared at the pirate. "What the hell is he doing on my ship?" he demanded of Keva. To Viktis, he turned and said, "You're like a bad disease that just keeps showing up."

Viktis grinned. "And you'd know all about bad diseases, Captain? I hope you were tested before you slept with our girl here."

Dear gods, would the man ever grow up? She rolled her eyes as Keva's mouth dropped open into a shocked O.

"I'm sorry, sir," Keva said. "He said he had information on the attack and that he'd been working with Renna. Should we throw him off?"

Viktis stepped aside. "Why don't we discuss my merits *after* we get the hell off this planet?"

Finn shook his head and strode past toward the CIC. "He can stay. But one Ileth toe out of line and he goes in the brig."

"Damn, Renna. This guy is a gem." Viktis frowned at her as they followed Finn through the ship. "I can see why you chose him over me."

Renna slanted him a look. "Enough. We barely made it out of there in one piece. We don't have time to ice your injured pride right now."

The *Athena*'s engines spun up, and the ship lifted off. Less than a minute later, they were through the atmosphere and away from the attack. Renna paused at the bridge window and looked down at the plumes of smoke drifting up from the city.

Aldani's had cost them more than time; it had cost those people their lives.

Viktis leaned against one of the railings in the CIC. "Captain, I have some information. That is if you'd like to take your head out of your ass long enough to hear it." He paused for effect. "The attacks aren't random."

Finn studied the monitor in front of him. "Tell me something I don't already know."

"Okay. How about each of the attacks hit MYTH bases in specific cities?"

Finn's hands paused on the keyboard, and he slowly turned to face Viktis.

Renna felt her jaw slip open. "How did you find that out? Aren't MYTH bases top secret?"

"They're supposed to be. But there's an interesting mechanical signature some of their machinery uses. The same signature of the *Athena* here."

"You had Gheewala track the signatures." It wasn't a question. Dammit. Why hadn't she thought of that? They might have learned about this days ago. The blame she'd felt toward Aldani faded, replaced by the sting of self-hatred. "But what does this mean?" she asked.

Viktis smiled slowly and crossed his arms. The damn Ileth was enjoying himself way too much. "I had her go back several years and search for each of the MYTH signatures in this quadrant of the galaxy. The first attack was on Banos Prime three years ago, the one that killed the kid's parents. It destroyed the MYTH research station there, but not before, I assume, the drug formula was intercepted. There was a gap in the attacks, but they started up again earlier this year. Each attack struck at one of the secret MYTH bases: Nath, Baeno, Hesperia, Lenue." He paused, letting his gaze shift between Renna and Finn.

Her whole body ached from her race through Lenue. Maybe her brain still wasn't working quite right, but what Viktis said didn't make any sense. "I don't understand. Then how is Myka involved? Why go to such trouble to kidnap him? And then destroy the worlds he was being held on?"

"Whoever is behind this is killing two birds with one stone. Isn't that the human expression?" Viktis asked. "I think they're eliminating MYTH strongholds and searching for Myka at the same time. Which begs the question. Where's the leak?"

Finn growled and turned away, his shoulders tense and hard as stone beneath his uniform. "There is no leak. Somehow the kid is leading them to MYTH. So we need to find out what's so special about Myka before we can stop these people."

"And there's only one person who can do that," Renna said.

After a long moment, Finn nodded. "Keva, patch us through to Aldani."

The lieutenant turned to her console, but after a moment of typing, she frowned. "I'm sorry, sir. It looks like enemy fire hit our long-range communicator."

"Dammit." Finn slammed his hand down on the railing.

"There's still another option." Renna let her eyes drift shut for a moment. "We have to go to Vall. Aldani said that's where his ex-partner and his business are located. If what Aldani says is true, Draven Navang has been behind all of this from the start."

Viktis growled. "I knew I should never have taken a job from a corporate type. Industrial espionage, my ass."

Renna thought back to the business card she'd found in Viktis's things when she'd drugged him. If only she'd done more research. Maybe she could have stopped Navang days ago. Yet another screw-up on an already messy job.

"Too late for principles now, pirate," Finn snapped. "If you hadn't started all this…"

"Someone else would have. You know how it works."

The two men glared at each other. Evidently she was going to have to play peacekeeper between them a little longer. "Hey! Save your pissing contest for a day when we don't actually have to save the universe. Until then, pack it away. We have work to do." When neither man relented, she ground out, "Right, Finn?"

He stared at her for a moment before finally letting out a huff of air. "Keva, set course for Vall. It's time to pay our esteemed doctor a visit." He spun on his heels. "I'll be in my quarters. I have some research of my own to do." And without another word, he stalked away.

"Moody, isn't he?" Viktis asked. "Where should I put my stuff? Am I bunking with you, Renna, love?"

"Hell no. Keva will find you a place to stay."

TWENTY-SEVEN

Keva's voice came through the intercom, and Renna sat up in her bed. "Thirty minutes out from Vall. Prep for landing." In two hours, maybe they'd have answers. Maybe they'd have Myka.

And then what?

Take the kid back to his uncle and start her new life? Stick around and see what happened with Finn? Disappear completely? She sighed and buried her hands in her hair. Why was everything so complicated? A month ago, she'd been all ready to retire. And then that one-last-job speech from Boyd had dragged her back into this life.

Renna pushed away from her bed where she'd been trying to sleep and paced the room. Her whole body thrummed with tension. Not long ago, she would have gone to find Viktis in his bunk for a much-needed distraction. Now, her thoughts strayed to Finn. To the feel of his hands on her skin, to his scent wrapping around her.

Stop it, Renna.

Being with Finn had been nice. More than nice, if she was being completely honest with herself. But down that road lay heartbreak and bitterness. They were completely different people, and Finn wasn't exactly a no-commitments kind of guy. She doubted he'd ever even heard the word "fling."

The only other option to work off her stress was the weight room. Not nearly as fun, but it would have to do.

When she arrived at the shuttle bay weight room, she paused in the doorway. Finn had a thin T-shirt on, his shoulder and back muscles rippling as he used the pull-up bar in the corner. She stared for a moment, mesmerized by the movement.

Gods, he was beautiful.

But the lust that surged through her left her with no doubt. She had to get away. The last thing she needed was another confrontation with the man. She had no doubt he'd win.

She turned to leave, and Finn's voice came from the corner. "Renna. Don't go." He didn't even turn around to talk to her.

"How did you know I was here?" she asked.

"I always know when you're close." He sighed and dropped from the bar, landing lightly on his feet. He wiped his hands on a towel from the stand beside him before turning to face her. "We need to talk."

Wasn't she the one who usually delivered the it's-not-you-it's-me speech? "About what?" she asked, sinking down onto one of the benches.

He swung a leg over, straddling the seat to face her. "I don't even know where to begin."

"How about starting with what happened to you after I thought you died seven years ago?" Her tone was sharper than she'd intended. Evidently she hadn't quite forgiven him for that yet.

Finn nodded. "After I found proof of Blur's activities, one of the Coalition agents on the case, Erik Dallas, convinced me I had to turn Blur and the gang in. He arranged for my death after I agreed to join the new organization he was forming."

His gaze drifted away over her head as he talked, like he was reliving the memory. "It seemed like the perfect way to start a new life. To become someone different. I thought everyone who knew my past was dead. Gone." He sighed and brought his gaze back to hers. "A few weeks ago, Dallas came to me. Wanted to bring in a new option to help us retrieve Myka, since we'd been unsuccessful. A thief by the name of Renna Carrizal."

Finn raked a hand through his dark hair. "The world I'd built so carefully came crashing down around me. You couldn't be the same Renna from my time with Blur. It wasn't possible. But there you were, large as life on that parking deck and obviously very good at your job. I wanted to run you through with my sword right then and there."

She nodded. "Yeah, that was pretty obvious."

"I was furious. You were a part of the life I'd worked so hard to forget. And you were a threat to everything I stood for. I tried to convince Dallas to arrest you or send you away, but he wouldn't listen. So I was determined to make you miserable. To make you feel as on edge as I did. Then you would laugh at something the kid said or smile at him, and even after all these years, I still recognized that girl I'd known. It killed me thinking you were part of Blur's slavery business."

"I wish you would have asked me about it. You were always so stubborn."

"Guess some things never change, no matter how hard you try."

His shoulders drooped, and Renna wanted to touch his arm, to comfort him. Instead she clutched her hands in her lap and let him continue.

"So when you went off with Viktis...I don't know what came over me. I was furious. But for some reason, I was also jealous. It didn't make sense." Finn stared down at the bench. Traced a finger across the worn plastic. "I expected to never see you again. Assumed that you'd run off with the merc and disappear. But when you came back, everything I thought about you shifted. And even before I knew the truth about you and Blur, I'd started to respect you."

Renna blinked at that. "You did?"

Finn nodded. "I saw how good at your job you were, at how much pride you took in doing things well. You're amazing at what you do, even if you don't always do it the way I'd approve of. We're lucky to have you here. I'm lucky to have you here. I would never have made it out of that facility without you."

She smirked. "You probably wouldn't have gotten in without me either."

His face hardened into a grim expression. "That's what I mean. I don't want to do it without you. And that scares the hell out of me."

"I know the feeling." It almost made it worse that Finn understood where she was coming from, that he was having the same conflict. "I had planned to sell my stuff, cash out my accounts, and change my name. I was going to retire to some tropical island and life on the beach. Alone."

"So what now?" he asked. Need and vulnerability warred in his expression. The silence stretched between them until it felt heavy and impenetrable.

How she answered him could change everything. For both of them.

Her mind flashed back to the series of men her mother had slept with. To the series of men Renna had slept with. The only difference was Renna had chosen her conquests, not had them chosen for her because they paid for her services.

She curled her shoulders in, wrapping her arms around her waist as the tightness in her chest grew. She wasn't her mother. Sometimes it was okay if life wasn't entirely in her control. It was okay to trust people, even if they didn't always live up to that trust.

A shuddering breath shook her to her core. Dammit. This was more terrifying than finishing her first job.

Finally, she raised her eyes to look at Finn. "You're not the only one it scares the hell out of. But then I remember that the best jobs always freak me out before I start."

"I know that feeling. It's the same one I get before starting a new mission. You just have to hold your breath and jump in."

She nodded. "Sometimes fear is good for you. It makes you sharper. More alert. It makes things more real. And if you have someone else to depend on…"

"You don't have to do it alone," he finished. His lips curled up slowly. "So does this mean you're going to stick around for a little while?"

Renna used her finger to draw a cross over her heart. "I promise."

His grin grew bigger. "I can't believe you're still using the Code."

"Hey, it's kept me alive for the last seven years. You were a smart guy back then."

Finn raised an eyebrow. "That was a backhanded compliment if I ever heard one."

She shrugged, trying to keep a serious face. "Too bad I'm still not convinced your merc skills have carried over. I might need a bit more convincing."

"Convincing, eh? I think we need to take care of that right now." He leaned forward and scooped her into his arms, pulling her across his lap. She felt him thicken as she settled against him.

"Why, Captain, is that a blaster in your pocket?" she asked with a wicked grin.

Finn let out a low growl and kissed her hungrily. His hands drifted lower to lift the hem of her shirt and stroke the soft skin of her stomach.

She shivered against him and let her own hands tangle in his hair, pulling him even closer.

"Captain, we have a distress call coming through." Finn jumped at Keva's voice over the intercom. He pulled his lips away from Renna's, but kept her in his embrace, pressed against his chest.

"Who's it from?" he asked, flashing Renna a look of disappointment.

"I can't tell. Looks like it's coming from Navang's facility. Maybe he has defectors."

"We'll be right there." Finn smiled at Renna. "Are we good?"

She forced a stern look to her face. "For now. But I can't wait for shore leave. You still owe me some more convincing."

He traced a finger across her jaw. "I promise."

Renna and Finn raced to the bridge where the crew was already working feverishly, talking into their comms and tapping at their consoles. An air of barely contained panic filled the space and set Renna's teeth on edge.

"Lieutenant Keva, status report." Finn stood in military stance behind his chair, legs apart, hands behind his back

Everyone else on the bridge snapped into military formality as well, straightening their backs, watching their posture. Except Renna. She leaned against the railing and crossed her arms, watching Finn with a smirk. He'd thrown on his uniform jacket as they'd run, but it hung open, displaying the muscled planes of his chest through his cotton shirt.

There were some perks to being a thief.

Keva bent over one of the comm screens. "I think we almost have the distress call located, Captain. Estimated landing in ten minutes."

"Any sign of attack? Have we been able to hail their airbase?"

Keva shook her head. "No answer yet."

Finn frowned and stared out the window at the approaching planet.

Gheewala stepped forward, her hands twisting the hem of her uniform jacket. "Sir, I'm not sure if this helps, but the strange electronic signatures are getting stronger the closer we get to Vall. From what I can tell, they're clustered around the facility. We should be careful."

He nodded. "Thank you, Sergeant. Renna, you think we can sneak in and see what we're up against?"

"Maybe. Can we cloak our landing? If these are the same ships that attacked us on Lenue, we don't want them finishing the job here."

"Already done." Kojima's voice came over the intercom. "There looks to be a small clearing off to the west of the facility. We should be able to land there and send a small team in."

"Then we go in quiet. Renna and I will head in first, then call for backup."

"But sir, after last time..." Keva shook her head. "We should assemble a team. You're going to need more support than just...Renna." She tilted up her chin defiantly.

Interesting. The lieutenant was finally growing a backbone.

Finn stared at Keva appraisingly. "Very well. Pull one together, Lieutenant. We'll split into two groups. Do we have the emergency transmission cleaned up yet?"

Viktis nodded from his chair in the corner and pressed one of the buttons on the comm device. "Here it is."

Static filled the bridge, and Viktis moved one of the controls. The noise sharpened into the sound of a woman's voice. "...out of control. Please help. Trapped in section two. Chemical leak in manufacturing has affected staff and production.... Send help."

The words cut in and out, covered by static and a strange beeping sound.

"What is that?" Finn asked.

"I can't tell. The signal is too degraded." Viktis tried to sharpen the loop, but the recording was still choppy.

Renna straightened from her lounging pose as her skin erupted into goose bumps. The one thing she could make out was the sheer terror in the woman's voice.

Finn crossed his arms. "I don't like this. Everyone gear up and meet in the shuttle bay in five."

The crew scattered, and Renna made her way back to her own cabin. She didn't need armor, but she did have a few tricks in her bag that might come in handy. She stuffed her pack with her lock-picking tools, some small thermal detonators, and an extra blaster pistol.

"Download map of Vall," she told her implant. A terrain map of the planet appeared. "Now the city map, please." She found Navang's lab at the edge of the spaceport, a large, sprawling building with spokes running off a central hub. From the satellite image, it seemed like a normal complex of buildings, but when she drilled deeper with the infrared scan, it looked like there was a whole other maze below ground level.

Where in all this was Myka?

She let out a sigh and let the image fade. She needed to focus, to get this job done no matter what. The kid was counting on her. The universe was counting on her.

No pressure.

TWENTY-EIGHT

The rest of the crew was already down in the shuttle bay when Renna joined them. Bokal and Gheewala were staying behind, but they stood off to the side inspecting the gear. Lieutenant Keva and two of the other MYTH agents wore their black ninja suits, only Keva's silver eyes betraying who she was behind the mask.

Captain Finn appeared from the locker bay, wearing a similar version, but it shone metallic in the helo lights when he moved and seemed thicker, more like armor. It clung to his thigh muscles, and as he turned to talk to Keva, Renna's gaze drifted lower to linger appreciatively on the view.

Viktis stood nearby, checking his blaster. "I think there's a little drool on your chin, Renna," he said, looking up with a smirk.

She shrugged. "Yeah? I saw you watching Lieutenant Keva as she bent to tuck her uniform into her boots."

"Damn, you caught me." He slid the chamber closed and holstered his gun.

Renna frowned. "What are you doing here?"

"I'm coming with you. These people killed my crew, remember?"

"Finn agreed to that?" Maybe there was hope for this mission yet.

"He didn't have a choice." Viktis's glance at the man was full of cold indifference. "So am I to assume he's the new fling of the week?"

"Viktis…"

"Don't worry. I promise I won't try to kill you this time. I'm more than over you."

Renna shook her head. "You never loved me, Viktis."

He smiled sadly, his violet eyes almost going soft. "You never let me."

Renna sucked in a breath like he'd punched her. What they'd had had been a convenient, friends-with-benefits kind of relationship. He couldn't have loved her. Or had she been too afraid to see it?

Before she could figure out how to answer, Kojima's voice came over the intercom. "Captain, we'll be landing in two minutes."

Finn stood with his arms behind his back to give orders. "Team, we're going in hot. Keva, take your crew to the east entrance of the facility and make your way to the center. Viktis, Renna, and I will head west. Keep in contact if possible. If this facility is anything like the last, they may have disabled comms. If that's the case, find the boy and get back here ASAP. Whoever finds him waits two hours and then leaves. His safety comes first."

Keva and the rest of the crew finished gearing up.

Renna's skin prickled, and she rubbed her hands up and down her arms. She hated this feeling, like things were about to go tits up and there was nothing she could do about it.

The *Athena* touched down with a soft tremor, and the cargo door slid open. Everyone drew their guns, and each group headed down the plank. Keva raised a hand in farewell and headed east with her crew.

"Renna, you have the map?" Finn asked.

She nodded. "Shouldn't be too far. I found an entrance that looks like it's through the forest here. Keva and her team will have to go farther around the building before they can get in."

"Let's go."

The trio headed through the jungle. The air pressed down on her like a weight, the smell of death and decay catching in her nose and hair. Strange animals screamed at them from the shadows as they approached the cement-gray building. At least it wasn't made of the same strange material the last place had used. Getting in would be much easier.

Walking through the wet heat felt like moving through water. Renna tugged at the neck of her shirt as sweat trickled down her back and her hair plastered to her face. Beside her, Finn used his sleeve to wipe the perspiration from his forehead.

Luckily they found a thick, steel door guarding the entrance at the corner of the building. A V'Mani lock glowed blue against the dull cement wall. Renna smiled. About time things started looking up. She had the lock disabled in moments, and Finn let out a low whistle.

"You get what you pay for," she said with a laugh.

Viktis shook his head. "Or, in this case, who she slept with."

Finn took a step forward. "Watch it, pirate."

Renna rolled her eyes and slipped through the door into a dim hallway. A fine coat of dust covered the floor, and cobwebs hung in the corners of the ceiling.

If the kidnapper was going for creepy, he'd nailed it on the head.

"Scan for security," she ordered. A few cameras and sensors popped up on the map her implant laid out for her, but none were close enough to worry about. "We're clear for now. I say we head toward the center of the facility and then down. The distress call said something about the problem being on level two."

Finn shifted his grip on his blaster, holding it more firmly. "Let's go. And stay quiet."

"This ain't my first brawl, soldier." Viktis shoved past him so that he was closest to Renna.

She ignored their bickering and focused on the doors dotting either side of the long corridor. Her implant said there were no heat signatures, but it wouldn't hurt to stay on guard.

The hall dead-ended after a few minutes. Their only choice forward was through a door and into a brightly lit passageway that led toward the center of the building.

Renna pulled back to check the map again. Her stomach plummeted. The central hub was at the end of this corridor.

Gathered in and around the area were at least a hundred heat signatures.

There was nothing for it; they were going to have to go right past that space to get to the stairwell. "Stay on guard. This section is crawling with people," she warned, before moving silently toward the main hallway.

Finn and Viktis followed close behind her, blasters drawn as they circled the main open space. It seemed to be some sort of auditorium, two stories tall, with the main floor on the lower level. She crept closer and risked a glance over the railing into the room below.

Human men and women filled the space, all standing perfectly still, staring straight ahead. Her gaze caught on one of the men at the edge of the group. He was tall, with closely cropped dark hair and olive skin like hers. He looked like someone she might see on a street in Hesperia. Someone she could be related to.

Until his eyes began to flash with a strange red light.

The same light that most implants made when they were downloading information. A quick glance around confirmed her suspicion. Every single person had the same flashing light in their eyes.

She clutched at the railing as everything inside her started to scream.

"What is it? What's wrong with them?" Finn's breath was hot against her ear, but for once, his closeness didn't distract her.

"I wish I knew." She swallowed back the nausea burning her throat as everything started coming together. The mercs, the facility, the drugs. "Navang must be experimenting on them, trying out the drug we found. We need to get out of here before they see us." Renna crept around to the emergency exit and ran her safety program through the lock. It opened with a snick, and the three slipped into the stairwell.

"What were they?" Viktis asked, scraping a hand over the bone plates in his head. "I've never seen anything like that before."

She shook her head. "I think they were...robots. But we don't have time to figure it out right now. Navang is here somewhere. We need to find him and Myka." She scanned through her implant's blueprints of the facility. "Looks like level two has a lot more security than the upper floors. Let me go first and disable the systems."

Both men nodded, and she eased open the lower level door to reveal a gleaming white hallway. Glassed-in labs and research pods lined the way. It reminded her of Aldani's station back on Iniros, but with one big difference.

Her implant detected no heat signatures, no movement in any of them.

She snuck forward and peered into the first lab. One of the lab chairs had fallen on its side, and a coffee cup sat steaming on the desk. Someone had been here. And recently.

Shit.

As she crept down the hall, she snuck glances into lab after lab. All empty. She disabled the sensors as she went, but it seemed like it didn't matter. There wasn't anyone around to catch them.

"Where is everyone?" Viktis whispered. His head whipped back and forth as he searched each of the rooms.

"I don't know. But I don't like it." Renna kept moving despite the goose bumps prickling her arms. Whatever that distress call had been about, it hadn't been a trick. Something had happened here.

They reached the end of the corridor, which led to another pair of doors. These were thick, opaque plastic with some kind of airtight seal, almost as strong as an airlock. She didn't recognize the flashing keypad beside the door, but she pulled out her tools and went to work. The silence around them—broken only by their breathing—stretched her nerves taut. Her skin crawled each time the air blowers kicked on or a computer beeped in the distance.

Something was very wrong here.

After a few tweaks of the wiring and a quick pass of her software, the airlock swooshed open, letting out a puff of metallic-smelling air. Behind it came the other scent she always dreaded: the choking, burnt-sugar odor of clay. But woven into the clay was a strange metallic undertone like the one she'd smelled in the facility on Banos Prime.

She spoke through gritted teeth, trying to breathe in as little as she could. "Layout is similar. One long corridor with labs. There doesn't seem to be anyone here either, but stay on your guard." She pulled her blaster from its holster, and they continued on. The smell grew stronger the deeper in they went, until her nostrils burned and her eyes stung.

"What is that?" Finn asked.

"I think it's the drug they were making at the other facility. Maybe that's what the distress call was about." She pulled her shirt over her nose, but it did little to block the heavy smell.

"Is it toxic?" Viktis asked, alarmed.

"I don't know. But I'm sure it can't be good." The last thing she needed was to get high in the middle of a job. "Wait." A heat signature flashed on the map in her head. "I'm getting a reading from the far end of the hall. Let's move."

They sprinted toward the last lab, and Renna pressed a palm against the autolock, letting the doors slide open. Inside, computers and holomonitors lined the wall, and a bank of strange machines beeped and hummed near the door.

As she did a quick sweep of the room, her gaze tripped over a familiar form. She sucked in a breath.

Myka lay in the center of the room on a surgical table.

TWENTY-NINE

The boy's eyes were closed, his chest barely moving with each shallow breath. His dark skin looked ashy against the white sheet covering his mostly naked body. An IV line disappeared into the crook of his arm, and his hair had been shaved to accommodate sticky probes attached to his skin.

Guilt burned in her belly, shooting bile up the back of her throat. For a moment, Renna thought she was going to be sick all over the sterile floor. She tore her gaze away from Myka and took several slow breaths, trying to steady herself.

"My gods." Finn's voice shook as he surveyed the boy. "How are we going to get him out of here?"

Viktis had already moved to the computers and was scanning the readouts. "They're monitoring his vitals. It looks like the IV is full of that new drug in liquid form. What the fuck are they doing to him?"

Renna forced her legs to carry her closer until she could stare down at the boy. Her fingers shook as she touched his bare shoulder. His skin felt hot and damp, as though he had a fever.

His eyes flew open.

She screamed, jumping back as Myka suddenly thrashed. The sheet that covered him slid down to reveal his thin arms were tied to the table.

Finn grabbed her shoulders to steady her. She wanted to turn her face to Finn's chest and hide there, but Myka's voice jerked her out of her own fear.

"You came," the boy whispered, staring up at her like she was some kind of hero. "I told him you would. You promised."

"Are you all right? What are they doing to you?" She tried to keep her voice calm, but a sob choked her on the last word.

"They're using my cells for something. They come in every day and take blood. They won't tell me what they're doing." His voice trembled. "I want to go home. Get me out of here, Renna. Please."

She forced the worry from her face. "Yes. Yes, that's why we're here. Just hang on a bit longer so we can figure out how to disconnect you. Viktis, what do you see?"

"I have no idea. There are two probes in his brain. Several Cida patches are keeping him mostly sedated, and the IV is pumping drugs into his bloodstream. There's also an external port currently hooked up to an interfaced hemodialysis machine. Like they're going to drain him."

Viktis's words circled her brain. She knew they were bad; she just couldn't let herself think too much about them or she'd be useless.

"Do what you have to and get everything out of him."

Viktis typed some commands into the control. Renna moved back to Myka and nodded at Finn, who took up a spot on the other side of the boy.

Renna smiled down at Myka. "I don't know if this is going to hurt, but we need to pull all of these needles out. Okay?"

Myka bit down on his lip before nodding.

Finn met her gaze over the table. "Are you sure?"

"As fast as you can. Keep the pain to a minimum."

He nodded. "One. Two. Three."

Together she and Finn pulled the tiny probes from the boy's temples. He screamed, high and shrill. His body jerked once, and then he went still.

"Myka! Myka? Are you all right?" Renna shook his thin shoulders

His head lolled loosely against the bed.

"Get the rest of these needles out of him!" She scrambled to pull the IV out of his vein. The patch on his shoulder was next, then the restraints tying his arms to the bed. Across the bed, Finn did the same. But the boy still didn't move.

"Viktis! What's his status?"

"Heartbeat is off the charts. Vital signs are unstable. There's some strange brain activity going on."

Her pulse raced as she studied the boy on the table. She'd never forgive herself if she'd hurt him.

"Renna, we need to get out of here. We can stabilize him once we're back on the *Athena*." Finn put a gentle hand on her shoulder.

Viktis's scalp ridges vibrated as he scanned the machines. "There should be a dose of clay on that table. It might help get his heart rate under control."

Renna eyed the needle. She hated the thing, hated the fact she was about to shoot up a kid with even more of that drug. But if it would save Myka...

"If he's already on clay, won't it make it worse?" she asked.

Viktis shook his head. "Whatever they're pumping him with is no longer clay, it's...different. I'm hoping this will stabilize him."

She pulled down the sheet to uncover the rest of Myka's thin body.

A wave of horror swept over her, so powerful that when it crashed, the room spun. She clutched at the edge of the table to stay upright.

A portion of the skin covering Myka's ribs was pinned back to reveal metal and tissue wrapped together in a nightmare of robotic engineering. His ribs seemed to be made of some kind of metallic material, and some of his veins looked synthetic. The rest of what she could see was obviously still human.

Finn tugged the sheet down on his side of the bed and said, "His arm, Renna. What have they done to him?"

Her gaze flew to Myka's forearm. The skin there was pulled back to reveal a mess of wires, nerves, and veins. She couldn't tell which ones were human and which were synthetic.

"The kid's a frakking robot." Viktis stared at the boy, his mouth clenched into a hard line. "There's no way he's still human with all of that cybertech inside him."

The taste of copper burned the back of her throat, and she swallowed. "I don't care what he is. We have to get him out of here." Steeling herself, she unpinned the skin on his ribs and folded it back to cover his insides. It disappeared seamlessly into his body. If she hadn't seen it a second ago, she would have never known.

Renna gasped. That wasn't possible. What the hell had they done to this kid? She seriously would like to meet this Dr. Navang in a dark alley some day. Quickly, she injected the clay into the boy's arm.

Viktis nodded across the room. "Looks like that helped. He's stable for now."

Finn wrapped the kid in the sheet and picked him up. "Is there a faster way out of here, Renna? We can't go back the way we came."

She pulled up the schematics. "There's a door not too far from here. We'll have to pass through the rest of the lab, but if it's as empty as this, it won't matter."

He nodded. "Make sure it's clear."

Renna pulled her gun and peeked out the door. She took a moment to suck in a deep breath and try to scrub her mind clear of the image of the boy's cybernetic insides. No matter how horrified she was, Myka was counting on her. She exhaled her fear out with her next breath. "It's clear. Let's go."

Together she and Viktis took point, scanning the hall as Finn carried the boy behind them. The labs they passed were still empty. No sign of the woman who'd sent the distress signal. No sign of whatever had happened.

Her skin prickled.

They reached the end of the hallway and turned left. "We're almost there," she said, glancing back over her shoulder. "One more set of doors and then the stairwell and we'll be outside. How's Myka doing?"

Finn shook his head. "Not moving, but I can feel his heart beating. He needs help."

Who could help him? They didn't even know what he was anymore. She pushed the thought away. One thing at a time. She needed to focus on getting them out of here.

Renna pushed open the door and gestured Finn and Viktis through. Just a little farther to the stairwell and they'd be almost out.

Two labs sat on either side of the hallway, and she expected them to be empty like all the rest. But as they approached, the doors slid open and a group of people marched out into the hallway from each lab. They fell into formation, three abreast, and one of the young men in the front row stepped forward. His eyes seemed to gaze past her, and a red light flashed once, deep inside the cornea.

They were the people from the auditorium.

"Intruder alert. You may not pass. Please come quietly with us."

His voice sounded human, but the cadence was off, as if he'd been programmed to say that. She risked a glance at Finn and saw that he was backing toward the doors. Viktis had his pistol out, aimed at the leader.

"Let us go and no one gets hurt," she said sternly.

"Assassination protocols have been engaged," the man said. "Please return the boy to his room immediately." He took another step toward her, and Viktis fired his gun into the man's head.

It erupted in a shower of metal and flames and screams. Organ tissue and blood splattered everywhere, coating her face and hands, and Renna pressed a hand to her mouth.

He spoke like a machine but bled like a human.

"What are you?" she whispered.

Another man stepped forward to take the leader's place. "We have been perfected."

Dear gods. These things were hybrids. Robot-human creations. Navang's drug was keeping the human bodies from rejecting the tech.

Had they done this to Myka?

"Viktis. Remember our job in New Holland?"

He raised an eyebrow. "You want to try that here?"

"Now."

Renna and Viktis dropped to one knee, opening fire on the robots. Renna focused on the column to the right, Viktis on the left. She aimed at each robot's head, squeezing off a shot with her blaster. Each one exploded in a mess of flying tissue and metal.

Blood splatters turned the walls into crimson rivers, and the rich metallic scent filled the air, mixing with the smell of the drugs. She gagged, forcing her nausea back down with every shot.

She fired again just as one of the robots surged forward. The bullet ripped a hole through the woman's chest, spinning her away, but not before Renna caught sight of a living, beating heart through the wound.

Bile burned her throat as her lunch tried for another return trip.

"There are too many of them! Get Finn and the kid out of here!" Viktis yelled, still shooting. He'd cleared a path down the left side. She glanced back at Finn. He dashed past, and she followed, shooting at anything that moved toward them. The sound of Viktis's blaster screamed through the narrow space behind them.

"Up the stairs and to the right. The exit is at the end of the corridor!" She turned back to keep shooting at the robots following them. These things moved fast, and there were mere yards between her and the front of the crowd. The only thing left to do was stop and fight. Finn needed enough time to get out of there with the boy.

"Take him to Aldani. He'll be able to help," she shouted over her shoulder. "Don't wait for us!"

"Renna!" Finn's eyes were wide and terrified as they darted between the limp boy in his arms and Renna's blood-smeared face.

She flashed him a smile. "I'll catch you later, Captain. You still owe me a shore leave."

He shook his head. "No. There's got to be…"

"Go!" she shouted, drilling two bullets into the head of the closest robot, then pivoting to hit the next one through the door.

She heard the airlock swish open behind her, and then he was gone.

Down the hall, Viktis' gunfire was slowing. Was his pistol charge running out, too?

Another surge of robots pushed through the door, and she picked them off until her gun whined and vibrated in her hand. She threw it to the floor and grabbed her knife from her boot.

She slashed through two human-metal chests before glaring at the oncoming pack. "Who else wants to rumble?" she taunted.

That's when they charged.

THIRTY

Renna woke with her head spinning. She kept her eyes closed. Any other motion might have sent her over the edge. She licked her dry, cracked lips, but her tongue felt like it had been coated with glue. Around her, the hum of machines vibrated against her skin. She'd bet her life she was still in Navang's station.

Slowly, she eased her eyes open. Her head was propped on something soft and white. A pillow. So someone had moved her after the attack.

She had a pretty good guess as to who.

Renna blinked again, trying to clear the fog from her eyes. Everything seemed hazy, indistinct. Even her thoughts felt fuzzy. A series of machines beeped near her head, and her arm itched where a needle was stuck into the vein. It felt like spiders crawling up and down her skin, and she shuddered.

A woman's voice cut through the room. "She's awake, Doctor."

Renna sucked in a breath. She'd had no idea someone was there with her.

"Very good. I'll be there shortly." The man's voice sounded as if it came from an intercom. Though tinny, it was firm and melodious.

The nurse moved around to Renna's head. "Please don't struggle. Dr. Navang wants to help you. You've been exposed."

"To what?" she croaked.

The nurse pressed a button, and the head of the bed rose enough so that Renna was propped upright. Then she handed her a glass with a straw.

Renna drank thirstily before sinking back against the pillows. Her heart raced like she'd run a mile. Even sitting up had sent her spinning. What the hell was going on?

The nurse smiled reassuringly at Renna's expression, her sharp blue eyes softening as she said, "Just try to relax. The doctor will explain everything once he's here."

Relax? That was the last thing she wanted to do. Had Finn and Myka made it out? Where was Viktis? And the robots? By her ear, the heart rate monitor beeps increased until they sounded like an alarm.

The nurse frowned and turned down the sound. "Please be calm. I don't want to have to sedate you again."

Renna's muscles twitched and rebelled, but she took a deep breath, trying to get her racing heart back under control. Her head began to ache, and everything had a strange halo of light around it.

What exactly had the doctor done to her?

Her hand drifted to the necklace at her throat, and she squeezed it like a talisman. Panicking was not going to help. This was bad, but she'd gotten out of worse. She was Renna Carrizal, the Star Thief. It was going to be fine.

Across the room, she heard the door slide open and turned her head to watch a man in a white lab coat enter the room.

"Miss Carrizal, I'm glad to see you've finally woken up." His smile didn't reach his cold, blue eyes. "I'm Dr. Navang."

"What did you do to me? To Myka?" The effort of talking left her out of breath and shaking. She forced herself to relax back against the pillows. She'd need all her strength to escape these people.

The doctor shook his head, his cropped white hair glowing in the helolights. "I did nothing, I assure you. The people you work for did that themselves."

Renna rubbed her eyes with a shaking hand. "You're saying MYTH created these…hybrids? I highly doubt it."

"Then you'd be mistaken. Let me show you." He flipped a switch near the door, and the monitors along the wall flickered on.

"Five years ago, the MYTH installation on Banos Prime discovered an interesting element in the soil. It had strange properties, ones that held promise in the medical industry. MYTH sent a research team to investigate and work with the element. Myka's parents, both MYTH doctors, headed up the project." He paused and adjusted one of the monitors to display an image of utter destruction. What looked to be some sort of building lay in pieces around a crater. Bodies lay everywhere, along with chunks of machinery.

"Two years into the project, there was an explosion. Many of the MYTH staff were killed or injured, and Myka was caught in the worst of the blast. His parents knew MYTH was developing advanced cybernetic implants in secret in another facility, against all regulations. They proposed an exchange. Use the new implants to save their son and the others injured, and in return, get a real-world test case."

Renna opened her mouth to protest, but the doctor held up a hand. "Let me finish. MYTH granted approval for the Aldanis to try out the implants, but there was an interesting wrinkle. Myka had been downwind of the mine when it exploded and cast the experimental element into the air. He was exposed for several hours before they could rescue him. The others, both MYTH agents and civilians, who were injured in a different area of the mine weren't exposed."

He pressed another button, this time bringing up an image of a lab full of bodies on tables. Some were obviously dead, bleeding out of wounds too horrific to fix. Others had the same sort of robotic hands and eyes and legs she'd seen on the mercs back on Banos Prime.

"The child was the only one who survived the experiment. The other human bodies rejected the implants, killing their hosts in days or weeks. But Myka…his body embraced them. Integrated with them until it was impossible to find where the boy left off and the machine began."

"I don't understand." Renna's head throbbed like her brain wanted to ooze out her ears. She forced her eyes to stay focused on the doctor. "Are you saying Myka was the first hybrid?"

Navang nodded. "Myka's parents were already familiar with the work Aldani and I had done on an anti-rejection drug. After seeing Myka's miraculous recovery, his parents hypothesized that the new element they'd found in the destroyed mine had been the missing key. They developed a new formula and tested their theory on other accident victims. Each one was given a cybernetic implant and put on the drugs. Sixty-five percent of the cases were successful. But Myka was the most important because his implants truly became a part of him. They changed him, and he changed them."

"So where do you come in?" she asked.

"I was part of their team in a consultant capacity. MYTH asked me to step in when the Aldanis were killed."

She shook her head. "Why you? David Aldani seems like a better choice."

"He wasn't given the opportunity. MYTH was afraid his emotions would cloud his judgment, and you must be impartial when running these kinds of experiments." Navang's lips curved into a smile. "Besides, they needed the best. Aldani is a washed-up has-been."

Renna snorted, then winced as her head pounded. "Aldani is a better man than you'll ever be."

Navang shrugged. "You know nothing of me. Of the work I've done for this organization. I've used my research to create an army for MYTH. One that will be unstoppable."

She stared at him. It couldn't be true. MYTH wouldn't have hired her to find the boy if they were already involved. None of it made sense. "You're saying that MYTH asked you to create an army of hybrids to take over the galaxy? That doesn't make sense."

The man was insane. Completely and utterly mad. He'd created a new race with the blessing of a government agency. They'd be completely undetectable once they assimilated into the humans.

If it was true.

"But it *does* make sense," Navang said. "Someone wants power, and undetectable assassins and spies are the perfect solution. I don't ask questions. I just get paid for my work. One branch of MYTH is the same as any other to me. Besides, who's to say the order came from MYTH headquarters itself? The bigwigs probably had no idea what we were working on. Dallas certainly didn't when he sent you after the boy."

She struggled to sit up. Enough of this mad man's ramblings. Aldani had said not to trust him. These were probably all lies. "Where is he? Where's Myka?"

"I was going to ask you the same thing." The doctor narrowed his eyes. "Seems like the good captain has escaped with our template. I want him back."

She forced her face to stay expressionless, but she felt herself relax against the pillows. Myka and Finn were safe. That was the most important thing. And if she could keep Navang talking, maybe she could figure out a plan to get out of here.

"So who was behind the attacks on the planets?" she asked.

"MYTH was, of course. I needed test subjects to build my army, and my contact was more than happy to oblige. Each attack gave me thousands of dead or dying humans to work with. A virtually unlimited stock of research subjects. It was the perfect solution."

Impossible. MYTH would never condone that. The people she'd met were honorable. But a sliver of doubt wormed its way into her mind. She'd wondered before about how easily the kidnappers had found Myka. About the attacks on the planets. But surely they wouldn't kill their own people. Unless...

There was a traitor within the organization.

Navang smiled as he watched her come to her conclusion. "Don't look so surprised, my dear. An organization as large and decentralized as MYTH has to have its share of bad apples. I don't care who I work for, as long as I get paid. You and I are alike in that way, I think."

"Never!" she spit. "I'd never murder thousands of people or torture innocent children."

"No. You'd just steal a priceless cultural artifact and let its people die in a pointless war."

She blinked at the doctor, going perfectly still.

"That's right. I know who you are. And I think you may be even more useful to us than Myka."

White-hot anger scorched through her, momentarily burning away the fog. "At least I can assure you you'll never get Myka back."

"We may not need him. We have enough of his genetic material to work with for now. And the new subjects are coming along very well. Most of them are on a steady dose of the drug and hooked into our neural network. They are completely under my control." He shrugged, looking smug and haughty. "And the few that we are unable to control are destroyed once we know they are no longer viable."

Navang pulled a pair of rubber gloves on and smiled over at the nurse. "Rebekka, please remove the IV from Miss Carrizal's arm. I think she's had enough. I'll be curious to see the effects of the drug at this dosage."

Renna's gaze flew to the needle in her arm, and then to the orange liquid that had been dripping into her vein. "What have you done to me?" she demanded.

"We've simply made you better, my dear." Navang's smile turned his face into a hideous mask. "I haven't been able to try our new dosing on the current subjects yet, and with the addition of Myka's DNA, I think the implant integration process will go even more smoothly than before. By using the antibodies and genetic material in Myka's blood, we've developed a way to allow the implants to fuse with your nervous system seamlessly, until you're able to control your implant like you would another limb. Or so we hope. Plus it's always interesting to deal with someone who already has one."

"How did you know about my implant?"

"You don't exactly keep it a secret, my dear. Now take a few deep breaths and calm down. I'd hate to have to knock you out again."

She stared at him, her heart racing beyond her control. The fog in her brain was swirling back in. What would the drug do to her? Would she become a machine like one of those…things?

"What's going to happen?" she asked, trying to keep her voice from shaking.

"I'm not entirely sure. Regular implants and transplants are superficial; their limitations well-documented. Even the most well-designed technology fails after a few years as your body attacks and rejects it. What I hope will happen is that this new drug will allow your nervous system to gradually integrate with your implant until it becomes a part of you. Something that physically ties you into the technological world."

He rubbed his hands down the front of his lab coat, tugging at the lapels as if he was giving a lecture to a university class. "Some of our subjects have almost been able to control the flow of information on the network. Others had brief integration with electrical systems, like power centers or computers, allowing them to turn entire power grids on and off with a simple thought. We haven't been able to make it work long-term yet, but you're strong enough. And now that we've integrated Myka's genetic material, I think it might finally take."

Okay. That wasn't too bad. When she thought about it rationally, it could actually be pretty useful. Especially if it helped her break through safes or into buildings. "What's the catch?"

"I don't know what you mean, Miss Carrizal." His smile was slimy and full of lies.

Fuck this. She flexed her muscles beneath the sheets. Luckily, they'd left most of her clothes on, only removing her shirt so they could stick her with the needle. She was grateful for the army bra keeping her girls firmly in place.

Before she could let herself think about what she was about to do, she jumped from the bed and snatched the scalpel from the tray nearby.

THIRTY-ONE

Dr. Navang's face paled, and he backed away.

The nurse held her hands out and approached Renna. "Just get back into bed, dear. It's the drugs making you do this," she said soothingly.

Renna shook her head. "Nope. This is all me." She stalked toward the doctor. He stumbled backward as she approached, his long legs looking oddly like a spider's as he tripped and scuttled away from her. When his back hit the wall, Renna pressed the blade of the scalpel to his neck.

"Tell me what's going to happen."

"I don't know." Navang's voice wavered, and he glanced at the nurse.

"No. Look at me." She yanked his chin so he was forced to meet her furious gaze. "What is going to happen?"

A trickle of sweat ran down Navang's cheek. "The drug we gave you has destroyed your antibodies and replaced them with Myka's. It's also begun to break down the neural connections between your implant and your nervous system. Once the process is complete, the technology will begin to fuse with you. It will grow and connect in ways we can't even imagine."

"Right. I got that. Then what?" The scalpel trembled in her hand, and she gripped it tighter, trying to steady it.

Navang shook his head. "I don't think you understand. The drug we injected you with is destroying your immune system. If the process isn't kept in check, your implant will take over your entire body. Or it will fail completely. Either way, you'll die."

Renna lowered her hand and blinked at him. Each breath she took felt like it was on fire. "How do I stop it? Reverse it?" she demanded. "There has to be a way to fix this!"

"We can keep your immune system working and the implant from being rejected, but you'll need a steady dose of the drug I developed. Once you've stabilized, any disruption in the protocol could cause the implant to fail or your organs to shut down."

Renna's voice trembled as she brought the edge back up to his neck. "You mean I have to take those drugs for the rest of my life now?"

He swallowed, the scalpel nicking his Adam's apple as it bobbed. A small bead of blood welled to the surface of his pasty skin. "Possibly. Or the implant could stabilize. It's hard to say since it was already installed in you when we started the process. Your body may already have accepted it. We had a sixty-five percent acceptance rate in most of our subjects."

"How would I know if my implant is failing?"

His eyes lit up. "You'd know. There would be tremors and headaches. You might feel like you're coming down with the flu or catching a cold. And then your muscles would go stiff. Eventually you'd lose your sight before your brain shut down. It depends on your body. It's a fascinating process."

"Fuck you."

She drew her arm back and punched him, throwing her entire weight into the swing. His head crashed back into the wall with a *thunk*. Blood streamed from his nose and splashed down the front of his white jacket. With one last whimper, he slid to the floor.

The nurse gasped and turned to flee the room.

"Not so fast." Renna gestured with the scalpel. "You're going to help me or this man is dead."

The nurse stopped just feet from the door.

"Pick up the restraints," Renna ordered.

The nurse glared at her, but moved to the bed and removed the restraints.

"Now bind his hands. Hurry up." Renna brandished her weapon again when the woman looked like she was going to protest. Her muscles were turning to rubber, and the headache Navang had warned her about already throbbed behind her eyes. She needed to get out of here.

The nurse obeyed, but Navang didn't put up a struggle. He whimpered as the tears mixed with the blood on his face.

"Hook the restraints to the metal bar," Renna said. "Then get the other ones from the foot of the bed." She leaned against the counter and tried to look bored while she inspected the rest of the machines.

Where was Viktis? Had they captured him, too?

When the nurse had tied herself to another bar across the room, Renna crouched in front of Navang. "I need answers, Doc. Or you're not going to like what happens."

He shook his head, blood splattering onto the white front of his lab coat. "You wouldn't. You don't have it in you."

"You should know enough about me to know I'm telling the truth. You've hurt my friends, and you've fucked up my life. I don't have much left to lose." A quiet life on Paradisio Prime was certainly out of the picture now. Her stomach churned as she thought about Finn.

Her hand shook, and she let the scalpel slide down his cheek, just deep enough to scratch. "Did you know I grew up in the Izan Tenements on Old-Earth?"

His eyes widened, and he shook his head.

"I see you've heard of them. Then you'll realize I have no problem gutting you like a frakking fish. Now tell me where my partner is. The Ileth who was with me?"

"He—he was being prepped for implantation down the hall. We haven't tested on aliens before. MYTH wanted to stick with humans until the process was perfected." The man's gaze darted toward the door as if help were just beyond.

Renna's heart constricted, but she forced herself to stay calm. To not shove the scalpel through his damn eye. "Tell me who's behind all of this. The people in MYTH that I know would never agree to this kind of thing."

The doctor shook his head. "I never saw more than a holovid. The person called himself Pallas, but I know that wasn't his real name."

"How high up does this go? Tell me." She bent down to get in his face, making sure the scalpel never left his field of vision.

"I...I don't know. I got the impression he was fairly important, but he didn't have unlimited resources for this project and he was adamant we keep it secret from the other MYTH agencies. He didn't want them to know what was going on."

"A splinter cell?"

The doctor nodded. "That was my guess. I usually worked through one of his men—a Major Larson."

Her chest tightened. Larson was part of this? Who else was involved? If what Navang said was true, she couldn't trust anyone at MYTH with Myka. He was still at risk. Even if Navang was out of the way, Larson and his boss could start up the experiments again if they had the boy.

There was only one thing left she could think to do. The old part of her twinged with regret. If she sold this information on the black market, she'd be set for the rest of her life—for three lives probably—but she couldn't unleash something like this on the galaxy. A human-robot hybrid army, completely at some traitor's beck and call?

If the wrong people got a hold of this...

She swallowed. "I'm sorry, Doctor. What you've created here must end. It's nothing personal." A sharp pain shot through her head, and she gritted her teeth. "Well, maybe it is."

"Please," Navang begged. "We can work something out. I have money. I know..."

"You know nothing." Her eyes drifted down his tear-streaked face to the crimson-stained white lab coat. He looked like he was about to piss himself. So much for the brave doctor.

The scalpel felt cool and heavy in her hand as she shifted her weight. Usually she only killed when it was necessary for self-protection, but she might enjoy this one more than a little.

In one fluid motion, she drew her arm back and slammed the scalpel into Navang's neck, just below the ear. It slid through the skin like it was butter, blood spurting from the wound as it pierced his jugular vein. Her push carried the blade almost half-way to the handle.

"How about you just take a few deep breaths and try to relax?" she taunted as his body slumped against the wall. Blood gushed down his neck and dripped on the floor, leaving a spreading pool of crimson against the white tiles.

The nurse whimpered in the corner.

Renna whirled on her heels and glared at the trembling woman. She marched toward her, stopping at the tray of surgical tools to pick up one of the gauze pads. Renna wiped Navang's blood from her fingers, then dropped the stained scrap of fabric back on the tray. Her hands still felt sticky, but she needed to get the hell out of there. She'd wash them back on the ship.

"You're lucky I don't have time to deal with you, too," Renna said as she grabbed the bag of orange pills from the counter.

"Please, let me go. I won't bother you. I'll disappear."

Renna stepped into the hall, slamming the door behind her. She ignored the woman's pleas as she headed toward the hall to where Navang said Viktis was being held.

A scream exploded from the next room and she raced for the door. Only to stop short just inside.

Viktis had gotten free and was making sure the orderlies would never touch him again. Even half-drugged, the Ileth grabbed each of the men, snapping their necks in a smooth, practiced move.

The men crumpled to the floor. Viktis spun toward her, his eyes rolling wildly as he braced for another attack. He stopped when she made no move toward him, then relaxed as if realizing who she was. He let out a shaky breath as he took in her battered form. "Like the new look. Who needs armor when you look like that?"

Renna glanced down. She'd forgotten she was only wearing a bra and pants. Bruises from the robot's attack blossomed on her ribs, and scratches ran up and down her arms. Somehow she couldn't bring herself to care. "Always glad to inspire. You ready to get out of here?"

"You have no idea."

She stumbled as they left the room, and Viktis slid an arm around her. "I think the bigger question is, are you all right?"

She blinked away the moisture fogging her eyes. "I don't know. But right now it doesn't matter. We need to destroy this place."

"I am more than happy to oblige," Viktis growled.

"Did you find out who killed your crew and destroyed your ship?"

He nodded. "The doctor said whoever hired me wanted no loose ends. Once they had the boy, we were expendable."

"I'm not surprised. Our friend, Major Larson, seems to be involved, too. According to Navang, they were both working for a splinter cell run by someone named Pallas. I'd bet my life MYTH doesn't know they've been betrayed from the inside. Unfortunately, that makes it even harder to figure out who to trust there."

"Renna Carrizal? Trust? That's a first." He chuckled as they limped along.

Renna spotted a lab filled with computers and paused. "I don't want to run into those hybrids again. You up for some hacking before we get out of here?" There was no way she'd be able see straight, let alone hack the network, with her head aching like this.

"What do you have in mind?"

She led him to one of the machines. "Shut them all down. Navang said they were all connected to the neural network."

Viktis started typing. In just a few moments, he'd gotten access to the lab's systems and was busy creating a virus to destroy the hybrids and put them out of their misery.

Renna sank down onto one of the stools and rubbed her temples. The pounding was getting worse, and the bite of nausea was a constant at the back of her throat. Her implant didn't feel any different yet, but Navang had said it was only a matter of time before it fused with her nervous system. Would she even still be herself at that point?

She swallowed. There wasn't time to think about that right now. They weren't out of here yet, and she couldn't afford to let herself freak out.

"Almost done here," Viktis said, glancing over his shoulder. He frowned at her as she leaned unsteadily against the desk. "Hey, you hanging in there?"

She shook her head. "I'll survive."

"Can we blow this place to hell now?"

She paused. Could she really blow this place up? Dr. Navang's research might be the only thing that could keep her alive.

"We don't have any other options, Renna. You know what will happen if this gets out. Robots masquerading as humans? Never a good idea."

She squeezed her eyes shut. He was right, even if she didn't want to admit it. "Fine. Just hurry up."

Viktis turned back to his computer. "I'm going to set the generator systems to overload. That should give us time to get the hell out of here. And when they blow, this whole place will come down." He tapped a bit more. "I'm also venting the chemical lines. That'll add some extra spark to the explosion."

Renna patted the drugs in her pocket. Once this place was gone, those little orange pills would be the only thing standing between her and a possibly painful death. Maybe she'd been smart to let Wall take a sample. If she got out of this, she might have to set up a manufacturing facility of her own.

"Okay. Done. Let's get the hell out of here."

Together, she and Viktis limped toward the exit. As they approached the hub, the hybrids stood frozen in place, eyes vacant. A series of beeps came from several of them, spreading through the crowd as the virus took hold.

"What will happen to them?" she asked. Her stomach twisted as the former humans shuddered and trembled. "Will they feel pain?"

"No, they shouldn't. It will shut down all mechanical components, leaving them immobile."

She blinked at him. Then back at the room full of people. "Viktis, they're not just machines. These were once people. Navang fused cybernetic implants to human bodies." Her voice cracked, and she studied the nearest hybrid, a matronly looking woman with graying hair and soft skin. Maybe she'd been someone's mother or wife. Now she was a monster created by MYTH.

His eyes widened, and he scanned the hundreds of hybrids in the room. "That's horrific," he whispered.

A rumble started somewhere deep within the facility, and he jerked. "It's too late for them, but at least this will put them out of their misery. Come on, Renna. We need to go. Now."

Together they made their way down the corridor and out the main door. They found themselves standing on a quiet street at the edge of town.

"Hurry, we have to get out of the blast radius."

"Make for the *Athena*. Maybe she's still there." Renna forced her legs to move, despite the pounding in her head and the tremors wracking her body.

Viktis paused, his amber skin still pale and ashy looking from the sedatives they'd given him. "What did they do to you? You're going to have to tell me, you know."

Her eyes burned, but she refused to let the tears fall. "I'm becoming one of the hybrids. I already had the implant. Navang injected me with the drug to integrate it into my system."

His hand tightened convulsively on her arm, and he swallowed. "You could have been infected with the virus I just released."

"No. Integration with his neural network hasn't happened yet. He said it would take a few days or weeks for the process to complete."

"Oh my gods." He shook his head and pulled her toward the shade of the forest. "We'll figure this out, love. Get you help. Reverse it somehow."

She let out a sad chuckle. "I appreciate it, but somehow I don't think there's getting out of this one, even for me. We need to focus on Myka right now and making sure he's safe. Even if Larson is involved, the real mastermind behind all of this is still out there. And we have no idea who he is. Or why he needed an army of hybrids."

They stepped out into the steamy forest, and Renna sucked in a deep breath of the thick air. It looked the same as it had earlier, yet everything had changed forever. She wiped a bead of sweat from her forehead, squaring her shoulders. "Let's move."

There wasn't much of a chance, but a tiny part of her held on to the hope that Finn had waited for her. That somehow they'd find a way to fix this together.

As they approached, that hope died. The clearing was empty, all signs of the ship long gone. Renna sagged against a tree. The world had gone fuzzy again, her eyes unable to focus on anything. She slid down the trunk to sit on the ground.

"Shit. What are we going to do now?" Viktis paced the clearing, his long legs eating up the ground. "We need to get you help. We need to get you out of here."

She thought about the communicator in her implant. Could she risk trying it? Would it even work anymore? At that thought, a sharp pain zapped through her brain, and then she heard the static as the communicator turned on and contacted the *Athena*.

"*Athena*, this is Renna. Do you copy?" she asked, voice shaking. The pain sliced through her again, and she let out a whimper. She needed to hold on long enough to reach them.

Her head hummed with a strange noise, and a moment later, Finn's voice echoed in her head. "Renna! Where are you? Are you safe?"

"We got out. We're in the clearing. The facility is about to explode."

"We're on our way. Hang on."

"Is Myka safe?"

"Yes. He's fine. Stabilized once we got him on board. It was like there was something in that facility affecting him."

"The neural network."

"What?"

She shook her head. "Never mind. Just hurry."

Viktis stared at her. "Are they coming?"

She nodded. Then her body slid sideways as the world went black.

THIRTY-TWO

When Renna regained consciousness, it felt like someone had stuck a stick of dynamite in her head and put the lid back on. When several minutes passed without her head exploding from the pain, she opened her eyes.

She half-expected to see Navang's lab again. Instead, she was surrounded by the familiar gray-white walls of the *Athena*. In her own bunk.

She squeezed her eyes shut against the humming that vibrated through her brain and tried to breathe.

Inhale calm.

Exhale pain.

Slowly her clenched muscles relaxed and the humming faded. No, not faded—it had shifted. Somehow, with every vibration, she could feel the movement of the *Athena*, the murmur of her drive core and the feeling of the crew moving through the ship. The vibration of the electronics and controls. Everything.

It was amazing. All the feelings she'd never even guessed lay below the surface of her mind.

Renna let out a slow breath and tried to reach out with her implant. There was a flash of the CIC, with Keva and Viktis chatting over a star map. Another flash of Lieutenant Kojima sitting at the helm.

A sharp zap burned through her body, and she seized on the bed. The world spun, crashing and screaming through her body until all she could do was clutch the edge of the bed and ride out the surge of agony. Seconds turned into long, torturous minutes as wave after wave rushed through her.

She was going to die. Her implant was being rejected.

Eventually, the pain withdrew, and she wiped away the tears that had trickled down her cheeks. She took a shuddering breath and opened her eyes. Somehow the cabin seemed brighter. Clearer. She shifted in bed so she could see the rest of the room.

Finn was sprawled out in the tiny chair, head back against the wall. The low rumble of a snore came from his lips. She smiled at him, then winced as her brain twinged again. She curled her fingers into the sheets, clutching them in case the pain came back. A moment later, the twinge was gone, replaced by a shot of fear, white-hot and burning as it all came rushing back.

Major Larson was a traitor. But that meant someone even higher up was behind everything.

How would she ever find out the truth?

Finn yawned and stretched in the chair as he came awake. His gaze fell on her, and his eyes widened. "How are you feeling?"

No sense in telling him how bad it was. The longer she could keep him safe, the better. "Like I got hit by a magnacraft. But it's getting better."

He crossed the room and sank down on the edge of the bed. His fingers traced the cut on her cheek, then brushed away a strand of her dark hair. "You had me worried."

"How long was I out?"

"Just a few hours. We're on our way back to Aldani's lab."

Renna stared up at Finn's worried expression. How was she ever going to tell him what had happened? She was dying. For all she knew, she only had hours left. An ache filled her chest. There was so much left she wanted to do. To say.

"Viktis said they'd...experimented on you?" he said gently. "Can you talk about it?"

Tears filled her eyes, and she blinked them away. Pull it together, Renna. She stared at the wall and quickly told Finn about Navang's drug, about the hybrids, about everything that had happened at the lab.

"He said he worked for someone at MYTH named Pallas," she said. "Major Larson was his contact."

Finn frowned. "That's not possible. I've never heard of anyone called Pallas."

"But MYTH is like a hydra. There are so many arms you may never know about all of them. And this is the only thing that makes sense. Who else would have the resources or be able to stay hidden so well? Who would know where all the MYTH installations were? Who else would know how to stay one step ahead of us?"

Finn chewed his lip. "Major Larson. I can't wrap my head around it. I would have bet my life he was trying to help us back on Lenue."

"He fooled everyone. How else would he still be in that position?" She squeezed his hand. "It also means that someone even more powerful is protecting him. Myka still isn't safe. We can't take him back to Aldani."

Finn shook his head. "He needs help and so do you. Based on what you said, Aldani is the only person who can fix this. He's got the resources and the experience to keep you both alive and healthy." He got to his feet. "We'll be there in another hour. Get some rest. I need to some time to digest all this."

"There isn't anything to think about, Finn. We need to take the boy and run. We need to find somewhere safe for him, and then we need to find the person behind all this." Renna struggled to sit up. The room whirled like a deranged merry-go-round, everything moving up and down. She forced herself to ignore the nausea burning her throat and swung her legs over the side of the bed. "I don't know what's going to happen to me, but you have to promise me to watch over the kid."

Finn glared at her. "Stop talking like that. You're going to be fine. Aldani will fix you."

"There's nothing he can do, Finn. My immune system is gone. The implant is going to integrate with my nervous system. I'll either survive the process or not. And when Navang's drugs run out…" Her voice broke off, and she looked away, not wanting Finn to see her watery eyes. Dammit. Just when life had finally started looking up.

"We'll find a way to fix this. I promise you." Anger vibrated in every line of Finn's body. "If you hadn't destroyed that facility, I would have killed the man myself."

"Did it blow?"

He nodded. "Just after we landed. Shook the whole ship. I can't imagine anything's left but a crater now. Now I'm going to do the same to Larson."

The image of those hundreds of hybrids would haunt her forever, but right now, Myka was her main concern. "No, you're not. We have to come up with another plan." She struggled to her feet, ignoring the feel of the *Athena* pulsing around her.

Her knees buckled, but Finn caught her.

Pressed against the hard planes of his chest, her eyes locked onto his. "I'm sorry we won't have time to figure this thing out between us." She stroked the strong line of his jaw, rough with a day's worth of stubble. "But it's been fun."

"This isn't over, Renna," he growled, capturing her mouth with his. Heat blazed through her, pushing away her aching head and the fear crawling along her skin. Maybe right now she could forget. Could lose herself in Finn and the way he made her feel. Her hands tangled in his dark hair as she pulled him closer. She'd crawl inside him if she could, but she settled for his touch, the taste of him, the feel of him against her.

His strong arms held her steady, his hands sliding down to the waistband of her pants, then lower to cup her behind. He pressed her against him, and she moaned. She could feel the heat pooling inside of her. She wanted him more than she'd ever wanted anything. She wanted one last time to feel human. To feel like herself before everything changed.

"Make love to me," she whispered in his ear.

"I thought you'd never ask."

He kissed her again before pulling away long enough to slip his shirt over his head. His hands slid the back of her bra open, and it fell to the floor. They kissed, each of them fumbling with the zippers and buttons on their pants, and then Finn scooped her into his arms and carried her to the bed, lowering his weight down on top of her.

He planted his hands on either side of her and smiled slowly. Her insides clenched at the look in his eyes. Like he'd devour her. Like he'd never let her go.

"What have you done to me?" he asked softly as he lowered his mouth back to hers. He nibbled at it, sucked at her lower lip.

She took a shuddering breath, tried to regain control of herself. "I could ask you the same question. I've never begged a man for sex before."

"I'm glad I'm the first. I hope I'm the last." His lips traveled lower, tracing the line of her collarbone, the outer curve of her breast. His tongue flicked against her, and she arched, burying her hands in his hair, pulling him closer. She could feel his smile against her skin.

His body fit with hers like they'd been made for each other, and she let him kiss his way down her stomach before reaching for him. Desire curled through her fiercely, pushing away her fear and worry. She slid her hands across his chest, tracing the scar he'd once told her about. She followed the trail of his hair lower, until she could touch him, hard and smooth.

He moaned, his arms trembling slightly as he held himself above her. And then he was between her legs, his thick heaviness pressed against her. She arched and let him slide slowly inside.

He captured her mouth with his as he thrust the rest of the way into her. She gasped against his lips at the feeling, at the exquisite pressure, and then moved her hips so he could slide in and out of her. His gaze never wavered, and she felt itchy and uncomfortable, like he was truly seeing her.

But if this was the end of the Renna as she had been, she wanted someone to have seen her. So she gazed back as the pleasure built, as each thrust made her whimper, and her hands clutched at his back. Finally she couldn't stand it; her eyes fluttered shut as her whole body exploded. She felt Finn stiffen against her, and she opened her eyes to watch him come. When he collapsed on her, panting, heart pounding, she wrapped her arms around his strong shoulders and blinked away the tears.

They had just started to get to know each other again. So much possibility in front of them. Now this might be the last time she could be with him. She was going to make the most of it.

THIRTY-THREE

Renna let herself lie in bed a few minutes after Finn left. She didn't know if she loved him, but she knew she cared about him more than she had anyone. Ever, maybe. Now she'd never get a chance to see what would have happened. Maybe they would have never worked. Maybe he would have broken her heart. But Navang had taken all of that away from her.

She felt the burn of tears again and growled. She wasn't going to spend her last few days feeling sorry for herself. She was going to find some way to stop this traitor and put an end to all of this. Somehow she needed to figure out how to use Larson to get to Pallas.

But first, she had someone she needed to visit.

The crew nodded and smiled at her as she made her way to Myka's cabin, but she didn't have the energy to do more than smile back. She paused in front of Myka's door and stared at the smooth metal. Would he even want to see her? Was he angry that it had taken so long to rescue him?

She sucked in a breath and knocked lightly at his door. Her heart skipped a beat before he finally called out, "Come in."

"Hey, kid." Renna sat down on the bed beside Myka. He was still pale and dark smudges shadowed his eyes, but he grinned at her and sat up. Relief washed over her. He didn't hate her.

"Renna! You're all right?"

"Damn straight. You didn't think that creep would stop me, did you?"

He shook his head. "I saw the explosion. I was glad."

"Good." She ran a hand over his shaved head. "Nice look. You'd fit right in with the mercs I used to run with."

"You're not going back to them, are you?" he asked, looking worried. "I want you to stay with Uncle David and me."

"No, I'm not going back to that. But I'm not sure what's going to happen. I'm going to be honest. They're still looking for you. You're the only thing left from that research now, and whoever commissioned it is going to be very pissed off. We need to keep you safe."

"But if you're with me, I'll be fine." He slipped his hand into Renna's, and her heart twisted.

"Myka, how much did you know about your parents' research after your accident?"

"About me being part-machine?" He shrugged. "I don't re-member any of it. I'm just me."

She blinked in surprise. He seemed so…accepting. "Do you feel any different? Do you notice your implants?"

He shook his head. "No, they're part of me now. And they help me sometimes. Run fast, lift heavy things. It's cool."

"Good. I didn't want you to be afraid after what happened..."

"No, I always knew there was something different about me after the accident. After my operation, Mom and Dad treated me different. Watched me more. But it's okay. When we were attacked, they said it would save my life. That I shouldn't be afraid."

She squeezed his hand. "I want you to know whatever happens, I'm out there watching for you, too, okay? We're going to make sure you're safe. Captain Finn promised."

"I saw that mercenary guy. I don't like him."

"Viktis? He's going to protect you, too. He's a good guy, even if he's made some mistakes."

Myka shrugged. "I'm not worried. When I'm bigger, I'll protect all of you."

"I bet you will. Now get some rest. We should be at your uncle's lab soon."

He snuggled back into the bed. "I'm glad you're here, Renna. Thank you for finding me."

She watched him drift off to sleep before getting to her feet. She'd told Finn and Viktis she'd meet them in the conference room when she was done. With her luck, they'd already started fighting.

The headache had eased somewhat, but she still felt unsteady on her feet as she made her way through the ship. The radio and electromagnetic waves around her felt like prickles of energy against her skin.

Gheewala watched her with wide eyes as Renna approached her station. "You have an electronic signature," the woman said.

"Lucky me." Renna grimaced. "At least you'll always know how to find me if I'm close."

"I'm so sorry." Gheewala stared down at her computer. "I wish there was something I could say."

"Hey, don't worry about it. It's thanks to you we made it this far. Make sure the rest of the crew know it." She squeezed the woman's shoulder and moved on. She could already hear the raised voices coming from the conference room.

When she walked in, Viktis and Finn were on opposite sides of the conference table, glaring at each other.

"What the hell is going on here?" she asked.

"Just a little disagreement. We'll handle it," Finn said, not moving his angry gaze from the Ileth.

Viktis shook his head. "Pretty boy here thinks he's in charge of me. I think otherwise."

"Well, you both need to stop it. We're almost out of time, and we have to figure out what our next steps are." She sank into one of the chairs and glared at both of them until they sat as well. "I have an idea, but it means both of you need to work together." She stared down at her hands. She had no problem asking Viktis to do his part, but what she was about to propose was going to send Finn completely over the edge.

"What is it?" Viktis asked.

"As I see it, we have two goals. We need to figure out who's leading the MYTH splinter cell. We also need to keep Myka safe and out of this person's hands. The *Athena* is the best ship in this sector, and you have Sargent Gheewala who can alert you to any-one following." She paused, took a deep breath. "I think the ship and crew should turn rogue. Hide out somewhere in the galaxy until we can figure out what's going on."

Finn blinked once and opened his mouth, but closed it before saying anything.

Viktis leaned back in his chair and slowly nodded. "I could make that work. I know how to stay ahead of the authorities, and I have contacts on most of the merc worlds. Not that I'm agreeing to help or anything," he added with a glare at Finn.

Finn shook his head. "Running from MYTH? Do you know how impossible that is?"

Renna watched him. Willed him not to fight her on this. "Not if you change the ship's signature and let Viktis help. It would keep you all safe. Keep Myka safe. Just until we know how to stop whoever is behind this."

His eyes met hers, and the expression in them felt like a knife twisting between her ribs. "You're asking me to be a traitor, Renna. To go back to that life."

She forced the words to her lips. "I know. And you know I would never ask unless it was the only way out. Really, you're acting in MYTH's best interest. They just won't know it at first." She smiled reassuringly, trying to hide her fear.

Finn arched an eyebrow. "What is it you're not telling me? What are you going to do?"

Heat flooded her face. She should have known Finn would catch her lie of omission. When she was younger, he'd always been able to tell when she'd purposefully left out things. Evidently he hadn't lost that skill either.

She looked down at the table. "I'm not going with you."

Both men shot to their feet. "What?!"

"Sit down and let me explain." She folded her hands on the table, trying to seem calm and composed. Inside, her mind raced as she fought for control. "I'm going after Larson. He's our only lead to the real traitor. MYTH has a main headquarters, right?"

Finn nodded. "It's on Newton Alpha."

"That's where Pallas is then. He went to a lot of trouble to build this hybrid army. I can't imagine he'll give up now. Which means he'll come after you or send Larson." She traced a finger across a scratch in the plastic table. "My guess is that a fuckup this big will trigger an internal investigation. His only choice will be to pretend that he's working on going after whoever did this. Either he'll pin it on Larson or he'll use the major to smoke you out to get Myka's tech. But what if the only other tech left from the facility is already in his hands?"

"Renna. I can't let you…"

She held up her hand. "Listen, Finn. Something is happening to me, and I don't know how to fix it or what's going to happen. Offering myself up as a test subject is the best way to infiltrate MYTH HQ. Once I'm there, I'll have the chance to look for whoever is behind this. And maybe stop him."

"No. Absolutely not." Finn waved his arm in a sweeping motion. "I am not letting you put yourself in danger."

She felt a surge of anger but pushed it away and kept her voice calm and reasonable. "You're not letting me do anything. And trust me, if there was any other way, I would be all for it. This way I can keep an eye on Larson. See who he interacts with. Maybe by me being there, it will take some of the pressure off finding the kid and you guys. Maybe it'll keep you safe."

Maybe they'd be able to find a way to save her.

Viktis didn't say anything. He just arched an eyebrow ridge and shook his head.

Finn paced the room. "But what if they find out you're a spy? What if you get sick?"

"Then Myka is still safe with you. He and his uncle can disappear on some remote world and live happily ever after."

He turned to glare at her. "And what about me?"

"If worse comes to worst, you can come back to MYTH. Tell them Viktis abducted you. That you had no choice. You're a pirate. I'm pretty sure you can take care of yourself. The pirate I used to know can take care of himself."

Viktis smiled wryly. "Your concern for me is touching."

"You know it's a compliment. You're more than capable of staying out of MYTH's way." She got to her feet. "When we land at Aldani's lab, we'll have a short time for him to check on the kid, grab some of his stuff, and then you need to leave like you've kidnapped him."

"You're staying behind?" Finn asked through thinned lips.

She nodded. "I'll call for help. Tell them I managed to escape. It's the only way," she added as Finn's face darkened.

"I don't like it."

"I don't either, but do you have another idea?"

He growled and started pacing again.

Renna turned to Viktis. "I know we haven't had the best relationship, but if you do this, I'll owe you. And you know I always fulfill my promises."

He shrugged. "My crew's dead, my ship's destroyed, and I don't have any jobs lined up. I'll help out." He got that calculating expression she knew far too well. "As long as you give me that little security deposit around your neck."

Her hand crept up and clutched the sapphire. Retirement was looking even further away than when she'd started this mission. And if it would keep Finn and Myka safe, she'd give up more than this. She yanked at the chain, and it snapped, burning the skin on the back of her neck.

She handed it over. "Deal."

Finn frowned. "Renna."

"What? It's mine to do with what I want." She shrugged. "It's a small price to pay."

"There's one more part of this deal, love," Viktis said, slipping the stone into his pocket. "When it's all over and we're safe, you have to tell me the story behind stealing this."

Renna shook her head. "Some things are better left untold, Viktis."

Keva's voice sounded from the intercom. "Renna, we've landed at the labs. Aldani's on his way."

Thank gods for small favors.

"Good. Finn, prep him as fast as you can. I'm going to get my stuff."

THIRTY-FOUR

Thirty minutes later, Renna had stashed her bag in one of Aldani's guest rooms and was sitting on a hard exam table as he flashed a light into her eyes.

"Why would you protect Navang?" she asked. "We could have stopped this days ago if you'd just told us the truth."

Aldani sighed and looked her in the face. "I needed to know how much Navang knew about Myka and the drugs before I went after him myself. And if you were captured, it was better that you knew nothing."

"You're a doctor. What exactly did you think you were going to do with him?" Renna frowned.

"I was going to offer a trade. Offer to work for him. Whatever he wanted in exchange for the boy."

"Blackmail never works out. You've been around long enough to know that. Navang would have killed you eventually or turned you into one of those hybrids."

He rubbed his eyes. "I know. It was stupid. But he killed my brother and sister-in-law. I wanted revenge, and this was the only way I could think to get close to him."

Renna's jaw dropped. "I thought they were killed in the attack."

"No, they were killed *before* the attack. Navang wanted them out of the way so he could get Myka and the formula. He's been searching for the boy ever since."

"I had no idea."

"I should have told you. Trusted you." Aldani shook his head. "I can't do anything to fix what Navang did to you, but I will do whatever I can to make you comfortable."

"Just make sure Myka is okay. I'll deal."

Aldani shook his head. "You're an amazing woman, Renna. We're lucky Dallas hired you to help. I can't think of anyone else who would have rescued a perfect stranger."

His gratitude made her uncomfortable, so she jumped down from the table to study one of the holopads on the counter. "Myka's not safe yet. And you need to get out of here. Have you gathered your research?"

"Downloaded and ready to go. Pulled a few things into a bag. Can't take too much or they'll get suspicious." Aldani's lips curved into a smile. "I don't know what's going to happen, Renna, but I want you to know I'm in your debt. And if things get too bad…" He opened a drawer and pulled out a medipatch. "This will put you in a peaceful sleep. You won't feel a thing. Your heart will stop, and you'll drift off. Painlessly."

Renna swallowed and took the patch. "Thank you, Doctor. I hope it doesn't come to that, but I appreciate it." Right now the pain in her head wasn't too bad, but it could change any second. It was nothing more than a ticking time bomb.

He squeezed her shoulder. "Enough of that. You're a strong woman, and I know you're going to save us all. You already have. And in the meantime, I'll do my best to work on something to save *you*."

Together they walked back to the hangar. Myka spotted his uncle and ran down the gangplank. The older man caught the boy up in his arms and kissed his head. "Glad you're feeling better, my boy. Now let's get back on board. We're leaving."

Myka frowned. "Is Renna coming with us?"

She shook her head. "I'm going to stay here for a while, but you'll have Captain Finn and your Uncle David and even Viktis to protect you. It'll be fine." She hugged the boy before stepping back. "I'll see you soon, kid."

"Promise?" His dark eyes shimmered with tears, and she nodded.

"Promise."

Aldani and Myka disappeared into the ship, leaving Viktis behind to fiddle with one of the tech panels.

She walked over and leaned against the ship. "Hey."

"Hey," he said, closing the door and turning to face her. "How are you feeling?"

"Doc gave me something for the pain. I'll be okay." She shuffled her boot against the cement. "Thanks for doing this."

He pulled her into a hug, and she inhaled his familiar scent of cedar and starfuel. "I figure I owe you one after trying to kill you. I'll keep your men safe."

She grinned at him. "I'm going to hold you to that. You know you're included, right?"

"I was hoping. Maybe I have a chance after all." He winked and squeezed her hand. "Looks like the captain wants to say his goodbyes, too. Take care of yourself, love." Viktis retreated back into the ship as Finn came down the gangplank.

"Everything all set?" she asked. Her gaze traveled across his broad shoulders to the cleft in his chin. Memorizing him. This could be the last time she saw him.

"As much as it can be. Gheewala's changed the *Athena*'s signature; I've had Keva take care of the ship's registry. Once Viktis finds us a place to hide, we'll be invisible."

"Good. He and I have an old merc trick we'll use to communicate. I'll send the all-clear as soon as I can. Stay out of trouble in the meantime." She smiled up at him. "And don't kill the pirate. We need him."

"Yeah, yeah." Finn stepped closer, and butterflies danced in her stomach. He trailed a finger down her cheek. "Rain check on that shore leave?"

She nodded. "It's a date. Don't go falling for any sexy mercenaries while I'm gone, or I'll have to track you down."

"Well, if that's all it'll take..." He smiled sadly. "I promised myself I'd never go back to that life, Renna. And here I am about to turn traitor."

She shrugged. "I promised myself I'd never get caught, and here I am handing myself in."

"If it helps, just remember that I caught you first." Finn pulled her to his chest, kissing her hard and deep. A goodbye kiss she'd remember.

"Promise me you'll be careful," he said.

"I can't promise that. Could you?"

He frowned and shook his head. "Probably not. But try, for me."

"Hey, you're talking to the Star Thief. Covering my ass is what I do best. Now get out of here before MYTH arrives."

He kissed her again, one last time, holding her for an extra heartbeat. And then he turned and walked back into the ship, not looking back.

The *Athena*'s engine's roared to life, and Renna backed away as it lifted off through the roof.

Her implant spun up as soon as she thought about contacting Major Larson. "Help me," she whispered. "They're escaping with the boy."

"Where are you?" Larson shouted in her ear. "Renna? Where is the ship? Do you have Myka?"

"I'm at Aldani's labs. Please hurry." She shut off the connection with her mind and then looked at the heavy pipes the mechanics had left behind.

"Might as well make it look convincing," she said, picking it up and testing the weight in her hand.

At least knocking herself out would stop the pounding in her head for a while.

THE END

Thanks for reading THE STAR THIEF. I hope you enjoyed it!

- Would you like to know when my next book is available? You can sign up for my new release e-mail list at http://eepurl.com/DDYhj.

- Reviews help other readers find books. I appreciate all reviews, whether positive or negative.

- You've just read the first full-length book in the Star Thief Chronicles series. The other books in the series are ATHENA'S ASHES, and a bridge novella, FORTUNES RISK. I hope you enjoy them all!

Read on for a peek at the first chapter of THE STAR THIEF sequel, ATHENA'S ASHES.

ATHENA'S ASHES

It's Renna's biggest job yet – convincing MYTH leadership that she's put away her lock picks and is ready to save the galaxy, despite the dangerous implant in her brain. But with the Athena on the run, she's working solo and facing her most ruthless enemy, the traitor Pallas, who'll go to any lengths to destroy the MYTH organization. Including framing Renna for a devastating assault on MYTH HQ that leaves their defenses crippled and hundreds dead.

Now that MYTH believes she's a dangerous double-agent, Renna escapes their firing squad before they put more holes in her than a pair of fishnet stockings. But the ticking time-bomb in her head is the one thing Pallas needs to complete his master plan and he's not about to let her get away. Even worse, he's discovered the only thing that will bring Renna to her knees – threatening Captain Nick Finn.

Out of time and options, Renna's got one shot to take down the traitor before he annihilates everything she loves, even though winning this battle may cost her everything.

Available on:

Amazon
Barnes and Noble
iTunes
Smashwords
Kobo

ATHENA'S ASHES
CHAPTER ONE

For someone who was supposed to be the best thief in the galaxy, Renna had been spending entirely too much time locked up lately.

Not that a high-security hospital room in a secret MYTH base was much of a prison for her, but the IV line snaking from her arm might as well have been a pair of Saltani iron handcuffs. She swung her feet over the edge of the lumpy bed and watched the holoscreen on the far wall. Stats scrolled past, red text on the black background. Her vitals were stable; blood pressure was fine. Looking at her chart, she was the picture of health.

Except for the cybernetic implant taking over her mind.

Renna rubbed the back of her neck where the original incision site had started to throb. It had been doing that a lot lately, thanks to Navang's depraved experiments and the drugs he'd injected her with. Drugs he'd used to create a whole army of human-robot hybrids.

Thana Samil, the MYTH doctor in charge of her case, said it was nothing to worry about, but Renna knew better. In the five days she'd been locked up here in the MYTH facility, the pain in her head had only gotten worse.

And then there were the weird side effects. She hadn't stepped foot outside her room, but she knew a bank of super-servers sat in the northeast corner of the facility, as if she'd drawn the blueprints herself. Communications relays resided on each corner of the roof. She'd even felt the throb of the automated defense cannons guarding the facility.

If the doctor and her team didn't figure out how to slow down the integration between the implant and her nervous system, Renna would be a walking machine before she had the chance to stop the person behind all this.

Pallas.

If Renna's hunch was right, the traitor was close enough to touch. Maybe even inside this facility. But she'd never find him if she was trapped here for the rest of her short life. She slid off the bed to pace the stark room, careful not to disturb the needles in her arm. Six steps to the door. Turn around. Six steps back to the bed.

She'd done this to herself. She'd volunteered to be locked away and dissected, just to keep Myka Aldani safe. To keep *Finn* safe.

Her pacing slowed as a pang of longing shot through her. Captain Nick Finn. Former gang member turned MYTH soldier and her first childhood crush. Now, she suspected that she'd fallen in love with him, which worried her. Renna had spent most of her life making sure that *didn't* happen. Yet somehow his bright blue eyes, square jaw, and straight-laced moral code had slipped through her defenses.

And oh, the way his fingers had tantalizingly stroked her most sensitive places...

Renna felt herself go warm as she remembered the last time she'd been with him. She'd escaped from Navang, but not before he'd started the process of taking over her implant. Finn had spent the night in her room, waiting for her to regain consciousness, and she'd practically begged him to make love to her. She could still feel the heat of his skin. She inhaled, half-expecting to smell his scent—sandalwood, gun grease, and something that was inexplicably him.

She needed to know what was going on between them, and if that meant more bunk-side exploration, she'd totally take one for the team. But until she knew how to stop Pallas and put an end to these experiments, she wasn't going anywhere, despite the urge she had to run back to Finn. She'd stay in this facility and let them poke and prod her, just to protect him and Myka. Even if it made her crazy.

The lock on her door beeped, and high-heeled shoes clacked across the threshold. Speak of the devil.

Renna turned as Dr. Samil entered the room. The young doctor wore a pleasant smile despite the slightly frazzled appearance of her long blonde hair escaping the messy bun she always wore. Renna leaned back against the edge of her bed. "Do you always have to look so happy at the prospect of stabbing me with those instruments of torture?"

Dr. Samil's blue eyes sparkled. "For someone who's done her share of killing, I can't believe you have a needle phobia."

"We all have our weaknesses," Renna said with a shrug. "Pointy, shiny, metal bloodsuckers just happen to be mine."

Samil set her holopad down on the counter and pressed her thumb to the scanner to unlock the drawer. She pulled out a tray of tools. "I guess it's time for the torture to begin."

The doctor brushed her bangs back off her forehead, and Renna gritted her teeth as she slid back onto the bed, preparing to be poked.

"How'd the last test go? Is the implant fusing normally?" Renna stared pointedly at the far wall as Samil fumbled with the glinting needles on the tray. "Or whatever normal is in this fucked-up situation."

The doctor shook her head, flicking a finger against one of the syringes before pushing the plunger. Pink-tinged liquid squirted from the needle. "I wish I knew. I haven't seen anything like this before. It's fascinating." Her voice was full of that breathless excitement Renna had come to hate. "Whatever Dr. Navang did prompted your ordinarily harmless implant to start fusing directly with your nervous system. If my hunch is right, any other cybernetic implants installed during this time would also fuse to your body. You could even start picking up other electronic signals."

Renna flinched. Not only because of the quick jab of pain as the doctor deftly slid the needle into her arm, but because she was already picking up those electronic signals. Things were progressing faster than the doctor knew.

"Relax. I promise this won't hurt."

"That's what Navang said." Renna tilted her head and fixed Samil with a frown. "And look how that turned out."

The doctor finished injecting Renna with whatever drug cocktail she was trying today, then smiled. "There. Wasn't so bad, was it? I promise I don't like torturing you any more than you like being tortured. Unfortunately, I need one more sample to check your antibody levels."

"Of course you do." Renna grudgingly let the woman extract a vial of blood and then crossed her arms as Samil slipped the vial into her pocket. "So what did you mean about the other implants?"

Dr. Samil nodded as she tapped some information into her tablet. "Navang wanted to create an army of hybrids he could control, right? Well, the first step was to keep their bodies from rejecting the modified implants he installed. But it didn't work. His technique destroyed some of their own tissue and risked the constant rejection of the implants. Hence the need for a steady infusion of the anti-rejection medications.

"The new formula he tested on you was a different attempt at the same thing. If he could find a way to make your body fuse with the implant, make it think it was part of itself, eventually technology could overtake biology. Even better, when the process was complete, depending on the type of implant, he could have different types of soldiers. He'd be able to control them all using his neural network. They'd be nothing but mindless robots until he gave them orders."

Samil's voice rose as she spoke, her gestures growing even more animated, but a dull ache had started in Renna's stomach. She remembered the expressionless eyes of the minions at Navang's lab as she'd slaughtered them to ensure Finn and Myka's escape. Her heart squeezed as she recalled Viktis's assurance that she would make it. Her skin crawled at the realization that she was nothing more than an experiment to the doctor, a shiny new toy to be studied until the novelty waned.

But this was Renna's life. She wasn't going to sit here helpless while other people tried to save her. "How long do I have?" she interrupted before Samil could get even more excited. The woman positively hummed.

Samil paused, blinking at Renna. "Of course. Right. My assistant has had some success in creating a new drug to slow the fusion. It's not exact, but I'm hopeful it will work." Wispy, flyaway hairs floated around her face like a halo as she shook her head. "I'm confident we'll have a breakthrough soon. I promise we'll figure this out."

"Don't make promises you can't keep, Doctor. The headaches are getting worse every day." Renna rubbed at her sore temples, closing her eyes as a wave of pain started to build. She shored up the walls surrounding her heart and refused to even think about losing the connection she'd made with Finn. "On the plus side, if your drugs don't work and the implant takes over my brain, I hear metal body suits are all the rage this year."

Samil crossed her arms and leaned back against the table, a frown marring her pretty features. "You're awfully calm about this whole situation."

Renna shrugged. She was ten years younger than the doctor, but she suddenly felt like she was a hundred years older. "I've learned to deal with the unexpected in my line of work, doc. If you can't change something, you figure out how to work around it. It's the only way to survive."

"That's a cynical view of life for someone who's only twenty-three."

"You saw my file. I grew up in the Izan tenements on Earth, with a prostitute for a mother and a background in stealing. I've worked hard to move on, but growing up like that leaves a scar.

Or two." Renna forced herself not to touch the physical scar on her neck, the daily reminder of that life and everything she'd worked so hard to forget.

Thinking about her mother's attempt to kill her in a drug-induced rage still made Renna flush with shame and hatred. Still made her wary of trusting anyone. Even Finn.

Samil's expression softened. "I know. And for someone with your past, you've come a long way. You're now part of an inter-galactic organization, doing your part to save the universe. You've become something bigger than just a thief. I admire you for that."

"If I had a choice, I would've been long gone by now. I'm no hero, and I certainly am not a team player. I don't need to depend on a galactic organization. I just need myself." Renna settled back against the pillows and crossed her arms. "MYTH can keep its good deeds. I'm just in this for the dental plan." And just maybe to make sure she got a shot at happily ever after.

Samil chuckled, and Renna felt a responding smile twist her lips. Despite the needles and the fact that the doctor viewed Renna as a science experiment, she liked the woman. Samil was whip-smart, and if anyone could solve this puzzle, it would be her.

"What am I going to do with you, dove?" the doctor asked with a shake of her head.

"Save me, I hope." But the doctor could stop using that stupid nickname any time now. Thinking of Renna as a meek little dove was laughable.

"I'm doing my best. I do wish Navang's facility hadn't been de-stroyed. If I had access to his drugs and research, it would make all of this so much easier. Or even Myka Aldani. At one time, he was the key to all of this."

Renna's pulse jumped, and she dropped her gaze to the stark white tiles on the floor. This was exactly why she'd sent Finn on the run with Myka. Destroying the facility had been the only way to stop the human-robot hybrid army Navang and Pallas were building, but it had also signed Renna's death warrant, and put the kid in even more danger.

Had she made the right choice? Could she have stopped Navang another way?

"Do you know why Captain Finn destroyed the place?" Samil asked. "It doesn't make sense. The captain doesn't disobey orders."

"You know Finn?" She clenched her hands in her lap at the unexpected pang of jealousy. The past seven years had changed Finn into a different person, and those years were wrapped in a protective cloak that seemed to surround his heart. He was different, but that Finn from her childhood still remained. She'd thought they'd have plenty of time to get to know him again, to figure out if there was, in fact, a relationship developing under her nose, but life never worked out the way she planned.

Samil nodded. "I was ship doctor for a year on the *Athena*. He's a good man. It must have been something big for him to turn his back on MYTH." Her blue eyes searched Renna's. "Are you sure he didn't tell you anything?"

A lump formed in her throat, and she had to swallow around it before answering. "Finn and I didn't exactly get along when I came on board." Sticking to half-truths was the safest bet for now, until she figured out who she could trust.

"Right. I'd heard he was angry that Major Dallas wanted him to work with a thief on the last mission. You, I presume?"

"Guilty as charged. He wasn't likely to confide in me either way."

"Probably not. I know how he felt about people like you." Samil's eyes widened. "I mean, people who don't follow the law." She shook her head with an apologetic frown. "I'm sorry, this isn't coming out right. I just mean Finn's a good man. For him to go on the run from MYTH means something is seriously wrong."

Renna nodded. "I get it. I'm a thief. Untrustworthy. But I was hired to do a job and that's what I did."

"I didn't mean anything by it, Renna. I'm sorry." The doctor glanced at the door. "Now that I've put my foot in it, I'm going to go make sure my assistant has your newest sample. Stay positive, Renna, it's going to be fine."

"I hope you're right because it feels like my brain is about to ooze out my ears."

Samil unlocked another drawer with her thumbprint and rummaged inside. She pulled out a small, flesh-colored disk. "Here, put this medipatch on. It should help with the pain."

Renna slapped it on her arm. "Thanks, doc. I'll see you later. Hopefully much, much later."

Samil smiled as she left. The door swished shut behind her, and the sound of the lock re-engaging echoed through the room.

ABOUT THE AUTHOR

Jamie Grey writes sci-fi and futuristic romance about smart women and the men who fall in love with them.

She spent most of her childhood writing stories about princesses who saved the day and pretending to be a daring explorer. It wasn't until much later that she realized she should combine the two. Now, as a tech-obsessed gamer geek, her novels mix amazing scientific developments, future worlds, and the remarkable characters that live in them.

Jamie lives in Michigan with her significant other and their pets, who luckily tolerate her overspending on tea, books, and video games.

You can learn more about her at www.jamiegreybooks.com

ALSO AVAILABLE FROM JAMIE GREY

Fortune's Risk – A Star Thief Novella

(Star Thief Chronicles #1.5)

Athena's Ashes (Star Thief Chronicles #2)

Ultraviolet Catastrophe

ACKNOWLEDGEMENTS

Writing this book was an amazing process, mostly because of the support structure I had in place. Thanks to Leigh Ann Kopans and Mandy Stagg for being the best Alpha readers anyone could ask for. I couldn't do this without you ladies.

Thank you to my early readers—Marie Meyer, Nazarea Andrews, and Nanci Schwartz. Your feedback was invaluable!

To my copy editor—Becks, thank you for helping me straighten out my comma tangles and keeping the words flowing.

To Ryan, who is always supportive and encouraging. I don't know what I'd do without you, babe.

And a huge thank you to all of the amazing readers and bloggers who've encouraged me and been excited for this book. You have no idea how much that means to an author!

Printed in Great Britain
by Amazon.co.uk, Ltd.,
Marston Gate.